More praise for *Are We Related?*:

'The stories in this wonderful collection are all concerned in one way or another with the family ties that bind us and tear us apart . . . There is quite a bit of fiction as well as autobiographical memoir, but all the stories share the same intensity of recollection' *Observer*

'An all-star cast struggles with fading heroes, strives to recapture lost voices, lost selves' *Psychologies*

'Writing as fine as this is consolation in itself – a reminder that, however desperate your circumstances, however difficult your life, you are not alone' *Herald*

'The whole collection sings with a depth of complex, contradictory feeling that is heartfelt, concise and awash with interior life . . . The sharpness – the cutting edge of piece after piece – is what imbues this book with its glorious, sometimes disturbing, memorability. From the very first sentence of Linda Grant's foray into the twilight world of her mother's descending dementia, all the way to Ali Smith's snapshot of her father, there isn't a dud: not even a whimper or hollow gesture to loosen the reader's rapt concentration' *Scotsman*

'Contemplative tales about family relationships, often describing commonplace situations. Their appeal comes not from exoticism or high drama, but from the sensitivity with which the authors pick apart their emotional complexities' *Star Tribune*

'This is one of those volumes you'll ingest ravenously then come back to again and again over the years. Rich, unsettling, by turns bleak, warm, tormented and beautiful, sources of comfort, love and pain, the families in these pieces bind with ties that can both bring together and divide, create and destroy. A stunning compilation' *Rock's Backpages*

ARE WE RELATED?

The New Granta Book
of the Family

Edited by
Liz Jobey

Granta Publications, 12 Addison Avenue, London W11 4QR

First published in Great Britain by Granta Books, 2009
This paperback edition published by Granta Books, 2010

A CIP catalogue record for this book
is available from the British Library.

1 3 5 7 9 10 8 6 4 2

ISBN 978 1 84708 145 2

Typeset by M Rules
Printed and bound in Great Britain by
J F Print Ltd., Sparkford, Somerset.

Family likeness has often a deep sadness in it.
Nature, that great tragic dramatist, knits us together by bone and
muscle, and divides us by the subtler web of our brains; blends
yearning and repulsion; and ties us by our heartstrings
to the beings that jar us at every movement.

George Eliot, *Adam Bede*

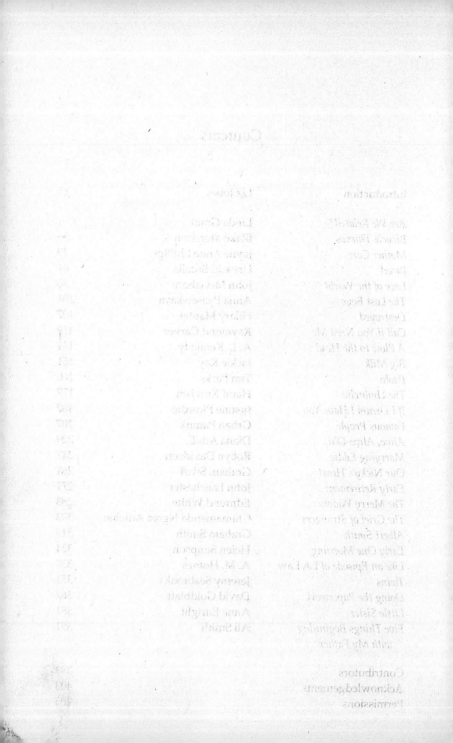

Contents

INTRODUCTION

Liz Jobey

Most family relationships are difficult, and sometimes they can become the most difficult human relationships of all. They tend to combine, as George Eliot wrote, 'yearning and revulsion', as we are bound by biology to people with whom we might have very little in common. I owe the prompt for the quote to Jeremy Seabrook, whose memoir, *Twins*, in this anthology, describes the almost complete alienation from his twin brother that lasted from birth until his brother's death. It was a separation orchestrated by his mother, who, Seabrook writes, 'whispered to each of us her dissatisfaction with the other, with the consequence that we viewed one another with distrust and a fierce defensiveness of our wronged parent.' The long-term consequence of this maternal divisiveness was that 'Separation has been, perhaps, the single biggest determining influence in my life.'

This may be an unhappy place to start, and yet for a writer, the difficulties of family relationships are fertile territory; not only does the family unit offer multiple opportunities to examine human conflict, whether parental strife, or sibling rivalry or filial angst or any of the painful variants in between, but it offers many examples of extreme behaviour, whether bitterness and cruelty, or – sometimes as alarming – doting parental care. Few of us, I hope, have ever had to suffer the remedies to which Edmund White's mother, a state psychologist, leapt at the suggestion that one of her children was physically or emotionally under par. 'If my sister or I ever spoke of general apathy, a broken heart, listlessness, anxiety, Mother would say,

"I think we should run an electroencephalogram on you," or, "Maybe you need a good neurological work-up." It's fair to say that in most aspects Lila Mae White was an unconventional parent, and she too, like Jeremy Seabrook's mother, exercised an uncomfortably intimate dominance over her son's every move. When, as a teenager, he started to go out, Lila Mae would tell her son, 'Remember, I won't be able to sleep a wink until you're safely back here . . . Please don't keep me up all night, honey.' And, when he did return: 'I'd stand in her doorway at midnight . . . she'd want me to rub her back; sometimes she'd turn on a light and ask me to press out the blackheads. Her skin felt clammy. I could smell the whisky seeping from her pores; in a kittenish way she'd call it "wicky".' With a mother like that, one might be tempted to say, what better son to have, than one who became a writer?

In selecting this anthology from more than fifty issues of *Granta*, from 1995 to 2009, I could hardly fail to be aware that the memoir, the first-person autobiographical form that generations of writers were taught to avoid, is the literary genre that marks this period more than any other. And what made memoir during this period more notable was that it was men, as well as women, who were writing about their personal experiences and their emotions. In America, an early example was Tobias Wolff's *This Boy's Life*, published in 1989, which proved that this autobiographical form could have a novelistic resonance. In Britain, Nick Hornby's *Fever Pitch* (1992) used football, and specifically a love affair with the north London club, Arsenal, as a means by which to chart a young man's emotional progress. It was followed, a year later, by Blake Morrison's *And When Did You Last See Your Father?*, which explored the relationship, rarely exposed so candidly in print, between an adult son and his dying father. It caught the frustrating, humiliating tension of a son trying to reconcile his love for a man who appears to him, in so many ways, an absurd figure: a self-assured cheat who has exploited his wife's loyalty and failed to recognize his own faults. The memory of his father's life allowed Morrison to examine his own and the book perfectly caught the moment when all children have to acknowledge that, however much we might hate to admit it, we have been formed, to a lesser or greater degree, by the character of our parents and by our experiences within family life.

The memoir soon became the fastest-growing genre in non-fiction. *Granta* had been in the vanguard of its literary form, publishing not only Morrison's book, but an early passage from what became Mikal Gilmore's 1995 memoir, *Shot in the Heart*, about his family, including his brother, Gary, who was executed for murder in 1977, and William Wharton's terrifying account of the losing his daughter, son-in-law and two small grandchildren in a multiple car accident caused by the smoke from field burning in Oregon. But beyond the magazine it was the worldwide popularity of Frank McCourt's 1996 memoir of his grim, poverty-stricken Irish childhood, *Angela's Ashes*, that developed the public appetite for ever more awful tales of family suffering, and by the turn of the century memoir appeared most frequently with the word 'misery' attached. As publishers vied with one another to produce an author whose traumatic experiences exceeded anything that had gone before, whole new sections in bookshops were devoted to the memoir, and creative writing courses, reacting to its popularity among would-be authors as well as readers, set up classes in life writing, as a new subdivision of literary non-fiction.

It was in the contemporary memoir, more than in any other form of autobiography, that the lines between accuracy of fact and accuracy of emotional description began to be blurred. All sorts of labels were used to describe this sleight of hand: 'creative non-fiction' (despite the pejorative echo of 'creative accounting') being one of the most popular. Against that background, *Granta* continued to publish memoir selectively. In Ian Jack, the editor of the magazine from 1995 to 2007, factual accuracy had its greatest defender, and any false flowering of adjectives or 'atmospheric' additions of, say, factory chimneys in northern towns long after they would have been demolished, would be quietly excised.

Whether or not it was related to the rise of the memoir, writing about the family, in the period covered by this anthology, was a particularly strong element in *Granta*. One only needs to glance at the list of writers collected here (and it would have been quite possible to assemble an alternative list, without loss of quality, from the wealth of available material) to recognize it. Omissions had to be made reluctantly. One positive decision, however, was to include fiction as well as non-fiction, on the basis that to exclude short stories about family relationships (which often have personal experience as their guide) would be to impoverish the reader to no good purpose. The longest story in the collection, John McGahern's 'Love of the World', seems to me a small miracle of storytelling, a novel in miniature, which follows the passage of two people through marriage to parenthood, from love to hatred, and leads us, thanks to a judicious narrator, to see how the factors that affect some people's lives move gradually to destroy them.

Many writers turn to fiction, even when using their own direct experience, because it gives them a greater freedom to discuss the characters of people they would otherwise have to identify, and, perhaps more importantly, to reveal the truth about their own emotions. Diana Athill, in a note at the end of her story, 'Alive, Alive-Oh!', which describes how a single professional woman's life is overturned by a late and unexpected pregnancy, explained her reasons for choosing the third person when she wrote about the events forty years later:

> My sense of recall ... was sharp, yet the woman to whom this happened, though not exactly a stranger – I knew her well – was no longer me. Retelling this experience in the third person is my way of acknowledging the difference between 'her' and me.

Emotional truth is something *Granta* has always valued; the old diktat, that writing should 'show not tell', still pertains, as does the need for an author to establish the underlying sense of human morality in a story, which characters abuse at their own risk. So in this anthology, fact and fiction are distributed almost equally, in the belief that it provides a more rewarding reading experience. And while on the subject of statistics, for once – and this, too, came without any massaging – the gender split has come out fairly evenly. As it should, the subject of the family appeals as much to men as to women.

For anybody discussing writing about the family, it's hard to avoid at least a mention of Philip Larkin. 'They fuck you up' provided a usefully provocative title for the first issue of *Granta* to concentrate on the family (*Granta* 37, Autumn 1991). But it is the final verse of that famous poem, less often quoted, that reveals Larkin's disgust at the entire family project. *Man hands on misery to man./ It deepens like a coastal shelf./ Get out as early as you can,/ And don't have any kids yourself.*

The instinct to procreate, though, is strong in most of us, writers included. One of the earliest pieces collected here is by the American writer Jayne Anne Phillips. When it was first published in *Granta* in 1996 it was a work-in-progress, part of what would become her novel, published in 2000, *MotherKind*. It describes a new mother's struggle to orient herself in the first week after childbirth. Her own mother, who comes to stay, decides, partly as a treat, partly because she is recovering from chemotherapy and too weak to provide that kind of help herself, to buy her daughter the services of a Mother Care agency nurse to look after the baby. Thus Phillips introduces the idea of balance, between the new life of the baby and the decline of the older woman, and between them, the new mother who gradually, reluctantly, moves from a state of dreamy post-natal semi-consciousness to the realization of her new responsibilities. 'She would not be alone again for many years, even if she wanted to be, even if she tried.'

The miraculous transfer of life, from mother to child, is consolidated at the breast, and in this, as in all her writing, Phillips is both accurate and poetic:

> Absently she traced the baby's lips, and he yawned and began to whimper. You're hungry? Kate thought, and he moved his arms as though to gather her closer. Her milk let down with a flush and a surge, and she held a clean diaper to one breast as she put him to the other. Now she breathed, exhaling slowly. The intense pain began to ebb; he drank the cells of her blood, Kate knew, and the crust that formed on her nipples where the cuts were deepest. He was her blood. When she held him, he was inside her; always he was near her, like an atmosphere, in his sleep, in his being.

The newborn baby in 'Mother Care' is the passive receptacle of his mother's emotions. The baby in Jackie Kay's story, 'Big Milk', is a more robust character altogether. As the narrator tells us at the outset, the baby isn't 'really a baby any more except in the mind of the mother, my lover,' and at the age of nearly two, the little girl is quite capable of the naming of parts, in particular, her mother's breasts, which come in two sizes: Big Milk and Tiny Milk. Big Milk, the left one, is 'enormous. The right one small and slightly cowed in the presence of a great twin.' This relationship, between mother and child and the breast, forms a unit that leaves the mother's partner out in the cold. She lies awake while they sleep soundly together; she is isolated, guiltily resentful of the baby that has taken her place in her lover's arms.

> The baby has the power. It is the plain stark truth of the matter. I can see it as I watch the two of them. Tiny puffs of power blow out of the baby's mouth. She transforms the adults around her to suit herself. Many of the adults I know are now becoming babyfied. They like the same food. They watch the same programmes. They even go to bed at the same time as the baby; and if they have a good relationship they might manage whispering in the dark. Very little fucking. Very little. I'm trying to console myself here. It's another day.

This grim, painful humour is part of Jackie Kay's strong literary voice: she is able to make us feel both the seriousness and the absurdity of a situation; the ways in which we are fools to our own desires, ambushed by emotion in the face of reason. In response to the baby's dominion, the jilted lover acts, in order not to be passive. Only when she is far away does she realize, 'that the baby has engineered this whole trip. The baby wanted me to go away. She wanted her mother all to herself in our big bed.'

One of the biggest changes in family life since the 1960s has been the gradual break-up of the nuclear family. These days, children grow used to having four parents – two biological ones and two step-parents – along with step-brothers and sisters. In 2007 the marriage rate in England and Wales dropped to its lowest since records began in 1862; in America, there has been a thirty per cent decline in marriage over the past twenty-five years – and separations, between couples whether married or not, have become accepted as part of life. When John Updike's novel, *Couples*, was published in 1968, the dizzying choreography of partner-swapping in a small New England town made marriage seem irrelevant, if not redundant. Updike said he was writing about sex as the 'emergent religion . . . the only thing left', but it was the arrival of the contraceptive pill that reduced the practical risks of adultery and allowed women to enjoy sex as carelessly as men. Towards the end of the novel,

Piet Hanema hands over his wife, Angela, to his neighbour, Freddy Thorne:

> Freddy asked, 'She's on the pill, isn't she?'
> 'Of course. Welcome to paradise.'

But if separation and divorce have become a social norm, that still doesn't limit the damage involved in trying to escape from a marriage, or trying to hang on to one. The way separating couples behave (and the way it affects their children) is drawn with horrible accuracy in Hanif Kureishi's story, 'The Umbrella', when the narrator and his wife resort to a level of pettiness and cruelty that only two people who once loved each other can muster:

> 'Give me one.'
> 'No'
> 'Sorry?'
> 'I'm not giving you one,' she said. 'If there were a thousand umbrellas there I would not give you one.'

The memory of the night his father left home for good, over forty years before, is the central image in Graham Smith's short memoir of his father, Albert Smith. Though he came to know his father eventually, Albert Smith was never reconciled with his wife, and lived alone, a few miles away from his family, for the rest of his life. What comes through in the writing is not a child's bitterness, but the mature recognition of his father's self-destructiveness and what that cost him. It isn't the only example in this anthology of the complicated emotional negotiation that has to be made when writing about a parent – between finding fault and paying tribute.

When *Granta* first published Raymond Carver in 1981, with his story 'Vitamins', it introduced a writer whose voice would become part of the magazine's character. To enter a Carver story was like slipping into a pool of water at body temperature; you were in it before you realized, and even if the people and places described were far from your own experience, you recognized that what you were reading was real. There was a momentum in Carver's plain, short sentences that meant the reader covered a lot of ground in a single paragraph. Near the beginning of one of his most famous stories, 'What We Talk About When We Talk About Love', the sense of instability, of something temporary about the characters' lives, is built in from the start.

> The four of us were sitting around [the] kitchen table drinking gin. Sunlight filled the kitchen from the big window behind the sink. There were Mel and me and his second wife, Teresa – Terri we called her – and my wife Laura. We lived in Albuquerque then. But we were all from somewhere else.

In 1998, ten years after Carver's death, Richard Ford wrote about the things he most admired in Carver's writing.

> ... to me the most arresting quality of Ray's stories was not how much they drew on life, or how dire or spare they were (they often weren't spare), but, rather, how confirmed *he* was, how unswerving was his election of art – stories – to be life's consoling, beautifying agent. In the very imagining of fictive events, in their committal to shapely, objectifying language, in their formal depiction of emotions we readers will perhaps never have to face in life, *there* is pleasure and relief and also beauty.

Carver was one of my favourite writers a long time before I joined the staff of *Granta* in 1998, so when we had the opportunity to publish 'Call if You Need Me', a story that Carver had not published in his lifetime, and which therefore risked the condemnation not so much of literary critics but of those who thought that what remained was best left undisturbed, it was – despite the sceptics – a thrill to have him in the magazine again. The story is about a couple who leave their respective lovers and their teenage son to attempt a marital reconciliation. The first two sentences give readers all the background they need:

> We had both been involved with other people that spring, but when June came and school was out we decided to let our house for the summer and move from Palo Alto to the north coast of California. Our son, Richard, went to Nancy's mother's place in Pasco, Washington, to live for the summer and work toward saving money for college in the fall.

If you are a fan of Carver, when you come to this story there will a shock of recognition at the familiar voice, and pleasure in the way it can put you into a room with a couple of bickering people and make the struggle that re-routes their lives feel like something universal.

There has always been a tension – sometimes creative, sometimes antagonistic – between *Granta*'s 'English' writing, by which I mean writers from Britain, and American writing, as exemplified by Carver, Ford, Tobias Wolff, Jayne Anne Phillips, all of whom appeared in what is probably *Granta*'s most famous issue: 'Dirty Realism' (*Granta* 8, Summer 1983). But though it was fashionable, then, to prophesy the demise of the English novel, the work of writers on this side of the Atlantic has somehow managed to survive. In 1993, Helen Simpson was one of *Granta*'s twenty Best of Young British Novelists, and few writers can match the naturalism of her stories of middle-class motherhood. Her female narrators, in recounting the small anxieties and compensatory pleasures of family life, nevertheless convey that underlying tension between fear and contentment so familiar to women with children. (I don't have children, but when I once bemoaned this to friend, she said, 'Once you do, you never stop being afraid.')

The story published here, 'Early One Morning,' is bounded by the duration of the school run. It is told from the point of view of Zoe, who, as she drives, is half-listening to the banter of her son and his friends in the back, but because she has sworn not to interrupt or join in, is left to ponder her life as an increasingly middle-aged, dispensable parent (her son, George, is nine; her other children are older). She replays the compromises she has made in leaving behind her professional life to take care of her children full-time.

> She'd done the sums, gone through the interviews in imagination, considered the no-claims bonus; she'd counted the years for which her work time would be cut in half, she'd set off the loss of potential income against the cost of childcare, and she'd bitten the bullet. 'It's your choice,' said Patrick. And it was

Now, so many years later, she is one of a dwindling number among her group of friends who is still married. She appears to herself as a tired, careless, absent-minded woman who even forgets to wear make-up, but as she thinks herself into old age she wonders whether she might bloom again.

> ... perhaps the shape of life would be like an hourglass, clear and wide to begin with, narrowing down to the tunnel of the middle years, then flaring wide before the sands ran out.

Death is part of family life and we all have to deal with it. We expect to lose our grandparents, and then our parents, in that order, and for their deaths somehow to prepare us for our own. But when death comes unexpectedly it subverts the natural order of things, forcing on to mothers and fathers and siblings a level of grief and suffering they could never be prepared for. In Graham Swift's story, 'Our Nicky's Heart', a mother is faced with a decision that few women will have to make, or few families have to live with. But this doesn't release the reader in any way from the agony of the struggle between the selfishness of maternal instinct and the pull of moral duty.

Nothing could have prepared David Goldblatt for the day his father, Ivor, was robbed and murdered at home in his flat by a couple of carpet fitters, and nothing could have prepared him for the aftermath. But in writing about it he found an episodic form that as it shifts between memories of his father, visits to the police station and trips to clear out his father's flat, communicates a real sense of his bouts of fury and grief. The matter-of-fact sentences only make his underlying hysteria more apparent.

> When anyone is murdered the police want to take a look at their home. When they're murdered in that home, the police want to take a good long look. In Ivor's case they examined his flat for almost a month. They looked at him for just as long – time enough for three autopsies, one for the prosecution and one for each of the two defence cases. We got to see him for ten minutes in the Uxbridge morgue, a low brick building of studied anonymity. Unadorned it is surrounded by stark beds of cracked earth and leggy municipal roses strewn with a thousand cigarette butts. Inside it's suffused with seedy, thin, yellow light, furnished like a cheapskate undertakers.

It would be a mistake, however, to think this is a collection without happiness. There are many more pieces than the few I have mentioned here, and among them are those in which family relationships are fond, respectful, equable, even funny. The exasperation with which Tim Parks describes the bond between Paolo, his brother-in-law, and Paolo's mother, who both sides of the family call 'Mamma', has a wonderful tolerance to it, though they drive him to the edge of his patience. Robin Davidson's journey across the Central Australian desert with four camels makes a great adventure story, even before her unexpected liaison with Eddie, an Aborigine. Some writers have found it sufficient to celebrate the people who nurtured and formed them. A.L. Kennedy writes about her grandfather, Battling Joe Price, an amateur boxer who would have defended her with his life. John Lanchester, in remembering his modest, hard-working father, writes this: 'He was a good man, in his unostentatious and shy way one of the best men I have known.' Ali Smith sums up her feelings for her father – and his for her – in a final brief, perfectly executed snapshot. This is the kind of familial closeness that many readers will recognize and others will wish they knew.

Linda Grant, aged seven, with her mother
on the ferry to Ostend, 1958

ARE WE RELATED?

Linda Grant

My mother and I are going shopping, as we have done all our lives. 'Now Mum,' I tell her, 'don't start looking at the prices on everything. I'm paying. If you see something you like, try it on. You are the mother of the bride, after all.' At long last one of her two daughters (not me) is getting married.

In recent years my mother has become a poverty shopper; she haunts jumble sales looking for other people's cast-offs. I don't like to think of her trying on someone else's shoes which she does not because she is very poor but because footwear is fixed in her mind at 1970s prices. Everything she sees in the shops seems to cost a fortune. 'You paid £49.99 for a pair of shoes?' she would cry. 'They saw you coming.'

'But Mu-um, that's how much shoes cost these days.'

'Yes, but where do you go looking?'

In my childhood, my mother had aspired far beyond her station to be a world-class shopper. Her role models were Grace Kelly and Princess Margaret, Ava Gardner and Elizabeth Taylor. She acquired crocodile shoes and mink stoles, an eternity ring encrusted with diamonds, handbags in burnished patent leather. In her shut-up flat in Bournemouth were three wardrobes full of beautiful, expensive garments all on wooden or satin hangers, many in their own protective linen bags – a little imitation Chanel suit from the Sixties that came back into fashion every few years; her black Persian broadtail coat with its white mink collar and her initials, RG, sewn in blue silk thread in an italic script on to the hem of the black satin lining, surrounded by a sprig of embroidered roses; her brown mink hat for high days and holidays.

And so today I want the best for her, as she and my father had always wanted the best for us. 'The best that money can buy,' my father always boasted when he bought anything. 'Only show me the best,' he told shopkeepers.

'So we're looking for a dress?' A nice dress. The sales are still raging through the summer's heat, hot shoppers toiling up and down Oxford Street. We should, I think, find something for £60 or £70. 'John Lewis is full of them,' a friend has said. She has an idea of the kind of dress someone's mother would wear, an old biddy's frock, a shapeless floral sack.

'I don't think that's her kind of thing,' I had told her, doubtfully. But then who knew what was left? Could my mother's fashion sense be so far eroded that she would have lost altogether those modes of judgement that saw that something was classic and something else merely frumpy?

'I'm not having a dress, I want a suit,' my mother says as the doors part automatically to admit the three of us, for tagging along is my nephew, her grandson, who also likes to shop.

'OK. A suit. Whatever you like.'

And now we're in the department store, our idea of a second home. My mother has never been much of a nature lover, an outdoors girl. We used to leave the city once, years ago, when we motored out of town in the Humber Hawk, parked in a lay-by, ate cold roast chicken from silver foil, then drove home early so my father could watch the racing and my mother refold her clothes. By the Sixties we considered a day out to be a drive to the new service station on the M6 where we enjoyed a cup of tea as the cars sped along to London below. My mother has never got her hands dirty in wellingtons, bending down among the flower beds to plant her summer perennials. Or put her hands to the oars of a boat or tramped across a ploughed field in the morning frost or breasted any icy waves. She shrinks in fear from sloppy-mouthed dogs and fawning kittens. But show her new improved tights with Lycra! They never had that in my day, she says admiringly on an excursion to Sainsbury's, looking at dose-ball washing liquid.

And no outing can offer more escape from the nightmare of her present reality than shopping for clothes, the easiest means we know of becoming our fantasies and generally cheering ourselves up all round. Who needs the psychiatrist's couch when you have shopping? Who needs Prozac?

Through the handbags, gloves and scarves and utilitarian umbrellas. Not a glance at fabrics and patterns for neither my mother nor I have ever run up our own frocks at the sewing machine, shop-bought always being superior to home-made in our book. Why do an amateur job when you could get in a professional?

Up the escalators to the first floor where the land of dreams lies all around us, suits and dresses and coats and skirts and jackets. And where to begin? How to start? But my mother has started already.

At once a sale rack has caught her eye with three or four short navy wool-crêpe jackets with nipped-in waists, the lapels and slanted pockets edged in white, three mock mother-of-pearl buttons to do it up. My mother says she thinks she is a size twelve. She tries the jacket on right then and there and it takes fifty years off her. She stands in front of the mirror as Forties Miss, dashing about London in the Blitz, on her way to her job in Top Ops. She turns to us, radiant. 'What do you think?'

'Perfect.' The sleeves are too long, but this is a small matter. We will summon the seamstress and she will take them up, her mouth full of pins. As my mother folds the sleeves under I steal a covert look at the price tag. The jacket is reduced to £49.99, and this, in anybody's book, is a bargain.

'Now I need a skirt and blouse. I've got to match the navy.'

She disappears between the rails and I am anxious for it is not hard to lose sight of her, she has shrunk so in recent years. Five feet two all my life but I doubt if she is that now; perhaps she is under five feet. Her only grandson, the one whose mother is belatedly marrying at long last, doing the decent thing by her mother, at eleven is taller than her. How long will it be before he can lean his chin on the top of her head?

She's back quickly with her selection. The navy of the skirt and blouse she has chosen match each other and the jacket exactly, which isn't the easiest thing in the world to do so that I know that her perception of colour is quite unaltered and whatever else is wrong with her, there is nothing the matter with her eyes. I take the garments from her as we walk to the changing rooms, for everything apart from the smallest and lightest of handbags is too heavy for her now. A full mug of tea is too heavy for her to pick up. In cafés where they serve coffee in those large green and gold cups from France, she is stymied, remains thirsty.

What she gives me to hold is a Karl Lagerfeld skirt and a Jaeger blouse, both substantially reduced, at £89.99 and £69.99, but not within the £60 budget I had estimated when the old biddy dress came to mind, like those which hang from rails ignored by my mother. She has obeyed my instruction. She has not looked at the prices. Half-submerged in whatever part of the brain contains our capacity to make aesthetic judgements, her old good taste is buried and my injunction to ignore the prices has been the key that released it. A young woman of twenty-five could attend a job interview in the outfit she has put together.

In the changing room, she undresses. I remember the body I had seen in the bath when I was growing up, the convex belly that my sister used to think was like a washing-up bowl from two Caesarean births. The one that I have now, myself. She used to hold hers in under her clothes by that rubberized garment called a roll-on, a set of sturdy elasticized knickers. She had been six and a half stone when she got married which rose to ten stone after bearing her daughters, and she would spend twenty years adhering to the rules of Weight Watchers without ever noticeably losing a pound. She more or less stopped eating when my father died, apart from cakes and sweets and toast with low-calorie marge, on which regimen she shed two stone and twice was admitted to hospital suffering from dehydration.

As she removes her skirt, I turn my head away. It is enough to bear witness to the pornography of her left arm, a swollen sausage encased in a beige rubber bandage, the legacy of a pioneering mid-Eighties operation for breast cancer which removed her lymph glands. The armpit is hollow.

The ensemble is in place when I look back. The pencil skirt, a size ten, is an exact fit but the blouse (also a ten) is a little too big, billowing round her hips, which is a shame for it is beautiful, in heavy matte silk with white overstitching along the button closings.

And now my mother turns to me in rage, no longer placid and obedient, not the sweet little old-age pensioner that shop assistants smile at to see her delight in her new jacket.

Fury devours her. 'I will not wear this blouse, you will not make me wear this blouse.' She bangs her fist against the wall and (she is the only person I have ever seen do this) she stamps her foot, just like a character from one of my childhood comics or a bad actress in an amateur production.

'What's the matter with it?'

She points to the collar. 'I'm not having anyone see me in this. It shows up my neck.'

I understand for the first time why, on this warm July day as well as every other, she is wearing a scarf knotted beneath her chin. I had thought her old bones were cold, but it is vanity. My mother was seventy-eight the previous week. 'Go and see if they've got it in a smaller size,' she orders.

My patient nephew is sitting beneath a mannequin outside watching the women come and go. There are very few eleven-year-old boys in the world who would spend a day of the school holidays traipsing around John Lewis with their aunt and their senile gran looking for clothes but let's face it, he has inherited the shopping gene. He's quite happy there, sizing up the grown ladies coming out of the changing rooms to say to their friends, 'What do you think? Is it too dressy?' or 'I wonder what Ray's sister will be wearing. I'll kill her if it's cream.'

'Are you all right?' He gives me the thumbs-up sign.

There is no size eight on the rack and I return empty-handed. My mother is standing in front of the mirror regarding herself: her fine grey hair, her hazel eyes, her obstinate chin, the illusory remains of girlish prettiness, not ruined or faded or decayed but withered. Some people never seem to look like grown-ups but retain their childish faces all their lives and just resemble elderly infants. My mother did become an adult once but then she went back to being young again; young with lines and grey hair. Yet when I look at her I don't see any of it. She's just my mother, unchanging, the person who tells you what to do.

'Where've you been?' she asks, turning to me. 'This blouse is too big round the neck. Go and see if they've got it in a smaller size.'

'That's what I've been doing. They haven't.'

'Oh.'

So we continue to admire the skirt and the jacket and wait for the seamstress to arrive, shut up together in our little cubicle where once, long ago, my mother would say to me: 'You're not having it and that's final. I wouldn't be seen dead with you wearing something like that. I don't care if it's all the rage. I don't care if everyone else has got one. You can't.'

My mother fingers the collar on the blouse. 'I'm not wearing this, you know. You can't make me wear it. I'm not going to the wedding if I've got to wear this blouse.'

'Nobody's going to make you wear it. We'll look for something else.'

'I've got an idea. Why don't you see if they have it in a smaller size.'

'I've looked already. There isn't one. This is the last . . .'

'No, I must interrupt you. I've just thought, do you think they've got it in a smaller size?'

'That's what I'm trying to tell you. They haven't got one.'

Her shoulders sag in disappointment. 'Anyway,' I say, to distract her, 'the seamstress will be along in a minute to take up the sleeves.'

She looks down at her arms. 'Why? They aren't too long.'

'That's because you folded them up.'

She holds the cuffs between her fingers. 'Oh, that's right.' She looks back at herself in the mirror, smiling. 'I love this jacket. But I don't like the blouse. Well, I do like it but it's too big round the neck. Why don't you nip outside and see if they've got a smaller one?'

'I've been. They haven't. I've told you already.'

'Did you? I don't remember. Have I ever told you that I've been diagnosed as having a memory loss?'

'Yes.'

Now the seamstress has come. My mother shows her the blouse. 'It's too big round the neck,' she tells her. 'Can you take it in?'

'No, Mum, she's here to alter the jacket.'

'Why? There's nothing the matter with it.'

'Yes there is. The sleeves are too long.'

'No they aren't.'

'That's because you've turned them up.'

'Well, never mind that. Go and see if they've got this blouse in a smaller size.'

And so it goes, like Alice in the garden, on the path where whatever she does always leads straight back to where she started. We are through the looking-glass now, my mother and I, where we wander in that terrible wilderness without landmarks, nothing to tell you that you passed here only moments before.

We pay for the jacket and the skirt which are wrapped, the jacket remaining, ready to be collected absolutely no later than the day before the wedding, which is cutting it a bit fine but what can you do? We leave John Lewis and walk a few yards to the next store which is D. H. Evans.

Up the escalator to the dress department and on a sale rack is the very Jaeger blouse! And there are plenty of them and right at the front what is there but an eight.

'Look!' I cry. 'Look what they've got and in your size.'

My mother runs towards me, she really does pick up her legs and break into a trot. '*Well*, they didn't have that in John Lewis.'

'They did but it was too big and they didn't have a smaller one.'

'Did they? I don't remember.'

She tries the blouse on in the changing rooms. The fit is much better. She looks at the label. 'Jaguar. I've never heard of them.' Her eyes, which could match navy, sometimes jumbled up letters.

'Not jaguar, Jaeger.'

'Jaeger! I've never had Jaeger in my life before.'

'You must be joking. You've got a wardrobe full of it.'

'Have I? I don't remember. Have I told you I've been diagnosed with a memory loss?'

'Yes,' I say. 'You've told me.'

'And now,' my mother announces, 'I need a jacket and a skirt.'

'We've bought those already.'

'Where are they then?'

'The skirt is in this bag and the jacket is being altered.'

'Are you sure?'

'Positive.'

'What colour are they?'

'Navy.'

'Well, that's lucky,' she says pointing triumphantly to the blouse, 'because this is navy.'

My mother wants to take the tube home (or rather to the Home in which we have incarcerated her) for a taxi is an unnecessary extravagance. 'I'm fresh,' she says. But I am not. A moment always comes, towards the end of these outings, when I want to go into a bar and have a drink, when I wish I carried a hip flask of innocuous vodka to sip, sip, sip at throughout the day. Most of all I want it to stop, our excursion. I can't put up with any more and I fall into cruel, monosyllabic communication. 'Yes, Mum.' 'No, Mum.' 'That's right.' 'Mmm.'

Here is a taxi and do not think for a moment, Madam, that despite the many burdens of your shopping, however swollen your feet or fractious your child, that you are going to take this cab before me.

'Get in,' I order. As we drive off up Portland Place I am calculating how much her old biddy outfit has cost. It has come to £209.97, which is more than I have paid for mine and has beaten out all of us, including the bride herself, on designer labels.

My mother holds on to her two purchases, from which floral prints have been rigorously excluded.

She looks at us both, her daughter and grandson. She's puzzled about something. She has a question she needs to ask. 'Just remind me,' she says. 'How am I related to you?'

What is wrong with her? It isn't Alzheimer's disease but something called Multi-Infarct Dementia or MID. Tiny, silent strokes had been occurring in her brain, mowing down her recollections of what she had said half a minute ago. They were not the kind of strokes that paralysed or blurred her speech, far from it. She isn't confined to a chair but can walk for miles.

'Why do we have to go back now?' she complains. 'I'm still fresh. You know I've always been a walker.'

Apart from the physical wasting, she looks normal – she looks like a sweet little old lady – and people start up conversations with her which proceed as they expected until a question answered a moment before would be asked again – 'No, I must interrupt, you haven't told me yet where you live.'

'As I just said, Birmingham.'

And then asked and asked and asked until you lost your patience because you thought you had been entering a dialogue which had its rules of exchange, and it turned out that what you were really talking to was an animate brick wall. Questions asked over and over again not because she couldn't remember the reply but because a very short tape playing in her head had reached its end and wound itself back to the beginning to start afresh. She knows the conventions of conversation – these have not deserted her – but she cannot recall what she has said herself a few moments before.

Sometimes the question is repeated before the person she is asking has finished getting through their response. There are little holes in her brain, real holes in the grey matter, where the memory of her life used to be and what she has done half an hour or even a few minutes ago.

She has no sense at all of the progress of her memory's ebb. I do. She does not know what lies ahead and I'm not going to tell her. Soon, she will no longer recognize me, her own daughter, and if her disease progresses as Alzheimer's does, her muscles will eventually forget to stay closed against the involuntary release of waste products. She will forget to speak and one day even her heart will lose its memory and forget to beat and she will die.

'Does she know you?' people ask, with that concerned, sympathetic tone in their voices. There is this thing which everyone can tell you about senile dementia, that after a while the most extraordinary event occurs – sufferers no longer recognize their closest relatives and believe that a wife of fifty years is an impostor and a beloved son changing his mother's sheets is a burglar who has entered the house to steal her valuables. When people ask me in that particular way, 'Does she know you?' what they imagine is a vacant drooling wreck in a chair from whom the last vestige of personality has fled, or perhaps a desolate wandering soul in house slippers Condemned until death to walk the halls of the asylum, mumbling. Not a screaming harridan with eyes sharp for matching navy.

When did it begin, this business with my mother? Where was the start of it? Even now, when we have tests and diagnoses and medical records, I still feel that who my mother was once and who she is now are bound up together. Where did her personality end and where did the dementia begin? There is another aspect of her condition; it is called by doctors emotional incontinence. It causes her to come out with the most surprising things – rages, tears, but also information that she has suppressed for the whole of her life.

Whenever I asked her what her father did for a living she said, 'He was a cobbler.'

I assumed he had a shop. I always thought that.

'And what did your father do?' someone asked her recently. My mother replied at once: 'He went round the houses where someone had died and bought their shoes then he did them up and my mother sold them on a stall at Bootle market.' She'd kept that quiet for nearly eighty years.

When I sent away for her birth certificate (because she had given her mother's maiden name as a password for a bank account and couldn't remember it any more) I saw that her father signed it with a cross. He lived, it seemed, the most scavenging of lives, a poor illiterate who in another country would have crawled across refuse dumps to find something he could sell. I come, after all, from a family with a dodgy memory, one which mythologized its own past to fill in the gaps it either did not want to tell us about, or didn't know itself.

'I don't remember' was the answer to so many of my insistent questions. And whenever they told me they didn't remember, I always assumed they had something interesting to hide: like the repressed existence of my older half-sister Sonia, whose phone call to the house when I was ten and picked up the phone before anyone else and said in my best telephone voice, 'Who's speaking please?' was the first, rude intimation that I was a middle, not an oldest child.

Or why there was an eight-year gap between my younger sister and me. Or what my father's name was when he came from Poland, or why the family later changed the one they took when they arrived. Did they drop Ginsberg after I was born, landing me with two complicated birth certificates, because my father had been called guinea pig when he was at school? Or was it that letter from Mosley's resurgent post-war fascists promising the extermination of my Daddy and all his line? I still don't know.

When I think about my mother's loss of memory I understand that remembering things implies continuity, but my grandparents on both sides had, nearly a hundred years ago, become immigrants, stepped off the edge of the known world into England and the twentieth century, the century in which my family was to all intents born. She was the last of her line, my Mum, the youngest of six who married one of six and all the brothers and sisters now dead and their husbands and wives. The world of my forefathers was locked up in her brain which, in certain places, had been turned off at the mains, so to speak.

On the day she revealed my grandfather's true occupation we were looking at old photographs and she began to talk about how her mother and father had come from Russia and how her father had said he would have stayed if only he could have got his hands on a gun to defend himself and 'your father told me that when he was a little boy he overheard his father talking – in Yiddish, you understand – and there was a girl and they came one night, and they came back every night and she went mad in the end and when it was born they killed it.'

'What are you talking about? Who came? Who was the girl?'

'What girl?'

'The one you were just talking about.'

'What was I saying? I can't remember.'

It was so ironic that Jews, who insist on forgetting nothing, should wind up, in my mother's case, remembering nothing.

If there was a beginning, I can't place a marker on it now. There is only the chronology of that year in which she went from being an independent widow in her own flat to her first involuntary steps through the doors of the Home, where she was living in the summer of 1996, the day of the shopping trip.

Whenever she had another stroke, she moved further down the stair into the dark cellar of her life. We got the diagnosis in April 1993 when we paid £60 to a man in Harley Street to tell us what was wrong. But the year which began for us at Christmas 1994 was the one in which great tracts of memory started to disappear in quick succession. And it was not just a matter of blouses, for the disease began to turn its malign attention to the very heart of her, her own identity.

We had always regarded Christmas as an entirely commercial festival, editing out the Infant Jesus and the manger and the carols and Midnight Mass. So when I invited my mother and sister and brother-in-law and nephew to my new flat for Christmas what we all anticipated was a good meal and the exchange of gifts.

They arrived on Christmas Eve and we sent her to bed in my room while I slept on an inflatable mattress in my study below. Michele said the next morning, 'I was up with Mum all night.'

'Why?'

'She kept getting up every five minutes and trying to leave because she thought she was in the wrong house. She didn't recognize the bedroom. I wrote out THIS IS LINDA'S NEW HOUSE, YOU ARE IN THE RIGHT ROOM on a piece of paper and propped it on the chest of drawers but she folded it up and put it in the drawer for safe keeping. I found all the keys to the front door in her handbag.'

My mother came down for breakfast: 'I've had a terrible night. I thought I was in the wrong flat and someone would come in and say, "What are YOU doing in MY room?"' She said it in the tone of Father Bear asking Goldilocks, 'Who's been sleeping in MY bed?'

She and Michele had gone out to buy me a house-warming present, a radio for the kitchen as I had requested which I had opened with delight and mock surprise. 'Ooh, a radio! Just what I wanted. I can listen to music now when I cook.'

Several times as I was preparing lunch she pulled me away from the stove. 'Now this is important. I haven't bought you a house-warming present so I want you to take some money and get it yourself.'

'You've already bought me a house-warming present.'

'Have I? What is it?'

'A radio. Look, there it is.'

She examined it with uncertain eyes. 'I don't remember buying it. Are you sure?'

'Positive.'

After lunch, which was surprisingly good given the circumstances, my mother said,

'I'll wash up.'

'Fine with me.' It would get her out of the way for three-quarters of an hour.

She came back a few minutes later. 'Linda, do you know you've got no sink in your kitchen?'

'What do you mean, no sink?'

'Come and have a look.'

She gestured round the room. 'Where is it?'

'There.'

'Oh, yes. I see it now.'

The following morning, taking a few glasses from the living room to the kitchen, I fell down a flight of stairs. Bruises blossomed across my back and legs. The pain was frightful. When I picked myself up and crawled to a chair Michele appeared. 'I've got the most stinking cold,' she said.

A summit conference was held. 'I vote we abandon Christmas,' I proposed. 'Let's just forget all about it.'

Mark said, 'The presents were lovely, the tree was lovely, the meal was lovely, the only problem was the people.'

We needed one of those smart weapons that would have vaporized the guests but left the trappings of Christmas intact.

'I want to go home,' my mother said. 'I don't like it here.'

Michele made a pretence of ringing the station to enquire about train times, though we had no intention of allowing her to travel home alone. 'There aren't any trains to Bournemouth on Boxing Day,' she said.

'Any to Liverpool?'

'But you don't live in Liverpool.'

'Don't I?'

'No.'

'Do I have a home any more?'

'Of course you do.'

'Where is it, because I can't remember?'

'It's in Bournemouth, where you moved with Dad.'

'Oh, yes, that's right. But sometimes, you know, I look round when I'm in my flat and I don't recognize where I am. Sometimes I start crying and I can't remember what I'm crying about.'

She began another sentence then broke off. 'I don't remember what I was talking about.' She cried again, easy tears that stopped as easily, for like cigarette smoke, the memory of her sorrow had disappeared without trace into the air.

Mark drove Michele and Ben back to Oxford, then my mother to Bournemouth and then back to Oxford. He spent the whole of Boxing Day on motorways, but that was better than spending it *en famille* Grant, he said.

April 1995. I went to Capri and stayed in a terracotta-coloured hotel built on the spot where the Emperor Tiberius once hurled his victims into the sea. Every morning I went to the deserted dining room for breakfast, came back and worked on my novel, and in the afternoon I ascended by the funicular railway to the town. The island was quiet; it was the week before Easter and the first tourist arrivals from the mainland were due but they weren't there yet. I did circular walks on paved paths in suede shoes and a pale lilac silk jacket and whatever fork I took, my wanderings always ended among the smartest of shops. One early afternoon I had a manicure. I bought my mother a musical box of inlaid wood which played 'Twas on the Isle of Capri that I met her'. Some friends who had driven from Rome to Naples took the boat over to spend the day with me. We had lunch overlooking a gorge and the blue Mediterranean spread itself in front of us, like the best kind of dress. This was what living was cracked up to be, privileged, effortless, exquisite. I was cut off from tragedy and tears. I dwelt that week in fairyland.

At home the new flat was full of plaster dust and builder's rubble, squalor on the grand scale. My mother rang me promptly the morning after my return.

'What are we doing for Pesach? You aren't going to leave me on my own in this flat with a box of matzo are you?'

'What would you like to do? Michele and Mark and Ben are in San Francisco but I could come to you.'

'I'm not staying here. I'm the only one who never goes away. I'm always here on my own.'

Later, searching through her things, I found a scrap of paper. On it she had written: <u>People</u> TAKe <u>STRAN</u>geares IN FOR <u>YONTIF</u> I HAVe <u>NOT</u> Bean <u>OUT</u>.

'That's not true,' I said. 'You were here at Christmas.'

'Was I? I don't remember.'

'Should I come and pick you up on the train?'

'Rubbish. I can manage on my own.'

But I didn't think that she could. She did not know any longer that Waterloo was the terminus station. 'Why isn't it called London?' she had asked me. This was the mother who when we took our annual Christmas trips to London confidently navigated buses and tubes and taxis. We went to the Tower of London and Kensington Palace, to little shops on Bond Street she had read about in a magazine at the hairdresser's, to the East End for Jewish food at Blooms. There were photos of me with pigeons on my head in Trafalgar Square, an outstretched hand filled with corn. Now she moved in a restricted universe, frightened of venturing beyond certain well-known routes near her own home.

So I took the train to Bournemouth and walked along the road from the station to her flat, in the bosky south coast air of a spring morning to the avenue lined with pine trees that were deceptively similar to the ones in Capri. I rang her entry phone buzzer and she let me in. I passed through the large empty lobby with chairs that no one sat in, vases with dusty silk flower arrangements which no one admired, came up in the small wood-panelled lift to her silent floor with its four flats. Her door was ajar.

I walked in. I called out, 'Where are you, Mum?'

'Here.'

The worst of her illness for me then and now was seeing her, sitting on the toilet, crying, struggling to put on her tights.

'I don't think I can handle myself any more.' She wept. 'Sometimes I think I'm so brave, what I manage to do. Do you think I'm ready?'

'Ready for what?'

'To go somewhere else.'

'What sort of place are you thinking of?'

'Somewhere they'll look after me.'

'Yes,' I said. 'I think you're ready.'

I saw her loneliness, her isolation from the world, the battle to make it through every day without major mishap, without getting lost or burning herself or falling in the bath or forgetting to take her tablets or turn the gas off or pay her phone bill or eat. I saw the programmes marked with a cross on the television pages of her *Daily Mail*, the programmes which were her only company day after day, her television friends. The casts of all her soap operas were the ones who said goodnight to her and the presenters of the breakfast shows said good morning. They smiled at her and spoke to her as if she had no memory loss at all, never irritated, never complaining. They did her the honour of assuming she had as much sense in her head as they had.

As if she lived in a house that was falling down, she ran hither and thither trying to repair her roof or mend her floor, anything to stop the place from tumbling down around her ears for she fought not just to manage her everyday life but to maintain her existence as a human being, a social animal with rights and responsibilities and likes and dislikes.

I could see now that my family had by necessity reconstructed itself and its past for the life it would live in a new land. Cut off from the previous century, from its own line of continuity with its memory of itself, it made itself up. All the lies and evasions and tall stories are what you must have when you are inventing yourself. Now my mother was bent on a similar task, that of continuously inventing for *herself* (and the rest of the world) a coherent identity and daily history.

For a lifetime of practising deceit had only prepared her for her greatest role, dementia, in which she did everything she could to pretend to the world that she was right as rain and could not stop to talk if she saw someone in the street for really, she had to dash, she was meeting a friend for morning coffee. Her neighbours told me that, later. They suspected that there was no date. Instead of cakes and gossip she would return to her empty flat, with neither husband nor children nor grandchildren, to cry her eyes out. Yet she went on presenting a bold façade, a fictitious person for inspection, hoping it would pass muster.

This was a battle which called up everything she had in her. It was her capacity for deception that armed her against the destruction of her self. Only to me, for a moment, who saw her alone and vulnerable, sitting on the toilet trying to dress, did she reveal the bruising exhaustion of that daily combat.

We took the train to London. 'Would you like to live in London or Bournemouth?'

'London. Definitely. You're not making me stay in Bournemouth.'

I knew why. Because of the humiliation; she who had once been a helper would now be the helped. She who had once held the hands of her old dears at the day centre, where she volunteered with other active Jewish ladies, would have her own clutched by her former equals.

There was no trouble that night remembering where she was but the next morning I found all my drawers and cupboards immaculately tidied. In her case, beautifully folded, were some of my clothes.

I raised again the matter of her moving on.

'I will have my own kitchen will I, because I'm not eating other people's food?'

'No, I don't think you would have your own kitchen.'

'I'm not going then.'

'But it's not like you cook much anyway.'

'Yes, but if I didn't have a kitchen I'd feel like I was in a home.'

'What sort of place would you like to move to?'

'Where they have a warden.'

'You mean sheltered housing.'

'That's right, sheltered housing.'

'I'm not sure if that's the right place for you.'

'Well I'm not going into a home and that's the end of it.'

Walking along the street she suddenly exploded like a match thrown into a box of fireworks, remembering an old grudge she bears against my sister.

'You're taking her side, are you? You're no better than her. Where's the bus? I'm going. I'm getting the bus home.'

'Well you can't. You can't get a bus from here to Bournemouth.'

She began to sob. 'I want to go home, I want to go home. I'll get a taxi, then, you can't stop me.'

We reached my house and she went and sat down and cried. I left the room. I came in ten minutes later. 'Do you want a cup of tea?'

'Yes. But tell me. Have I had a row with someone? I think I've had a row but I can't remember who with. Was it Michele? I don't remember.' It was an excellent new tactic this. Whatever was upsetting her, if you left her alone for a few minutes she couldn't remember it.

The next day I mentioned Michele.

'Michele. Who's Michele?'

'Your daughter.'

'I've got a daughter called Michele.'

'Who lives in Oxford.'

'Who lives in Oxford.'

We were at Piccadilly Circus. 'Where are we, Mum?' I asked her. She looked around.

'Bournemouth.'

Like Michele at Christmas I developed a violent, atrocious cold, the kind where you feel nauseous and dizzy if you stand up. How could I take her to Bournemouth and come back in one very long afternoon? We went by taxi to Waterloo and I put her on the train in the care of another passenger. I went home and as soon as I thought she might have returned I rang. She answered the phone without concern.

'Was the journey all right?'

'Yes. Why shouldn't it be?'

The following day she rang me. 'You've left me like a dog all over Pesach. I haven't budged from this flat for a week. I've been all alone with just a box of matzo. What kind of daughter are you to do this to your own mother?'

'Mum, you were here, yesterday. You've been in London.'

'Don't you lie to me, you liar. I've not been out the door.'

'Don't you remember being in London? At my flat. You stayed here.'

'In Brixton?'

'No, the new flat.'

'When did you move?'

'In December.'

'And you've never bleddy invited me for a cup of tea.'

'You were here. You stayed here. You've only just got back.'

'I'm not listening to you another minute. You're telling me I'm mad.' The phone slammed down at the other end.

I rang her back at once. She was crying her eyes out. 'You bitch,' she screamed and the phone went down again. This went on for the next hour.

I rang her the next morning. 'What's new?' she enquired in a calm, bright voice. 'I haven't spoken to you for ages.'

She wanted me to do something. When she asked me if she was ready, she knew she was but she could not accept responsibility for making the decision for herself. She wanted to rest now, to let go of all the burden of her life, but she needed someone to make her. So she could say, 'I was advised to. I wanted to stay in my own home but they wouldn't let me.' A member of that superior breed, the 'specialist', would be called in and then pride could be satisfied and indignity stared out.

But Michele and I were too taken in by the current fashion in social work and the advice columns: respect the rights of the elderly; consult them; do not force them to do what they do not want. Michele had already rung the Help the Aged helpline. The thinking went like this: old people with dementia were best left to stay in familiar surroundings for as long as possible, where they were habitualized. It was moving that caused crises, where they would have to deal with unaccustomed rooms and would not have, secure in an undamaged portion of their minds, the routes to and from home. When they were taken away, like dogs they tried to find their way back. Then they were locked in, the keys and the bolts got heavier until in the end only a secure mental institution could hold them. Better to keep her where she was. And anyway she had rights. We could not put her away just to suit us, we were told. My mother's rights allowed her to spend twenty-three hours alone, crying, overdosed or under-medicated because fifteen minutes after her taking her tablets she couldn't remember if she had swallowed them or not. Her nightmare went on and on.

I read these sentences from other people's lives: 'Just because I'm old doesn't mean I'm stupid.'

'Just because I'm old doesn't mean I don't see, don't understand.'

So for several more months my mother was treated like an adult, like a fully paid-up member of the human race.

October 1995. Yom Kippur, the Day of Atonement, the most important day in the Jewish year when even the least observant Jew makes their way to the synagogue.

Yom Kippur is also a day of remembrance. It is the day when we say the prayer of Yiskor that offers up our words to God for the souls of the dead. Children are ushered out and adults whose parents are both still living leave voluntarily. First there are spoken the names of the congregants who have passed away in the last twelve months. Then come the prayers for the dead whose relatives in the congregation have offered money to charity to hear their names uttered aloud. Then there is our public memory of the nameless dead of the Holocaust.

Those who remain offer their own individual prayer for their dead relatives, their mother or father, husband or wife. So we cast our chain of memory down through the generations and link ourselves with all the forgotten ones of the past who have nobody left to mourn them. The synagogue is at its fullest. The old and the sick and frail stumble there any way they can to say Yiskor. To do less is to have done nothing.

This was the most important day of the year, when my mother would pray for the souls of her dead parents, and for her brothers Abe and Harry and her sisters Miriam and Gertie, and Gertie's only child, Martin, who died of leukaemia when he was only twenty-six, and for her own husband. But I thought she was too confused to travel to London and that it would be best if I came to her.

'I will not, I will not stay in Bournemouth,' she shouted at me down the phone. 'This place reminds me too much of your father at this time of year. I want to come to London.'

'I'll come and get you on the train.'

In fact it was all to the good that she had decided that London was the place to be because my long-lost cousin Sefton, who had lived in Israel for the past twenty-five years, was back in town and so I invited him to come and see my mother. 'Sefton!' she cried. 'My favourite nephew.' She remembered everything about him, who his wife was and how they had married and when he had gone abroad.

I rang her just before I left the house to remind her what time my train arrived. I explained that if she was there to meet me with her small suitcase we would only have a brief wait until the return journey.

'Yes,' she said. 'Don't worry. I've got it written down.'

I did not know if she would be there but she was, only a few minutes late, standing without any luggage. 'I've got to buy my ticket,' she said. 'I've been to the bank.' She no longer kept money in a purse or wallet but in a small plastic bag.

'Mum, where's your case?'

She looked around. 'Where's my case. Bugger it, I don't need any clothes.'

'Of course you do. What have you brought with you?'

'Nothing.'

'Have you got your pills?'

'Yes, they're in my bag.'

'Show me.'

'Bugger off. I've got them.'

'I want to see.'

Meekly, she gave me her small handbag, the lightest of all those she owned and held across her shoulder by its strap. She was so little now. Little and old and confused. A mugger's ideal target.

There were no pills.

'We're going to go back now and pack properly.'

'Oh, do we have to?'

'Yes.'

We walked along the road to the flat. She let us in and sat down for a few minutes with her eyes closed, exhausted, in what used to be my father's chair. Then she opened them and said: 'Well, I'm delighted you've come for the weekend. How long are you staying?'

'I'm not staying. I've come to pick you up. You're coming to London.'

She burst into tears. 'Now you tell me. Do we have to?'

'But it was you who insisted. You said you wouldn't stay here.'

Her mood changed like a radio clicking to another station, from sobbing violins to angry drums.

'You're not going to make me stay in Bournemouth. I'll cut my throat if I've got to stay here.'

'Well that's good, because Sefton is coming to see us in London.'

'Who's Sefton?'

'Uncle Louis's son.'

'No, doesn't ring a bell.'

I watched her pack, a few things that didn't belong to each other thrown into a small case.

'Underwear, Mum.'

'I don't need that, do I?'

We went back to the station and caught the train. The orange signal lights inside the tunnel at Waterloo caught her eye as we approached the platform. 'Ooh,' she said. 'Isn't it beautiful, like fairyland.'

As we went towards the tube I saw a newspaper placard announcing that O. J. Simpson had been found guilty. 'I'm just stopping to buy the *Evening Standard*, Mum.'

'Why, anything interesting in it?'

'The verdict on O. J. Simpson,' I told her. Of course she would not know what I was talking about.

'Well, I think he did it, don't you? I've been addicted to the trial.' Thus my mother, who did not know what day of the week it was, what was up and what was down, had for many months been following one of the most complex criminal cases of the century.

I went in to see her as she was getting ready for bed. She was standing with her nightdress on over her clothes.

'Mum! What are you dressed like that for? Are you cold?'

'No. Why?'

'You've got your nightie over your clothes. You don't do that.'

She looked down, uncertainly. 'Don't you?'

The following morning we went in the rain by taxi to the synagogue at Muswell Hill. She gave out little cries and ran to embrace people, complete strangers as it turned out. They saw my embarrassment. I saw the look of pitying understanding in their eyes. She did not follow the service.

On each seat was the congregation's community magazine. It contained an article about a nursing home adjacent to the synagogue. It was called Charles Clore House after the famous Jewish philanthropist who had once owned Selfridges, exactly the kind of man my parents admired and longed to be like themselves.

She read it over and over again. 'Do you think I'm ready?' she asked.

'Shush. Don't talk so loud. Whisper. Remember where you are.'

'Why? Where am I?'

My mother's diabetes ruled out fasting so I took her for lunch in a café where she had a bowl of soup and a sandwich. Someone I knew came in and I saw him start to come over to speak to us but I shook my head. Her voice was so loud though she wasn't deaf, she smiled so brightly at people she did not know and they all, without exception, said, 'Oh, she's so sweet.'

'I must give you some money,' she offered.

'What for?'

'For the pictures.'

'What pictures?'

'Where we've just been. We've been to the pictures. I can't remember what the film was but I know we've been. Have I told you I've been diagnosed with a memory loss?'

And it was then that I thought, 'That's it. This has gone far enough. She's got to go into a home whether she likes it or not. I must do something.'

I saw that the mother, who for so long I thought had made my life such a misery, was gone. That I was never going to win the great argument with her about the kind of daughter she expected me to be for my adversary had left the field. In her place was a bewildered infant whom the world insisted on treating as an adult with no one to protect her. My mother, my child.

After half a lifetime of being an inadequate, undutiful daughter, now I was to take on a role I had refused elsewhere, that of a parent. It was up to me to do what I thought was best for her, to tell her how she could and could not behave, to protect her from danger, make sure she was properly housed and fed, to find her the best attention money could buy. Like many women of my generation, I thought I had won freedom and independence. I hadn't of course. Now I was to become my mother's guardian, as tied to her as if she were my baby.

My cousin Sefton came for lunch and as soon as he walked into the room my mother ran to greet him. After an absence of a quarter of a century the visual recognition portion of her brain was intact.

'You're as handsome as you ever were,' she told him. 'My favourite nephew.'

We looked at old photographs.

'Who's that?' she asked, pointing to a picture of his father.

'That's my father.'

'Who is your father?'

'Louis.'

'But you're Louis.'

'No, I'm Sefton.'

'How am I related to you?'

'I'm your nephew.'

'So who is your father?'

'Louis.'

'That's right. How's your wife? She was very beautiful, you know. She used to be a beauty queen.' It was true, she had been.

Why could she remember Anne, met perhaps two or three times and not since the 1960s? Why could she whisper to me when he was out of the room, 'His wife isn't Jewish, you know'?

And why was it, as we waved goodbye to Sefton, that she turned to me and smiled and said, 'He's lovely. Who is he?'

I took her back to Bournemouth on a packed train. I watched her lips moving as she tried to capture the thoughts that drifted through her mind like fast clouds. A woman opposite us was watching her too. She looked at her in pity. She looked at me and I saw in her face what she thought, 'The poor bloody daughter, having to look after her.' Perhaps she thought I was one of those selfless, dedicated women who loved their mothers so much they would never put her in a home. I stared back at her, eyeball to eyeball. I sent out a telepathic message. I'm not what you think. This situation is not as you imagine. I am going to put her in a home.

'Mum,' I said. 'Show me your chequebook.' She handed it over. On the day she left Bournemouth she had withdrawn two lots of £30. She only had £30 when she met me at the station. Thumbing back through the stubs, I saw that on various days she had withdrawn multiple amounts of money. I imagined that she had gone to the bank, written a cheque, then forgotten later that she had been.

She rang me the next morning. She was crying.

'I've left my chequebook at your house. Will you send it back to me.'

'No, you definitely haven't left it here because I was looking at it on the train and you put it back in your bag yourself.'

'I haven't got it. Why won't you listen to me?'

'Honestly, Mum, I promise you that you have got your chequebook. It is there.'

'It isn't. Why are you doing this to me? I've got no money for food. I'm hungry and I've got no money. Please, please send me my chequebook.'

'I can't because I haven't got it.'

The familiar routine began. The phone slammed down then a minute or two later rang again.

'Linda, it's Mum. I can't find my chequebook. Have you got it?'

'No, we just had this conversation.'

'When?'

'Two minutes ago.'

'We didn't.'

'Yes, we did.'

'Well never mind that. I want you to send me my chequebook.'

'I can't. I haven't got it.'

'Please, please, I'm so hungry.'

It went on for two days. The phone calls every hour or so as if they had never occurred before. I went out for a while. My cleaner said, 'Linda, I was cleaning your office and there was the most terrible message on the answering machine. Whoever it was was in the most awful distress. I didn't know what to do. It was something about a chequebook.' The last call came at twenty past midnight on Saturday, the latest my mother had ever phoned me. The first began at ten to eight the next morning.

In the evening people were coming to dinner. It was early October and unusually warm. The last of the first phase of redecorating was over and I was free to entertain, to be gracious, to lay my marble table with my canteen of cutlery and place there the squat, cut-glass tumblers that I had stolen from my father's cocktail cabinet. To be on the safe side I put the answering machine on. The phone rang and everyone went quiet as my mother's demented voice formed a faint but audible back-drop to the Delia Smith beef casserole which we ate in defiance of threats to our own future sanity, just before the BSE scare went ballistic. 'I'm hungry, I've got no money for food. Why won't you help me?'

First thing on Monday morning I rang my mother's bank. I don't think anyone has been so pleased to hear my voice as that young clerk who, it turned out, dealt with my mother's account.

And that phone call, followed by others to social workers and doctors and matrons of homes, marked the end of my mother's adult life. From that day on, she was to be my dependant. When she went into the Home we took her money away from her, her door keys, her chequebook, her credit card, her kitchen, her cupboard with its boxes of dinner services for best, her furniture. We left her in a small room with some photographs and a fraction of her once-fabulous wardrobe. The jewels were gone already, stolen down the years by window cleaners and home helps.

The actual day she went into the Home, I was away. It was Michele and Mark who took her there. To the place of old men and women, drooling wrecks, Alzheimer's cases. Jewish old people's homes had unusual problems. There was a Holocaust survivor there, severely damaged by dementia. When they took him to the shower he thought he was being led to the gas chamber.

I got back and the phone was ringing. 'They've made a new woman of me,' she said. 'I'm ready to go back to Bournemouth now.' They had, in a way. She was fed three times a day, properly medicated, no longer had to struggle to preserve herself intact for daily life.

'No, Mum, you can't go home.'

'Do you mean I've got to stay here for the rest of my life?'

I did not want to tell her, yes. There was silence at my end.

'You bitch,' she said.

BICYCLE THIEVES

Blake Morrison

Late June, scorched grass and sprinklers, the sky as if scuffed and beaten. Too hot to work, too lazy to think, I've knocked off early to play tennis. I'm sitting on the edge of the bed, putting on my trainers, when my son crashes in, a raspberry lolly bleeding in his hands, huge breaths and distraught between them, dragging the words from a well: 'My bike . . . they took . . . I left . . . when I came out . . . my bike . . .'

'Don't cry, don't cry, we'll sort it out,' I say, pulling his wet head to me. 'What is it, what's happened?'

'The bike. It was outside the shop. Two boys took it.'

'What about the chain lock? I've told you.'

'But I was only a minute.'

'Did you see them?'

'No, two little kids said. But I saw them outside before.'

'How old?'

'Bit bigger than me. Twelve or thirteen. The little kids pointed where they'd gone.'

'OK. We'll go and have a look.'

We get in the car. It would have taken him ten minutes to run back. Five minutes more have passed. They're quarter of an hour away at least.

The shop is at the edge of a small estate, HAPPY SHOPPER it says over the window, which is covered by a metal grille. This is one of the better estates: one people try to move into, not out of. You can tell because the shop has only a grille, not metal shutters or wooden boards. Behind his sloping rack of sweets, the Asian owner is upset.

'Sorry, no, I didn't see. I served the boy, yes. It's happened before. You have to lock your bikes. I try to tell them.'

'I've tried to tell him too. But it was only a minute. You didn't notice any boys outside?'

'No. Only two schoolchildren at a time in here. That's my rule. It keeps down incidents. But outside . . .'

I duck out again, angry at these bullying great kids who've taken my son's bike, and also excited. We pause by the shuttered off-licence next door, CHEERS, long past its last closing time.

'Which way did they go?' I ask.

'The kids said here,' he says, pointing to a walkway between garages. We go down, glancing to left and right, in case the bike has been abandoned. At the end is a metal barrier, a pedestrian crossing over the road and, beyond, the Ferrier Estate. I've heard stories about the Ferrier – about murders, rapes and stabbings; about crack dealers ripping each other off; about the dangers of parking. You get the same stories about other estates. But I'm new to this bit of south-east London. I didn't realize the Ferrier was so close. I've not been paying attention.

We cross over and follow the dust-groove of a path across the grass. It runs by a high metal fence, like tennis-court mesh, but the concrete square beyond the wire has no markings – a compound of nothing. Where the high fence ends, a lower wood-slat fence begins, with a sign saying ANTI-CLIMB PAINT. A big-windowed building, some sort of institution, squats peeling beyond – a school, with spiked railings to keep the pupils in by day and out by night. We walk over the grass to where the first block of flats looms up on our left, like a docked cruise liner.

'I think those are the kids who saw,' says my son.

A boy and a girl, black, about six. They're holding a small plastic holey bat each, like a pair of waffles, the sort you're supposed to use with spongy-light balls. When they strike their yellow tennis ball, the bats flop limply, and the ball dies. Seeing us, they stop the game, curious, waiting.

'You saw his bike being stolen?'

'Yeh.'

'It was two boys?'

'Yeh.'

'Do you know them? Did you see where they went?'

'Up there. Past the yellow block, the next one, that begins with number twenty. One of them lives at number twelve.'

'So you know him?'

'No, but he lives there.'

'Do you know his name?'

'Andy, yeh, innit.'

The boy has done all the talking, but now the girl says: 'We're visiting. From Wandsworth. We don't live here.' She picks up the ball and whacks her bendy racket at it: 'Come on, Stephen.'

'Thanks,' I say, not knowing which of their answers is true – if any. A stolen bike: in my day, that would have been something, and if a boy and his father were out looking for it, you'd want to help, you'd join in the hunt, you'd ... And yet they'd not been unhelpful. The spareness, the wariness: I recognized it from my own kids; it is how the young are taught to be with strangers. So we were looking for a bike; so they had seen the bike being stolen. It didn't mean they should trust us, cooperate, go out of their way. How they'd been was as unobstructive as anyone could be without running risks. To answer when strangers ask you questions: this is plenty, this is more than enough.

We press on, under the unfiltered sun, past the first block and into the square beyond – concrete slabs with weeds growing between them. The square is a giant courtyard, the four cruise liners (each with five decks) round the sides, a fenced-off adventure playground in the middle – slides, climbing frames, ravine bridges. Among the dozen or so boys here – shaven-headed, bare-chested, earringed – two are riding bikes. As we move towards the playground for a better look, I try to remember what the bike looked like – silver wheels, furry grey saddle, black foam bits (like the sort used to insulate copper pipes) over the handlebars. My son hangs against the wire like a prisoner. Then he says, 'Nah, not mine.'

'Are you sure?' I ask, wondering if – his father's son – he merely fears the confrontation.

These bikes all look the same to me. High above, men in vests lean from balconies, watching, waiting. I'm glad, really, that I don't have to challenge these bikes' owners, or putative owners. And I'm glad I'm not black or Asian, not Jamaican or Pakistani or Tanzanian or

Vietnamese or Somali, much riskier here – to judge from the stories I've
heard – than being a middle-class white.

We pass on to the next square: no sign of a bike. Beyond, there's
a light-blue map-board saying FERRIER ESTATE, and I try to get my
bearings. Some of the names – faint and faintly foreign: Pinto, Gallus,
Dando, Romero, Telemann – I can read, but most have been defaced,
as if it's wartime and the signpost has been blanked out to confuse the
enemy. The estate's much bigger than I thought. A railway runs
through it, dividing east from west. A four-wheel drive nought-to-
sixties in five seconds down the abbreviated street.

'Keep up,' I say to my son, noticing the kicked-in front gates, the
flaky window frames, the front doors grinning broad and toothless
where letterboxes must once have neatly gleamed. 'Keep up,' I say
again, wondering how conspicuous we look, how much like strangers.
We're in the second square now, and for a moment we lean against a
wall, cupped by its shadow. Like all the other walls here, it's battleship
grey and ribbed in texture. Searching for deeper shade, we sit in a gully
of broken steps. Around us, pigeons purr and tick, scanning the
concrete, something stuck in the back of their throats; the balconies
above us are covered in chicken wire to stop them sitting and shitting
there. A tyre-less old Escort sits on its arches. That fallout of glass must
have been its windows once. Under the sun, the shards are like ice: I
want to gather a handful and wipe them across our faces. Up ahead,
the windows and vents are painted yellow, not blue. The next block on
our left must be the one the little boy meant, if the first door is number
twenty, which it is. We get up. We move on. 'Stay near me, pretend
we're not looking,' I say, as if we're stalking a murderer, not a kid who
may or may not have stolen a bike. The numbers run down to twelve:
a front yard with a rusting washing-machine, a barbecue, a baby's car-
seat, a toddler's scooter, a plastic patrol car, a box of empties. No bike.
I hadn't expected it, out in the open. If I was bolder, I'd knock at the
door. But I can't do that, not on the say-so of two six-year-olds. And
what use would it be, even if I had the nerve? No answering kid would
shop himself; no parent would shop him either.

We walk on, to the next square, painted red. Beyond there's a tall
chimney, like a factory chimney, except that there's no factory. There's
no sign of a bike, WHAT MUST I DO TO BE SAVED? asks an advertisement
posted on what looks like a bus shelter but, windows intact, turns out

to be a lift lobby. We search the brambled slope of a railway embankment. We search the next square and the squares beyond: green, purple, brown, pink, navy-blue. I'm getting the hang of the estate now, its fierce symmetries and sudden departures: the ground-floor yards and then, above, the decks of glass and metal, some with ensigns of washing, some with the foghorn of a satellite dish. It's like a gaudy chessboard, a square of squares, vertical squares of glass, horizontal squares of stone, different shades and different colours. But just when I think I've worked it out, I'm lost again, away from the thronging squares on a patch of broken concrete, the only sign of life a dog snarling from behind a wooden fence and then a second dog, snappish, running towards us.

'Fuck off,' I say, ready to kick it. Rather than harass us, it sniffs at the fence confining the bigger dog, driving it to new fits of frenzy. We move away.

'I don't think we're going to find it,' I say. 'I think we should go home and call the police.'

The sun presses down, unforgivingly hot, as if this were a foreign country we'd slipped into from some hole in the map. An ice-cream van ting-tangs an ancient pop song. On the path, disposed of, a disposable nappy. Did the child who was its wearer, toddling in these canyons, drop it here? No, some adult has tried to roll it up, to fold its odour in on itself, though not, in this heat, successfully. It seems an odd place for a nappy to have strayed, though I've known odder. One summer when my son was small, we parked in a rush at Stansted Airport and left the passenger window open half an inch. By the time we came back two weeks later, someone had posted a nappy through the gap. It sat there on the passenger seat, a welcome-home banner.

No sign of a bike. Disappointed and relieved, we soodle homewards back to square one, hoping to see the kids who'd seen the other kids, but finding only their tennis ball, the spoor of their limp game.

Back home, I phone the police, who take down details and promise to send an officer round, 'when one becomes available'.

'When will that be?'

'That I can't say, Sir.'

This is what being middle-aged means: not avoiding the police but needing them to come round and feeling pissed off when they don't. My son is pale still and bleared by his earlier weeping. But it isn't some ultimate, shaking grief: he knows how the world works, that possessions can't any longer (or not for long) be possessed. Boys steal bikes – and car radios and anything not nailed down in shops – as casually as they once stole apples. And those are the good boys. The bad ones take the cars as well as the radios. The worst ones take the cars, then crash them, or set fire to them, or both. Once, if something went, there was the belief, consoling to the liberal-minded, the guiltily affluent, that someone less well off must have needed it: that car, that bike, would be riding around somewhere, under different colours. Now the old motives – need, greed – can't be relied on: as often as not, stolen possessions pass into oblivion, wrecked or set alight. I remember seeing a piece of graffiti in the 1970s: I DON'T BELIEVE IN NOTHING. I'D LIKE TO SEE THEM BURN THE WHOLE WORLD DOWN, JUST LET IT BURN DOWN BABY. I'd imagined it to have been written by some druggy, disaffected twenty-eight-year-old, a nihilist philosopher of the streets. Now there are twelve-year-olds who think like that, kids for whom life holds out no promise except failure, kids who know for sure what most of us spend our lives not wanting to acknowledge as a possibility: that life is shit, and at the end of it we die.

Easy come, easy go, cheering himself up with Weetabix, my son seems resigned now – more resigned than I am, still angry at the world I've brought him into, which has now carried off his favourite thing. I tell him not to worry, that it wasn't his fault, that there are other bikes, that we'll buy him a new one, which he'd have needed soon enough anyway. We're sitting in the kitchen, under the old fifties built-in cupboards we've never bothered to tear out, and I think of how the scene might have played itself out then: one of those epiphanies of childhood, bringing with it the end of innocence and a lesson in the epistemology of loss: the boy dries his tears and, harder, wiser, learns how to watch out for himself, how to mourn, how to stand up. But these are the nineties. It's only a bike, for Christ's sake. There are queues for them every day at Argos. Things get broken or go missing, and you replace them. What more is there to say?

Later, alone, I drive back through the hot night to number twelve and park. Small children pass in and out through the open door into the front yard. A teenager tinkers with his motorbike. The man of the house comes out with a can of Kestrel and leans against his wall. I duck down behind my newspaper till he goes back in to the flickering neon square beyond the net curtains. I sit on for an hour, until the ebb and flow of small children has ceased. But there is no twelve-year-old returning on his – or someone else's – bike. I drive back home, still scanning the estate, certain it's there. My car was stolen once, from outside a flat I had in Greenwich, and afterwards, convinced it was just kids taking a quick way home after the pub, I drove round the streets of south-east London, in a friend's car, madly exhilarated for hours, on the case like Holmes or Maigret, only belatedly getting out the *A–Z* and seeing what a small patch I'd covered. But a bike . . . it couldn't have gone far.

Later still, I lie awake in bed and hear sirens and more sirens. The estate seems close now, scarcely beyond the bottom of the garden. The late trains clattering down to Dartford, the sex screams of foxes, the whooshy tides of traffic on the A2: these, the usual night sounds, are drowned tonight by sirens. Infringements, impingements. I drift back to sleep and dream of a man entering the room, his knife bisecting my torso from neck to navel. I wake sweating and imagine blue lights surrounding the estate, police cars and fire engines and ambulances, and a solitary boy on a stolen bike at the centre of their arc light. But the sirens are speeding all over the city and suburbs, to diverse domestic incidents, the humdrum nightly toll, stabbings and smashed windows and stolen VCRs. It's up to me to solve this smaller crime. I lie awake, the same thoughts playing over, unable to exit from the file. I begin putting my clothes on. As I reach for my trainers, Kathy wakes.

'Where you going?'

'To look for the bike.'

'You're mad. It's three in the morning. It's only a bike. We can get it back on the insurance.'

'It's the principle. Plus I feel sorry for him.'

'He's OK about it. I've talked to him. It's you that's the problem. Anyway, they didn't hurt him, did they, they didn't beat him up? It could have been a lot worse.'

'He's my son. It was his bike. I should try my best to get it back. My father would have done.'

'Jesus, you have tried. He knows you've tried. Come back to bed. Leave it to the police. Didn't they say they'd be round?'

'When an officer becomes available,' I say, starting to undress. 'Meaning never.'

But an officer stands on the doorstep the following morning. I go through the incident again. I show him the 'owner's manual' for the bike, a four-page leaflet. I confirm that no, the bike hadn't been engraved or tagged with an ID number. I describe the conversation with the kids and mention the address they gave.

'Number twelve? Ah, yes, a family known to us, I think I'm right in saying: we'll pay them a little visit, though I don't hold out much hope.'

'Well, you never know . . .'

'There's a trade in stolen bikes, you see. The boys don't rob them for themselves: they sell them on. We think they're being shifted to second-hand shops up north. You really have to get your bike coded or make your boy use a lock.'

'He does, usually. But it was only a minute . . .'

The days pass, and the police don't ring back. Gradually, I stop scrutinizing every child's bike I pass: I'm not going to run into it; it's not going to run into me. But I acquire the habit of leaving work half an hour early and parking near number twelve on my way home. They're always about somewhere, in this hot weather: him with his chest hair spooling over the top of his vest; her with the black-sheen cycling shorts and the figure she's already getting back now the baby's eight months; and the older kids, Michael and Leah, and baby Charlene: yes, I've heard them shouted so often in reproach, I've learned their names. All of them small, though, no twelve- or thirteen-year-old bicycle thief. Where is he? It can't be Michael, who's nine at most. Nor the lurky biker, seventeen at least, who turns up on Tuesdays and Thursdays for a quick tea and fiddle with his Yamaha and who can only be a younger brother of one of the parents. Why did the police say they knew about number twelve? They seem a harmless lot; there'll be rent arrears and unpaid bills, but nothing big. They watch telly, sit in the yard when the sun comes round, take the kids off to school, drive off in the blue Transit to Safeway and that's about it. They don't look to have the energy for crime.

Sometimes, as well as parking there, I get out and walk, not in search of the bike, not for exercise, just to get the feel of the estate. It seems less scary now. I notice things I didn't before: tenderly wired saplings; a woman cradling a cat leaning down to gossip from her sliding window, as if this were the old quarter of some distant city. 'He's a bastard, they all are,' says an eighteenish mother by her pushchair to two other mothers by their pushchairs, and they laugh together, happily conjoined in derision of the shittiness of men. Two boys are throwing something, their arms raised like stone-throwers in Belfast or the Gaza Strip; when I get nearer I see it's only a tennis ball. There are flats whose fronts are pretty with hollyhocks and hanging baskets, though round the back they've gone to hell. In the Wat Tyler pub, the rotor blades of huge fans sweep the ceiling. I buy myself a Guinness while Otis Redding, deep from the speakers, is just sitting on the dock of the bay. A man in shorts goes past, a rose tattooed on the back of his thigh, CHARLTON ATHLETIC and AC MILAN compete as graffiti opposite, as if Milan were as local as Charlton – and tonight, in this heat, it feels as though it is. When the sun eases off round eight and there's a pink glow over the roofs, the estate seems almost happy, relaxed, a good place to be, and for a moment I see it as the architect who designed it must have seen it, as if in miniature, in the glass case at the town hall, with green felt and fuzzy trees and someone's dreams invested in it. Light catching the westward panes, I'm back to the drawing-board of high intentions – wide spaces, protected acres, light-blessed windows, walkways like Venetian bridges, streets in the sky. There's glass under my feet, bottle glass, windscreen glass, bus-shelter glass, but at dusk, the lights coming on, it shines like scattered jewels. I know that the local papers say this is a sink estate, and sinking. I know that I have a score to settle. But for the moment, the sun goes down, and all this place was supposed to be is there in ghostly silhouette.

Another week passes. Now I stop off at the estate on my way to work as well as on the way back. I get my kids off to their schools, and there's still time to be round at number twelve to see Leah and Michael trooping down to theirs – reception class in her case, middle school in his, or so I deduce, watching them go in at different times and by different entrances. Once, I keep an eye on Charlene, not trusting the pushchair to stay where her mother has left it just inside the playground, the compound of the peeling barracks. These mothers, don't they read the papers, haven't they learned there are some funny people about? I nearly say something as she comes out past the classroom window with its pasted cut-out dragons and Indian deities and smiling suns. She wears black leggings and a white embroidered blouse. She has a long nose and a no-crap manner. She could pass for pretty. She is pretty. The same this evening, in her cut-off denim shorts and yellow flop top, her bare legs slender and mulberried with varicose veins. It's hot still, even at eight, even with the engine running and the air-conditioner on. The dog days whine. Tonight it's a family barbecue: he's leaning over a rack of briquettes, turning sausages and chicken wings with his tongs. She hands him a Kestrel, and he stands there gripping it like a torch. All over London men are standing or walking with similar torches, tubes to light up with, to take the dark away. The kids pedal in and out of the yard. I should be at home with my own kids, having our own barbecue, but, for the moment, they've become anonymous: it's this surrogate family that obsesses me instead. I hang on at a safe distance, feeling conspicuous, a voyeur. This isn't Saab country, yet here I sit twice daily in my red 900i. It's as well that there are trees, and cars left by commuters at the station, and the indolence of a London estate in mid-July.

One night I come much later than usual, a bit drunk after a party. The estate is dark and silent. I park in the usual spot, between the rusting Bedford and the Escort with beaded seats. I step out on to the walkway, and light – from the moon or street lamps I can't tell – catches silver in the yard of number twelve. I hesitate in my stride, then adjust it like a hurdler, an extra step in it before I reach the gate. I stare in as I pass, and the bike's there, high above the plastic patrol car and the lowly scooter, black and gleaming like a timing device. I walk by, wondering if it's chained to something or if it's simply been forgotten. I turn after the last house, like a busby at the end of his beat, and cursor back along the line I've made, once more past the gate. No chain that I can see, no lock; it must be a mistake, the kind of mistake most kids have learned not to make, that their parents wouldn't make either, a mistake made tonight only through distraction or exhaustion. A bike for a ten-year-old shining brightly. I walk back to the car and sit there for a while and scan the line of flats for signs of life: not a bleep, not a chimmer. I wonder if I dare do what I want and feel a surge of elation, that once-in-a-decade certainty of being in the right. Tracy Chapman, on Jazz FM, dies with the ignition. I get out and listen. I ooze across the grass on my

soft heels and I don't even need to open the gate, only reach over to
where the bike is leaning against the low wall and tilt it away to
upright. I pause and listen again, holding it there, my stomach muscles
tensing as I raise it off the ground, one hand under the saddle, the other
squeezing the mudguard and front wheel; no chain noise, no scraping
against the wall, the thing hanging mid-air now as I draw it back and
up towards my face like a giant pair of spectacles; one wheel revolving
slowly as I lift it higher, raising it to my lips, over the summit of the
wall, safely and in silence down this side on to the pavement, gently
down, still not a noise. A last pause before I carry it up the walkway,
not daring to put it down yet in case it squeaks. Then, ten yards on, I
set it down at last, my wrist muscles tight and pinging, and I lift my leg
over and clamber on, forcing the right pedal down as I do, wobbly for
a second, far too big for it, my knees absurdly winging out each side.
Inside, I'm a silent scream of triumph and reparation, the scales tipping
back to middle, the world put to rights again. I'd do tricks if I could –
no hands, see – but I spin over to the shadows by the railway
embankment, look round to see all's clear, then leave the bike under
the darkness of the fence while I go back for the car. All quiet at
number twelve, no lynch-mob, no torchlights of outrage: I drive the
Saab the hundred yards up to the sprawl of spokes, swing the big
mouth of the boot open and lift the bike in, doubling back the front
wheel to squeeze the whole frame in free of the catch. Boot locked,
doors locked, I drive back through the spotlights and security glare of
street after street, preparing my story should the police stop me and
demand to see the contents of my boot: easy enough, 'my son's bike,
officer', which is true. Then I'm home; I stow the bike in the garage and
climb the stairs to Kathy under the duvet, saying nothing, saving my
surprise for later.

I lie awake, listening for sirens, resisting the temptation to wake my
son, thinking back to my own childhood and its deferred gratifications,
the surprises my father once prepared for me. I remember the
extravagant secrecy of his Christmas presents – the huge train set in the
attic, which he must have worked at for weeks, joining the tracks,
ensuring the points worked, painting fields and sticking down model
bushes, and all the while me banned from the attic because, he said, he
was redecorating, the ban lifted only on Christmas morning; and then
the next Christmas, the pedal car in the garage, my old pedal car,

which I'd nearly outgrown but into which he'd had the engine of a moped fitted so I could learn to steer and brake and accelerate, so I could bat around the outside of the house like Stirling Moss. For my father, the surprise had been more important than the giving. I grew up expecting surprises. Now I'd prepared one myself. I get up and scribble a note and leave it by my son's bed: A SURPRISE FOR YOU IN THE GARAGE.

In the event, though, I wake before him and have to rouse him to make him read the words on the note. He's confused and doesn't understand why I wrote the message and why I can't just tell him now what the surprise is, rather than making him trail downstairs. He dresses. We go below together. I turn the garage light on, waiting for triumph to light in his eyes as it has in mine.

'There,' I say. 'Your bike.'

He goes over to look, takes hold of the handlebars.

'It's second-hand, Dad.'

'Well, third-hand, I suppose. But at least you've got it back. Everything's OK.'

'But it's not my bike.'

'Well it may be a bit more scratched than it was but . . .'

'No, it's not mine. It's a different make. It's a Raleigh and it's got a fur saddle.'

He goes off to school, I drive to work, putting the bike in the boot while I try to work out what to do. I could go and knock at the door of number twelve and try to explain, but who'd believe me, or believe me before beating me up? I could go to the police, but they might charge me – 'It's an offence, stealing: this was police business, Sir.' I could try to leave the bike in the night, just as I'd stolen it in the night, but won't they be looking out, extra vigilant? And if they aren't looking out, who can guarantee the bike won't be gone before they wake? I could hide the bike, and write a note telling where to find it, an anonymous tip-off, but how could I get the note delivered safely? The post takes too long, a courier would have my name and address, leaving the note myself means going to the door. I could do nothing, and keep the bike, but even if my son consented to ride it, would it be worth the shame and guilt?

I try to work, but can't. I feel stupid, criminal, a failure. Now, two bikes have been stolen instead of one. Seeking to cure my son's misery,

I've made another child miserable. Setting the world to rights, I've
added to its sum of little wrongs. God knows, the Ferrier is deprived
enough without me depriving one of its children some more. I think of
my father again, and of how pathetic a father I look beside him – he
who gave, I who can't even repossess; he who seemed so certain of
what was right, I who don't know what to do.

What I do is this: drive to the estate, get the bike out of the boot and
wheel it over the quiet grass, in sight of Leah and Michael's school. It's
three-twenty, coming out time, and I wait till I see them walking in my
direction with their mother and Charlene. I turn and wheel the bike
around the corner, ahead of me and them, then leave it in the middle
of the path, sprawled there like an accident. It's risky, I know. They
might choose a different route. They might not recognize this bike as
the bike gone from their yard. It might be nicked in the two minutes
before they reach it. But I remember the trap my father laid the night
we lost the hamster: lumps of cheese placed across the wash-house
floor, then up a ramp and abundant in the bottom of a deep cake-tin,
tempting the hamster below. It couldn't work, we knew, and yet it did.
And this will, too, if a man's to be allowed one small act of reparation:
a bike returned as if from heaven.

MOTHER CARE

Jayne Anne Phillips

After the birth and the overnight in the hospital she didn't go downstairs for a week. She'd lost some blood and she felt flattened, nearly dizzy, from the labour and then the general anaesthetic. She wept frequently, with incredible ease, and entertained the illusion that she now knew more than she'd ever questioned or known before. The illusion pursued her into sleep itself, into jagged pieces of sleep. She slept and woke, naked except for underpants, sanitary napkins, chemical ice packs. The ice packs, shaped to her crotch, were meant to reduce swelling and numb the stitches; the instructions directed her to bend the cotton to activate the solution; inside, the thick pads cracked like sticks. This bathroom looks like a MASH unit, Matt would say. But it's not your unit that's mashed, Kate would think. In fact, her vagina was an open wound. Her vagina was out of the picture. She couldn't believe she'd ever done anything with it, or felt anything through it.

She couldn't use tampons; there were boxes of big napkins, like bandages, piles of blue underliners – plastic on one side, gauze on the other – to protect the sheets, haemorrhoid suppositories, antibiotic salve, mentholated anaesthetic gel, tubes of lanolin, plastic cups and plastic pitchers. She drank and drank: water, cider, juices. The baby slept in a bassinet right beside her bed but her arms ached from picking him up, holding him, putting him down. On the third day her milk came in, and by then her nipples were already cracked and bleeding. The baby was nursing colostrum every hour but he was sucking for comfort, losing a few more ounces each day. His mouth was puckered, and a large clear blister had formed on his upper lip; he was thirsty, so thirsty; finally Kate gave him water, though the nurses had said not to. *He needs to nurse, to pull the milk in.* That night she woke in the dark, on her back, her engorged breasts sitting on her chest, warm to the touch, gravid, hard and swollen. She woke the baby to feed him. He began to cry, but she held him away until she could sit and prop her arms with pillows, pour a glass of water for the thirst that would assail her. In the beginning she'd moaned as he sucked; then, to move through the initial latching on, she did the same breathing she'd used throughout labour. She breathed evenly, silenced vocalizations cutting in like whispers at the end of each exhalation. The pain cracked through her like a thread of lightning and gradually eased, rippling like something that might wake up and get her.

She called LaLeche League every couple of days for new suggestions. Kate's favourite counsellor was in Medford, a working-class part of Boston Kate didn't remember ever having seen. But the woman had no accent; she was someone else far from home. You'll battle through this, she would say. Be stubborn and hang on. Women are made to nurse, she'd declare in each conversation; any woman can nurse. And then she'd say, in a softer tone, that people forgot how hard it was to get established the first time. 'Don't let the pain defeat you,' were her exact words. 'The uterine pain actually helps you heal, and your nipples will toughen.'

'What about stress?' Kate asked once. 'Will I have enough milk –'

'Stress?' was the response, 'are you kidding? Any woman with a new baby is stressed to the max. She doesn't sleep, she's bleeding, she's sore, she might have other kids or a job she'll go back to. The baby is sucking for life. As long as you eat and drink – drink constantly – your body responds. You don't need unbroken sleep. You don't need a perfect situation. Refugees nurse their babies, and war victims; theirs are the children more likely to survive, even in the worst of times.'

I understand, Kate wanted to say, I understand all about you, and I understand everything.

'Have your husband buy you a manual breast pump at the hospital infirmary,' the counsellor had said, 'and a roll of disposable plastic bottles. The pump is a clear plastic tube, marked in ounces. Use it each time your breasts aren't completely emptied by the baby. Increase production; you can't have too much milk. Freeze all you express.

That's how some women work full-time and still nurse their babies. I'll send you some information in the mail. And if you feel discouraged, call back.'

I just want to hear your voice, Kate wanted to say. We're in a tunnel flooded with light.

But she spoke an accepted language, words like air-dry, lanolin, breast rotation, demand schedule. And there was light all around her, great patches angling through the naked windows, glancing off snow piled and fallen and drifted, hard snow, frozen, crusted with ice, each radiant crystal reflecting light. Kate had brought her son home in the last week of December, and the temperature was sixty degrees, sun like spring; her neighbour Carmela had festooned the fence with blue balloons. Kate and Alexander posed for photographs, then she took him in the house, shutting the front door behind them. Immediately the cold came back, and the snows began. At night Kate was awake, nursing, burping the baby, changing odourless cloth diapers, changing his gown, nursing, nursing him to sleep; all the while, snow fell in swathes past the windows, certain and constant, drifting windblown through the street lamp's bell of light. Each day Kate stayed upstairs, and her mother padded back and forth along the hallway connecting their rooms. Just before Christmas she'd finished a full round of chemo, and the tumours in her lungs had shrunk; she had a few weeks of respite now before the next group of treatments and she came to Kate's room to keep her company, to hold the baby while Kate slept, to pour the glasses of juice.

'Are you awake, Katie?' She sat in an upholstered chair that had once graced her own living room; Kate had moved that couch and chair to Boston and covered them in a vibrant 1920s print, navy blue with blowzy, oversized ivory flowers.

'I'm always awake, more or less,' Kate said. 'How was your night?'

'No complaints,' her mother said. 'No nausea.'

'Good.' Kate smiled. 'It's nice to see you sitting in that chair. I always see it in photographs, in one of its guises. In the old house.'

'Yes,' Kate's mother said. 'By the time we moved into town, this chair was in the basement.'

'Now you might admit I was right to drag it to Boston. The cushions may be shot, but at least you have a comfortable place to sit.' Watching her mother, Kate realized the print she'd chosen for the chair, dark blue with white, was nearly the reverse of her mother's choice. 'Remember the fabric of your slip-covers, what you used on that chair? What did you always call that print?'

'It was a blue onion print, white with blue vines –'

'Thistle-like flowers,' Kate interrupted, 'like fans, with viney runners –'

'Yes,' her mother continued patiently, 'wild onions, hence the name.'

'And you had those glass pots with lids in the same print on the coffee table. I remember. There they sit, in all the Easter pictures. When we're wearing our good clothes. You always matched things. But before, there was that dark living room.'

'Dark?'

'The walls were dark green, and the drapes on the picture windows were dark green with gold, and the furniture in its original upholstery, dark beige with a raised texture.'

'Well, when kids are young, you want things that are dark and tough, to last. When you were older, we had the white fibreglass drapes and the lighter slip-covers. That first upholstery was chosen to last through climbing and sliding and whatever – your brothers gave it a workout.'

'It did last,' Kate said, 'it was what I covered up. It seems ageless.'

'Yes,' her mother agreed, 'but it darkened. This was your father's chair, and the fabric darkened just in the shape of him.'

'Really?' Kate asked. 'You mean, as though his shadow sank into it?'

Her mother frowned, exasperated. 'No, I mean it was worn. Worn from use. Am I speaking English?'

Kate laughed. 'Your energy level is better, isn't it? You're your old feisty self, and I'm just lying here.'

Her mother peered over at the bassinet. 'I thought I might hold Alexander for you, but he's sleeping so beautifully. I've been downstairs already, to let that little girl in, the Mother Care worker. It's been wonderful to have her for a week. She came this morning with her arms full of groceries. She's just putting things away and then she'll be up to see what you want her to do.'

'It was so nice of you to buy help for me, Mom, such a great present.'

'Well, I'd be doing all the cooking myself, if I were able. But I must say, your requirements are pretty daunting.'

Kate smiled. She'd asked for someone versed in preparing natural foods. No additives, no preservatives. No meat with hormones. 'Your colour is good today, Mom,' she said. 'You're sitting right there in the sun and you look all lit up.'

'I'm sure I do. It's so bright in this room. Why do you paint everything white? And not a thing on the windows, not even shades to pull down.'

'The walls are linen white,' Kate said, 'and the trim is white. And I don't need shades; I'm not worried about snipers.'

'Snipers?'

'My LaLeche League lady,' Kate said. 'She was telling me how war victims can go right on nursing their babies, even in foxholes.'

Her mother frowned. 'Some of these people are way out there. What do war victims have to do with you? You're not in a foxhole.'

'Not yet,' Kate said. 'But really, if you want shades on your windows, I'll get some. You should have told me sooner.'

Her mother waved away the suggestion. 'I don't care. That big tree is in front of one of the windows, and the other faces Carmela's house. I certainly don't care if she sees me, not that there's much to see at this point.'

'But there's always Derek,' Kate said slyly, referring to their neighbour's live-in boyfriend. 'What about him?'

'Derek is occupied in greener pastures. I hope not too occupied. If he lives with Carmela, I don't know why he has to have his own place downtown. And his own crystal and china. And his own art collection.'

Kate shrugged. 'He's a lawyer. Maybe he needs a place downtown. Anyway, he's cute. I remember how they charged over here the first day we moved in, on their way to some swank thing, and there's Carmela, nearly six feet tall, in one of those long satin capes her daughter made her, and all her Navajo jewellery, with a huge tray of assorted handmade cookies and a raspberry pie.'

'Carmela is wonderful. Mark my words, though, Derek is not in it for the long haul.'

'Not everyone is into hauling,' Kate said. 'She's been divorced twice; he's been divorced once; maybe they're better off just relaxing.'

Her mother shook her head impatiently, signalling her annoyance with a click of the tongue. 'She's certainly suggested he give up the apartment. Carmela loves taking care of people; she'd like to be married. But he is not the right fellow.'

'Gotcha,' Kate said. She realized she often knew in advance her mother's response to a given topic, but she elicited the responses anyway, sometimes to her annoyance, more often for pleasure. She so valued her mother's sheer dependability, the slight cynicism of the old wives' tales she favoured, her bedrock common sense, even the rigid provincial innocence with which she approached discussions of what Kate referred to as 'modern life'. There were so many topics on which her mother held strong opinions based on scant experience. Like serial monogamy and live-in arrangements. Interracial relationships. Homosexuality. Literature. Film. When I go to a movie, she liked to say, I want to be *entertained*, not upset.

Kate leaned back on her pillows. She didn't want to be entertained; entertainment was far too demanding and gave so little in return. Kate wanted someone to read stories to her or speak intensely about a private matter. She wanted to be fed. The Mother Care worker brought Kate lunch on a tray, numerous plates of soft, warm tastes, samples of the various entrées she'd made to freeze, and sliced vegetables so cold and crisp they wore ice fragments. Her name was Moira, but Kate liked to think of her only as Mother Care; Mother Care put a flower on the tray, the head of a hothouse daisy or rose, never in a bud vase – too likely to topple in the journey upstairs, perhaps – but floating, the first day, in a cup. Then the flower always appeared in an antique shot glass. It was so pretty to see a flower, yet Kate felt that the daisy and its lissom petals seemed sacrificial. The soft sphere of the scarlet rose sank inward, pulled from its stem. Kate touched the flowers, their surfaces, as though they were already gone. 'It may be January in New England,' Moira had said, 'but it's still important to see something blooming. And don't worry, I work with unprocessed foods. I'm a vegetarian though I don't mind cooking meat if that's what you want. My objections are strictly personal.' Kate heard her now, her tread on the stairs and the subtle shifting of cutlery. The smell of food came closer and set up a dull fear in Kate, like nervousness or excitement.

'Here we are,' Moira said. 'And I brought the mail up too.' She placed the bed tray squarely before Kate and pulled her pillows back. 'Might want to sit up a bit more. There's a tomato-arugula salad and French bread, and I made you a really hearty vegetable soup with barley. I froze five pints.'

'Great,' Kate said. 'We'll be thinking of you into next month, blessing the fact of your existence.'

Moira nodded. She was so efficient, Kate thought, and she had a quiet, non-intrusive presence, but she seemed a bit humourless. Now she smiled her quick, disappearing smile. Perhaps she was only shy.

'This is my last day with you,' she said, 'so maybe we should come up with a plan. I know you want to do everything with the baby yourself, but the freezer is almost full of food. There's just room for a few pans of lasagne, which I'll make this afternoon. I'll do all the laundry again, but don't forget I could also give you a massage or a manicure.'

'Or you could read to me,' said Kate.

'Don't waste the time you have left,' her mother said. 'I could read to you.'

'How about a massage?' Moira asked.

Kate felt so sore, so weak, the thought of anyone touching her was alarming. But she thought Moira had a dreamy voice, soft, a bit insubstantial; Moira's voice would carry words and disappear in them. 'A massage, maybe,' Kate said, 'and then a story.'

'Sure.' She nodded and took the mail from the tray. 'There's a little package for you and some cards. I left the bills downstairs. Now I'll go and get another lunch, so the two of you can eat together.'

Kate's mother nodded in her direction. 'No, I'll eat later, I'm coming down soon. You go ahead, Katie, before he wakes up, and your arms are full.'

'I'm coming down later too,' Kate announced. 'I hope you both realize that I'm dressed today. It's a nursing gown, but still –'

'You're right,' Moira said. 'I didn't even notice. There you sit, clothed to the elbows.'

'Well, I've always been clothed below the waist, in my various bandages.'

'Exactly.' Moira busied herself straightening the covers of the bed. 'And when you're nursing every hour and you're so sore, it hardly seems worth it to take clothes on and off, or lift them up and down.'

'It's amazing how the two of you think alike,' Kate's mother said wryly. 'Anyway, I wasn't going to say anything. You've been mostly covered with sheets and blankets, and I figured you'd get your clothes on by spring.'

'I have my gown on.' Kate picked up her spoon. 'That's all I'll commit to.'

'And you do feel warm,' Moira said, 'when you're making milk. But I know you don't have a temperature, because I've taken it every day.'

'You certainly have,' Kate's mother said. 'You've taken good care of her.'

'Why don't we plan on the massage then?' Moira gathered used cups from the bedside table. 'You eat all that, then he'll wake, and you'll nurse, and by the time he goes down again, I'll be ready. I'll bring up my oils and a tape to play. All right?'

'You're in charge,' Kate's mother said.

When Kate woke, the bed tray was gone. Her mother was gone too, and the house was perfectly quiet. She remembered finishing the food and leaning back in bed, and then she'd fallen asleep, dreamlessly, as though she had only to close her eyes to move away, weightless and pure, skimming the reflective surface of something deep.

She heard a small sound. Alexander lay in the bassinet, his eyes open, looking at her. His swaddling blankets had come loose. Propped on his side by pillows, he raised one arm and moved his hand delicately. Kate sat up to lean near him and touched her forefinger to his palm; immediately he grasped on hard, and his gaze widened. 'They're your fingers,' she told him. 'You don't know them yet, but I do.' Everyone had told her to leave him be when he was happy, she'd be holding him and caring for him so ceaselessly, but she took him in her arms, propped up the pillows and put him in her lap. He kicked excitedly and frowned. She bent her knees to bring him closer and regarded him as he lay on her raised thighs; the frown disappeared. 'You're like me,' Kate said softly. 'You frown when you think. By the time you're twenty-five, you'll have two little lines between your eyes. Such a serious guy.' He raised his downy brows. He had a watchful, observing look and a more excited look; he'd open his eyes wider, compress his lips, strain with his limbs as though he were concentrating on moving, on touching or grasping. He could feel his body but he couldn't command it to move or do; his focus was entirely in his eyes. And he did focus; Kate was sure he saw her. He wasn't a newborn any longer; today he was one week old. Perhaps his vision was still blurry, and that was why he peered at her so intently. His eyes were big and dark blue, like those of a baby seal. One eye was always moist and teary; his tear duct was blocked, they'd said at the hospital; it would clear up.

Now Kate wiped his cheek carefully with the edge of a cloth diaper, then drew her finger across his forehead, along his jaw, across his flattened, broad little nose. 'Mister man,' she whispered, 'mighty mouse, here's your face. Here are your nose, your ears, your widow's peak. Old widower, here are your bones . . .' She touched his collarbones and the line along his shoulder under his gown. His skin was like warm silk. She cleaned him with warm water, not alcohol wipes, and powdered him with a product that contained no talc. The powder was fine as rice flour and smelt as Kate thought rice fields might smell in the sun, when the plants bloomed. Like clean food, pure as flowers.

Across the world and in the South, those young shoots grew and moved in the breeze like grass. 'Rice fields are like grass in water,' she said to Alexander. 'We haven't seen them yet. Even in India I didn't see them.' Outside the wind moved along the house; Kate heard it circling and testing. Suddenly a gust slammed against the windows, and Alexander, startled, looked towards the sound. 'You can't see the wind,' Kate murmured, 'just what it moves.' The wind would bring snow again, Kate knew; already, she heard snow approach, like a whining in the wind. Absently she traced the baby's lips, and he yawned and began to whimper. You're hungry? Kate thought, and he moved his arms as though to gather her closer. Her milk let down with a flush and surge, and she held a clean diaper to one breast as she put him to the other. Now she breathed, exhaling slowly. The intense pain began to ebb; he drank the cells of her blood, Kate knew, and the crust that formed on her nipples where the cuts were deepest. He was her blood. When she held him, he was inside her; always he was near her, like an atmosphere, in his sleep, in his being. She would not be alone again for many years, even if she wanted to be, even if she tried. In her deepest thoughts she would approach him, move around and through him, make room for him. In nursing there would be a still, spiral peace, an energy in which she felt herself, the debris of her needs and wants, slough away. It seemed less important to talk or think; like a nesting animal, she took on camouflage, layers of protective awareness that were almost spatial in dimension, like sonar. The awareness had dark edges, shadows that rose and fell; Kate imagined terrible things. That he might stop breathing. That she dropped him, or someone had. That someone or something took him from her. That she forgot about him or misplaced him. There were no words; the thoughts occurred to her in starkly precise images, like the unmistakable images of dreams, as though her waking and sleeping lives had met in him. Truly, she was sleeping; the days and nights were fluid, beautiful and discoloured; everything in her was available to her, as though she'd become someone else, someone with a similar past history in whom that history was acknowledged rather than felt, someone who didn't need to make amends or understand, someone beyond language. She was shattered.

Something new would come of her. Moments in which she crossed from consciousness to sleep, from sleep to awareness, there was a lag of an instant in which she couldn't remember her name, and she didn't care. She remembered him. Now his gaze met hers, and his eyelids fluttered; she could see him falling away, back into his infant swoon. His sleep closed around him like an ocean shell and rocked him within it. In this they were alike, Kate thought, though he had no name known to him, no name to forget. He was pure awareness and need. She took him from the breast and held him to her shoulder, patting and rubbing him, softly, a caress and a heartbeat.

Moira came into the room so quietly that Kate was unaware of her until she reached the foot of the bed. She carried blankets, a tape recorder, plastic bottles of oils, a small cardboard box. Depositing her burdens on the floor, she mouthed, 'Shall I take him?' And Kate gestured, no, not yet. She whispered, 'I'll set up,' and disappeared from view. Kate smelt the sulphur of lit matches and then citrus and gardenia, Moira's scented votives. Kate put Alexander carefully into the bassinet and looked through the books stacked beside her table. She chose one. Which passage? The beginning would do.

'I'm going to put the tape on very low. As he sleeps more deeply, I'll turn it up just a bit.' Moira was beside her. 'Is that the book you want?' She smiled and took it, then indicated the rug at the foot of the bed. 'I've made a space. It's better to have a firm surface.'

'A space,' Kate said. She stood and saw that Moira had made an alternative bed, blankets precisely folded, a pallet covered with terry towels. Sheets and more blankets were arranged over it, neatly turned down. Six votives were lit in a row of little flames at the head. 'This looks quite ritualistic,' Kate said. 'Do I need a chaperone?'

'I don't believe so.' Moira turned the tape on. 'But I won't lie, it is a ritual. I'm sorry I can't lower the light. Evening is a better time, but I don't work nights.'

'It doesn't need to be dark,' Kate said. 'Look how the sun falls across. I love the sun.'

'Yes, you'll feel it. Can you lie on your front comfortably? I'll go out while you get ready.'

'No need.'

'No, I will. And take everything off. I'll bring the warm oils from the kitchen.'

Kate watched her go and sighed. What a lot of work this was. She walked past the pallet into the bathroom, pulling the door to. There, the water running, getting warm. She took off her gown and pants, folded the pads and wrapped them in paper, threw them away. Slowly, she began to wash, water cooling on her legs in rivulets. They'd told her not to bathe yet; she stood like this, cloths and soap, carefully. At first, when she stood or walked, she'd felt as though she were moving on the deck of a ship, as though some rhythm pulsed in the ground, the floor. Rooms subtly shifted. The effects of the general, Matt said, but Kate could see the movement even from her bed, from her window. The way the angles of the ceiling met the walls, how the floor slid to its four corners. How the earth turned. This is the way it's always been, Kate thought; she hadn't known. Now she did. She rocked the baby in the rocking chair and imagined sailing through the window, rocking, with no interruption, into the cold, the air billowing around them. You OK? Matt would ask. I'm fine, Kate would answer. As a child, an adolescent, an adult, she had almost never cried. Now she could. She didn't feel depressed, she felt amazed and moved and out of sync. Or she was in sync, but she couldn't explain how. She left her gown where it fell, dried herself and opened the door.

The music was a little more noticeable now, classical music, strings. A shaft of sunlight poured across the rug, and motes of dust swam in the light. Moira knelt by the empty fireplace, waiting for her. 'Sorry,' Kate said, 'I wanted to get clean.' Moira nodded and pulled back the sheets of the pallet for Kate to slip inside. Slowly, Kate was on her knees, and then prone.

'We won't wake him?' she said, before turning over.

'You wouldn't be comfortable away from him,' Moira answered. 'We won't disturb him.'

Then the sheets and blankets were a silky covering. Moira moved her hands along Kate's form as though to gain some innate sense of her, pausing, exerting a gentle pressure. It's a New-Age thing, Kate thought, and it's from the oldest days, when floors were swept earth. Behind the music she heard Moira breathing, exhaling in time to the movement of her hands, as though she were draining Kate of fatigue or discomfort, releasing it through herself. Surely that was the idea. 'So, Moira,' Kate said softly, 'what are your personal objections?'

The hands never slowed. 'To what?'

'Meat. To meat.'

'Oh. Health, basically, at first, theories about nutrition. But after I stopped eating meat, the smell of my body changed, and the taste in my mouth. I don't mind handling meat – I cook and do catering, and sometimes it's part of my job – but I don't want it inside me. And I didn't want my daughter growing up on a meat diet.'

'You have a daughter?'

'Yes. She's three. I'm a single mom.'

So she works days, Kate thought. Nights at home with her daughter. 'You seem so content and organized,' she said aloud. 'Were you always single?'

'Yes, pretty much. It was a bit difficult at first, but for now, we're content. We do very well.'

'Little women,' Kate said. 'But in those mother-daughter stories, there's always a virtuous hero offstage, the father off at war, or the rich neighbour.'

'And so there may be,' Moira said. 'But I'll do whatever's best for my child. I don't need to be saved.'

'What a relief,' Kate said.

'Yes.' Moira laughed softly.

'But we do have to save ourselves, don't we,' Kate murmured. 'Such a project.'

'You're stronger each day,' Moira said. 'And you're doing exactly what you should be doing with this baby. It's so important to nurse and to have him constantly with you.'

Now the light of the sun had shifted; it seemed winter light again, flattened and diffuse, and the flames of the votives burned higher. Moira's hands were at Kate's hips, lifting her from behind, tilting heat into her abdomen; she moved up along Kate's spine with her fists, a hard and soft pressure, repetitive, patterned with heat Kate felt in her forearms, in her thighs. She felt herself knit together, handled like something wounded; she realized how far she was from herself, and how she might begin to live here again, in her body. Slowly it would happen. She might call and call now for her own return, but she only floated, inhabiting so many former selves with more conviction: just now she saw the backs and jostling shoulders of her hometown girlfriends, all bundled in their coats and descending into snow down dormitory stairs; they still looked like high-school blondes and brunettes in fur hats and boots, bright twine in their hair, but they were getting off on mescaline, falling into the first tinges of visuals, and someone was crooning, *Pleased as punch, pleased as punch.* In India, on the vast terrace of the Taj Mahal, boys had approached Kate with open arms. *Sell blue jeans? Buy hashish? Extreme hashish. You sell blue jeans?* The young men, the slim ones, looked like boys, smooth skinned and lithe. The middle-aged men on the train to Agra were toadish and portly in their tailored clothes; they seldom looked up from their newspapers. Mist rose from the steaming fields as though daybreak would go on for weeks, and Kate saw silhouettes of movement, squatting forms, their morning toilette a slow, dark ballet. An old man, skeletal in white, hunkered by the tracks, brushing his teeth with a twig. On the tortuous mountain track to Chitwan, the Nepalese bus had stopped in a town; farmers disembarked with their caged chickens, and the women with their saronged babies; the Gurkha soldiers piled out with their guns. The women merely lifted their layered, intricately sewn skirts to relieve themselves, standing to straddle the sewage ditch that ran along one side of the only road. Water rattled in it, and the men walked further up, discreetly, but Kate wandered behind the shack-like kiosks to pick her way down a rocky bank to the river. Ropes of faeces blackened among the stones. The riverbank flattened in a broad sweeping curve, and the water was low; outcroppings strewn with boulders rose in crescents from glistened sweeps too still and silver to seem fluid. Kate dropped her loose cloth trousers to her knees and crouched, urinating; to her left, two men appeared at the bend of the river, balancing on their shoulders a long pole bent with the weight of a body. The body swung in delicate motion, bound to the pole at wrists and ankles, the swathed, faceless head flung back.

Kate wanted to look away but could not. Moira's voice came from above her. 'It's time for me to go now,' she said.

'Yes, I know.' Kate turned and lay on her back. Behind her eyes she saw a darkness reddened by light. 'Goodbye, Moira.'

Moira touched Kate's forehead with her fingertips. Her touch lingered deliberately, a firm little bruise specific as a kiss. Kate lay still and felt Moira close to her, just over her, her clove-scented breath, the oil of her dark hair. Perhaps she always ended her massages this way. Perhaps she thought Kate ridiculous, a privileged woman not yet alone with her child. Kate raised her gaze to Moira's. 'You look so grave,' Kate said. 'But then, goodbye is a grave word.'

'It's just a wish,' Moira said and moved away. Her hands pressed in a careful pattern above the tucked blankets, finishing evenly. 'He's sleeping,' she said softly. 'You sleep too, if you like, but here's your story.'

Kate heard a ruffling of pages.

'Chapter one,' came a voice. 'I am born . . . To begin my life with the beginning of my life, I record that I was born (as I have been informed and believe) on a Friday, at twelve o'clock at night . . .' Kate closed her eyes. The river was a high rattling murmur, and the barefoot men moved ceaselessly forward in the islanded riverbed. The men never looked at her. They were there still, Kate thought, making progress down the Narayani to the mouth of the Bagmati, two days' trek. The cremation sites, in view of the blue-eyed stupas and their gold spires, were raised earth bound by stones, and the flaming pyres were set afloat, heaped with burning flowers. Kate smelt that scent, like blackened oranges, sticky and boiled, so close she was enveloped. It was remarked that the clock began to strike . . . and I began to cry, simultaneously . . . She knew she must stand up now and walk, or the bus would ascend into the mountains without her.

Kate sat at the kitchen table, dressed in her clothes. Mother Care was finished; Kate herself was Mother Care. The downstairs of her own house looked strange to her, larger, more impersonal, as though she were a visitor with some dimly realized connection to this place. She lay other mail aside and opened only the little package from LaLeche League, postmarked Medford.

Sealed into a white envelope were two small plastic objects and a handwritten instruction sheet: *How to Use Nursing Shields*. The shields were gently conical and extremely simple. Kate considered regarding them as unpretentious S&M aids or punk-rock falsies, but in fact they were objects seemingly more conducive to plastic food storage than to anything used for enhancement, protection or pleasure. Kate got the impression they'd been passed on to her from other women, other breasts. Circular plastic discs that snapped apart, they had a hole in the inner disc where the nipples fit through. They were meant to keep the nipple erect and dry, so it healed, and they had the added benefit of collecting the flow of milk that seeped into one's clothes before the baby could latch on. Milk seeped into Kate's clothes; milk sweetened and soured her chest and the cleft between her breasts every time she heard the baby cry, as soon as he cried. Milk wet her shirt when she sat down alone near her bedroom window and saw the exposed brown grass in the yard, rents in the snow; when she read some item in the newspaper about a child falling out a window; or when she saw a commercial for long-distance dialling on television. Sixty seconds of manipulative human-interest images, and her eyes were wet, and she didn't bother wiping her face. Her breasts let down, and her uterus cramped sharply, turning like a small animal inside her, contracting in its nest. When her eyes got wet, her breasts performed, as though she wept milk. She could cry and she could nurse, or when she nursed, she didn't have to cry; her body wept. She wept food, and he grew on sorrow.

'What are those things?' Kate's mother stood behind her, peering over her shoulder.

'They're nursing shields. Look, they're like something out of *Barbarella*.'

'What's *Barbarella*?'

'You know, that Jane Fonda movie where she's a blonde space bimbo and she wears pointy warrior shields over her breasts, and silver gladiator boots and tights, and she gets picked up by an eagle –'

'An eagle?'

'Yes. She wakes up in this huge bird's nest looking – soporific . . .

anyway, the LaLeche woman sent these things to me for my breasts. They go inside a nursing bra, now that I'm wearing a bra, to keep the cloth from sticking and making everything worse.'

'What else did she tell you to do?'

'Well, there's the wet method and the dry method. One school of thought is to feed through the pain and keep the cuts moist with lanolin, because otherwise the baby breaks them open anyway every time he nurses. But then nothing ever really heals. Or, you hope you heal, but it might take a long time. The other is to stop nursing, go naked and air-dry, express into a pump to feed the baby, but then the baby might refuse the breast when you start up again, or the nipples heal and just crack repeatedly –'

'What do these things have to do with it all?'

'They keep you dry and pull your nipples out if they're inverted, so the baby latches on better. And I guess they beat going topless. I mean, suppose I want to answer the doorbell or leave the house someday.' Kate put one of the plastic shields inside her shirt, in her bra, over the sorest breast.

'Of course you'll leave the house again. My God, after what you went through, you needed to stay in bed for a week. You had a general anaesthetic after that long labour. And then all this with the nursing.' Kate's mother sighed and sat down in the chair opposite. 'It's amazing how nature slaps women with everything at once – you take care of a new baby twenty-four hours a day, just when you're most exhausted.'

Kate gazed at her mother's face and felt her wholly familiar presence. In this place, this house where they'd all lived less than three months, her mother was so real, so connected to all they'd come from, to everything Kate had taken with her, the burden and the weight and the furious beauty she kept trying to turn around and see. She wondered if she would see anything of that first world anymore, when her mother was gone. 'Yes,' she said aloud, her voice faltering, 'it's so unrelieved. You never really wake up or sleep. Time stands still.'

'And later,' her mother went on, 'you forget. You don't think you will, but you do. I must have gone through all this with nursing, but I don't remember. I do remember the time your brother bit me.'

'Which brother?' Kate put her forefinger into the hole of the other nursing shield and began to spin it slowly on the table top directly in front of her. It made an unsatisfying, lopsided axis.

'I'll never forget that,' her mother said. 'He took a bite right out of me. He came away with blood all over his little face.'

Kate looked up. 'But I thought I was the only one you nursed.'

Her mother frowned. 'You're right. It must have been you.'

'It had to be me.' Kate laughed.

'What's so funny?'

'I'm thinking about the song. You look confused. Never mind.'

'Oh,' her mother said. 'That song. That's "It Had To Be You". No, I'm just surprised. Aunt Maud, who was the closest I had to a mother-in-law, told me I'd never be able to nurse because I was a smoker, though I stopped each time I was pregnant. So I didn't try with your older brother but I was determined to nurse you. I drank beer and milkshakes by the hour and I had plenty of milk. You were so fat your boobs hung to your waist.'

'That was fleeting,' Kate said, 'until now.'

'You'll get back into shape. Actually, nursing takes the weight faster – it all goes to the baby. But with my third, I was too tired. I had three kids under four. Think about it.'

'I can't,' Kate said. 'But I think bottle-feeding would be so much more trouble, all those bottles to wash and sterilize, and have you ever tasted formula? It's just chemicals and water. I think babies only drink it because they're starved to it.'

'Maybe. Mine sure sucked it down.' She paused. 'They were skinnier babies, much skinnier.'

'No one would ever advise you to drink beer to nurse now. You must have been slightly looped all the time. Think of all the IQ points I lost. No wonder I bit you.'

Kate's mother gave her an exasperated look. 'I don't think it hurt you any.'

Kate smiled. 'By the way, how old was I when you gave me that IQ test? Fourth or fifth grade, I believe. Just think, if not for all that beer, I might have scored solidly in the genius category.'

'I didn't tell you what your score was,' her mother said, abashed.

'No, but you told me approximately what it was, within precise parameters. I'm sure you remember. I lost out by a few points, and see, it was all your fault.'

'Fine, fine,' her mother said. 'In any case, you're smart enough. If you were any smarter, you'd have been unbearable. I couldn't have coped.'

'I'm not feeling smart,' Kate said. 'I feel as though half my brain is missing.' She positioned the other nursing shield in her bra. The top of her breast felt hot. Under her palm, her fingers, she felt a hard spot, like a knot. What was that?

'You look a little flushed,' her mother said. 'Your cheeks are red. Maybe you'd better go lie down.' She reached out to touch Kate's wrist. 'Just rest. Soon you'll be yourself again.'

'No,' Kate said, 'I won't. And why should I?'

She had mastitis. Desperately she wanted to walk outside into the cold, up and down the snow-bound streets. Antibiotics, her doctor said. Hot compresses and bedrest, fluids, said her LaLeche League counsellor. Give it a day. Antibiotics are a last resort; no one can really know how they'll affect the baby. Nurse even more frequently and pump and change compresses as soon as they begin to cool. If the fever reaches 102, take Tylenol. Is there someone to help you?

'Mom, please,' Kate said, 'open the window.'

'Don't be ridiculous. You're feverish and you have an infant here. Lie back and cover up. The water is good and hot. I just don't want to burn you.' She came to Kate's bed with an aluminium basin in her arms, and Kate looked dully inside it at the steaming cloths. 'Let me change the compress again,' her mother said. 'How long would you say the heat really lasts?'

'Oh, a hundred years or so.'

'I know you're restless. Could you read?' her mother said. 'Shall I turn on the TV?'

'No,' Kate said and threw off the coverlet. 'You're terribly efficient, Mom, but I don't see how we can go on like this all day. Weren't you just here three minutes ago?'

'Matt will take a shift when he comes home.' She removed the cooling cloth and lay the hot one delicately across Kate's breast. 'Should we see if Moira could come back?'

'That's not necessary.' Kate held her hand above the steaming cloth and imagined the heat on her breast increased. 'We can't afford another week of Mother Care. And this is not rocket science, it's hot washcloths.'

'We have to keep them this hot,' her mother said. 'The more constant we keep the heat, the more likely you are to get results. You've worked so hard at this, I don't want you to have to stop nursing.'

'I'm not stopping,' Kate said, incredulous. 'Who said anything about stopping?'

'Well, no one,' her mother said worriedly. 'You would only stop if your health were at stake.' She put down the basin and took up the edge of the wrinkled duvet, smoothing the white flannel.

Kate sighed. 'I see you've got the coverlet in your hand. Don't come at me with it. Unless someone has chills, you really don't bundle up a person with a fever. You only make them hotter. Where did you go to medical school, anyway? Mastitis is not serious; it's almost de rigueur. Nursing mothers who don't get it are really not even respectable veterans.'

'I wouldn't be concerned about your status. With all you've got on your plate, you'll surely come out of this a veteran of something. Is that cloth cool yet?'

'Mom, you'll make yourself tired. Please, sit down. If you want to distract me, read to me from something panoramic. There, read from what Moira started. Not the first lines, I don't want to hear them again, but start anywhere on the first page.'

Kate watched as her mother pulled the rocking chair close to the bed and felt for the book behind her on the seat, where Moira had left it. '*I was born with a caul . . .*' she began uncertainly.

'No, no,' Kate said. 'Let's skip the whole beginning. I heard it earlier today and came down with a fever. Go near to the end, when it's all coming right. Didn't you ever read this book? Doesn't everyone have to read it in high school?'

'Good heavens, I don't remember what I read in high school. Do you want the very last pages?'

'No, a little earlier. Do the reunion scene; you'll like it.' She took the book from her mother's outstretched hand and turned it to the right page. 'Start with, *Agnes, shall I tell you what about? I came to tell you.* Right here.'

'This print is so small. I feel as though I need my glasses changed.' Her mother leaned back slightly and peered at the page through her bifocals. '. . . *do you doubt my being true to you . . . what I always have been to you . . .* that part?'

'Right. *You have a secret, said I. Let me share it, Agnes.*'

'Now, if you know it from memory, why do you want me to read it to you?'

'Because I *love* it, of course. And who wouldn't? *Said I. Let me share it.* And the way he keeps repeating her name. My God, why don't people speak to one another that way every day, every hour?'

'People don't necessarily want to share secrets,' her mother said. 'And maybe I should read something else. The point of this was not for you to get upset.'

'I'm not upset!' Kate leaned back on the pillows, took a breath and lowered her voice to a near whisper. 'Just read, please. I beg of you.'

'*Said I*,' her mother intoned. 'All right. I'll start at the top of this next page.'

She began to read, and Kate trained her eyes on a middle distance, a space informed by winter light. It was the space behind her mother's chair, a shape consisting of bare floor and air just in front of the window. When Kate peered into that space correctly, the snowy view of descending streets and drifted roofs lost specificity and interest. Her eyes rested in emptiness that held nothing but a particular light of day and time. The space seemed concave, difficult to hold or see if one tried, but effortlessly present within a certain focus. The mode of the listener was that focus, and Kate let herself enter it, drifting and aware. Like active dreaming, infant dreams, dreams in which the body subtly flexes while the mind moves into other stories. Dickens's language was a story Kate knew, shadowed, burnished and detailed, even the descriptions of filth and ruin rendered in a language so controlled and rich, so confident that stories exist and listeners hear. Dickens's listeners were gone now; gone, all those living souls who'd paid to hear him speak in lecture halls, on stages, who'd stood within reach of his voice, all companions to a homeless boy, travellers to the death house, the poor house, all of them moving along streets made of stones, the horse-drawn wagons creaking, the clotted mud on flanks and boots. It was always winter in Dickens's London boyhood, always cold and foggy, and the bridges so long one couldn't see to the other side through wet, cloying mist. Everyone's hands looked chapped and old; so Western, Kate thought, that white, mottled skin, like the faintly mauve hands of kids from the coal towns, kids with old eyes. They knew how to say goodbye, those children, lined up in school hallways in their wrinkled coats, their chafed wrists delicate and dirty, the lines and whorls of their skin etched with old dirt. They were children from her mother's classrooms, children her mother had taught to read and write, children she'd clothed with whatever her own kids had outgrown. They boarded school buses at day's end and never waved, only looked, sideways glances through the rectangular windows. Kate had thought no one kissed them; she'd thought they'd be cold forever. Now in her mind's eye they cast their clear gaze through Dickens's unfurled words . . . *toiling on, I saw a ragged way-worn boy, forsaken and neglected . . .*

In Sri Lanka, in India, babies burnt with cholera or malaria. Moist skin, dark, lustrous hair. And ripe, endless gardens, fertile riots, fecund with colour and smell. Those babies could drown in dense scent, even through the membranes of their mother's bodies, through the protective caul of Dickens's story, any story. Kate watched her mother's mouth, a mouth not so generous as Kate's, a rosebud mouth perfectly suited to the bright red lipstick she'd worn all the years Kate had stood near her, looking up, the daughter so small in stature; or followed her, skipping to keep pace, her mother's black coat disappearing along grocery aisles, corridors, slushy streets. Dimly she heard the words her mother read: *Long miles of road then opened out before my mind . . .* Goodbye was not so simple as a kiss. Goodbye went on and on.

'Mom, wait,' Kate said softly.

Her mother stopped speaking and raised her eyes, startled.

'I'm sorry,' Kate said. 'I wasn't concentrating and I missed the part I really wanted to hear. Can you go back a bit and read the underlined paragraph?'

She glanced at the book and moved her chair closer to the bed, then half stood, remembering the compress, reaching to touch the cooled cloth that lay across Kate's breast. But Kate gestured to leave it be and nodded, encouraging her to go on.

'I went away, dear Agnes,' her mother read, 'loving you. I stayed away, loving you. I returned home, loving you. And now, I tried to tell her of the struggle I had had, and the conclusion I had come to. I tried to lay my mind before her, truly, and entirely.'

There was a hush in the room. Kate's mother looked back at the lines once. Then she leaned forward and touched her open palm to Kate's face. Kate touched her own hand to her mother's wrist and inclined her head as her mother stood to embrace her. Listening, she heard the beating of her mother's heart as snow brushed the windows in sweeps of wind.

Urvashi Butalia's mother's family outside their house in Model Town, Lahore, mid-1930s. Back row, l to r: Vikram, Urvashi's uncle, who died in an air crash; Dr Paras Ram Sood, Urvashi's grandfather, who built the house; Sumitra, her mother's oldest sister. Front row, l to r: Suniti, her mother's second-oldest sister (standing); Rana, or Bricoder (his real name), the brother who stayed in Pakistan and became a Muslim (called Ghulam Muhammad Sheikh); Sudha, her mother's youngest sister; Dayawanti (later Ayesha), Urvashi's grandmother; Brijeshwar, called 'Billo', her mother's younger brother, Shubniti, her younger sister, and Urvashi's mother, Subhadra. The youngest, Savita, is still to arrive.

BLOOD

Urvashi Butalia

The political partition of India caused one of the great human convulsions of history. Never before or since have so many people exchanged their homes and countries so quickly. In the space of a few months, about twelve million people moved between the new, truncated India and the two wings, East and West, of the newly created Pakistan. By far the largest proportion of these refugees – more than ten million of them – crossed the western border which divided the historic state of Punjab, Muslims travelling west to Pakistan, Hindus and Sikhs east to India. Slaughter sometimes prompted and sometimes accompanied their movement; many others died from malnutrition and contagious disease. Estimates of the number of dead vary from 200,000 (the contemporary British figure) to two million (a later Indian speculation), but that somewhere around a million people died is now widely accepted. As always, there was sexual savagery: about 75,000 women are thought to have been abducted and raped by men of religions different from their own. Thousands of families were divided, homes were destroyed, crops left to rot, villages abandoned. Astonishingly, the new governments of India and Pakistan were unprepared for this convulsion. They had not anticipated that the fear and uncertainty created by the drawing of borders based on headcounts of religious identity – so many Hindus and Sikhs versus so many Muslims – would force people to flee to what they considered 'safer' places, where they would be surrounded by their own kind. People travelled in buses, cars and trains, but mostly on foot in great columns, called *kafilas*, which could stretch for dozens of miles. The longest of them, said to comprise 800,000 refugees travelling east to India from western Punjab, took eight days to pass any given spot on its route.

This is the generality of Partition; it exists publicly in books. The particular is harder to discover; it exists privately in the stories told and retold inside so many households in India and Pakistan. I grew up with them. Like many Punjabis in Delhi, I am from a family of Partition refugees. My mother and father came from Lahore, a lively city loved and sentimentalized by its inhabitants, which lies only twenty miles inside the Pakistan border. My mother tells of the dangerous journeys that she twice made back there to bring her younger brothers and sister to India. My father remembers fleeing to the sound of guns and crackling fires. I would listen to these stories with my brothers and sister and hardly take them in. We were middle-class Indians who had grown up in a period of relative calm and prosperity, when tolerance and 'secularism' seemed to be winning the argument. The stories – looting, arson, rape, murder – came out of a different time. They meant little to me.

Then, in October 1984, the prime minister, Mrs Gandhi, was assassinated by one of her security guards, a Sikh. For days afterwards Sikhs all over India were attacked in an orgy of violence and revenge. Many homes were destroyed and thousands died. In the outlying suburbs of Delhi more than three thousand were killed, often by being doused in kerosene and then set alight. Black burn marks on the ground showed where their bodies had lain. The government – headed by Mrs Gandhi's son, Rajiv – remained indifferent, but several citizens' groups came together to provide relief, food and shelter. I was among hundreds of people who worked in these groups. Every day, while we were distributing food and blankets, compiling lists of the dead and missing, and helping with compensation claims, we listened to the stories of the people who had suffered. Often older people, who had come to Delhi as refugees in 1947, would remember that they had been through a similar terror before. 'We didn't think it could happen to us in our own country,' they would say. 'This is like Partition again.'

Here, across the River Jamuna, just a few miles from where I lived, ordinary, peaceable people had driven their neighbours from their homes and murdered them for no other readily apparent reason than that they were of a different religious community. The stories from Partition no longer seemed quite so remote; people from the same country, the same town, the same village could still be divided by the politics of their religious difference, and, once divided, could do terrible things to each other. Two years later, working on a film about Partition for a British television channel, I began to collect stories from its survivors. Many were horrific and of a kind that, when I was younger and heard them second or third hand, I had found hard to believe: women jumping into wells to drown themselves so as to avoid rape or forced religious conversion; fathers beheading their own children so that they would avoid the same dishonourable fate. Now I was hearing them from witnesses whose bitterness, rage and hatred – which, once uncovered, could be frightening – told me that they were speaking the truth.

Their stories affected me deeply. Nothing as cruel and bloody had happened in my own family so far as I knew, but I began to realize that Partition was not, even in my family, a closed chapter of history – that its simple, brutal political geography infused and divided us still. It was then that I decided I would find my uncle Rana – Ranamama as we called him, though he wasn't mentioned often.

Nobody had heard from Ranamama in almost forty years. He was my mother's youngest brother. In 1947 my mother, who was working in the part of the Punjab that became Indian, had gone back to Lahore to bring out her younger brother, Billo, and a sister, Savita. Then she went back a second time to fetch her mother – her father was dead – and Rana. But Rana refused to come and wouldn't let my grandmother go either. Instead he promised to bring her to India later. They never came, but my family heard disturbing news.

Rana had become a Muslim.

My family didn't think that God had played much part here. They were convinced that both Rana's refusal to leave and his conversion were calculated decisions that would allow him to inherit my grandfather's property – a house, land, orchards – when my grandmother died. Letters were exchanged for a while but they began to draw the attention of the police and intelligence officers. They were opened, and questions were asked. Pakistan and India had so much in common – if not religion then certainly language and ways of life – that the barriers of a nation state became especially important to their governments as proof of difference and nationhood. Travel between the two countries, for the people who lived in them, became nearly impossible. My mother gave up hope of returning to Lahore and soon abandoned correspondence. What was the point of trying to communicate with someone who was so mercenary? And so, though Rana continued to live in my grandfather's house in Lahore, which is fewer than three hundred miles from Delhi, forty minutes in a plane, he might just as well have been on another planet. We heard rumours that my grandmother had died, but no one really knew. My mother's grief at losing her home, her mother and brother, gave way to bitterness and resentment, and eventually to indifference. The years passed; Pakistan and India fought two wars; Ranamama's fate remained obscure.

Then, in the summer of 1987, I managed to get a trip to Pakistan, to Lahore. I told my mother I wanted to meet her brother. She was sceptical. Why? What was the good? I felt as though I were betraying her; once in Lahore, it took me three days to pluck up the courage to go to my grandfather's house. I first saw it late one evening – an old and crumbling mansion set in a large bare garden – and found it hard to believe that this was the house we'd heard so much about. Through a window I could see a bare bulb casting its pale light on cracked green walls.

I rang the bell, and three women came to the barred window.

Yes, they said, this was Rana's house, but he wasn't in – he was 'on tour' and expected home later that night. I said I was his sister's daughter, come from Delhi. Door-bolts were drawn, and I was invited in. The women were Rana's wife – my aunt – and her daughters – my cousins. For an hour we made careful conversation and drank Coca-Cola in a luridly furnished living room, and then my friend Firhana came in her car to collect me. I'd met her sister in Delhi and was staying at their house.

At midnight, the phone rang. It was my uncle. He called me *beti*, daughter. 'What are you doing there?' he said, referring to my friend's house. 'This house is your home. You must come home at once and you must stay here. Give me your address, and I'll come and pick you up.'

This was a man I had never seen, who had last seen my mother five years before I was born. We argued. Finally I managed to dissuade him. But the next day I went to his house and stayed there for a week.

Rana looked like a solid citizen of Pakistan. He was six feet tall, strongly built and always dressed in a long cotton shirt and pyjamas – a style Zulfikar Ali Bhutto, the former prime minister who was deposed by the military and executed, had popularized as the *awami*, or people's, suit. He had a deep, enjoyable voice, which I heard a lot that week. I asked questions, he answered them; some facts emerged. My grandmother had died in 1956 (the seven of her eight children who lived in India dated her death variously as 1949, 1952 and 1953), and Rana had married a Muslim.

Why had he not left with his brother and sisters at Partition?

Well, Rana said, like a lot of other people he had never expected Partition to happen in the way it did. 'Many of us thought, yes, there will be change, but why should we have to move?' He hadn't thought political decisions could affect his life and by the time he understood otherwise it was too late. 'I was barely twenty. I'd had little education. What would I have done in India? I had no qualifications, no job, nothing to recommend me.'

I had enough imagination to understand those reasons. In Lahore, Muslims, Hindus and Sikhs had lived alongside each other for centuries. Who could have foreseen that as a Pakistani rather than an Indian city it would become so singularly Muslim, that 'normality' would never return? But his treatment of my grandmother was harder to forgive. She had lived on for nine years after Partition – nine years in which her six daughters heard nothing of her – hidden, alone, isolated. Why had he forced her to stay with him?

'I was worried about your mother having to take on the burden of an old mother, just as I was worried when she offered to take me with her. So I thought I'd do my share and look after her.'

I didn't believe him. What about his decision to become a Muslim?

'In a sense there wasn't really a choice. The only way I could have stayed on was by converting. I married a Muslim girl, changed my religion and took a Muslim name.'

But did he really believe? Was the change born out of conviction or convenience?

He said he had not slept a single night – 'no, not one night' – in forty years without regretting his decision. 'You see, my child,' he said, and this became a refrain in the days we spent together, 'somehow a convert is never forgiven. Your past follows you; it hounds you. For me, it's worse because I've continued to live in the same place. Even today when I walk out to the market I often hear people whispering, "Hindu, Hindu". You don't know what it is like.'

That last answer chilled me and softened me. There is a word in Punjabi that is enormously evocative and emotive: *watan*. It's a difficult word to translate: it can mean home, country, land – all and any of them. When Punjabis speak of their *watan*, you know they are expressing a longing for the place they feel they belong. For most Punjabis who were displaced by Partition, their *watan* lay in the home they had left behind. For Rana, the opposite had happened: he continued to live in the family home in Pakistan, but his *watan* had become India, a country he had visited only briefly, once. He watched the television news from India every day; he rooted for the Indian cricket team, especially when they played Pakistan; he followed Indian soap operas.

By the end of my week with him I had a picture of his life. As forty years had gone by, he had retreated into himself. His wife and children, Muslims in a Muslim nation, worried for him; they couldn't understand his longings and silences. But perhaps his wife understood something of his dilemma. She had decided early in their marriage, sensibly I thought, that she would not allow her children to suffer a similar crisis of identity. Her sons and daughters were brought up as good Muslims; the girls remained in purdah and were taught at home by a mullah. One of his younger daughters told me once: 'Apa, you are all right, you're just like us, but we thought, you know, that *they* were really awful.' She meant a couple of distant relatives who had once managed to visit and who had behaved as orthodox Hindus, practising the 'untouchability' that Hindus customarily use in Muslim company. They had insisted on cooking their own food and would not eat anything prepared by Rana's family. They were the only Hindus this daughter had met. Who could blame her for disliking them?

One day, as Rana and I talked intimately into the evening, stopping only for some food or a cup of tea, I began to feel oppressed by him. 'Why are you talking to me like this?' I said. 'You don't even know me. If you'd met me in the marketplace, I would have been just another stranger.' He looked at me for a long time and said, 'My child, this is the first time I have spoken to my own blood.'

I was shocked. I protested: 'What about your family? They are your blood, not me.'

'No,' he said, 'for them I remain a stranger. You understand what I'm talking about. That is why you are here. Even if nothing else ever happens, I know that you have been sent here to lighten my load.' And in some ways, I suppose, this was true.

I went back to India with gifts and messages, including a long letter from Rana to his six sisters (his brother had died by this time). They gathered in our house and sat in the front room in a row, curious but resentful. Then someone picked up the letter and began reading, and soon it was being passed from hand to hand. They cried, and then their mood lightened into laughter as memories were shared and stories recounted. Tell us what the house looks like now, they demanded. Is the guava tree still there? What's happened to the game of *chaukhat*? Who lives at the back these days? Rana's letter was read and reread. Suddenly my mother and my five aunts had acquired a family across the border.

We kept in touch after that. I went to visit Rana several times. Once he wrote to my mother: 'I wish I could lock up Urvashi in a cage and keep her here.' Then, before one of my visits, my mother said to me: 'Ask him if he buried or cremated my mother.'

Muslims bury their dead. Hindus burn them. I looked at her in surprise. Hinduism has never meant much to her – she isn't an atheist but she has little patience with orthodoxy.

'What does it matter to you?' I said.

'Just ask him.'

When I got to Lahore, I asked him.

'How could she have stayed here and kept her original name?' he said. 'I had to make her a convert. She was called Ayesha Bibi. I buried her.'

Late in 1988 I took my mother and her eldest sister back to Lahore. One of Rana's daughters was getting married, and there was a great deal of excitement as we planned the visit. They hadn't seen their brother, their home or Lahore for forty-one years. They had last seen Rana as a twenty-year-old. The man who met them at Lahore airport was in his sixties, balding and greying, and the reunion was tentative and difficult. We made small talk in the car until we reached Rana's house, which had once been home to his sisters but was now occupied by strangers, so they had to treat it politely, like any other house. The politeness and strain between brother and sisters went on for two days, until on the third day I found them together in a room, crying and laughing. Rana took his sisters on a proper tour of the house: they looked around their old rooms, rediscovered their favourite trees, and remembered their family as it had once been.

But as Rana and his sisters grew together, his wife and children grew more distant. Our presence made them anxious – understandably so. A girl was being married. What if her in-laws objected to Hindus in the family? What if the Hindus were there to reclaim their land? What if we did something to embarrass the family at the wedding? Small silences began to build up between the two sides. I was struck by how easy it was to rebuild the borders we thought we'd just crossed.

After that, I managed to go to Pakistan to see Rana again. But it wasn't easy. He began to worry that he was being watched by the police. His letters became fewer and then stopped altogether. For a while my mother continued to send him letters and gifts but eventually she stopped too. I went on sending messages to him via my friends, until one of them returned with a message from him. Try not to keep in touch, he said; it makes things very difficult. The pressure he felt was not just official but came also from inside his family. His sons urged him to break contact with his relations in India. And then the relationship between India and Pakistan, which had grown more relaxed in the 1980s, became stiffer again, and it was more difficult to travel between the two.

It's been many years now since I last saw Ranamama. I no longer know if he is alive or dead. I think he is alive. I want him to be alive. I keep telling myself, if something happened to him, surely someone in his family would tell us. But I'm not sure I believe that. Years ago, when he told me that he had buried my grandmother, I asked him to take me to her grave. We were standing by his gate in the fading light of the evening. It was, I think, the first time that he'd answered me without looking at me. He scuffed the dust under his feet and said: 'No my child, not yet. I'm not ready yet.'

On the night of 14 August 1996 about a hundred Indians visited the India-Pakistan border at Wagah in the Punjab. They went there to fulfil a long-cherished objective by groups in the two countries: Indians and Pakistanis would stand, in roughly equal numbers, on each side of the border and sing songs for peace. They imagined that the border would be symbolized by a sentry post and that they would be able to see their counterparts on the other side. But they came back disappointed. The border was more complicated than they thought – there is middle ground – and also grander. The Indian side has an arch lit with neon lights and, in large letters, the inscription MERA BHARAT MAHAN – India, my country, is supreme. The Pakistan side has a similar neon-lit arch with the words PAKISTAN ZINDABAD – Long live Pakistan. People bring picnics here and eat and drink and enjoy themselves.

The suffering and grief of Partition are not memorialized at the border, nor, publicly, anywhere else in India, Pakistan and Bangladesh. A million may have died but they have no monuments. Stories are all that people have, stories that rarely breach the frontiers of family and religious community; people talking to their own blood.

LOVE OF THE WORLD

John McGahern

It is very quiet here. Nothing much ever happens. We have learned to tell the cries of the birds and the animals, the wing-beats of the swans crossing the house, the noises of the different motors that batter about on the roads. Not many people like this quiet. There's a constant craving for word of every sound and sighting and any small happening. Then, when something violent and shocking happens, nobody will speak at all after the first shock wave passes into belief. Eyes usually wild for every scrap of news and any idle word will turn away or search the ground.

When the Harkins returned with their three children to live in the town after Guard Harkin's heart attack on Achill, they were met with goodwill and welcome. The wedding of Kate Ruttledge to Guard Harkin, ten years before, had been the highlight of that summer. A young, vigorous man struck down without warning elicited natural sympathy. Concern circled idly round them – would Kate take up work again, would he find lighter work? – as if they were garden plants hit with blight or an early frost. The young guard, an established county footballer with Mayo when he came to the town, was tipped by many as a possible future all-star. We'd watched Kate grow up across the lake, go away to college in Dublin and come home again to work in Gannon's, the solicitors, turning into a dark beauty before our eyes. She was running Gannon's office at the time they met, and was liked by almost everybody. The excitement that ran through the town and near countryside when Harkin declared for the local club was felt everywhere. Excitement grew to fever over the summer as he led the team from victory to victory, until he lifted high the beribboned silver cup in Carrick on the last Sunday in September. Nineteen long years of disappointment and defeat had been suddenly kicked away, and the whole town went wild for the best part of a week.

Kate, who had shown no interest in sport of any kind up till then, spent every Sunday of that rainy summer travelling to football matches all over the country. She'd seen Harkin prostrate on the field at Castlebar when Mayo lost in the Connacht Final, but everywhere else she attended was victory and triumph. She'd witnessed men and boys look long and deep into his face, lost in the circle and dream of his fame. She'd held her breath as she'd seen him ride the shoulders of running mobs bearing him in triumph from the pitches. There were times when he fell injured on the field, and she could hardly breathe until she saw him walk again when he was lifted to his feet.

On an October Sunday at the end of the football season Kate took him out to the farm above the lake to meet Maggie and James for the first time. They parked the car at the lake gate to walk the curving path through the fields above the water and down to the house in its shelter of trees. Girls didn't take men to their homes at the time unless they had made up their minds to marry. These visits were always tense and delicate because they were at once a statement of intent and a plea for approval. There was little Kate had ever been denied. Now all her desires and dreams were fixed on this one man. In her eyes he stood without blemish. These small fields above the lake were part of her life. Away from here she often walked them in her mind, and, without her noticing, this exercise had gradually replaced the earlier exercise of prayer. She was light, almost tearful with happiness as she closed the lake gate. Now she was leading her beloved through the actual fields to meet the two people who meant most to her in the world, and she felt as close to Harkin and as certain of her choice as she was of her own life. The lake below them was like a mirror. The air was heavy and still. The yellow leaves of the thorns were scattered everywhere with the reds of the briars and the thick browns of the small oaks. Blackbirds and thrushes racketed in the hedges. A robin sang on a thorn.

'What do you think of the place?' she asked as they crossed the hill to go down under the tall hedges to the house.

'It's a bit backward and quiet,' he said. 'The views, though, are great. They'd pay money to have this in the middle of a city.'

In the house the young guard was polite, even deferential, as he enquired about the fields and the lakes and the cattle. Her father, James, was quiet and attentive, asking in his turn about the sheep and cattle they kept on the Mayo farm the guard had grown up on. Maggie was herself as always, quietly there, large and easy, withdrawing only to make the sandwiches and tea. Whiskey was offered, but at that time Harkin did not drink. Already he felt comfortable in the house. It was a house where he felt he wasn't expected to be anything other than himself. There was a generous side to the guard's nature; among footballers he was known as an unselfish player. After they'd eaten, and he'd praised the tea and the sandwiches, he felt moved in some clouded way to give something of himself back for the simple courtesy he had been shown. The generous virtues are at times more ruinous than vices.

'I don't expect to stay a guard for much longer,' he said. 'I've already passed the sergeant's exam, and I expect to go much further.'

'To get to be a sergeant is a big step,' James responded. 'Not many get that far in a whole lifetime.'

'I expect to be a super or an inspector at the very least. The Force is awash with old fools. It needs a big shake-up.'

The young guard went on to ridicule his immediate superiors and to expand his sense of self to very attentive listeners. When he finished the free run of untrammelled self-expression, he was taken aback by how much time had flown.

The old couple walked their daughter and the guard all the way out to the car at the lake gate.

'What do you think?' James asked his wife anxiously as they made their slow way back to the house.

'There's no use worrying,' Maggie said. 'Kate will have her way. To go against him would only make her more determined.'

'Kate isn't going to have an easy life. She needs somebody easier.'

Maggie pressed his shoulder as they walked. 'When we married, and you came in here, everybody was against it. Yet it worked out all right.'

'I can't help wishing she had found somebody easier. That poor young man is full of himself.'

'There's no use wishing,' Maggie said. 'We'll have to make the best fist of it we can.'

'Still, we sent her to school. She has pleasant work, plenty of friends. I wish . . . I wish . . .' But Maggie did not encourage him to complete the wish.

All the people who lived around the lake were invited to the wedding. His people travelled from Mayo. They were tall and good-looking, forthright in their manner and very proud of Guard Harkin. Famous footballers came from all over the country and formed a guard of honour outside the church. Girls who had been to college with Kate in Dublin travelled from as far as New York and London, to attend the wedding. The church was full. The whole town turned out. The crowds spilt into the church grounds and even on to the road, and the wedding was talked about long after the couple had gone to live in Athlone. Guards were transferred automatically once they married.

We saw little of them in the years that followed. Harkin's football career was at its height. He was much in the newspapers, and there were pictures of Kate by his side at the celebratory dinners and dances. In all the photos she looked glamorous and happy. For a while Kate had temporary work in Athlone, but James told me that Harkin didn't like to see his wife working. They came for short visits in the winter and a few times appeared with Maggie and James at Sunday Mass where they were the centre of all eyes. At the church gate after Mass people would crowd round them to grasp their hands, and the talk of what Kate was wearing and how she looked and what a nice plain man Harkin was in spite of everything would sound around the place for days. They were admired and envied. Once Kate did come for a visit on her own and must have stayed two or three weeks. I was over helping James with cattle, and we came together into the house. She was wearing a blue dress and sitting with her elbows on the table looking out of the back window towards the old apple tree heavy with green cooking apples. She was far more like a young girl dreaming about her life than a settled married woman. Once she noticed me, she rose quickly and smiled and stretched out her hand. We were cousins as well as good neighbours.

I was told that Harkin was studying hard for the new sergeant's exam. The last time he passed but failed the interview. Now he was more determined than ever.

'Kate says he finds it easier to study when he's on his own in the house,' Maggie said while James sat looking down at the floor without adding a single word.

That summer Mayo won the Connacht Championship and beat an Ulster team to reach the All-Ireland Final against Cork. James and Maggie were offered seats in the Hogan Stand, but used one excuse or another to get out of going. I walked round the lake to watch the match with them on television. Their near neighbour, Michael Doherty, had crossed the fields to watch the match as well. There was a long dry spell of weather that September. The Sunday was warm and golden. All the time I was in the house, the front door was left open on the yard. Outside the back window, the old Bramley was heavy again with cookers. Maggie poured us a large whiskey before the match began and filled our glasses at half-time. When it was over, we all had tea and sandwiches. Mayo lost, but Harkin had played his heart out at centrefield. If Mayo had had even one more player like him, they'd have won. Once we thought we saw Kate's face in the rows of heads in the Hogan Stand. When I got up to leave, James took his hat and insisted on walking me all the way out to the lake gate. Michael Doherty stayed behind to chat with Maggie. We were going in different directions anyhow.

'Thanks for the day, for everything. It would have crowned it had they won,' I said as we parted.

'What's it but a game? We had the day. Thanks yourself for coming all the way over.' James waved, and I saw him wait at the gate until I passed out of sight behind the alders along the shore.

That game and year must have been close to the very best of the Harkins' life together. Kate was expecting their first child. In the new sergeant's exam he came first in the whole of Ireland. He was certain he'd be promoted before the next year was out. Maggie went early to Athlone to help Kate around the birth, and James went for the little girl's christening.

'The little girl is a treasure,' Maggie told me when they got back. 'Outside that, though, things could be better.'

'How could that be? Aren't their whole lives in front of them? He's going to be a sergeant before long?' I asked though I wasn't all that surprised by what she said.

'He's not so certain now. When he walked into the room for the interview, whom did he find sitting behind the table but the same officers who turned him down the first time.'

'How could they turn him down after him coming first in the whole country?'

'He says that if they're against you enough they'll turn you down no matter what. There were no older guards at the christening, just foolish young fellas who looked up to him as if he were God. Even if you have to come in first everywhere, you must learn to wait and bide your time along the way. A man can only do so much; after that, it's people who do everything. When God made us, He didn't allow for us all to be first all the time.' The words were very strong coming from James.

I saw Maggie look hard at him as he spoke. When he caught her eye, he stopped; nothing more was said, and I asked nothing more. Harkin came with Kate and the child a few times to the farm that year but did not stay for long. They never appeared together at Mass. Another girl was born the following year. Maggie went to help Kate as before, but this time James refused to go to Athlone for the christening. Harkin was no longer playing football. A nagging knee injury had worsened, and he had no interest in continuing to play at club level. He joined a gun club with a new friend, Guard McCarthy. He also started to drink.

'I couldn't wait to get away,' Maggie said when she came home. 'I fear Kate knows now she has her work cut out.'

In spite of what she said, she went again to Athlone to help Kate with her third baby, a boy. It was a difficult birth, and Maggie was several weeks away. During this time, Michael Doherty crossed the fields nearly every night to sit with James for company. When Maggie was at home, he came to the house a number of nights each week but not as frequently as when she was away. Some weeks after Kate's son was born, he stopped in fear when he came into the yard to find the house in darkness. The door was open. He switched on the lights. The rooms were all empty. There was a low fire in the cooker. Outside he heard a dog barking in the fields and then a tractor running. He found the body lying by the transport box. The ground all around was trampled, but the cattle hadn't walked on the body. James had scattered the hay before falling. Each of the baler twines had been cut.

James had married into the place and he cared for the fields more than if they were his own. Not only were he and Maggie man and wife but they were each other's best friend. 'I should never have been away. I should have been at home minding my own business,' Maggie complained bitterly for months and could not be consoled.

'You shouldn't take it so hard. A boy has come in so that an old man can go out,' one of those foolish people who have a word for everything said.

'He was not old to me,' she cried.

Harkin was in the newspapers again, but not the sports pages. He had been with his friend Guard McCarthy late one night when their patrol car was called to a disturbance at an itinerant encampment on the outskirts of the town. A huge fire of car tyres and burning branches lit up the vans and mobile homes, the cars and mounds of metal scrap. Stones and burning branches were thrown at the Garda car. They radioed for reinforcements before getting out.

The guards said that as soon as they left the car they were set upon by youths and men wielding sticks and iron bars. All the itinerant witnesses swore that both guards had jumped from the car with drawn batons and provoked the assault. In the bloody fight that followed, the guards stood and fought back to back, the short, leaded batons thonged to their wrists. When the reinforcements arrived, three tinkers lay unconscious on the ground. The rest of the men had escaped into the fields, and McCarthy and Harkin were being attacked by a crowd of hysterical women. McCarthy's face was covered with blood. He had a serious head wound. An ear hung loose. Harkin's left arm was broken, and he was cut and bruised.

When one of the tinkers died in hospital without recovering consciousness, a terrible furore started in the newspapers, on the radio and television. Itinerants' rights organizations denounced the two guards and Garda treatment of itinerants in general. At the trial the guards were exonerated of criminal wrongdoing. Whether excessive force was used or not remained unanswered. Once the uproar subsided, an internal Garda inquiry was held after a civil action brought by the itinerant families was settled out of court. As a result, McCarthy was transferred to a coastal town under the Cork-Kerry mountains. Harkin was sent to Achill Island. Any lingering hope he held of advancement in the force was gone.

On Achill the heart attack came without warning. For several weeks it was touch and go whether he'd live or die. He came through a number of serious operations. Strangely, he was very happy in hospital and an ideal patient. By the time he was released it was known he'd never be fit to resume normal police duties. For the first time in a marriage that had slowly emptied of everything but caution and carefulness and appearances, Kate took a decisive part. If Harkin accepted the desk work he was offered in a station in one of the big towns, he would have to go there alone. With him or without him Kate was going back to what she knew.

It was one of those rare moves in life which appear to benefit everybody. Maggie made no bones then or later that Kate saw it as a last chance to climb back into some kind of life of her own. The town had not won a county championship since that great summer ten years before, and Harkin was greeted like a returning idol.

He had been deeply shaken by the way people turned away from him once he ceased to be a star, the same people who had crowded around him on pitches and in hotel lobbies, had stopped him in the street to ask for autographs. This constant attention had been so long a part of his everyday life that he had come to take it as much for granted as air or health. When suddenly it disappeared, he was baffled: he was the same person now as when he had dominated centre-fields, and it gnawed at the whole structure of his self-esteem, forcing in on him the feeling that he no longer amounted to anything, he who had meant the world to cheering, milling crowds. Back in this small town where he was well remembered he felt he could breathe again, and the welcome and sympathy he was shown soon brought immediate, practical benefit.

During the ten years the Harkins had been away, tourism had grown rapidly. There were now many guesthouses, and foreigners had built summer houses by the lakes and were buying and converting old disused dwellings. They were mostly Germans and French, with a scattering of Swiss and Dutch: highly paid factory workers from industrial cities, attracted more to the hunting and fishing and cheap property prices than to the deserted beauty of the countryside. A local guard, Guard Tracy, had developed a lucrative sideline looking after their summer houses and soon had more work than he could handle. Some of this he passed on to the disabled ex-guard, with promises to put more business his way if things went well, but when Tracy was transferred suddenly to Waterford, Harkin got control of the entire business. Suspicion grew that he had brought about Tracy's transfer by reporting his dealings with the foreigners to the Garda authorities, but it could as easily have been any one of several people. While Tracy had managed the properties only, Harkin threw himself into the whole lives of the tourists. Soon he was meeting them at Dublin airport and taking them back. He organized shooting expeditions. He took them on fishing trips all over. These tourists did not return their catch to the water. The sport was in the kill. As well as pheasant, duck, woodcock, pigeon, snipe, they shot songbirds, thrushes, blackbirds, even larks.

His damaged heart meant Harkin wasn't able to go with them over the fields. Often he stood on the roads with his new repeater and guarded access to where they were shooting. In the summer they came with freezer vans, and Harkin took them to lakes rich in pike and perch and eel. He helped them net the lakes in broad daylight as well as at night. Heads of gutted pike were scattered round every small shore. Because of his contacts in the guards he was able to obstruct complaints, and most people did not bother to complain. Harkin was well known and admired – the disabled guard was entitled to a living like every other. The lakes had been there for so long and were so little used, except by eel fishermen from the north, that they were taken for granted; but everybody disliked the slaughter of the songbirds. When the day's shooting and fishing was done, the tourists loved to party and drink. In the same way as he disregarded the plunder of the lakes and the growing hostility to the shooting of songbirds, Harkin drank pint for pint, glass for glass, with his new friends without seeming to care for his health. At parties he would pull off his shirt to display the scars of his operations.

At weekends and in the winter evenings, Kate's two daughters often accompanied their father on his rounds of the empty tourist houses, while the boy went with his mother to visit Maggie, sometimes to stay the night. Kate must have felt the changes ten years can bring as she walked the curving path through the fields above the lake and down by the tall trees to the house. It was her son's hand she now held instead of Harkin's, his grip more demanding than ever her husband's had been. All that drowsy love had gone: she feared him now and feared closeness, not distance. The path and the lake and the fields were the same. Her father was gone, his dear presence nowhere but in her mind, and everything continued on as before. The blackbirds and thrushes racketed. A robin sang. Maggie was still there, praise be to everything that moves or sings. A red shorthorn left the small herd and walked with them on the path, frisking its long tail excitedly while trying to nuzzle her hand. 'Will it bite us?' the child asked. 'No. It's just looking for nuts. Your grandfather was always trying to stop your grandmother turning them into pets.'

'You left the two lassies behind today?' Maggie met them, her broad face creased with smiles.

'They went with their father on his rounds of the houses.'

'My little man is in his lone glory, then.' She stretched out and lifted the boy high above her head.

For days at a time and whole nights of the summer, Kate and the children didn't see Harkin, but when they did he was usually in good humour. He had plenty of money. He had always been generous, and Kate now had more money than she needed. His life became so intertwined with the tourists that in the off-season they sent him air tickets to join them in various cities. Kate thought little of the trips. When he was leaving, she wished him a good holiday and had the children wish him the same. He always brought back presents.

The tourists congratulated him on having an obedient, old-fashioned wife. They raised their glasses and wondered if he could find such a wife for Pierre or Helmut. Harkin took out his notebook and, with the mock solemnity of a policeman raiding a public house for after-hours drinking, wrote down the names, warning each man that anything said could be used in evidence against them once he found them such a wife.

They roared with laughter. 'Harkin can do anything. Harkin is the devil . . .'

As Kate was walking back through the town one morning after taking the children to school, Jerome Callaghan's car pulled up along the curb.

He pushed open the door on the passenger side for her to get in. She hesitated. They'd once been in the same class at school. He now owned his uncle's auctioneering business and had a reputation for going with older women.

'I've been looking out for you, Kate,' he said. 'How would you like to work again?'

She was taken aback because it was as if her most secret thought had been taken from her and offered casually back. 'There aren't many jobs for women my age.'

'There's one,' he said. 'They are looking for someone to run the office in the market.'

It was what she had hoped for but had never expected to find in this small place. As they talked, she knew she could do the work. All she doubted were his motives. She refused his offer to drive her home, saying she had things to get for the house. She also said she'd make her own way to the mart for an interview with McNulty, the manager, later the same day.

At twelve o'clock she went to the big galvanized building outside the town in the middle of a huge, gravelled space for cattle trucks and trailers. In spite of dressing with great care, she felt nervous and vulnerable offering herself for work again after all these years. McNulty could not have been more friendly. He seemed to know a great deal already about her training, and after a short conversation offered her the job there and then. He wanted her to begin work the following morning.

Confronted suddenly with an offer she had long wanted but only dared to think about in secret, her first instinct was to back away: she didn't know how her husband would react when he got back; she'd like time to think it over. McNulty couldn't give her time. If she wouldn't take the job, he'd be forced to look for someone else. More than a million pounds passed through the mart each week. She was always free to hand in her notice if, after a few weeks, she found the work didn't suit her.

She began the following morning. Men were already hosing the cattle pens when she came in, the arc light high in the steel girders shining down on the wet concrete. Annie and Lizzie who worked in the office were friendly and helpful. They'd worked in the mart for years and feared that the new person would be hostile or distant; either of them could have done her work, but they didn't want the responsibility. A few of the small farmers, who came in about cheques or cattle cards, she'd known since she was a girl, men like her father, rough and ready and anxious; but her father was not rough, and she knew that much of the rough manner was a shield, a working uniform. The dealers were more polished and better dressed and more interesting, and they too wore uniforms. Cattle she had grown up with. She loved their faces. She found their lowing hard at first, lowing for what fields and company they'd been taken from. They'd be driven round the sale rings, loaded on to trucks or trailers and carried through the night to ships or abattoirs. Only a few would reach the lives of new farms. All that passed through her office were their cards, their bills of sale, the cheques, the dockets. She was so busy on mart days that the voices of the auctioneers calling out their rhythmic numbers over the loudspeakers were only a distant sound.

On mart days and the days that followed, which were even busier, when the accounts had to tally and any irregularities of sale or purchase reported to McNulty, Maggie would come into the town to pick up the children from school. On all other days Kate had time to see to the children herself. As long as the work was done, they didn't care what hours she kept.

The days flew. In the quiet morning after leaving the children at school, as she came up the back lane to the mart by gardens and the yards of the bars and engineering works savouring the morning, she began to realize how much she had missed the independence of work. Now it was through this new concentration – and the simple walk from the school to the mart a prelude to the work itself – that each day had been given back to her in its long light and depth, all the actions and interactions of the day, between the setting out and the returning, a reflection of the mystery of the whole blessed gift of life. She had nearly lost that gift. She had given up thinking of her marriage. Though she had searched for hours, she had never been able to isolate any single day, or even month or incident, when it had taken that wrong turning; but it had turned, and they had never talked. How or when or why would never be known. She had no other wish but to live her life and to bring up her children in peace – without her husband, or any man. With her husband in the house, she felt more alone than in his absence. Her nervousness in the face of his return quickened the speed with which the days flew. They seemed to race. Jerome Callaghan was in the mart most days. When they met, he was polite and careful. Once he asked her how she liked the work.

'I'm very happy.'

'Everybody's delighted with you, anyhow,' he said.

'You can say that again.' Annie looked up from her chair far down the counter and echoed his words so vigorously that Kate knew that they were happy with her work and wanted her to stay. Her husband's visit abroad was prolonged much more than usual. She was relieved at the first postponements, but then her nervousness grew greater in the face of his return. The days no longer raced. They were fixed on his return like a held breath.

Harkin brought many presents back at the end of seven weeks. The three children were very excited, and he was full of plans for making a video of the area with a German company. If the video took off it could bring the many abandoned houses in the mountains on to the market as well as increase interest in the lakes, and it would make sense for him to set up as an auctioneer as well as to expand his present business. They could all wind up as millionaires. He had been drinking earlier in the day but he was far from drunk. Kate knew he would dislike that she had found work and that it was better that he heard it directly from her, but such was the atmosphere of the house and her own deep horror of confrontation that she kept putting it off. As the children were getting ready for bed, having eked out the day well past their usual bedtime, the boy blurted out proudly, 'Mammy's got work. Some days she takes us into her office after school.'

'What sort of work?'

'In the mart – in the office,' she answered quickly.

'Who gave you this work?'

'They were looking for someone in a hurry. Mr McNulty gave me the work.'

'So Horsey McNulty is a mister now all of a sudden. Did you need the money?'

'No. We've never had so much money.'

'Were you short of money before?'

'We were never short.'

'Why did you want the work?'

'The children are growing up. It was a chance to get out of the house.'

'Of course I didn't need to be consulted.'

'I tried to put off taking the job till you came home, but they couldn't give me the time. They needed somebody that week.'

The mood of the house changed. Instead of trying to postpone their bedtime, the three children were anxious to be away and under the blankets. When the doors of their rooms were closed, he took a whiskey bottle from the press and poured a large glass. She was always apprehensive when she saw him drink whiskey.

'Those crowd of wide boys knew well what they were doing. As well as McNulty, Jerome Callaghan is stuck to his elbows in the mart and he's nosing after the one thing.' He suddenly drained the glass but didn't reach for the bottle again. 'You'll have to throw it up. That's all. I'm not going to have my wife working up in the cow shit with a pack of wide boys. It's not as if I don't make enough money. You'll give it up tomorrow and get the hell out of the place.'

She said she couldn't. She liked the work, and it didn't interfere with the running of the house or the children. She said that the people were pleasant, especially the two women who worked with her in the office, and she had given them her word.

With the empty glass in his hand he rose and came towards her. It was as if all the resentments he'd held half in check over years had gathered into a fist. He had married her when he could have had his pick of women. He had given her a house, car, children, clothes – everything a woman could want. What had she given back? Nothing, nothing. She had given him no help at all. Their life had been a dog's life. He hadn't even the life of a dog. 'Have you ever asked yourself if there's anything wrong with you?' He didn't seem to know or care what he said.

'Be careful, you're saying too much,' she warned, but he did not hear her.

'I'll bring you up to date. I'll soon bring you up to date. Two nights ago I went to a hotel in the Black Forest. The Germans aren't stuck in the dark ages. We were ten couples. A divorced woman was with me. Helga. Every man had two keys to his room. After drinks, each man threw a key on the table and went to his room. The women stayed behind to pick up a key. The woman who came to my room said when she opened the door, "I won the prize. I got the Irishman." We did everything man or beast can do and we were the last couple to come down. Everybody clapped as soon as we came into the bar and wanted to buy us drinks. You mightn't think much of these people, but they know what I am worth.'

'This time you've gone too far,' she said.

'Not half far enough.' He came towards her. 'You'll either do what you're supposed to do in this house or get out.' He seized her with both hands and raced her to the door. She tried to stop herself falling as she was flung but before she realized what had happened she found herself reeling to a stop in the middle of the small lawn. She didn't fall. Behind her she heard the door lock.

It was cold and later than she thought. She was wearing a cardigan over a light dress. Not a single television set flickered behind the curtains of the little road. No music played anywhere. She thought of the children. She knew they would be safe and she could not go back to the house again. A car went slowly past on the main road. She would walk. She went out from the bungalows into the centre of town. A man was standing at one of the corners and shifted his feet and coughed as she passed. A full moon above the roofs shone down.

She started to sob, then to laugh headily before she regained a sort of calm. Once she left the street lamps of the town, the moon gave her a long shadow for company. Now and then she broke into short runs. The cold never quite left her shoulders.

So intent was she on getting to her mother's house that it closed out all other thoughts. Close to the lake she smelt the rank waterweed and the sharp wild mint. The moon was amazing on the lake, flooding the water in yellow light, making it appear as deep as the sky. The path through the fields was sharp and clear above the lake. Around the house it was like day. She tapped on the bedroom window, but Maggie was already awake.

As she told her mother what happened, Kate was suddenly so tired that listening to her own voice was like listening to the voice of another. Even with the children there, awake or sleeping, the bungalow that had been locked against her seemed as far away as Africa.

*

As Michael Doherty hadn't a car at that time, Maggie cycled round the lake to ask if I'd drive them into town the next morning. There was trouble and Kate needed to see the solicitor. They were waiting at the lake gate an hour later. Kate looked pale but beautiful that morning. She was unusual in that she grew more beautiful with age. Maggie's face was always interesting but never beautiful. Except for paleness and tiredness nobody could have guessed from either of them that anything was wrong.

We stopped at the mart on the way into town. The great spaces were empty. A few beasts waiting within the sheds were lowing and listening before lowing again. Compared to the bellowing of market days, the lowing of the isolated animals sounded hollow and lonely and futile. When Kate came from the mart she told us that she had telephoned the school. Their father had taken the children to school that morning. From the mart Maggie and Kate went together to the solicitor's.

Old Mr Gannon received them. He was now partly retired but had been very fond of Kate ever since she'd worked for him as a young woman, but the advice he had to give them wasn't good. By leaving the matrimonial home, Kate had forfeited all her rights. She couldn't, though, be stopped from entering their house to see the children. Neither could her husband prevent her from leaving the house.

Kate went to work in the mart, and I drove Maggie home. She told me everything on the way. 'I know you won't talk.' Kate was going straight from work to see the children. I said I'd drive them anywhere they wanted to be driven to over the next few days. That is how I came to take Kate and her belongings from the house late that same night.

Maggie asked me to stay in the car while she went into the bungalow. Kate opened the door and it was kept open. I saw the children near the door and once I thought I saw Harkin's shadow fall across the light. The two women started carrying loose clothes and a suitcase out of the house. It was a relief to get out of the car to open the boot and the back doors, besides sitting and watching in the mirrors. I only got back into the car when I saw the women kissing the children. The boy was clinging to them, but the two girls looked withdrawn.

It wasn't anything you'd want to watch too often. Kate cried in the
back all the way out, but at the lake she was the first out to open that
gate. She told us not to wait while she closed the gate. She wanted to
walk the rest of the way in. Maggie and I had all her belongings taken
from the car by the time she crossed the yard. She had stopped
crying.

'I'm sorry,' she said to me as she came in.

'There's nothing to be sorry about.'

'I should have more control,' she said as she reached into the press
for the whiskey bottle and poured me a large glass. Neither Kate nor
Maggie ever drank. I dislike drinking on my own, but it was easier to
drink than to refuse. I drank the whiskey down and left. I could see
that the two women were tired out of their minds.

I drove Kate in and out of town for most of a week. Maggie always
came with me when I went to the house at night. I never saw Harkin
once on any of these nights. They were worried about taking up too
much of my time and tried to give me money. I would gladly have
driven Kate in and out for a whole year, but when she found rooms
above the hairdressing salon on Main Street I wasn't needed any
more. The one thing I wasn't sorry to miss was seeing the way Kate
looked as we drove away from the house each night.

A slow, hard battle began, all of it silent and underground. Nothing
ever came out into the open. After work she went to the house and
stayed with the children till their bedtime. Harkin never spoke. As he
would not allow her to cook or eat in the house, she delayed coming
until after they'd eaten. Weekends were the worst. Often she would
turn up at the house and find it locked. He would have taken the
children with him on his rounds of the houses.

Once when she suggested that she take the children out to
Maggie's for the weekend, he stared at her in silence before turning
away. Gradually the children got used to their changed lives. There
were times when they complained that she was not like other
mothers. Knowing this, she was careful in everything she did outside
the house. After more than a year had gone by, on certain evenings
she found an attractive German woman in the house. On those
evenings she left early.

When Jerome Callaghan was in the mart on business, he would

nearly always come into the office. His ease and charm only increased her wariness. The silence between herself and Harkin over the children was like inching across a glass roof. She could risk nothing. She could only live within the small worlds of her work at the mart, her mother's house and company, the haven of her own rooms and the cramped confines she was allowed with her children. If Kate had continued living with her husband, any sexual attraction she held for Jerome Callaghan would have been suppressed, but once she left the house and moved into rooms, that changed. He was not put off that she gave no sign of reciprocating his interest. It was in his nature to be patient and he was used to getting his way.

At school Jerome Callaghan had belonged with Kate to a small group distinctly better than the rest, and he belonged there easily, without effort. He could have gone to university, but instead went to work in his uncle's insurance and auctioneering business in the town. Again, without much effort, he succeeded in expanding the business while getting on well with his uncle, his mother's brother, who had never married, and when the uncle retired it was Callaghan who took over.

Once the business was his own, he left it as it was. Hardly anything changed. The uncle came in to work as before, and often they had lunch together at the Royal Hotel. His nature was so well known that he was never suspected of courting the uncle in the hope of inheriting his money; and when his uncle died leaving him everything, the plain grief he showed did not look put on like a dark suit for the day.

His uncle had been an original shareholder in the mart, and when Callaghan asked Kate to see McNulty, he was using the manager as a cover. The position was already Kate's for the taking. While his modest way of life and manner and the underplaying of his increasing wealth were greatly approved of, his sexual inclination was nowhere liked. From a very young age he was drawn to older women: 'Callaghan doesn't want the trouble of schooling them; he likes his breaching done,' was joked to cover suspicion and resentment of any deviation.

An affair with the headmistress of the school Kate's children attended continued over several years, an intelligent, dark gypsy of a woman who had many suitors once but had let the years run on without naming a wedding day. No matter how much care or discretion was used, word of this and other affairs always got out. On a Friday evening the headmistress would leave her car at the railway station. Callaghan would meet her at a distant station, and they would drive away towards two whole nights and days together; but there was nearly always someone connected with the town who saw them in a hotel or restaurant or bar, and once, during the long school holiday, together on a London street. Harkin and Callaghan viewed one another with innate dislike. Callaghan was working for his uncle when Harkin first came to town. Football didn't interest him, and he resented the popular athlete's easy assumption of an animal superiority. Spoiled with adulation, Harkin saw the polite but firm distance Callaghan kept as criticism, all the more chafing since it was too hidden to be challenged.

Once Harkin became involved with the tourists, an involvement that led naturally to property dealing, he was probably relieved to be able to turn their mutual antipathy into rivalry because of the enormous change in the strength of their relative positions over the years. All property dealings that came his way he directed towards Callaghan's competitors, and now he was moving to set up as an auctioneer in his own right.

'What does Callaghan ever do but fiddle with old ladies' buttons while lying in wait for any easy game that comes along?'

A change had come to Callaghan's life that made him more vulnerable than he knew. His beloved mother died. His brother married. The newly married couple's protestations when he suggested that he should move and leave them to their own young lives – 'You're no trouble to us at all, only help, and we hardly ever see you anyhow' – strengthened his conviction that he should move out into his own life; but what life? Lazily he had believed that one day he'd marry a young woman, a doctor or a teacher, somebody with work and interests of her own. Years before, he'd bought part of an estate by a lake, with mature woods, oak and beech and larch. Above the lake he'd built a house he neither finished nor furnished, never making up his mind whether it was to be his life or an investment he would sell on a rising market. Several times he thought of finishing the house and going to live there while continuing to live with his brother and sister-in-law. During all this time he was careful not to pester Kate, and, if anything, visited her office in the mart less often than before, but the small courtesies he showed her could not be mistaken. When he did ask her openly out for an evening, she was able both to meet and turn aside the open sexual nature of the invitation.

'We're old school friends. We know one another too well,' she said.

'That's not knowing,' he smiled but did not press her further.

He appeared no longer to be seeing any of the women he had been linked with. Most weekends he spent alone about the town, unheard of before, weekends when she, as often as not, found the bungalow empty and locked, and they could not avoid running into one another.

'I'm not free,' she said to him bluntly when they had coffee together in the hotel one Saturday. She had come back into the town after finding the house deserted, the car gone.

'How not free? You live alone.'

'I don't even feel safe to be seen with you here over coffee in daylight.'

'Why?'

'Talk. Rumour. You know how little it needs to be fed.'

'Such scruples do not seem to bother your husband.'

'That's his business,' she told him sharply. 'He has charge of the children.'

'You are worried about losing the children?'

'I think of nothing else.'

She asked him as a favour to stay behind when she left. She wanted to be seen leaving alone. He agreed readily, ordered fresh coffee and was soon joined by two men from the bar who wanted to discuss a property deal.

One of the few liberties she was allowed with the children was to take them to Mass. One Sunday came when she found the children gone and the house locked. Always the same excuse was used – when any excuse was offered – that the children were taken with him on his rounds of the tourist houses for their own safety. She became very upset and decided to walk all the way to the lake to talk to Maggie before going back to the solicitor to see if there was any way she could obtain more regular fixed access. Every week there was some new twist or difficulty. She was afraid that soon she would not get to see her children at all, Jim and Kate and young Maggie, all brought up in the same air and world, and all so different. As she walked outside the town with these images and anxieties moving through her mind, sometimes with the charm of their individual faces and endearing gestures before her, and then again turning away from her with the woodiness of placards or a picket line, a car drew in ahead of her. Before she recognized the car or driver she knew it was Jerome Callaghan.

'I was just passing,' he said when he saw her reluctance to enter the car.

'I don't want to avoid you but I can't afford to be seen with you either.'

'I'm offering a lift. That's all,' he said.

'It's too dangerous.' He saw she was not herself, excited and troubled.

'I'm just going that way,' he said.

'An hour ago I called to the house and it was shut; the children gone again. I'm not free. Sometimes I think I'm worse off now than before I got the job in the mart.'

'You are free as far as I'm concerned.'

'I'm aware of that.' She smiled. 'I'm still not free as far as I'm concerned.'

'And I'm ready to help you in any way I can – and even wait.'

At the lake gate he stopped the car, and as she was about to shut the door, she said, 'If you'd like to come in to meet my mother, you are welcome.'

'Maggie and I have known each other for years.'

'We'll have to drive, then. The car would be seen by too many at the gate.'

When the car crossed the hill and was going down to the house under the tall trees, he eased it to a stop, letting the engine run.

'What's going to happen to us?' he asked.

'I don't see how someone like you would want to get involved in my situation.'

'I love you.'

In spite of his rational or common-sense self, he'd been drawn into the town in the early morning because of nothing but her presence in the rooms above the hairdresser's. He had this obsessional desire to

see her, if only with her children at Mass. He'd watched her leave the
rooms and walk to the bungalow on the outskirts of the town. From
a safe distance he'd observed her attempts to enter the locked house.
When he saw her walk out of the town in the direction of the lake, he
guessed where she was going.

'You are only making things bad for yourself. Even if I wanted to
help, there is nothing I can do. You see how I am. It is as if I've
already had my life.'

'What's going to happen?'

'I don't know but I know it can't go on like this. On Achill it was
this bad, but in a different way, and I knew then it couldn't go on. I
knew something had to happen. What happened was the last thing
I wanted or wished, but it did happen. I have the same feeling that
something is about to happen now that will change everything. It has
to happen.'

'Tell me one thing. It is all I ask. If you were free, would you be
interested at all?'

'Yes. But what use is that?'

'It's use to me. I know you well enough to know you would not
say it for the sake of saying. Even I feel something has to happen. I
hope to God it can set us free.'

She thought of kissing him lightly but then drew back. She had not
even that right. He drove to the house. In the house he had tea with
the two women and chatted agreeably with Maggie before leaving
them alone after a half-hour.

If they had kissed when the car was stopped under the trees that
went down to the house, if they had even lain bone to bone in the
empty night above Main Street in the solace and healing that flesh
can bring to hurt desire, they would not have gone halfway to satisfy
all the rife rumour implied they did with one another: 'Old Ireland
is coming along at a great rate. There was a time you lay on the bed
you made, but now it's all just the same as a change of oil or tyres.
The Harkins have split. Harkin has a German woman and scores of
others when he feels like rising. The heart, my dear, may be wobbly
but it appears everything is healthy enough in other departments.
The wife, I hear, hasn't let any grass grow either. She works at the
mart and is seen with Jerome Callaghan, who, they say, can tip a cat
on the way out through a skylight. Yes, my dear, old Ireland is

certainly coming along.' None of those who discoursed so freely above supermarket trolleys or bar counters, or just standing or sitting about, could trace their words to any source, but it did not lessen the authority with which they spoke. I even heard things quoted that I was supposed to have said of which I had never spoken a word.

At the height of these rumours, Harkin came all the way round the lake to see me. I was in the house when I heard the beat of a heavy diesel. I listened for it to go past the gate, but the sound stopped. After a while, a low tapping came on the front door. A small boy stood outside. I failed to recognize him.

'Daddy wants to see you.'

'Who's Daddy?'

'Guard Harkin.'

'What does he want?' It was too late now to try to make any amends to the boy. If he had been with Kate or Maggie, I'd have known him and given him coins or chocolate or cake or apples.

'He said he wants to see you.'

Harkin sat beside the wheel of the blue Mercedes outside the gate in the shade of the alders. His door was thrown open. The two girls sat in the back. He had put on a great deal of weight since his playing days. His features had coarsened. I assumed he did not get out of the car because of his heart condition.

'What kind of fish are in the lake?' he demanded though he already knew. He had helped to net the lake.

'Pike, eel, perch . . .'

'Is there much?'

'Not any more. They say the tourists netted the lake.'

'The foreigners are blamed for everything nowadays.'

'I wouldn't know.'

'Of course you wouldn't know but you'd talk.'

'The boy said you wanted to see me. Is there something you want?'

'I just wanted to get a look at you,' he said and shut the car door. I watched him back the Mercedes away from the gate and turn down to the lake, the children grave and silent in the back.

Maggie told me Jerome Callaghan came alone a few times to the house during those months. She also said there was never truth in the rumours flying around about him and Kate. He liked Kate and wished to help her, but that was all there ever was to it. Maggie was right and wasn't right.

One evening Kate left the children early because the German woman was making her presence felt in the house. She was walking back towards Main Street when Callaghan's car drew up. He wanted to take her to see his unfinished house.

'It's too dark for us to be seen, and it's normal for the car to be driving there.'

The night was dark. She had to imagine the woods on either side, the lake in darkness below the house, the mountains at the back. When the front light came on, she saw a small concrete mixer, a barrow and wooden planks scattered about on what could have been intended as a long lawn. A paint-splattered table stood in the centre of the large living room with some wooden chairs. All the other rooms were empty and held hollow echoes.

'It came cheap on the market, another man's misfortune, but I've never been able to let it go. I know they laugh: "Callaghan's built a big cage without first finding a bird."'

Kate went with him from room to room, looking with curiosity at everything but without speaking. As they prepared to leave, she said, 'It could be a fine house. A rich man's house.'

'Maybe some day,' he said, and she was glad he did not complete the wish. Without touching or speaking, they had drawn very close, as if they were two single people setting out on a journey from which they could return together. On the outskirts of the town she asked him to stop the car so that she could walk in to the first street light alone but before she left the car she kissed him firmly on the lips. 'I know it's dangerous and I can promise nothing.'

The silent, almost unbearable strain in the evenings with Harkin and the children changed without warning. He became alarmingly friendly. He must have heard some rumour about Callaghan and Kate. The German woman disappeared from the house. His voice could not have been more conciliatory when he spoke to her for the first time in months.

'We want to forget everything, Kate. We'll start all over again, as if nothing happened.'

She could find no words. She was grateful for the noise of a passing car. 'It's too sudden,' she said. 'I don't know what to say.'

'We want you to think about it anyhow. The children want that as well.' Later he asked, 'Have you thought about it, Kate?'

'For the children I'd do anything, but I don't see how we . . .' Mercifully she was able to leave the rest unsaid.

'Will you think about it? We all want to get back to square one. All the children as much as myself.'

Harkin and the children were there every time she called that week. The friendliness increased. Her nervousness grew intense. She had to force herself to go to the house.

'Will you be coming back to the house at the end of the week, Mammy?' young Kate asked as they were playing draughts together before their bedtime. She'd been playing badly, and the girls were beating her easily.

'I don't think so, love.'

'Daddy said we'd all be happy again,' little Kate added.

'I know,' she said.

She told Jerome Callaghan about the new pressure she had come under to return to the marriage, the way the whole weather of the house had turned.

'What will you do?'

'I can't go back. I know everything is about to change. That is all I know.'

'Do you think you should go to the house at all?'

'I have no choice. I have no other way to see the children.'

The next day Maggie came into town, and they spent a long time talking. They agreed to go together the following week to see a young solicitor Jerome Callaghan had recommended, no matter what happened. When Kate went to see the children that evening, it was Callaghan who drove Maggie out to the lake. Kate was sick at work the next day but couldn't be persuaded to go home. In the evening Jerome Callaghan insisted on driving her to her rooms, and she allowed him to come with her into the house in full view of the busy evening street. She seemed to be past caring; but when he offered to drive her to the bungalow after they had tea together she responded fiercely. 'You must be out of your mind.'

'In that case, I'm waiting here, and if you're not back before eleven I'm coming to look for you.'

'I'll be back before eleven,' she said.

As soon as she entered the house, she saw the strain in Harkin's friendliness.

'Well, have you made up your mind?'

She was calmer now. She said it was impossible. She felt the stone-faced silence return. Only by shutting everything out and going from moment to small moment with the children was she able to get through the long evening which suddenly started to race as the time to leave drew near.

The two girls were reserved as she kissed them goodnight. She was afraid the boy would cling to her so she lifted him high in the air. Beforehand she had been eating currants nervously from a glass jar on the sideboard and she lifted him awkwardly because the currants were still in her hand and she did not want them to scatter.

'I want you to know that if you leave tonight you'll never set foot in this house again.'

She bowed her head. 'I'll have to take that risk.' As she turned her back she heard a sharp click but did not turn to see him lift the gun. One hand was reaching for the door when she fell, the other closed tight. When it was opened, it held a fistful of small black currants.

Jerome Callaghan sat waiting without moving in the one chair. Not until after ten did he begin to grow anxious. At half past ten he moved to the window. Several times he went to leave, then held back, but once the hand of his watch moved past eleven, he ran down the stairs and drove to Harkin's house. A Garda car already blocked the entrance to the short road. There were other police cars in the street. The guard and Callaghan knew one another well.

'There's been a shooting. Mrs Harkin . . .'

'Is she . . .'

'I'm sorry,' Guard Sullivan said.

Callaghan restrained the urge to rush to her, the futile wish to help and succour what can be helped no longer, and turned slowly back to his car. Numbly he turned the car around and found himself driving out to the lake, parking at the gate. As he got out, he disturbed wildfowl in the reeds along the shore, and they scattered, shrieking, towards the centre. There was no moon but there were clear reflections on the water. Never did life seem so mysterious and inhospitable. They might as well all be out there in the middle of the lake with the wildfowl.

The lights were on in the house. When he knocked, Maggie came to the door. Later when the guards called at the house with word of the death, it was Callaghan who answered the knock.

After being charged, Harkin was transferred to a mental institution for a psychiatric report as part of the preparations for his trial. He took great interest in his case and consulted regularly with his solicitor. He tried but was unable to prevent the children from going to Maggie. Other than his solicitor, the only person he asked to see was Guard McCarthy, who had fought back to back with him against the tinkers on that terrible night years before.

McCarthy had settled in Cork and married a teacher. When Harkin's letter arrived, he was alarmed and took it straight to his sergeant, who consulted his superiors. To McCarthy's dismay, he was asked to visit his old friend and to write down everything that was said during the visit in case it could be of use in the forthcoming trial. All the expenses of the visit would be paid by the state.

On a summer's day the two men met and were allowed through locked doors into a walled ornamental garden. They sat on a wooden bench by a small fountain. Almost playfully Harkin examined McCarthy's ear for stitchmarks and asked, 'Do you think Cork has much of a chance in the All-Ireland this year?'

'Not much,' McCarthy answered. A silence followed that seemed to take a great age. The visit could not end quickly enough for him.

'What makes you say that?' Harkin eventually asked.

'The team is uneven. They're short of at least two forwards.'

'I'd hate to see Dublin winning it again.'

'They have the population,' McCarthy said. 'They have the pick.'

There was another long silence until Harkin asked, 'How do you think my case will go?'

In the heart-stopping pause that followed, McCarthy could hear the water splashing from the fountain, the birds singing. He said he had no earthly clue. The silence returned, but nothing came to break it. 'Was there anything in particular you wanted to see me about, Michael?' he ventured cautiously.

'No. Nothing. I just wanted to get a look at you again after all these years,' and he placed his hand on the guard's shoulder as they both rose.

McCarthy wrote down everything that Harkin said, but it was never used as evidence. That same evening Harkin swallowed an array of tablets that he had managed to conceal, and before he slipped into unconsciousness he reached beneath the scar on his chest to tear out the mechanism that regulated his heartbeat.

A silence came down around all that happened. Nobody complained about the normal quiet. Bird cries were sweet. The wing-beat of the swan crossing the house gave strength. The long light of day crossing the lake steeped us in privilege and mystery and infinite reflections that nobody wanted to break or question.

Gradually the sense of quiet weakened. The fact that nothing much was happening ceased to comfort. A craving for change began again. The silence around the murder was broken. All sorts of blame was apportioned as we noticed each year that passed across the face of the lake, quickening and gathering speed before swinging round again, until crowds of years seemed suddenly in the air above the lake, all gathering for flight.

With the years, Maggie and I had drawn closer. Whenever I had to go into the town I nearly always called at her house to see if she wanted to come and I often took the children to the train or met them when they came for weekends from Dublin.

All three children were at university. They were well mannered and intelligent and anxious to please, but compared to Maggie's rootedness they were like shadows. It was as if none of them could quite believe they had full rights to be alive on earth under the sky like every single other.

Every year I drove Maggie to the Christmas dinner and party for senior citizens in the parish hall. I am now almost old enough to go to the dinner in my own right, but it is one meal I want to put off for as long as I can. When Maggie was made Senior Citizen of the Year, it was natural that I'd drive her to Carrick for the presentation. All of us who knew her were delighted, but there was great difficulty in getting her to accept.

'Well, all of us here think it's great, Maggie, no matter what you say,' I said to her as we drove to Carrick.

'It's a lot of bother,' she answered. 'The old people used always to say it was never lucky to be too noticed. The shady corners are safer.'

'Even the shady corners may be safe no longer, but isn't it wonderful how well all the children did, and all you were able to do for them.'

'They were no trouble. They did it all themselves. I think they were making sure they'd never be left behind a second time,' and then she laughed her old, deep laugh.

'The two lassies will be fine, but I'm not so sure if his lordship will last the course. When he set out to be a doctor I don't think he realized he was in for seven years. Now his head is full of nothing but girls and discos. He thinks I'm made of money.'

As Maggie entered the ballroom of the hotel, everybody stood, and there was spontaneous clapping as she was led to her place. I saw Jerome Callaghan and his young wife at one of the tables. It was said he gave Maggie all the help she would allow over the years in bringing up the children – and I can't imagine her ever taking very much – and that he had played a part in her being chosen. I waited until she was seated behind an enormous vase of roses. Then I left as we had agreed. I walked about the empty town, had one drink in a quiet bar that also sold shoes and boots, across from the town clock, until it was time to take Maggie home.

'How did you enjoy it anyhow?' I asked as we drove towards the lake.

'Enjoy it?' she laughed. 'I suppose they meant well but I wouldn't like to go through the likes of tonight too often. The whole lot of them would lighten your head. What did I do? I did nothing. What else could I do? I was – in life.'

She was silent then until we turned in round the lake. 'Even where I am now, it's still all very interesting. Sometimes even far, far too interesting.'

The moon was bright on the lake, turning it into a clear, still sky. The fields above the lake and the dark shapes of the hedges stood out. Maggie sat quietly in the car while I got out to open the gate. Only a few short years before she would have insisted on getting out and walking the whole way in on her own. Wildfowl scattered from the reeds along the shore out towards the centre of the lake as soon as the car door opened. They squawked and shrieked for a while before turning into a dark silent huddle. Close by, a white moon rested on the water. There was no wind. The stars in their places were clear and fixed. Who would want change since change will come without wanting? Who this night would not want to live?

Nikolai Nikolaevich Pyasetsky, *c*.1994

THE LOST BOYS

Anna Pyasetskaya

My son Nikolai Nikolaevich Pyasetsky – Kolya to his friends and family – was called up into the Russian army on 24 May 1994. He was twenty.

He went for training at the Special Air Force centre in Omsk and then to the Ryazan regiment of the Tula division of the Special Air Force. The base isn't far from our home in Moscow, and I was glad he would be so near. We spoke on the phone on 28 November. He promised to find out when it would be convenient to visit and asked me to arrange a telephone call to him on 4 December. This was my last conversation with my son. On the following day, 29 November, he was flown with the rest of his battalion to Chechnya, though I didn't discover this till much later.

On 22 December we learned – from unofficial sources – that Kolya had been sent for duty in a 'southerly direction'. We knew by then that Russian troops had invaded Chechnya. We immediately wrote to ask: where is our son?

From the newspapers I found out that the Committee of Soldiers' Mothers of Russia was collecting parcels for young men who had been sent to Chechnya. I went to their headquarters on 25 December. They took a parcel for my son. I still didn't know where he was. I found out the telephone number of his division headquarters and rang every day from 26 December to ask about him. I was always given the same answer: he is not among the dead and wounded. Then, on 5 January, I was told that my son Nikolai Pyasetsky had been killed in Grozny.

For five days I walked around like a shadow unable to eat or drink. I prayed to God for our boys, the thousands of them, who had died in the battle of New Year's Eve. I cried for them all.

It wasn't until 11 January, after the holidays had ended, that I was able to appeal to the Tula division for my son's body to be returned to me. They told me that my son had disappeared without trace. I rang the headquarters again and was told to wait. New information: 'all the bodies are being collected in Rostov-on-Don, and from there your son's body will be sent to Moscow'.

I rang military section No. 41450 again to ask how my son had died. I discovered that Kolya was in personnel carrier No. 785 which had entered Grozny on 1 January. Of the twelve members of the crew only three remained alive. It wasn't clear what had happened; the vehicle had not been found. I managed to contact one of the survivors, Seryozha Rodionov. He was recovering from his wounds in Novocherkassk hospital. He said that my Kolya had been killed inside the vehicle close to the railway station. The Russian soldiers did not know the town: they had no maps. On 25 January I discovered that the vehicle had been found but that the body of my son was not in it.

On 26 January I flew with a group from the BBC a thousand miles south to the town of Nazran in Ingushetia, the state which borders Chechnya. Thousands of refugees had gathered in the town, and hundreds of mothers had come from all over Russia to look for their sons, though only a few managed to find them alive. On the first day in Nazran I discovered that a Chechen woman who conveyed the wounded from Grozny to Stariye Atagi had Kolya's military card. I wanted to find her and see if she knew anything of my son and so I went to Grozny. In the basement of city hospital No. 2 I met Maria Ivanovna Kirbasova, the chairperson of the Committee of Soldier's Mothers of Russia. I learned from her that Kolya was not on the list of prisoners.

Planes bombed the town every day and there was constant shooting. I was not afraid, I just wanted to know the fate of my son. I didn't manage to track down the Chechen woman until 31 January. She was called Zarema. She gave me my son's military card but couldn't tell me how or where she had come across it. The thread was broken. I went back to Nazran, but didn't stay long.

I decided to try to discover more from the military headquarters in

Beslan and then to travel to Rostov-on-Don where they were collecting the bodies of dead soldiers. At the headquarters they told me that my son's body must be in Rostov. I flew north to Rostov early in the morning of 2 February and looked through the books where the names of dead soldiers were registered. Kolya was not on any of the lists. I was told that only forty per cent of the bodies had been identified. I had to look through all the railway carriages filled with dead bodies. I will never be able to forget this horror.

The carriages were packed full. Many bodies were already unrecognizable: bitten by dogs, cut into pieces, burned. A month had already passed since the start of the war. Rostov was simply unable to cope. Apart from the train carriages, there was also a tent city near the hospital. The tents were also packed with bodies. I went through all the carriages and tents looking at every boy, the faces, the hair, and if there was no head, the hands and feet. My Kolya would be easy to find, he had a birthmark on his right cheek. There were some other mothers with me. One of them recognized her son, but I was not able to find Kolya. The soldiers told me that not all the carriages were in Rostov – there were more in Mozdok, close to the Chechen border. So I went south again to Mozdok, to the 'Mir' cinema. Hundreds of mothers gathered here every day. Each one was trying to find her son.

I needed to look through the carriages of dead bodies which had come from Grozny to Mozdok. I approached an officer who said he would help me, but the next time we met he said he could do nothing. 'What do you expect to be able to achieve? Your son is listed missing without trace.' I was overcome with despair.

Again I went to Grozny. Together with a young Japanese journalist I visited the cemetery where corpses from the whole town had been assembled: men, women, Christians, Muslims, all made equal in death. I did not find my son. Now, despairing of finding his body, I decided to look for him alive. I thought that in the mystery of God's plan he might have been taken prisoner.

On 4 April a group of us from the Soldiers' Mothers of Russia went to the village of Vedeno, the headquarters of Asian Maskhadov, the Chechen leader. Each woman had made her own way there. There were twenty-two of us and we met up at the Chechen military headquarters. The Chechens are a hospitable people and all the women were offered overnight accommodation. Three other Russian mothers,

Svetlana Belikova, Tanya Ivanova, Olya Osipenko and I were put up in a flat whose inhabitants had gone to Voronezh. We lived for almost two months in Vedeno, periodically going to mountain villages to look for our children.

Day followed day. In May there came a splinter of hope. We heard that some of the prisoners were in the mountains of Shatoi and my son's surname was mentioned. On 5 May we were received by Asian Maskhadov. A ceasefire had been negotiated but the Russians had not fulfilled their obligations: the exchange of prisoners could not take place. The front got closer and closer to Vedeno, Russian bombing raids became frequent, and seven times the village was hit. One bomb reduced a two-storey building to rubble and it took three days to dig out the dead. There were eleven of them, mainly women and children. We were seized by despair. We were Russians, the bombs were Russian bombs. Can people who sit in aeroplanes and deliver death be called human beings? A few mornings later we experienced the full horror of bombing for ourselves. The planes came suddenly as we were sitting down at the table for breakfast. The first bomb exploded thirty metres away. The windows blew out. As we ran towards the door, a second bomb hit the corner of our house. The floor above us collapsed, doors were wrenched off their hinges, the air was filled with dust and flying glass. We hid in the basement for the next half-hour until the raid ended. We were lucky. Sveta [Svetlana] had been lacerated by the glass, her leg swelled up and she found it difficult to walk, but the rest of us were unhurt.

We stayed on in Vedeno for a few days after the bombing. The bazaar was closed, it was impossible to buy food, and, because our house was destroyed, we had to sleep in the open. The sky was starry and the planes flew across it with their signal-lights on. Against the background of the stars it was difficult to make them out and they bombed with no fear that they would be hit by fire from the ground. I often recall those nights. We lay down under a blanket and tried to distinguish the planes from the stars. If a star began to fall it meant that a plane was preparing to bomb.

I thought that only the love of a person for all that lives could stop this madness.

We sent Olya with Sveta to another village where it was less dangerous, and then Tanya and I managed to persuade the Chechen fighters to take us with them into the Shatoi mountains where we thought our children might be. It was a tough journey along mountain paths, moving only at night without any lights or torches because planes were always in the sky. For two months we went from village to village. The fighters helped as much as they could, sharing their bread and distributing details of our children. We were bombed and fired upon several times. But we did not find our sons.

We headed back to Grozny along a road which was littered with burned and abandoned Russian vehicles and hundreds of dead Russian soldiers. There were many mass graves by the roadside. It was impossible to see all this without tears.

In Grozny I met some Chechen women whom I'd got to know on my previous visit, and we exchanged information. But there was nothing they could say to encourage our hope. I felt it was time to go home to Moscow – I'd been looking for my son now for seven months. Tanya decided to stay and continue looking for her son Andrei. I left Kolya's photo with her.

I reached Moscow on 20 August and on 4 September Tanya rang: she had recognized my Kolya from a video made on 21 February. Under the name Yevgeny Sergeyevich Gilev he had been buried 2,000 miles east of Moscow, in the Altai Mountains in a village called Stepnoe Ozero. Yevgeny's parents had opened the coffin when it arrived in their village but it was no longer possible to recognize the body. So they buried my son instead of their own. Six months later they buried another person; this time it was their son. He had been in carriage No. 162; his name was hidden in a pendant. His mother came to Rostov and recognized him and took him home. They buried him not far from my Kolya. The two lay together for a while until, on 15 October, my son was dug up and taken to Moscow, where I had requested that he be reburied.

Tanya Ivanova came to the funeral. In Rostov she had identified her Andrei, although the word 'identify' is not appropriate. He was completely burned: experts named him after taking X-rays of his skull and his chest and determining his blood group. Tanya had just buried her only son, but still she came to my son's funeral and responded to my grief. I am very grateful.

And how did the army help? Not at all. Only one person from my son's unit came to the funeral. The coffin was carried not by paratroopers but by my son's school friends. I was told there would be no government funding for the funeral because there were so many dead. And yet in his next breath the man who told me this, the representative of military unit No. 41450, spoke about the call of duty which my son had obeyed.

What is this debt? What do we owe this state which has taken from me my most precious thing?

Translated from the Russian by Patricia Cocrell and Galina Orlova

DESTROYED

Hilary Mantel

When I was very small, small enough to trip every time on the raised kerbstone outside the back door, the dog Victor used to take me for a walk. We would proceed at caution across the yard, my hand plunged deep into the ruff of bristly fur at the back of his neck. He was an elderly dog, and the leather of his collar had worn supple and thin. My fingers curled around it, while sunlight struck stone and slate, dandelions opened in the cracks between flags, and old ladies aired themselves in doorways, nodding on kitchen chairs and smoothing their skirts over their knees. Somewhere else, in factories, fields and coal mines, England went dully on.

My mother always said that there is no such thing as a substitute. Everything is intrinsically itself, and unlike any other thing. Everything is just once, and happiness can't be repeated. Children should be named for themselves. They shouldn't be named after other people. I don't agree with that, she said.

Then why did she do it, why did she break her own law? I'm trying to work it out, so meanwhile I have a different story, about some dogs, which perhaps relates to it. If I offer some evidence, will you be the judge?

My mother held her strong views, there's no doubt, because she herself was named after her cousin Clara, who died in an accident. If Clara had lived she would have been 107 now. It wasn't anything in her character that made my mother angry about the substitution, because Clara was not known to have had any character. No, what upset her was the way the name was pronounced by the people in our village. Cl-air-airra: it came sticky and prolonged out of their mouths, like an extruded rope of glue.

In those days we were all cousins and aunts and great-aunts who lived in rows of houses. We went in and out of each others' doors the whole time. My mother said that in the civilized world people would knock, but though she made this observation over and over, people just gave her a glassy-eyed stare and went on the way they always had. There was a great disjunction between the effect she thought she had on the world, and the effect she actually achieved. I only thought this later. When I was seven I thought she was Sun and Moon. That she was like God, everywhere and always. That she was reading your thoughts, when you were still a poor reader yourself, because you were only up to *Far & Wide Readers, Green Book III*.

Next door to us in the row lived my aunt Pauline. She was really my cousin, but I called her aunt because of her age. All the relationships were mixed up, and you don't need to know about them; only that the dog Victor lived with Pauline, and mostly under her kitchen table. He ate a meat pie every day, which Pauline bought him specially, walking up the street to buy it. He ate fruit, anything he could get. My mother said dogs should have proper food, in tins.

Victor had died by the time I was seven. I don't remember the day of his death, just a dull sense of cataclysm. Pauline was a widow. I thought she always had been.

When I was seven I was given a watch, but for my eighth birthday I had a puppy. When the idea of getting a dog was first proposed, my mother said that she wanted a Pekinese.

People gave her the look that they gave her when she suggested that civilized people would knock at the door. The idea of anyone in our village owning a Pekinese was simply preposterous; I knew this already. The inhabitants would have plucked and roasted it.

I said, 'It's my birthday, and I would like a dog like Victor.'

She said, 'Victor was just a mongrel.'

'Then I'll have just a mongrel,' I said.

I thought, you see, that a mongrel was a breed. Aunt Pauline had once told me,

'Mongrels are very faithful.'

I liked the idea of fidelity. Though I had no idea what it implied.

A mongrel, after all, was the cheap option. When the morning of my birthday came I suppose I felt excitement, I don't know. A young boy fetched the puppy from Godber's Farm. It stood blinking and shivering on the rug before the fire. Its tiny legs were like chicken bones. I am a winter-born person and there was frost on the roads that day. The puppy was white, like Victor, and had a curly tail like Victor, and a brown saddle on his back which made him look useful and domestic. I put my hand into the fur at the back of his neck and I judged that one day it would be long enough to hang on to.

The boy from Godber's Farm was in the kitchen, talking to my stepfather, who I was told to call Dad these days. I heard the boy say it was a right shame, but I didn't listen to find out what the shame was. The boy went out, my stepfather with him. They were chatting as if they were familiar.

I didn't understand in those days how people knew each other. They'd say, you know *her, her* who married *him. Constant was her name before she married him, or, her name was Reilly*. There was a time when I didn't understand how names got changed, or how anything happened, really. When somebody went out of the door I always wondered who or what they'd come back as, and whether they'd come back at all. I don't mean to make me sound simple, my infant self. I could pick out reasons for everything I did. I thought it was other people who were the sport of fortune, and the children of whim. One day about a year back, my father had gone out of the front door, looking so happy that I thought he was off to the corner for twenty cigarettes. If he had luggage, I didn't notice it. An hour had scarcely passed when the back door flew open and another man dumped a case down. He occupied a bed and tried to thieve a name.

So, when my stepfather had gone out, I found myself alone in our front room, before the slumbering and low-burning fire; and I started talking to the puppy Victor. I had read manuals of dog training in preparation for his arrival. They said that dogs liked a low, calm, soothing tone, but they didn't suggest what to say in it. He didn't look as if he had many interests yet so I told him about the things that interested me. I squatted on the floor next to him, so my great size wouldn't intimidate him. I looked into his face. Know my face, I prayed. After a certain amount of boredom from me, Victor fell to the floor as if his legs had been snapped, and slept like the dead. I sat down beside him to watch him. I had a book open on my knees but I didn't read it. I watched him, and I had never been so still. I knew that fidgeting was a vice, and I had tried to combat it, but I did not know stillness like that was in me, or calm like in the half-hour I first watched Victor.

When my stepfather came back he appeared to be himself, and no other; you could say that at least. He had a worried frown on his face, and something under his overcoat. A foxy muzzle poked out, noisily snuffling the air. 'This is Mike,' my stepfather said. 'He was going to be destroyed.' He put the new puppy on the ground. It was a bouncing skewbald made of rubber. It ran to the fire. It ran to Victor and sniffed him. It raced in a circle and bit chunks out of the air. Its tongue panted. It jumped on Victor and began to pulverize him.

Mike – let it be understood – was not an extra present for me. Victor was my dog and my responsibility. Mike was the other dog: he was everyone's, and no one's responsibility. Victor, as it proved, was of sedate, genteel character. When he was first put on his lead, he walked daintily, at heel, as if he had been trained in a former life. But when the lead was first clipped on to Mike's collar, he panicked. He ran to the end of it and yelped and spun into the air, and hurtled out into space, and turned head over heels. Then he flopped down on his side, and thrashed around as if he were in danger of a heart attack. I fumbled at his collar, desperate to set him free; his eye rolled, the fur of his throat was damp.

Try him again, when he's a bit older, my mother suggested.

Everybody said that it was nice that Victor had got his brother with him, that they would be faithful to each other, etc. I didn't think so, but what I didn't think I kept to myself.

The puppies had a pretty good life, except at night when the ghosts that lived in our house came out of the stone-floored pantry, and down from the big cupboard to the left of the chimney breast. Depend upon it, they were not dripping or ladies or genteel; they were nothing like the ghost that drowned Clara would have been, her sodden blouse frilled to the neck. These were ghosts with filed teeth. You couldn't see them, but you could sense their presence when you saw the dogs' bristling necks, and saw the shudders run down their backbones. The ruff on Victor's neck was growing long now. Despite everything my mother had vowed, the dogs did not get food out of tins. They got scraps of anything that was going. Substitutions were constantly made, in our house. Though it was said that no one thing was like any other.

'Try the dog on his lead again,' my mother said. If a person said, 'the dog', you knew Mike was the dog meant. Victor sat in the corner. He did not impose his presence. His brown eyes blinked.

I tried the dog on his lead again. He bolted across the room, taking me with him. I borrowed a book from the public library, *101 Hints on Dog Care*. Mike took it in the night and chewed it up, all but the last four hints. Mike would pull you in a hedge, he would pull you in a canal, he would pull you in a boating lake so you drowned like cousin Clara, when her careless beau tipped her out of the rowing boat. When I was nine I used to think quite a lot about Clara, her straw hat skimming among the lily pads.

It was when my brother P. G. Pig was born that my mother broke her own rule. I heard the cousins and aunts talking in lowered voices about the choice of name. They didn't take my views into account – no doubt they thought I'd recommend, Oh, call him Victor. Robert was mooted but my mother said Bob she could not abide. All those names were at first to be ruled out, that people naturally make into something else. But this left too few to draw on. At last my mother made up her mind on Peter, both syllables to be rigidly enforced. How did she think she would enforce them when he was a schoolboy, when he went to the football field, when he grew up to be a weaver or a soldier in a khaki blouson? I asked myself these things. And, mentally, I shrugged. I saw myself in my mind. 'Just asking?!!' I said. My fingers were spread and my eyes were round.

But there was something else about the baby's name, something that was going to be hidden. By listening at doors, by pasting myself against the wall and listening at doors, I found it was this: that the baby was to be given a second name, and it was to be George, which was the name of my aunt Pauline's dead husband. Oh, had Pauline a husband, I said to myself. I thought widow, like mongrel, was a category of its own.

Peter George, I said to myself, P.G., PG, PIG. He would have a name, and it would not be Peter, nor would it be Pete. But why so hushed? Why the averted shoulders and the voices dropped? *Because Pauline was not to be told*. It was going to be too much for her altogether, it would send her into a fit of the hysterics if she found out. It was my own mother's personal tribute to the long-destroyed George, who to my knowledge she had not mentioned before: a tribute, to pay which she was prepared to throw over one of her most characteristic notions. So strong, she said, were her feelings in the matter.

But wait. Wait a minute. Let logic peep in at the window here. This was Pauline, was it not? Aunt Pauline who lived next door? It was Pauline, who in three weeks' time would attend the christening? As Catholics we christen early, being very aware of the devil. I pictured the awful word 'George' weighting the priest's tongue, making him clutch his upper chest, reducing him to groans until it rolled out, crashing on the flags and processing down the aisle: and Pauline's arms flung up, the word 'Aa . . . gh!' flashing from her gaping mouth as she was mown down. What an awful death, I said to myself. Smirking, I said, what a destruction.

In the event, Pauline found out about the naming in very good time. My mother said – and thunder was on her brow – 'They told her in the butcher's. And she'd only gone in, bless her, for her little bit of a slice of–'

I left her presence. In the kitchen, Victor was sitting in the corner, curling up an edge of liver-coloured lip. I wondered if something had provoked him. A ghost come out early? Perhaps, I thought, it's George.

Pauline was next door as usual, going about her tasks in her own kitchen. You could hear her through the thin wall; the metal colander knocking against the enamel sink, the squeak of chair legs across the linoleum. In the days following she showed no sign of hysterical grief, or even nostalgia. My mother watched her closely. 'They never should have told her,' my mother said. 'A shock such as that could do lasting harm.' For some reason, she looked disappointed.

I didn't know what it was about, and I don't now, and I doubt if I want to. You can say 'how strong are my feelings', but be smiling all the while; and pay back obscurely for some obscure injury inflicted, maybe before I was born. It blights my life, trying to fill these gaps: I'm glad if I can persuade other people to do it for me. As far as I could see then it was just some tactic one person was trying on another person and it was the reason I didn't like to play cat's cradle, patience, cutting out with scissors or any indoor games at all. Winter or not, I played outside with Victor and Mike.

It was spring when P. G. Pig was born. I went out into the field at the back, to get away from the screaming and puking and baby talk. Victor sat quivering at my heel. Mike raced in insane circles among the daisies. I pushed back my non-existent cowboy hat. I scratched my head like an old-timer and said, 'Loco.'

My brother was still a toddler when Victor's character took a turn for the worse. Always timid, he now became morose, and took to snapping. One day when I came to put on his lead he sprang into the air and nipped me on the cheek. Believing myself an incipient beauty and afraid of facial scarring, I washed the bite then rubbed raw Dettol on it. What resulted was worse than the bite and I rehearsed to the air the sentence 'Hurts like hell.' I tried not to tell my mother but she smelled the Dettol. Later he chased P. G. Pig, trying to get him on the calf. P. G. marched to the German goose-step. So, he escaped by inches, or even less. I plucked a ravelled thread of his towelling suit from between Victor's teeth.

Victor didn't attack grown people. He backed off from them. 'It's just the children he goes for,' my mother said. 'I find it very perplexing.'

So did I. I wondered why he included me with the children. If he could see into my heart, I thought, he would know I don't qualify.

By this time we had a new baby in the house. Victor was not to be trusted and my mother said a sorting-out was overdue. He went away under my stepfather's overcoat, wrapped tight, struggling. We said goodbye to him. He was pinioned while we patted his head. He growled at us, and the growl turned to a snarl, and he was hurried out of the front door, and away down the street. My mother said that she and my father had found a new home for him, with an elderly couple without children. How sad! I pictured them, their homely grieving faces softening at the sight of the white dog with his useful brown saddle. He would be a substitute child for them. Would they dip their old fingers into the ruff at his neck, and hold on tight?

It was strange, what I chose to believe in those days. P. G. Pig knew better. Sitting in the corner, he took a sideways swipe at his tower of blue bricks. 'Destroyed,' he said.

About a year after that, we moved to a new town. My surname was changed officially. Pig and the younger baby had the new name already, there was no need for them to change. My mother said that generally, the gossip and malice had got out of hand, and there were always those who were ready to do you a bad turn if they could contrive it. Pauline and the other aunts and cousins came to visit. But not too often. My mother said, we don't want that circus starting up again.

So the years began in which I pretended to be someone else's daughter. The word 'daughter' is long, pale, mournful; its hand is to its cheek. The word 'rueful' goes with 'daughter'. Sometimes I thought of Victor and I was rueful. I sat in my room with compass and square-ruled book, and bisected angles, while outside the children shrieked, frolicking with Mike. In truth I blamed Mike for alienating Victor's affections, but there is a limit to how much you can blame a dog.

With the move to the new house, a change had overtaken Mike, similar in magnitude though not in style to the one that had overtaken his brother x years before. I call it x years because I was beginning to lose track of that part of my life, and in the case of numbers it is allowable to make a substitution. I remembered the facts of things pretty well, but I had forgotten certain feelings, like how I felt on the day Victor arrived from Godber's Farm, and how I felt on the day he was taken away to his new home. I remembered his straitjacketed snarling, which hardly diminished as he was carried out of the door. If he could have bitten me that day, he would have drawn blood.

The trouble with Mike was this: we had become middle-class, but our dog had not. We had long ago ceased trying to take him for walks on a lead. Now he exercised himself, running away at all hours of the day and night. He could leap gates and make holes through hedges. He was seen in the vicinity of butcher's shops. Sometimes he went to the High Street and stole parcels and packets from baskets on wheels. He ate a white loaf, secretly, in the shadow of the privet. I saw that he looked dedicated and innocent as he chewed it, slice after slice, holding the dough carefully in paws that he turned inwards, as if praying.

When my mother saw the neighbours leaning over the larchlap, imparting gardening tips, she thought they were talking about Mike. Her face would become pinched. She believed he was letting the family down, betraying mongrel origins. I knew the meaning of the word now. I did not get involved in any controversy about Mike. I crouched in my room and traced the continent of South America. I stuck into my geography book a picture of Brasilia, the white shining city in the jungle. I placed my hands together and prayed, take me there. I did not believe in God so I prayed provisionally, to genies and ghosts, to dripping Clara and old dead George.

Mike was less than five years old when he began to show his age. He had lived hard, after all. One year, he could catch and snap in his jaws the windfalls our apple tree shook down. Those he did not catch as they fell, the babies would bowl for him, and he would hurtle after, tearing skidmarks in the turf as he cornered; then with a backward jerk of his neck he would toss the fruit up into the blue air, to give himself a challenge.

But a year later, he was on the blink. He couldn't catch the windfalls if they rained down on his head, and when old tennis balls were thrown for him he would trot vaguely, dutifully, away from the hue and cry, and then turn and plod back, his jaws empty. I said to my mother, I think Mike's eyes are failing. She said, I hadn't noticed.

The defect didn't seem to make him downhearted. He continued to lead his independent life; smelling his way, I supposed, through gaps in wire netting and through the open doors of vendors of fine foods and High Class Family Butchers. I thought, he could do with a guide-person really. Perhaps I could train up P. G. Pig? I tried the experiment we hadn't tried in years, clipping lead to collar. The dog lay down at my feet and whimpered. I noticed that the foxy patches of his coat had bleached out, as if he'd been in the sun and the rain too long. I unfastened the lead and wrapped it around my hand. Then I threw it at the back of the hall cupboard. I stood in the hall and practised swearing under my breath. I didn't know why.

On New Year's Day, a fortnight before my twelfth birthday, Mike went out in the morning and didn't come back. My stepfather said, 'Mike's not come in for his tea.'

I said, 'Mike's bloody blind.'

They all pretended not to have heard me. There was an edict against quarrelling anywhere near Christmas, and it was still near enough; we were lodged in the strange-menu days leading to the Feast of the Epiphany, when babies daub jelly in their hair and *The Great Escape* is on TV and no one notices what time it is. That's why we were less alarmed than we would usually have been, yawning off to bed.

But I woke up very early, and stood shivering by the window, the curtain wrapped around me, looking out over land that was imagined because there was no light: leafless, wet, warm for the time of year. If Mike were home I would feel it, I thought. He would whine and buffet the back door, and someone would hear if not me. But I didn't know. I couldn't trust that. I ran my hand through my hair and made it stand up in tufts. I crept back to bed.

I had no dreams. When I woke up it was nine o'clock. I was astonished at the leniency. My mother needs little sleep, and thinks it a moral failing in others, so usually she would have been bawling in my ear by eight, inventing tasks for me; the Christmas truce did not apply in the earlier hours of the morning. I went downstairs in my spotted pyjamas, the legs rolled up above the knee, in a *jeu d'esprit*.

'Oh, for God's sake,' my mother said. 'And what have you done with your hair?'

I said, 'Where's my dad?'

She said, 'He's gone to the police station, about Mike.'

'No,' I said. I shook my head. I rolled down my pyjama trousers to the ankle. Fuckit, I wanted to say. Why pretend I mean him? *Answer the question I put to you.*

The next day I went out calling, through the small woods that belted open fields, and along the banks of the canal. It rained part of the day, a benign and half-hearted precipitation. Everything seemed unseasonable, forward: the rotting wood of fences shimmered green. I took my redoubtable brother with me, and I kept my eye on the yellow bobble of his bobble hat. The minute he went out of sight, in undergrowth or copse, I called him, Peegie pig, Peegie pig! I felt him before I saw him, loping to my side.

I had penny chews in my pocket and I fed them to him to keep him going. 'Mike, Mike!' we called. It was Sunday, the end of an extended holiday which had added to the dislocation of Advent. We met no one on our quest. Peegie's nose began to run. After a time, when the dog didn't answer, he began to cry. He'd thought we were going to meet Mike, you see. At some place pre-arranged.

I just tugged Peegie along. It was all I could do. The word 'interloper' was rolling around my mind, and I thought what a beautiful word it was, and how well it described the dog Mike who loped and flapped his pink tongue in the open air, while Victor squatted in the house, thin like myself, and his skin leaking fear.

On the banks of the canal at last we met a man, not old, his jacket flapping and insufficient even for the mildness of the day; his hair cropped, his torn pocket drooping from his checked shirt, and his gym shoes caked in mud. Who was Mike, he wanted to know?

I told him my mother's theory, that Mike had been mowed down by a Drunken Driver. Peegie sawed his hand back and forth under his snuffling nose. The man promised he would call out for Mike, and take him if recovered to the police or the RSPCA. Beware of the police pounds, he said, for the dogs there are destroyed in twelve days.

I said, that within twelve days we would be sure to hear from them. I said, my step my step my father has been to the police: I managed the word in the end. I swear by Almighty God, the man said, that I will be calling for young Michael day and night. I felt alarmed for him. I felt sorry for his torn pocket, as if I should have been carrying needle and thread.

I walked away, and I had not gone a hundred yards before I felt there were misunderstandings that needed to be corrected. Mike is only my step-dog. Supposing I had misinformed this stranger? But if I went back to put the facts to him again, perhaps he would only forget them. He looked like a man who had forgotten almost everything. I had gone another hundred yards before it came to me that this was the very kind of stranger to whom you were warned not to speak.

I looked down at Peegie in second-hand alarm. I should have protected him. Peegie was learning to whistle that week, and now he was whistling and crying at the same time. He was whistling the tune from Laurel and Hardy, which I can't stand. I knew full well – 'full well' is one of my mother's expressions – that Mike was dead in a ditch, where he had limped or crawled away from the vehicle that had smashed him up before he saw it. All day I'd been searching, in defiance of this fact.

Oh, I'm tired, Peegie wailed. Carry me. Carry me. I looked down and knew I could not, and he knew it too, for he was such a big boy already that it could almost have been the other way around. I offered him a penny chew, and he smacked my hand away.

We came to a wall, and I hoisted him on to it. He could have hoisted me. We sat there, while the air darkened. It was four o'clock, and we had been walking and calling since early morning. I thought, I could drown Peegie Pig, and blame it on the man with the torn pocket. I could haul him across the towpath by the hood of his coat, and push him under the bright green weed; and keep pushing, a hand on his face, till the weight of his clothes pulled him under; and I saw myself, careless beau, other life, lily pad and floating hat. As far as I knew, no one had been hanged for Clara. 'What's for my tea?' Peegie said. Some words came to me, from the Shakespeare we were doing. *When the exigent is come, that now is come indeed*. The damp was making me ache, as if I were my own grandmother. I thought, nobody listens, nobody sees, nobody does any bloody fuckit thing. You go blind and savage and they carry on making Christmas trifles and frying eggs. Fuckit, I said to Peegie, experimentally. Fuckit, he repeated after me. Mike, Mike, we called, as we trod the towpath, and early night closed in on us. Peegie Pig slipped his hand into mine. We walked into the dark together, and our fused hands were cold. I said, to myself, I cannot kill him, he is fidelity itself; though it did occur to me that if he drowned, someone would be named after him. 'Come on, Peegie,' I said to him. 'But cut out the whistling.' I stood behind him, put my cold hands into the hood of his duffel coat, and began to steer him home.

There was a lot of blame flying in the air about where had we been, up by the canal where vagrants live and anybody. My mother had already washed Mike's dishes out, and put them to drain. As she was not much of a housewife, we knew by this sign that he was not coming back, not through our door anyway. I cried a bit then, not out of the exhaustion of the day, but sudden scorching tears that leaped out of my eyes and scoured the pattern off the wallpaper. I saw Peegie gaping at me, open-mouthed, so I was sorry I'd bothered crying at all. I just wiped my fist across my face, and got on with the next thing.

CALL IF YOU NEED ME

Raymond Carver

We had both been involved with other people that spring, but when June came and school was out we decided to let our house for the summer and move from Palo Alto to the north coast country of California. Our son, Richard, went to Nancy's mother's place in Pasco, Washington, to live for the summer and work toward saving money for college in the fall. His grandmother knew the situation at home and had begun working on getting him up there and locating him a job long before his arrival. She'd talked to a farmer friend of hers and had secured a promise of work for Richard baling hay and building fences. Hard work, but Richard was looking forward to it. He left on the bus in the morning of the day after his high school graduation. I took him to the station and parked and went inside to sit with him until his bus was called. His mother had already held him and cried and kissed him goodbye and given him a long letter that he was to deliver to his grandmother upon his arrival. She was at home now finishing last-minute packing for our own move and waiting for the couple who were to take our house. I bought Richard's ticket, gave it to him, and we sat on one of the benches in the station and waited. We'd talked a little about things on the way to the station.

'Are you and mom going to get a divorce?' he'd asked. It was Saturday morning, and there weren't many cars.

'Not if we can help it,' I said. 'We don't want to. That's why we're going away from here and don't expect to see anyone all summer. That's why we've rented our house for the summer and rented the house up in Arcata. Why you're going away, too, I guess. One reason anyway. Not to mention the fact that you'll come home with your pockets filled with money. We don't want to get a divorce. We want to be alone for the summer and try to work things out.'

'You still love mom?' he said. 'She told me she loves you.'

'Of course I do,' I said. 'You ought to know that by now. We've just had our share of troubles and heavy responsibilities, like everyone else, and now we need time to be alone and work things out. But don't worry about us. You just go up there and have a good summer and work hard and save your money. Consider it a vacation, too. Get in all the fishing you can. There's good fishing around there.'

'Waterskiing, too,' he said. 'I want to learn to water ski.'

'I've never been waterskiing,' I said. 'Do some of that for me too, will you?'

We sat in the bus station. He looked through his yearbook while I held a newspaper in my lap. Then his bus was called and we stood up. I embraced him and said again, 'Don't worry, don't worry. Where's your ticket?'

He patted his coat pocket and then picked up his suitcase. I walked him over to where the line was forming in the terminal, then I embraced him again and kissed him on the cheek and said goodbye.

'Goodbye, Dad,' he said and turned from me so that I wouldn't see his tears.

I drove home to where our boxes and suitcases were waiting in the living room. Nancy was in the kitchen drinking coffee with the young couple she'd found to take our house for the summer. I'd met the couple, Jerry and Liz, graduate students in math, for the first time a few days before, but we shook hands again, and I drank a cup of coffee that Nancy poured. We sat around the table and drank coffee while Nancy finished her list of things they should look out for or do at certain times of the month, the first and last of each month, where they should send any mail, and the like. Nancy's face was tight. Sun fell through the curtain on to the table as it got later in the morning.

Finally, things seemed to be in order and I left the three of them in the kitchen and began loading the car. It was a furnished house we were going to, furnished right down to plates and cooking utensils, so we wouldn't need to take much with us from this house, only the essentials.

I'd driven up to Eureka, 350 miles north of Palo Alto, on the north coast of California, three weeks before and rented us the furnished house. I went with Susan, the woman I'd been seeing. We stayed in a motel at the edge of town for three nights while I looked in the newspaper and visited realtors. She watched me as I wrote out a cheque for the three months' rent. Later, back at the motel, in bed, she lay with her hand on her forehead and said, 'I envy your wife. I envy Nancy. You hear people talk about "the other woman" always and how the incumbent wife has the privileges and the real power, but I never really understood or cared about those things before. Now I see. I envy her. I envy her the life she will have with you in that house this summer. I wish it were me. I wish it were us. Oh, how I wish it were us. I feel so crummy,' she said. I stroked her hair.

Nancy was a tall, long-legged woman with brown hair and eyes and a generous spirit. But lately we had been coming up short on generosity and spirit. The man she had been seeing was one of my colleagues, a divorced, dapper, three-piece-suit-and-tie fellow with greying hair who drank too much and whose hands, some of my students told me, sometimes shook in the classroom. He and Nancy had drifted into their affair at a party during the holidays not too long after Nancy had discovered my own affair. It all sounds boring and tacky now – it is boring and tacky – but during that spring it was what it was, and it consumed all of our energies and concentration to the exclusion of everything else. Sometime in late April we began to make plans to rent our house and go away for the summer, just the two of us, and try to put things back together, if they could be put back together. We each agreed we would not call or write or otherwise be in touch with the other parties. So we made arrangements for Richard, found the couple to look after our house, and I had looked at a map and driven north from San Francisco and found Eureka, and a realtor who was willing to rent a furnished house to a respectable middle-aged married couple for the summer. I think I even used the phrase second honeymoon to the realtor, God forgive me, while Susan smoked a cigarette and read tourist brochures out in the car.

I finished storing the suitcases, bags and cartons in the trunk and backseat and waited while Nancy said a final goodbye on the porch. She shook hands with each of them and turned and came toward the car. I waved to the couple, and they waved back. Nancy got in and shut the door. 'Let's go,' she said. I put the car in gear and we headed for the freeway. At the light just before the freeway we saw a car ahead of us come off the freeway trailing a broken muffler, the sparks flying. 'Look at that,' Nancy said. 'It might catch fire.' We waited and watched until the car managed to pull off the road on to the shoulder.

We stopped at a little café off the highway near Sebastopol. Eat and Gas, the sign read. We laughed at the sign. I pulled up in front of the café and we went inside and took a table near a window in the back of the café. After we had ordered coffee and sandwiches, Nancy touched her forefinger to the table and began tracing lines in the wood. I lit a cigarette and looked outside. I saw rapid movement, and then I realized I was looking at a hummingbird in the bush beside the window. Its wings moved in a blur of motion and it kept dipping its beak into a blossom on the bush.

'Nancy, look,' I said. 'There's a hummingbird.'

But the hummingbird flew at this moment and Nancy looked and said, 'Where? I don't see it.'

'It was just there a minute ago,' I said. 'Look, there it is. Another one, I think. It's another hummingbird.'

We watched the hummingbird until the waitress brought our order and the bird flew at the movement and disappeared around the building.

'Now that's a good sign, I think,' I said. 'Hummingbirds. Hummingbirds are supposed to bring luck.'

'I've heard that somewhere,' she said. 'I don't know where I heard that, but I've heard it. Well,' she said, 'luck is what we could use. Wouldn't you say?'

'They're a good sign,' I said. 'I'm glad we stopped here.'

She nodded. She waited a minute, then she took a bite of her sandwich.

We reached Eureka just before dark. We passed the motel on the highway where Susan and I had stayed and had spent the three nights some weeks before, then turned off the highway and took a road up over a hill overlooking the town. I had the house keys in my pocket. We drove over the hill and for a mile or so until we came to a little intersection with a service station and a grocery store. There were wooded mountains ahead of us in the valley, and pastureland all around. Some cattle were grazing in a field behind the service station. 'This is pretty country,' Nancy said. 'I'm anxious to see the house.'

'Almost there,' I said. 'It's just down this road,' I said, 'and over that rise.' 'Here,' I said in a minute and pulled into a long driveway with hedge on either side. 'Here it is. What do you think of this?' I'd asked the same question of Susan when she and I had stopped in the driveway.

'It's nice,' Nancy said. 'It looks fine, it does. Let's get out.'

We stood in the front yard a minute and looked around. Then we went up the porch steps and I unlocked the front door and turned on the lights. We went through the house. There were two small bedrooms, a bath, a living room with old furniture and a fireplace, and a big kitchen with a view of the valley.

'Do you like it?' I said.

'I think it's just wonderful,' Nancy said. She grinned. 'I'm glad you found it. I'm glad we're here.' She opened the refrigerator and ran a finger over the counter. 'Thank God, it looks clean enough. I won't have to do any cleaning.'

'Right down to clean sheets on the beds,' I said. 'I checked. I made sure. That's the way they're renting it. Pillows even. And pillowcases, too.'

'We'll have to buy some firewood,' she said. We were standing in the living room. 'We'll want to have a fire on nights like this.'

'I'll look into firewood tomorrow,' I said. 'We can go shopping then too and see the town.'

She looked at me and said, 'I'm glad we're here.'

'So am I,' I said. I opened my arms and she moved to me. I held her. I could feel her trembling. I turned her face up and kissed her on either cheek. 'Nancy,' I said.

'I'm glad we're here,' she said.

We spent the next few days settling in, taking trips into Eureka to walk around and look in store windows, and hiking across the pastureland behind the house all the way to the woods. We bought groceries and I found an ad in the newspaper for firewood, called, and a day or so afterwards two young men with long hair delivered a pick-up truckload of alder and stacked it in the carport. That night we sat in front of the fireplace after dinner and drank coffee and talked about getting a dog.

'I don't want a pup,' Nancy said. 'Something we have to clean up after or that will chew things up. That we don't need. But I'd like to have a dog, yes. We haven't had a dog in a long time. I think we could handle a dog up here,' she said.

'And after we go back, after summer's over?' I said. I rephrased the question. 'What about keeping a dog in the city?'

'We'll see. Meanwhile, let's look for a dog. The right kind of dog. I don't know what I want until I see it. We'll read the classifieds and we'll go to the pound, if we have to.' But though we went on talking about dogs for several days, and pointed out dogs to each other in people's yards we'd drive past, dogs we said we'd like to have, nothing came of it, we didn't get a dog.

Nancy called her mother and gave her our address and telephone number. Richard was working and seemed happy, her mother said. She herself was fine. I heard Nancy say, 'We're fine. This is good medicine.'

One day in the middle of July we were driving the highway near the ocean and came over a rise to see some lagoons that were closed off from the ocean by sand spits. There were some people fishing from shore, and two boats out on the water.

I pulled the car off on to the shoulder and stopped. 'Let's see what they're fishing for,' I said. 'Maybe we could get some gear and go ourselves.'

'We haven't been fishing in years,' Nancy said. 'Not since that time Richard was little and we went camping near Mount Shasta. Do you remember that?'

'I remember,' I said. 'I just remembered too that I've missed fishing. Let's walk down and see what they're fishing for.'

'Trout,' the man said, when I asked. 'Cut-throats and rainbow trout. Even some steelhead and a few salmon. They come in here in the winter when the spit opens and then when it closes in the spring, they're trapped. This is a good time of the year for them. I haven't caught any today, but last Sunday I caught four, about fifteen inches long. Best eating fish in the world, and they put up a hell of a fight. Fellows out in the boats have caught some today, but so far I haven't done anything today.'

'What do you use for bait?' Nancy asked.

'Anything,' the man said. 'Worms, salmon eggs, whole kernel corn.

Just get it out there and leave it lay on the bottom. Pull out a little slack and watch your line.'

We hung around a little longer and watched the man fish and watched the little boats chat-chat back and forth the length of the lagoon.

'Thanks,' I said to the man. 'Good luck to you.'

'Good luck to you,' he said. 'Good luck to the both of you.'

We stopped at a sporting goods store on the way back to town and bought licences, inexpensive rods and reels, nylon line, hooks, leaders, sinkers, and a creel. We made plans to go fishing the next morning.

But that night, after we'd eaten dinner and washed the dishes and I had laid a fire in the fireplace, Nancy shook her head and said it wasn't going to work.

'Why do you say that?' I asked. 'What is it you mean?'

'I mean it isn't going to work. Let's face it.' She shook her head again. 'I don't think I want to go fishing in the morning, either, and I don't want a dog. No, no dogs. I think I want to go up and see my mother and Richard. Alone. I want to be alone. I miss Richard,' she said and began to cry. 'Richard's my son, my baby,' she said, 'and he's nearly grown and gone. I miss him.'

'And Del, do you miss Del Shraeder, too?' I said. 'Your boyfriend. Do you miss him?'

'I miss everybody tonight,' she said. 'I miss you too. I've missed you for a long time now. I've missed you so much you've gotten lost somehow, I can't explain it. I've lost you. You're not mine any longer.'

'Nancy,' I said.

'No, no,' she said. She shook her head. She sat on the sofa in front of the fire and kept shaking her head. 'I want to fly up and see my mother and Richard tomorrow. After I'm gone you can call your girlfriend.'

'I won't do that,' I said. 'I have no intention of doing that.'

'You'll call her,' she said.

'You'll call Del,' I said. I felt rubbishy for saying it.

'You can do what you want,' she said, wiping her eyes on her sleeve. 'I mean that. I don't want to sound hysterical. But I'm going up to Washington tomorrow. Right now I'm going to go to bed. I'm exhausted. I'm sorry. I'm sorry for both of us, Dan. We're not going to make it. That fisherman today. He wished us good luck.' She shook her head. 'I wish us good luck too. We're going to need it.'

She went into the bathroom and I heard water running in the tub. I went out and sat on the porch steps and smoked a cigarette. It was dark and quiet outside. I looked toward town and could see a faint glow of lights in the sky and patches of ocean fog drifting in the valley. I began to think of Susan. A little later Nancy came out of the bathroom and I heard the bedroom door close. I went inside and put another block of wood on the grate and waited until the flames began to move up the bark. Then I went into the other bedroom and turned the covers back and stared at the floral design on the sheets. Then I showered, dressed in my pyjamas, and went to sit near the fireplace again. The fog was outside the window now. I sat in front of the fire and smoked. When I looked out the window again, something moved in the fog and I saw a horse grazing in the front yard.

I went to the window. The horse looked up at me for a minute, then went back to pulling up grass. Another horse walked past the car into the yard and began to graze. I turned on the porch light and stood at the window and watched them. They were big white horses with long manes. They'd gotten through a fence or an unlocked gate from one of the nearby farms. Somehow they'd wound up in our front yard. They were larking it, enjoying their breakaway immensely. But they were nervous too; I could see the whites of their eyes from where I stood behind the window. Their ears kept rising and falling as they tore out clumps of grass. A third horse wandered into the yard, and then a fourth. It was a herd of white horses, and they were grazing in our front yard.

I went into the bedroom and woke Nancy. Her eyes were red and the skin around the eyes was swollen. She had her hair up in curlers and a suitcase lay open on the floor near the foot of the bed.

'Nancy,' I said. 'Honey, come and see what's in the front yard. Come and see this. You must see this. You won't believe it. Hurry up.'

'What is it?' she said. 'Don't hurt me. What is it?'

'Honey, you must see this. I'm not going to hurt you. I'm sorry if I scared you. But you must come out here and see something.'

I went back into the other room and stood in front of the window and in a few minutes Nancy came in tying her robe. She looked out the window and said, 'My God, they're beautiful. Where'd they come from, Dan? They're just beautiful.'

'They must have gotten loose from around here somewhere,' I said. 'One of these farm places. I'll call the sheriff's department pretty soon and let them locate the owners. But I wanted you to see this first.'

'Will they bite?' she said. 'I'd like to pet that one there, that one that just looked at us. I'd like to pat that one's shoulder. But I don't want to get bitten. I'm going outside.'

'I don't think they'll bite,' I said. 'They don't look like the kind of horses that'll bite. But put a coat on if you're going out there; it's cold.'

I put my coat on over my pyjamas and waited for Nancy. Then I opened the front door and we went outside and walked into the yard with the horses. They all looked up at us. Two of them went back to pulling up grass. One of the other horses snorted and moved back a few steps, and then it too went back to pulling up grass and chewing, head down. I rubbed the forehead of one horse and patted its shoulder. It kept chewing. Nancy put out her hand and began stroking the mane of another horse. 'Horsey, where'd you come from?' she said. 'Where do you live and why are you out tonight, Horsey?' she said and kept stroking the horse's mane. The horse looked at her and blew through its lips and dropped its head again. She patted its shoulder.

'I guess I'd better call the sheriff,' I said.

'Not yet,' she said. 'Not for a while yet. We'll never see anything like this again. We'll never, never have horses in our front yard again. Wait a while yet, Dan.'

A little later, Nancy was still out there moving from one horse to another, patting their shoulders and stroking their manes, when one of the horses moved from the yard into the driveway and walked around the car and down the driveway toward the road, and I knew I had to call.

In a little while the two sheriff's cars showed up with their red lights flashing in the fog and a few minutes later a fellow with a sheepskin coat driving a pick-up with a horse trailer behind it. Now the horses shied and tried to get away and the man with the horse trailer swore and tried to get a rope around the neck of one horse.

'Don't hurt it!' Nancy said.

We went back in the house and stood behind the window and watched the deputies and the rancher work on getting the horses rounded up.

'I'm going to make some coffee,' I said. 'Would you like some coffee, Nancy?'

'I'll tell you what I'd like,' she said. 'I feel high Dan. I feel like I'm loaded. I feel like, I don't know, but I like the way I'm feeling. You put on some coffee and I'll find us some music to listen to on the radio and then you can build up the fire again. I'm too excited to sleep.'

So we sat in front of the fire and drank coffee and listened to an all-night radio station from Eureka and talked about the horses and then talked about Richard, and Nancy's mother. We danced. We didn't talk about the present situation at all. The fog hung outside the window and we talked and were kind with one another. Toward daylight I turned off the radio and we went to bed and made love.

The next afternoon, after her arrangements were made and her suitcases packed, I drove her to the little airport where she would catch a flight to Portland and then transfer to another airline that would put her in Pasco late that night.

'Tell your mother I said hello. Give Richard a hug for me and tell him I miss him,' I said. 'Tell him I send love.'

'He loves you too,' she said. 'You know that. In any case, you'll see him in the fall, I'm sure.'

I nodded.

'Goodbye,' she said and reached for me. We held each other. 'I'm glad for last night,' she said. 'Those horses. Our talk. Everything. It helps. We won't forget that,' she said. She began to cry.

'Write me, will you?' I said. 'I didn't think it would happen to us,' I said. 'All those years. I never thought so for a minute. Not us.'

'I'll write,' she said. 'Some big letters. The biggest you've ever seen since I used to send you letters in high school.'

'I'll be looking for them,' I said.

Then she looked at me again and touched my face. She turned and moved across the tarmac toward the plane.

Go, dearest one, and God be with you.

She boarded the plane and I stayed around until its jet engines started and, in a minute, the plane began to taxi down the runway. It lifted off over Humboldt Bay and soon became a speck on the horizon.

I drove back to the house and parked in the driveway and looked at the hoofprints of the horses from last night. There were deep impressions in the grass, and gashes, and there were piles of dung. Then I went into the house and, without even taking off my coat, went to the telephone and dialled Susan's number.

A.L. Kennedy with her grandfather, Joseph Henry Price, *c.*1970

A BLOW TO THE HEAD

A. L. Kennedy

I am looking for my dead grandfather in the British Library. Around me the new building is calm and white, a little like a hospital for books. I peck my way through layers of computer filing looking for copies of his favourite, long defunct, magazine *Health and Strength*. Here, according to the story he always told, I will find his photograph: a picture of a young man, a boxer: a middleweight before his marriage, before his daughter, before me.

I wait for the delivery of 1935 and 1936 and, without intending to, remember his scents. My grandfather smelled of Lifebuoy soap and Brylcreem and soft, soft skin. Although he was a fighter and a steelworker most of his life, his hands and feet never hardened. Each new pair of work boots crippled him. His boxing stories were filled with magical strategies for toughening his fists. When I stayed with him and my grandmother in the school holidays, I would be given the task of picking tiny metal pieces from his uncallused fingers and palms with a needle's point. I realized this was a kind of honour, he usually did the work himself, but now he was trusting me, making his hands a helpless weight in mine. The whole process made me feel sick, all the same: I knew that I hurt him.

On the desk in front of me the Reminder to Readers warns that 'Books and manuscripts are fragile objects. Please take care and do nothing which might damage them.' The living and reading are intended to be gentle when they visit, to remember that the information stored here is vulnerable, quite easy to destroy. I don't believe my grandfather ever considered his weekly bible might end its life in such sickly company. Then again, he neither liked nor anticipated his own decline into frailty.

He was, after all, a man of certainty and solutions. A tool setter for most of his life, he spent hours calibrating machine tools, measuring out their tolerances for error, refitting and modifying them to meet every conceivable demand, the trickier the better: in retirement, he mended old radios, televisions, doorbells, clocks. His unshakeable assumption that I had inherited his general physical confidence and dexterity meant my childhood was littered with unmanageable gifts: the bicycle I couldn't balance, the roller skates that scared me – I only dared to use them over gravel – and the gleaming, implacable pogo stick. We both wanted me to enjoy these things, but I never could.

Far more comforting were his remedies for likely and unlikely threats. Crouching between his shins, my arms slung over his supporting knees, I would watch old horror films long past my bedtime and we would discuss the fatal weaknesses of vampires, werewolves and monsters of all types. We knew how to finish them, every one. And he would tell me, in only the twitch and surge of television light, how to deal with any real attacker. There, with the safest man in the world, I learned how I should stamp on insteps and scrape shins, gouge eyes and chop at windpipes, or jab with the heel of my hand at the base of noses in a way which he neglected to mention might well prove fatal if it sent the assailant's nasal septum spearing back into his brain.

Which my grandfather would not have minded. It was a gently accepted fact that he would have killed anybody who harmed me, who even thought of it. These were among his quieter gifts, the ones I didn't notice at the time: his unconditional belief that I was precious enough to be so very well defended, and my certainty that I can defend myself. I have many of the usual kinds of fear, but fear of attack is not among them. I have never, it so happens, lost a fight and I have never seen the strength and size of the male body as a threat. I have had full freedom, if I've wished, to find it only beautiful. My grandfather, Joseph Henry Price, he gave me this.

When it arrives, in leather-bound volumes, *Health and Strength* has its own kind of beauty. Billed as 'The National Organ of Physical Fitness', it mingles articles on the perfect punch and sexual advice with photographs of the physically fit. Men in leopard-skin trunks and gladiator boots tense and grimace happily. A man carries a small live pony draped resignedly around his neck. Here and there, sturdy Nordic women brandish hoops or beach balls in states of noticeable undress. 'Greek' scenes are recreated in homoerotic tableaux involving a good deal of oil and sometimes fig leaves. A range of small ads offers trunks, boots and leaves, all available for convenient purchase by mail.

The effect is chaotic and hardly what I'd expected Joe Price to find comfortable – I recall him as a man who thought twice before removing his jacket and who had no time at all for homosexuals. But there is a unifying theme here, something I know he understood: the need to be admired, to be an obvious success. It's most visible amongst the amateurs: the clerks and NCOs, the shopkeepers and factory workers who once hoped to make their own fabric a thing of pride. Six decades adrift, they still look out, perpetually pale and young and keen, snapped balancing on park benches, kicking in a brief Sunday's surf. They're three years away from a world war and showing their bodies as precious things, their best assets. A Mr Harvey stands alone in 1936, braced and British and facing the desert near Cairo, naked with his back to the camera. His arms and calves are tanned, the rest strikingly white from his knees to the bared nape beneath his savage army haircut. Other articles in the same year praise 'George VI – our Athletic King' and feature, without irony, Cary Grant and Randolph Scott lounging together in trunks – 'two noted Paramount stars who believe in the value of Physical Culture.' This is the promise of health and strength, the longed-for gift of physical democracy: film stars, commoners and kings all equal when stripped to the skin.

As I turn though the cheap, yellowed pages I realize how much my grandfather lived by what he found here. He left school in 1930 at the age of fourteen, walking straight into the mouth of the Depression. His family was working class with pretensions to gentility, his father a handsome man who dressed well but was violent in drink. One of four children, Joe wanted to defend what he found precious: to guarantee safety for his mother and himself, to assure his own dignity and success. It would have been tempting to believe that positive thinking and hard exercise could bring him all he wanted by acts of will. Variations on the theory were popular at the time. By the late 1930s

Health and Strength includes more and more German snapshots: worthy National Socialist bodies, stripped and staring towards horizons bright with eugenic promise.

Joe Price didn't embrace the politics or the spurious science, but he did put his faith in the logic of effort and will. He believed that he could and must fight to build a life worth living. More an individualist than a pacifist, he would spend his war in a reserved occupation, avoiding the daily risks of steel. He once told me he thought all conflicts should be settled by champions, squaring up, the only blood shed in the ring. His idea of combat was always individual. To build a character and a future, solitary effort was the key, and the most worthy drove themselves the hardest, took the greatest punishment: the boxers. Boxing suited his philosophy, his expectations and temperament. The magazine is filled with their faces, the men who made Joe's choice and boxed. Amateur and professional, each one measures himself against the classic pose: shoulders cocked, head ducked, hands ready and high, eyes confidently alert, perhaps that touch brighter with the possibility that, 'If you do achieve success, then your fists may well be the means of your seeing the world and meeting some of its most famous inhabitants.'

The path to personal advancement through sport: it's never offered with much enthusiasm to anyone outside the underclass, the risks are too great, the rewards too ephemeral. Boxing is held in reserve for the special cases, the young and poor who might be needed by the military, who might be troublesome if they weren't given discipline early enough. The myth is as powerful today as it was in the 1930s, the thought that – as *Health and Strength* put it – 'There is no sport like boxing to develop and cultivate a feeling of assurance and self-control. It gives you an aggressive spirit, properly leashed.' Watch African American and Hispanic kids trying to knock each other's lights out in any United States amateur bout, watch every nation offering up representatives of its least prosperous groups in Olympic competition or televised professional spectacles, and you'll realize boxing remains an occupation for the hungry.

I remember sitting in a Brooklyn church gym hall, watching a young Irish fighter losing, the only white boxer of the evening. His father, a small man who had obviously led an outdoor life, was behind me, trying to smoke away his nerves – he never normally touched cigarettes. He quietly rationalized the proceedings for me. This was a chance for the boy – coming to America – he'd never even, no offence, seen a black man at home and people had been very kind and, as long as he didn't get hurt, it could all be great for him. As long as he didn't get hurt.

Another father had brought along his son, a boy of eight or nine, who was a fan of World Wrestling Federation wrestling, but was already slowly pacing and turning his fist in the air ahead of him, working through the proper motions of a punch. Weaned on the glamour and choreographed fakery of the wrestlers, this was his first time at a boxing match and he was enjoying it well enough, tolerating the lack of pyrotechnics while his father tried to make a lesson of the evening. He wanted the boy to understand how fit a boxer has to be, how hard he has to try, about winning and losing and being only a few generations away from Ireland themselves, and this somehow having to do with life's realities. The boy kept on practising his punches, hardly listening, the man looking at me now, his voice softened, his eyes making it plain that this was something too hard to say, too hard to consider all at once. Then we both looked away while I remembered that my grandfather took my mother to watch boxing bouts and wondered what it might have been that he was trying to teach her. I'd only really agreed to come there that night in case it let me feel nearer to him, edged me back towards all the things I could no longer learn.

Joe Price's aggressive spirit may not have been leashed by boxing, but it was undoubtedly given expertise. Before he was twenty, he left Staffordshire for London after a confrontation with his father. It must have been a good day for a man who liked solutions, the day he fought for himself and for his mother, for what he loved. When I was very young, I met his mother, my great-grandmother, a few times: the last in a hospital. She lay motionless in an oxygen tent, the ward around her somehow distorted by the presence of a person so near to death. My grandfather couldn't bear to look at her, or even go close. He couldn't win her back – there was nobody to fight.

In London, Joe Price was apprenticed into the steel trade, learned how to dodge molten metal when it flew, played cards with a suspicious efficiency and slept in a hostel with a knife kept close to hand, because the Queensberry Rules don't cover everything. He kept on learning how to take his lumps and, even though he'd told his mother he would stop, he kept on boxing. She realized this was the case when she opened the March 7 issue of *Health and Strength* in 1936. There she discovered him, just as I do now, standing at the edge of a group from the Corinthian Athletic Club, Stoke Newington. (My mother and I have both inherited his photographic reticence, we all lurk at the frame's edge, if we can.) I can see the slight dip in his sternum – the place where he always told me he was hit by a cannon ball, a lie we both enjoyed. He's smiling a little, a muscular twenty-year-old in neat black trunks and boots. And (I may, of course, be biased) he seems to have a confidence, a presence, that none of the other Corinthians matches. Something about his expression suggests he is standing a little apart, not out of shyness, but because he is special.

And he's right, he knows he's special: as special as human beings prove to be when given any kind of close examination. He knows, for example, that he has 'short arms' – he grinds through his opponents' defences until he can infight. In the process, he soaks up punches to the eyes, the left eye especially, and to his head. Although he only fights for something like ten years and solely as an amateur, boxing will close down his eyesight and leave him using a magnifying glass for near work, squinting at splinters of metal that he can't find in his hands. What the punches will do to his thinking, no one will really be able to tell. Joe Price, like many boxers, wasn't educated to be an intellectual and his life rarely encouraged him to lower his guard among strangers, he was a largely closed and quiet man. His handwriting was never expected to be anything more than the fiercely angular printing I recognized on envelopes at Christmas and birthdays, or on the wildly over-wrapped parcels he sometimes sent. As I write in the hush of the room, I miss his lettering. I miss him: his secrets and evasions, even the ones about his eyes.

Joe made sure until late in his life that no one he loved would be able to tell exactly how much he couldn't see. With doctors, he would be adamant his weakness had nothing to do with boxing, most particularly when they said it was. With me, he would admit his style meant he'd had to battle – that was why they'd called him Battling Joe Price. He admired Sugar Ray Leonard, marked out his life according to a calendar of all the middleweight champions, but he always had a special affection for Marvin Hagler, another infighter, another brawler.

Because Battling Joe, when I think about it, didn't fight clean. Although with me he was never anything but tender, having no son and now no grandson, he told me his secrets of victory in the ring. How to stand on your opponent's feet, how to elbow, headbutt, rabbit and kidney punch and hit below the belt, how to wet the old-style leather gloves to make them hard and how to work your fingers through their horsehair stuffing to put some knuckle in your punch. It was his own fault when he broke his hands fighting – it would have been someone else's when he broke his arm. And for the eyes, he had no mercy, because an opponent blinded by swelling or blood is no real opponent at all. The gloves Joe fought with still had separate thumbs that could gouge into sockets and untaped lace ends he could use to open cuts above the eye, just as every twisting punch he landed on the eyebrow would be meant to. He fought, as they say, 'with bad intentions'. When he acknowledged that sometimes these tricks had been used against him, he still seemed both puzzled and aggrieved. Listening to the familiar purr in his voice, I never could understand why anyone would want to hurt him, why anyone would want to punch him in his eyes.

Joe's eyes, the same blue as mine, were built in the usual way, with a lens and muscles for focus to the front and a relatively gristly exterior behind which formed an almost spherical hollow filled with a translucent gel called vitreous humour. Like the eyes you're using to read this, they were miraculous; organs of sense so delicately complex and elegant that they gave Charles Darwin pause for thought. He wondered how gradual evolution could have created something only functional in such a highly developed state. The curved back of the eye has three layers: the outer sclera, then the choroid and then the retina. Our retinas receive the images which pass through the clear cornea, lens and vitreous humour. The retina is arguably where we start truly to see. If the eye were a camera, you might say the retina was its film.

But I hope it would come as no surprise that the human retina is far more lovely than any film. Freshly dissected, it is semi-transparent with a gentle purple tint, although it quickly clouds and whitens, fading. It is, after all, a fragile thing, never intended to be exposed. Under a microscope, the retina's ten layers appear more vegetable than animal, like impressionistic wood grain. Nutrition and sensitivity combine as the nerves within the layers transmit, and their cells consume and grow, entirely interdependent for the transfer of information and nourishment. This is a balanced system, cells sometimes intertwining across layers and sometimes simply resting against each other. Which is the retina's weak point – a hard blow to the eye can distort it for a moment and split the retina's layers apart, ripping the pigment cells away from the receptors which feed them and carry the impulses to generate our sight. Rents, even holes may form. An especially traumatic blow can rupture the eye itself, allow it to lose vitreous humour, but more commonly the retina suffers. Any detached section dies and the eye becomes, to a greater or lesser extent, blinded.

Joe Price boxed at a time when ringside doctors might not be present, when referees were none too anxious to stop fights, when boxers – if they could find the matches – might fight two or three times in one night, under a false name if they had to. He took more punishment than he would today, but the laws of physics haven't changed. Multiple hard blows will do more damage to an eye, may even 'punch your man blind', but it still only takes one significant impact to damage a retina. Laser surgery can fuse the retina back into place – my grandfather was offered the option, but didn't like the sound of it. Recently, minority medical opinion even suggested that eyes repaired in this way were stronger than they had been before. This has proved, unsurprisingly, not to be the case and boxers who have suffered retinal damage or any other serious eye pathology are not legally permitted to box in Britain, or to take part in world title bouts. A detached retina effectively ended British heavyweight Frank Bruno's career. Worldwide regulations are similar, although sometimes less stringent and more easily evaded, particularly when boxers choose to change their identities. No regulations can reach the unlicensed boxing underground which quietly eats up former contenders at the bottom of their downward slope and hard men who need money more than health.

Hard men: my grandfather haunted my childhood with them as if they were entirely natural companions for a young girl's mind. In my earliest years, I suppose, he was still hard himself. I would swing from his straight-extended arm, at least as pleased as he was with his strength, but I had no cause then to consider what such strength could do. I would read the descriptions he sent me of Victorian bare-knuckle battles to the death, or the marathon bouts between giants like Jim Corbett, John L. Sullivan and Jack Dempsey (he of the lead-pipe-weighted gloves) and the carnage would seem as genuine as a World Wrestling Federation contest. Joe Price and all the ghosts were just friends. Still, I've heard the stories of the way he was as a young married man, anxious to flatten any face that stared too long at my grandmother, looking for a fight.

Joe Price met Mildred Archer in 1938 during an uninspiring period for middleweights – Al Hostak was the NBA champion, soon to be ousted by Solly Krieger who lost the rematch in 1939, the year that Miss Archer became Mrs Price. In 1940, another steelworker, Tony 'Man of Steel' Zale, was on top of the world, and the Price's first and only child was born: my mother, Edwardine Mildred.

The Prices made a tight couple, almost too tight for a daughter to fit. They wore suits cut from the same cloth and had their hairstyles matched, my grandmother sporting an Eton crop. Their arguments and reconciliations were equally close-quarter and intense. By the time I knew them, they still worked singly – my grandmother as a French polisher with spectacularly roughened hands – but otherwise they were rarely apart and seemed to need few friends. Milly would shop and Joe would cook and clean and bring her tea and magazines when she took her regular afternoon naps. Every Sunday he would dust the Venetian blinds and make lunch before his wife came home from church.

For many years I didn't realize the facts upon which this intimacy rested, the reason for my grandmother's anxiety when her husband was even a few minutes late home. Her marriage to Joe was her second. Mildred Price, a woman of some passion, had courted Jack Peace and loved and married him, just as she should, and they had gone to bed on their wedding night and in the morning she had found him beside her, quite dead. He had been suffering from cancer, but had told nobody.

For a while, Mildred weathered an entirely understandable nervous breakdown. She would be eccentric all her life, but now she saw ghosts. She couldn't bear to be alone and had to be put out on a chair in the street if no one was left in the house. The family sent her to London for a change of air and this gave her a lifelong fear of the place – she never liked to hear that I was there, risking a city where she'd spent so much unhappy time. She never managed to meet Joe in the unfriendly size of the capital, but did when they were both back home again, safe in Staffordshire.

Joe Price must have been the perfect man for Milly. He was demonstrably, tangibly healthy, more than ten years her junior and fiercely ready for anything. Joe was happy to be utterly devoted, despite his family's certainty that he was marrying beneath him, and he had that smile, that air of being out of the ordinary. Once he married, he even agreed to stop boxing – the risks would have made his wife entirely demented – and contented himself with training policemen in combat and self-defence. But he still took his wife and daughter to fights. My mother can remember attending a civic hall bout where an Irish Catholic boxer made a great point of crossing himself before the opening round. Then, in front of the almost exclusively Nonconformist audience, he hit the canvas unconscious, having caught the first punch.

My grandfather told the same story, it held another secret he intended to pass on – don't be too sure of God's protection. Never mind Providence, Joe Price believed in being personally prepared, from his indestructible parcels to his ease with a half nelson. To underline the point, he also told me the tale of Randy Turpin, a man who was thoroughly ready at just the right time. He was one of my grandmother's favourites – she liked the way he wore his initials, RAT, on his shorts. Turpin came out against the odds and beat the great Sugar Ray Robinson in Earls Court in 1951. Robinson had been overcommitted and was probably tired but was said to have been complacent, to have spent the night before the fight playing cards until the small hours. Turpin, a fine British middleweight with two equally useful hands, had arrived unawed and in peak condition. He fought the distance fluently and, by the end, Robinson was bleeding and the crowd was singing 'For He's a Jolly Good Fellow' to Turpin. If Joe Price had a dream, it must have been something like this, to slip in as an underdog and win the world.

I wasn't told that Turpin lost the title to Robinson only sixty-four days later in a rematch in New York, and never flew so high again, or that his last days were penniless, or that he committed suicide in Leamington Spa, the genteelly depressing town where I lived as a student. Robinson ended up equally poor and with Alzheimer's disease.

Depression, unmanageable anger, Parkinson's disease, substance abuse, Alzheimer's: they're among the unhappy ghosts that seem to flurry around boxing, no matter how hard it tries to be the Noble Art. John Tate: alcohol and cocaine addiction, became homeless and died in a car crash. Wilfred Benitez: brain-damaged. Michael Dokes: coke addict, now in jail for sexual assault and attempted murder. Tony Tucker: former coke addict and now religious convert. Jimmy Bivins: brain-damaged and broke. Pinklon Thomas: formerly coke addict, currently youth worker. Jerry, Mike and Bob Quarry: all brain-damaged, Jerry now dead. Oliver McCall: coke addict, jailed for assault. Floyd Patterson: brain-damaged. Riddick Bowe: currently under house arrest after abducting his estranged wife and children. All were champions once, or contenders.

The problem lies in identifying cause and effect. No matter how stunned or revolted observers were by Ali and Frazier slogging it out in the 'Thriller in Manila' in 1975, no one can definitively state that Muhammad Ali's genes hadn't always determined he would spend his later years hemmed in by Parkinson's disease.

And then there's Tyson, the poor monster, Don King's punching freak show – a money machine for everyone with the possible exception of himself. Tyson's temperament was never docile, even in the sunny days of his old coach Cuss D'Amato, when boxing looked as if it would save a ghetto kid from more jail time and an invisible, wasted life. Now the business of boxing allows him to behave badly and go easy on the sporting discipline. A truly iron Mike, after all, is bad for the pay-per-view; an out-of-shape Tyson, weakened by character defects and deficiencies in the ring, promises a positively Shakespearean spectacle. But are his flaws caused by bad character, bad company, or blows to the head? Tyson, even now, is hardly known for catching punches.

Both sides try to carve out their own moral high ground. To quote Golden Gloves of America Incorporated, which organizes America's most influential amateur championships, boxing supporters promote a sport which 'encourages a positive lifestyle for today's youth', although your average Golden Gloves competition will be heavily policed to keep all those disciplined gentlemen, and now ladies, from – possibly armed – combat outside the ring. And, for the few, we're reminded, there's the chance of fame, maybe wealth, some foreign travel. Boxing's opponents see self-destructive dupes being injured in the ring to provide promoters and ghouls with a gladiatorial spectacle. While some professionals hit the big time, in their opinion, all boxers, including juniors and amateurs, risk serious injury or death.

The physics of boxing is slightly less ambivalent. And when the will, the imagination, when thought is removed – that's what we all come down to: physics. It might be said that our lives represent an elaborate flight from the inevitable return to inanimate matter and the laws that govern it. When Ali managed not to drop before Frazier did in Manila, he proved we can buck the trend for a while, despite extreme pressure. He is, after all, the man who kept on going against Ken Norton in San Diego in 1973, even with a badly broken jaw. When Joey Gamache went down in the second round to Arturo Gatti in Madison Square Garden last spring and then sat up, looking about him – a man in bloodstained shorts with the face of a waking child – he was diminished, but on his way back from the fall. The fall, when his head met a dreadfully effective triple combination of punches, when his body dropped beyond his control – that was when Gamache was matter and nothing more, a mindless, tumbling mass. His utter unconsciousness was as plain as a tiny piece of death: as clear as – say – Tommy Hearns's knockout at Caesar's Palace in Las Vegas in 1985. Marvin Hagler had worked neatly, methodically, through three vicious rounds, one eye eventually clouded over with his own blood, while Hearns's long arms whipped in at him, increasingly powerlessly. Then, the swagger still in his shoulders, Hagler punched Hearns back into a spin, caught him with a final right and Hearns's face emptied, took on the puzzled look of a post-mortem photograph, while his body drooped over Hagler, fell without a will. Physics.

Various researchers have tried to calculate the force of a punch, placing accelerometers in punching bags, asking boxers to swing at force plates. A more realistic experiment studied the British heavyweight Frank Bruno when he punched a sixteen-pound ballistic pendulum – sixteen pounds is roughly the weight of a heavyweight opponent's head and neck. The punch travelled at a little under nine miles per second and the force it exerted was calculated at 0.63 tons. Naturally, a range of boxers would have to be tested to average out the blows for various weights and levels of ability. Still, it gives us some idea of what one punch amounts to, which is, in this particular case, equivalent to the impact of a thirteen-pound padded mallet being swung at twenty miles per hour.

In a street fight, the swing can connect where it likes; in the ring it has rules to follow, a target area for scoring blows. If the fist is correctly positioned and lands a technically proper punch to the torso or the front of the head, it is deemed 'effective'. Punches to the head, carrying with them the possibility of a knockout, or at least a knockdown, are understandably popular. What happens when the head suffers an impact depends greatly upon the physics of the skull and brain. There is a slim, fluid-filled space between the brain and the skull, which means that, when the head moves violently, the brain can literally twist on its stem inside the skull and can collide repeatedly with the surrounding bone as the skull's acceleration and deceleration fail to match that of its contents. The resultant stretching and shearing within the different structures of the brain can stress neurons beyond their tolerance. Damage to the two membranes (the septum pellucidum) that separate the two fluid-filled ventricles deep inside the brain is thought to indicate other, as yet invisible, penetrating stress. The septum pellucidum is close to the limbic lobe, an area of the brain associated with aggression. Injury here is thought to have links with violently dysfunctional behaviour. For all that the brain has a phenomenal capacity for reorganization and survival, it will always be limited by the fact that nervous tissue cannot regenerate.

A membrane, the dura, designed to hold the brain in place, can be damaged, as can blood vessels inside and outside the brain. Bleeding can increase the pressure inside the skull, even forcing the brain down towards an impossible exit, the point where the brain stem feeds out into the spinal column. Blood clots within the brain, or between the brain and skull, can cause anything from localized areas of dead tissue to coma and death. Dead tissue in the brain can, of course, affect anything and everything that we think of as ourselves: our ability to move, our senses and our personalities.

It's hard for anybody to imagine their own destruction. Boxers may find it harder than most, trained as they are to pare down their thinking to the moment, an eternally present tense of speed, attack, response, a sometimes self-destructive belief in the attainability of success. Their trainers and supporters surround them with uplifting lies. In Brooklyn, the young Irish kid and all the other losers heard their share as their opponents pummelled them – 'Stick a jab on him when he charges', 'Punch when he punches', 'Don't feel bad, you did well', 'Even if you lose this now, you've won it'.

Win or lose, they grow from sporting teens with the usual sheen of immortality into men of certainty and solutions – because that's how they have to be, the ring would be intolerable without a mental defence. This kind of individualistic, almost magical training in faith and faith in training may be one reason why boxers, despite so many generations of uneven breaks and destitute retirements, have never formed an effective association in any country. It is always their patrons who organize. Meanwhile, alone in the ring, the boxer works in a place where self belief is all that will move a body against pain, against an opponent who is equally alone. Injury and failure are too close to consider, in case the thought might bring them on.

And the brain, in any event, is always shy when it comes to thinking of itself. Sitting in the library, I can turn my head to look around and know that I'm turning – among other things – about forty-two ounces of brain. My whole sense of myself and the world: up there in a weight I can't notice. It would fit, cradled very comfortably, in my palms, almost surrounded by my fingers. A man's brain might be three or four ounces more – either way, this seems light, considering all it represents. If I set it down on the table beside me, it would subside just a little, showing that it's surprisingly soft, vulnerable. This is what you and I carry under the scalp, above the face: the familiar coils and curves that give the organ's form a peculiar, fluid grace. Sliced cleanly through from – as it were – ear to ear, the brain looks almost like agate, the layer of grey matter undulating gently, surrounding the layer of white, the ventricles opened in twinned, seashell curves. The septum pellucidum is of an almost impossibly delicate, milky transparency. The brain makes a beautiful, unsettling study – a fascinating object with a form that gives little indication of its function. It is left unscarred by thought. I couldn't guess where, or quite how, it held scraps such as my liking for raspberries, the movements necessary for a kiss, my kiss, my past, all the memories upon memories that deal only with my grandfather's way of walking – so much I wish to be defended.

And, if I decided to enter the ring today, boxing medics would try their best to defend me. In fact, if I didn't conceal my medical history, they'd bar me immediately for the sake of my health. I have suffered serious concussion and migraines, both of which would lead to my exclusion from any kind of reputable organized boxing. The British Boxing Board of Control is arguably at the forefront of boxing safety. It submits professional boxers to an exhaustive number of tests and investigations before granting them a licence to fight. MRI scans were made compulsory in 1995. Any discovery of weakness, psychological instability, drug use or prior damage and the licence is not granted. The tests are repeated annually. There are cooling-off periods for recuperation between fights and a series of weigh-ins to pick up fighters who are trying to make their weight by dehydrating. Dehydration may slightly increase the space between the brain and the skull, intensifying injuries – it certainly weakens boxers and leaves them open to greater risk from their opponents. Participants are examined before and after bouts with particular attention paid to those who have suffered any period of unconsciousness. Doctors and an ambulance with trained staff and resuscitation equipment are on standby during bouts. Of course, safety provisions and testing for juniors and amateurs are not so extensive, although they run the same risks as professionals, without the benefit of experience.

When I asked the British Boxing Board of Control's chief medical officer, Adrian Whiteson, about the safety conditions surrounding my grandfather's boxing life, he mouthed 'appalling', as if he would rather not criticize the sport out loud. He presents modern boxing with a reformer's quiet evangelism – the professional game is conducted in a medically responsible manner, fielding boxers who are all thoroughly screened for optimum safety and psychological stability, fighting fit, chemically clean and engaged in an occupation with social benefits. In a professional boxing scene still heavily connected with organized crime, and where financial risks and pressures are high, Whiteson's portrait of the noble art admits no pressure to compromise, no lies, no evasions. The mystifying fact that Mike Tyson is able to pass a British psychological examination and gain his licence to fight here goes unmentioned. Whiteson contrasts licensed, responsible boxing with the underground scene, the legendary turf where mobster enforcers meet gypsy champions. He doesn't mention the current rise in British unlicensed public boxing – a high-risk affair with few safeguards for often poorly prepared participants – and the popularity of the even more gladiatorial no-holds-barred fighting codes such as Vale Tudo. In his, and the British Boxing Board of Control's, opinion, keeping licensed boxing popular offers the best chance of keeping boxers safe, or as safe as anyone involved in a contact sport might reasonably expect to be. Whiteson is not a member of the British Medical Association which, like its American counterpart, calls for a total ban on boxing, licensed and unlicensed. He genuinely loves boxers as individuals, loves the sport. This, many fellow medics would argue, involves him in a degree of double-thinking.

He appears absolutely sincere when he states that: 'The sport is irrelevant. At the end of the day, it's their health that matters.' He denies the existence of hard evidence that repeated exposure to head trauma produces a high chance of brain damage and points out that too few examinations of brains have been carried out to determine what a 'normal' level of damage to structures such as the septum pellucidum would be. Nevertheless, he does admit that, in such an extreme sport, it is impossible to prevent injuries, sometimes of the very worst kind: 'Not the acute brain damage, sadly no one can stop that.' Health matters, then, but boxing will continue in spite of the consequent unavoidable acute brain damage. Whiteson makes it plain that the British Boxing Board of Control's policy is to stop a fight continuing, or even taking place, if there is any doubt over a boxer's condition, because: 'One punch and he could die.' And yet he has a touching faith in the ability of an 'equally matched' fight to reduce both boxers' risks to acceptable levels.

Dr Whiteson is the kind of man my grandfather would have trusted, a proper gentleman with a Wimpole Street private practice and an OBE. Intelligent, soft-spoken and charming, he tells me how natural boxing is – that two infants in a playpen would fight over a toy. As it happens, the example undermines his point. The infants might well scrap over the toy, but then the winner would generally win and the loser would cry and that would tend to be that. Bouts of formalized, punching combat certainly wouldn't ensue. Studies show that children fighting tend to wrestle. If blows are struck at all, they are more likely to be slaps than punches and the head seems to be protected by something akin to a physical taboo. When tired or inexperienced fighters fall to clinches and slapping blows, they are withdrawing from their training into, one might say, more natural techniques. The pugilistic toddlers provide the sort of anecdotal evidence that stops comfortable people being too uneasy about less comfortable people's pain by making it a natural necessity. They have little connection with fact.

I would be the first to agree that violence exists in nature, but I also know it has nature's economy. Whether it proves dominance or provides food, it's too quick and too definitive to provide paying entertainment. Boxing exists in an artificial middle ground between death and retreat – in very human territory that encompasses humiliation, bravery, fear and the kind of sympathetic magic which creates the worship of champions. Human beings do attack each other, of course. I've been attacked and I've defended myself, once against a Parisian pickpocket and once against a Scottish drunk, but upper cuts and timed rounds didn't come into it. I did what my grandfather taught me to do, which was quick and worked. Punching someone in the head (so much a part of boxing) is an unnatural act and is often outside, or marginal to, even combative experience. Ask anyone who's stepped in the ring, or watch young fighters try to press themselves into truly trading blows – the giving and accepting of that type of pain, that particular shock, takes a lot of getting used to, no matter how much adrenalin and training lends a hand. My grandfather got used to it, he had the knack. Joe Price said he only ever lost one fight, his first, because he was frightened. He made sure he wasn't frightened again. His life had prepared him to see that as a good choice.

Go into a gym and you'll see the ones who have it and the ones who don't. Dancing and dipping through combinations, their trainers singing out, counting out, blows that will contact faster than they can be named: 'Hook, hook. One, two,' you'll realize the boxer's unopposed speed. Bodies slip and angle round each other, the presence or absence of commitment achingly obvious. Men stare themselves down in mirrors, hit the treadmill, skip and sweat, finding personal walls and breaking through them, finding and breaking through. This is where Joe Price lived, amongst the down-time tenderness of sparring partners, the small breaks of nudging play and the docile binding of hands: the willingness to let them be a helpless weight, before they take their proper place and swing, express a will. Neurological tests found one other effect of boxing, the improvement of motor functions, the increased ability to master human physics.

In training and in the ring, here is what Mildred Archer fell in love with – the flush under the skin that might be passion or pain, shame or heat. Here are the men who move with uncanny precision, even outside the ropes – soft-shoed, soft-footed men who have a constant, unusual sense of direction, a firm expression of will. When I watch old boxers – the set of their shoulders, the fix of their heads, the slightly softened mouths – I realize how much of my grandfather was burned into him by boxing. He walked like a middleweight, with that particular blend of solidity and lightness.

I've heard Tyson talk in an interview about the sheer excitement of 'being able to outsmart a man . . . to out-time them, to out-think them . . . they make one mistake and you outsmart them and then you have their wallet.' I didn't expect him to remind me of my grandfather, but he did. Joe Price was the man who would beat you every time. A burglar once decided to break into what should have been just one in a row of pensioners' apartments. But it was my grandfather's home and, even in his sixties, he was more than able to knock the intruder out cold. He was so pleased that all he could wish for was to be able to do it again. My grandfather took exception to being robbed, of course, but he also punched the man out just because he still could. Thirty years earlier, Joe Price would be the one to join you casually in a game of cards as you both whiled away a train trip, the one who would somehow manage to clean you out by the time you reached your station. That was how he got his holiday spending money. He did it because he could and you were stupid enough to let him.

At our final meeting, we got out the cards and, for the first and only time, my grandfather played as he would have against a stranger. We both knew that he was very ill and that we might not see each other again. He asked me to cut the deck whenever I dealt and named every card I cut to before I showed it. He was a man with hardly any eyesight left, with a body that was comprehensively betraying him, and he beat me soundly, thoroughly, arrogantly, beautifully. He knew what the ring was all about before he ever climbed inside: it was a place where he could win in a life where – beyond the card games – he would spend a great deal of time never even being able to compete. I know that he deserved better, because boxing rewards few and damages many – it damaged him. Boxing is not, by its nature, safe. Span your hand across the crown of your head and you'll be measuring out the greatest distance the force of a punch will ever travel, the greatest distance over which it will ever be able to dissipate. You'll be cupping your palm perhaps half an inch above the greater part of what you are. Joe Price, the little-known amateur, risked that every time he sparred, or fought, just as any world champion did, just as anyone who boxes does today. There is no audience, no manager, no promoter, no association, no doctor, no trainer worthy of that commitment.

My grandfather made the best of it, just as he made the best of an unusual marriage, of plans to be his own boss that never quite materialized, of his ulcers, his heart attacks, of the night when his wife was suddenly ill, fell asleep and never woke, of the last six years he spent as a widower growing frail. Even when it took him some effort to cross a road, he still had that air of being special, the dignity he'd fought for. If he went slowly, it was because he intended to stroll, if he leaned on my arm it was because he had decided we'd walk close. Still, make no mistake, he hated being old and unable to see. He didn't want to have lost his power, the shadow he'd always boxed, now slow beside him, uneasy in its balance. Providence was catching up with him. Used to fighting, to pushing himself where his will needed him to be, he decided to go for heart surgery, in the hope that it would free him from the problems of old age. He wanted to die on the table. In fact, the set of tests before the operation gave him his wish.

I thought his last gift came when he told me he was going for the surgery and gave me the chance to say goodbye. I was wrong. In researching this piece, I've discovered another. *Health and Strength* would have called me a 'brain worker' and, sifting through the Internet files and libraries, working away, I've found the secret he left for me to find.

My grandfather always called me Tiger, which is an unusual nickname in Britain, especially for a girl. It was something else between us that only we had and that no one ever questioned, although he allowed it to fall out of use as I grew up. I remember going back to his house just after my grandmother died, climbing the narrow stairs and walking into a room full of silent relatives. His chair faced away from the door, as it always had, and he turned round to me softly and said, as I'd known he would, 'Hello, Tiger', wishing us back to a time when I could still swing on his arm and his wife was alive. And now I understand why I was Tiger. Checking the middleweight champions he followed all his life, I found that the World Champion in the year I was born, 1965, was the British-based Nigerian fighter Dick Tiger. Before I even knew myself, my grandfather had made up his mind and privately christened me for a champion of the world. So now I thank him for that.

BIG MILK

Jackie Kay

The baby wasn't really a baby any more except in the mind of the mother, my lover. She was two years old this wet summer and already she could talk buckets. She even had language for milk. Big Milk and Tiny Milk. One day I saw her pat my lover's breasts, in a slightly patronizing fashion, and say, 'Silly, gentle milk.' Another day we passed a goat with big bells round its neck in a small village near the Fens. The light was strange, mysterious. The goat looked like a dream in the dark light. The baby said, 'Look, Big Milk, look, there's a goat!' The baby only ever asked Big Milk to look at things. Tiny Milk never got a look in.

I never noticed that my lover's breasts were lopsided until the baby started naming them separately. The baby was no mug. The left breast was enormous. The right one small and slightly cowed in the presence of a great twin. Big Milk. I keep saying the words to myself. What I'd give for Big Milk now. One long suck. I was never that bothered about breasts before she had the baby. I wasn't interested in my own breasts or my lover's. I'd have the odd fondle, but that was it. Now, I could devour them. I could spend hours and hours worshipping and sucking and pinching. But I'm not allowed. My lover tells me her breasts are milk machines only for the baby. 'No,' she says firmly, 'they are out of bounds.' I should understand. 'You are worse than a man,' she tells me. A man would understand, she says. 'A man would defer.' I'm not convinced. A man would be more jealous than I am. Two years. Two years is a long time to go without a single stroke. I look over her shoulder at the baby pulling the long red nipple of Big Milk back and forth.

At night I lie in bed next to the pair of them sleeping like family. The mother's arms flailed out like a drowned bird. The baby suckling like a tiny pig. The baby isn't even aware that she drinks warm milk all night long. She is in the blissful world of oblivion. Limbs all soft and gone. I test the baby's hand, full of my own raging insomnia. The small fat hand lands back down on the duvet with a plump. She doesn't even stir. I try my lover's hand. She can tell things in her sleep. She knows the difference between me and the baby. In her sleep, she pulls away, irritated. I lie next to the sleeping mother and baby and feel totally irreligious. They are a painting. I could rip the canvas. I get up and open the curtains slightly. Nobody stirs. I take a peek at the moon. It looks big and vain, as if it's saying there is only one of me buster, there's plenty of you suckers out there staring at me. It is a canny moon tonight, secretive. I pee the loudest pee I can manage. I pour a glass of water. Then I return to bed next to the sleeping mother and daughter. The baby is still suckling away ferociously, her small lips going like the clappers. It is beyond belief. How many pints is that she's downed in the one night? No wonder the lover is drained. The baby is taking everything. Nutrients. Vitamins. The lot. She buys herself bottles and bottles of vitamins but she doesn't realize that it is all pointless; the baby has got her. The baby has moved in to occupy her, awake or asleep, night or day. My lover is a saint, pale, exhausted. She is drained dry. The hair is dry. Her hair used to gleam.

I'm not bothered about her hair. I am not bothered about not going out any more, anywhere. The pictures, pubs, restaurants, the houses of friends. I don't care that I don't have friends any more. Friends without babies are carrying on their ridiculous, meaningless lives, pretending their silly meetings, their silly movies, their crazy avant-garde theatre matters. Tottering about the place totally without roots. Getting a haircut at Vidal Sassoon to cheer themselves up. Or spending a whole summer slimming. Or living for the two therapy hours per week. That's what they are up to. A few of them still bang away at ideas that matter to them. But even they sound tired when they talk about politics. And they always say something shocking to surprise me, or themselves. I don't know which. I don't see any of them any more.

I see the baby mostly. I see her more than I see my lover. I stare into her small face and see her astonishing beauty the way my lover sees it. The big eyes that are a strange green colour. The lavish eyelashes. The tiny perfect nose. The cartoon eyebrows. The perfect babysoft skin. The lush little lips. She's a picture. No doubt about it. My lover used to tell me that I had beautiful eyes. I'd vainly picture my own eyes when she paid me such compliments. I'd see the deep rich chocolate brown melt before me. The long black lashes. But my eyes are not the subject these days. Or the object, come to think of it. My eyes are just for myself. I watch mother and daughter sleeping peaceably in the dark. Dreaming of each other, probably. There are many nights I spend like this, watching. I haven't made up my mind yet what to do with all my watching. I am sure it will come to some use. The baby dribbles and the lover dribbles. The light outside has begun. I've come round again. The birds have started up their horrendous opera. I'm in the best seat, next to the window with the theatrical tree. The baby has power. It is the plain stark truth of the matter. I can see it as I watch the two of them. Tiny puffs of power blow out of the baby's mouth. She transforms the adults around her to suit herself. Many of the adults I know are now becoming babified. They like the same food. They watch the same programmes. They even go to bed at the same time as the baby; and if they have a good relationship they might manage whispering in the dark. Very little fucking. Very little. I'm trying to console myself here. It's another day.

In the morning the baby always says 'Hello' to me before my lover gets a word in. To be fair, the baby has the nicest 'Hello' in the whole of the world. She says it like she is showering you with bluebells. You actually feel cared for when the baby talks to you. I can see the seduction. I know why my lover is seduced. That and having her very own likeness staring back at her with those strange green eyes. I can never imagine having such a likeness. I tell myself it must be quite creepy going about the place with a tiny double. A wee doppelgänger. It's bound to unsettle you a bit, when you are washing your hair, to look into the mirror and for one moment see a tiny toddler staring back at you. It can't be pleasant.

The feeding itself isn't pleasant either. Not when the baby has teeth. I've heard my lover howl in pain on more than one occasion when the baby has sunk her sharp little milk teeth into Big Milk. A woman is not free till her breasts are her own again. Of this I am certain. I am more certain of this than a woman's right to vote or to choose. As long as her breasts are tied to her wean she might as well be in chains. She can't get out. Not for long. She rushes home with her breasts heavy and hurting. Once we went out for a two-hour-and-twenty-minute anniversary meal. When we got home my lover teemed up the stairs and hung over the bathroom sink. The milk spilled and spilled. She could have shot me with it there was so much. Big gun milk. It was shocking. She swung round and caught me staring, appalled. She looked proud of the quantities. Said she could have filled a lot of bottles, fed a lot of hungry babies with that.

I tried to imagine the state of my life with my lover feeding hundreds of tiny babies. I pictured it for a ghastly moment: our new super king-size bed (that we got so that all three of us could sleep comfortably and are still paying for in instalments) invaded by babies from all over the world. My lover lying in her white cotton nightie. The buttons open. Big Milk and Tiny Milk both being utilized for a change. Tiny Milk in her element – so full of self-importance that for a second Tiny Milk has bloated into the next cup size. The next time she mentioned having enough milk to feed an army, I told her she had quite enough on her hands. And she laughed sympathetically and said my name quite lovingly. I was appeased for a moment until the baby piped up with a new word. 'Did you hear that?' she said, breathless. 'That's the first time she's ever said that. Isn't that amazing?' 'It is,' I said, disgusted at myself, her and the baby all in one fell swoop. 'It is totally amazing – especially for her age,' I added slyly. 'For her age, it is pure genius.' She plucked the baby up and landed a smacker on her smug baby cheek. The baby patted Big Milk again and said, 'Funny, funny, Milk. Oh look Mummy, Milk shy.' I left the two of them to it on the landing outside the toilet.

Even when I go up to my attic I can still hear them down below. Giggling and laughing, singing and dancing together. 'If you go down to the woods today, you're in for a big surprise.' The rain chaps on my tiny attic windows. Big Milk is having a ball. I climb down the steep stairs to watch some more. Daytime watching is different from night-time. Tiny details light up. The baby's small hands are placed protectively on the soft full breasts. The mouth around the nipple. Sometimes she doesn't drink. She just lies half asleep, contemplating milk or dreaming milk. I am never sure. It makes me wonder how I survived. I was never breastfed myself. My mother spoon-fed me for two weeks then left. I never saw her again. Perhaps I've been dreaming of her breasts all my life. Maybe that's what rankles with the baby taking Big Milk for granted. When her mouth expectantly opens there is no question that the nipple won't go in. No question. Every soft open request is answered. I try and imagine myself as a tiny baby, soft black curls on my head, big brown eyes. Skin a different colour from my mother's. I imagine myself lying across my mother's white breast, my small brown face suffocating in the pure joy of warm, sweet milk. The smell of it, recognizing the tender smell of it. I imagine my life if she had kept me. I would have been a hairdresser if I hadn't been adopted. I'm quite sure. I would have washed the dandruff off many an old woman's head. I would have administered perms to give them the illusion of their hair forty years before. I would have specialized in tints and dyes, in conditioners that give full body to the hair. I would probably have never thought about milk. The lack of it. Or the need of it.

I lie in the dark with the rain playing soft jazz on the window pane of our bedroom. I say our bedroom, but it is not our bedroom any more. Now teddy bears and nappies and ointment and wooden toys and baby clothes can be found strewn all over the floor. I lie in the dark and remember what it was like when I had my lover all to myself. When she slept in my arms and not the baby's. When she woke up in the night to pull me closer. When she muttered things into my sleeping back. I lie awake and remember all the different places my lover and I had sex. All the different ways, when we had our own private language. The baby has monopolized language. Nothing I say can ever sound so interesting, so original. The baby has converted me into a bland, boring, possessive lover who doesn't know her arse from her elbow. There are bits of my body that I can only remember in the dark. They are not touched. The dawn is stark and obvious. I make my decision. I can't help it. It is the only possible thing I can do under the circumstances.

I love my lover and I love her baby. I love their likeness. Their cheeks and eyes. The way their hair moves from their crown to scatter over their whole head in exactly the same place. Their identical ears. I love both of them. I love the baby because she is kind. She would never hurt anybody. She is gentle, silly. But love is not enough for me this time. I get up, get dressed and go outside with my car keys in my hand. I close my front door quietly behind me. My breath in my mouth. I take the M61 towards Preston. I drive past four junction numbers in the bleached morning. There are few cars on the road. I stop at a service station and drink a black coffee with two sugars. I smoke two cigarettes that taste disgusting because it is too early. I don't smoke in the day usually. I smoke at night. Day and night have rolled into one. The baby's seat in the back is empty. The passenger seat has a map on it. There is no lover to pass me an apple. There is just me and the car and the big sky, flushed with the morning. I put on a tape and play some music. I am far north now. Going further. I am nearly at the Scottish border. I feel a strange exhilaration. I know my lover and her baby are still sleeping, totally unaware of my absence. As I drive on past the wet fields of morning, I feel certain that there is not a single person in the world who truly cares about me. Except perhaps my mother. I have been told where she lives up north. Right at the top of the country in a tiny village, in a rose cottage. She lives in the kind of village where people still notice a new car. If I arrive in the middle of the day, the villagers will all come out and stare at me and my car. They will walk right round my car in an admiring circle. Someone might offer to park it for me.

I will arrive in the daytime. When I knock at the door of Rose Cottage, my mother will answer. She will know instantly from the colour of my skin that I am her lost daughter. Her abandoned daughter. I have no idea what she will say. It doesn't matter. It doesn't matter if she slams the door in my face, just as long as I can get one long look at her breasts. Just as long as I can imagine what my life would have been like if I had sucked on those breasts for two solid years. If she slams the door and tells me she doesn't want to know me, it will pierce me, it will hurt. But I will not create a scene in a Highland town. I will go to the village shop and buy something to eat. Then I will ask where the nearest hair salon is. I will drive there directly where a sign in the window will read, ASSISTANT WANTED. I will take up my old life as a hairdresser. When I say my old life, I mean the life I could have, perhaps even should have, led. When I take up my old life, old words will come out of my mouth. Words that local people will understand. Some of them might ask me how I came to know them. When they do,

I will be ready with the answer. I will say I learned them with my mother's milk.

I am off the M6 now and on the A74. I read somewhere that the A74 is the most dangerous road in the country. Something new in me this morning welcomes the danger. Something in me wants to die before I meet my mother. When I think about it, I realize that I have always wanted to die. That all my life, I have dreamed longingly of death. Perhaps it was because she left. Perhaps losing a mother abruptly like that is too much for an unsuspecting baby to bear I know now this minute, zooming up the A74 at 110 miles per hour, that I have wanted to die from the second she left me. I wonder what she did with the milk in her breasts, how long it took before it dried up, whether or not she had to wear breast pads to hide the leaking milk. I wonder if her secret has burned inside her Catholic heart for years.

I can only give her the one chance. I will knock and I will ask for her to let me in. But if she doesn't want me, I won't give her another chance. I won't give anyone another chance. It has been one long dance with death. I have my headlights on even though there is plenty of daylight. I have them on full beam to warn other cars that I am a fast bastard and they had better get out of my way. The blue light in my dashboard is lit up. It and the music keep strange company. Is there anyone out there behind or before me on the A74 who has ever felt like this? I realize that I am possibly quite mad. I realize that the baby has done it to me. It is not the baby's fault or her mother's. They can't help being ordinary. Being flesh and blood. The world is full of people who are separated from their families. They could all be on the A74 right now, speeding forwards to trace the old bloodline. It is like a song line. What is my mother's favourite song? 'Ae Fond Kiss'? 'Ae fond kiss and then we sever.' There is much to discover. I picture the faces of all the other manic adopted people, their anonymous hands clutched to the steering wheel in search of themselves. Their eyes are all intense. I have never met an adopted person who does not have intense eyes. But they offer no comfort. This is all mine.

I arrive in the village at three o'clock, exhausted. My mouth is dry, furry. It is a very long time since I have slept. I spot a vacancies sign outside a place called the Tayvallich Inn. It has four rooms, three taken. The woman shows me the room and I tell her I'll take it. It is not a particularly pleasant room, but that doesn't matter. There is no view. All I can see from the window is other parts of the inn. I close the curtains. The room has little light anyway. I decide to go and visit my mother tomorrow after sleep. When I get into the small room with the hard bed and the nylon sheets, I weep for the unfairness of it all. A picture of the baby at home in our Egyptian cotton sheets suckling away and smiling in her sleep flashes before me. My lover's open nightie. It occurs to me that I haven't actually minded all my life. My mother shipping me out never bothered me. I was happy with the mother who raised me, who fed me milk from the dairy and Scots porridge oats and plumped my pillows at night. I was never bothered at all until the baby arrived. Until the baby came I never gave any of it a moment's thought. I realize now in room four of Tayvallich Inn under the pink nylon sheets that the baby has engineered this whole trip. The baby wanted me to go away. She wanted her mother all to herself in our big bed. Of late, she's even started saying 'Go Away!' It is perfectly obvious to me now. The one thing the baby doesn't lack is cunning. I turn the light on and stare at the silly brown and cream kettle, the tiny wicker basket containing two sachets of Nescafé, two tea bags, two bags of sugar and two plastic thimbles of milk. I open one thimble and then another with my thumbnail. They are the size of large nipples. I suck the milk out of the plastic thimbles. The false milk coats my tongue. I am not satisfied. Not at all. I crouch down to look into the mirror above the dressing table. I am very pale, very peelie-wally. Big dark circles under my eyes. I do not look my best for my mother. But why should that matter? A mother should love her child unconditionally. My hair needs combing. But I have brought nothing with me. I did not pack a change of clothes. None of it matters.

I pass the nosy Inn woman in the hall. She asks me if I need anything. I say, 'Yes, actually I need a mother.' The woman laughs nervously, unpleasantly, and asks me if I'll be having the full Scottish breakfast in the morning. I tell her I can't think that far ahead. She hesitates for a moment and I hesitate too. Before she scurries off to tell her husband, I notice her eyes are the colour of strong tea. I open the door that now says NO VACANCIES and head for Rose Cottage. I can't wait for tomorrow, I must go today. I must find her today. My heart is in my mouth. I could do it with my eyes shut. I feel my feet instinctively head in the right direction. It is teatime. My mother will be having her tea. Perhaps she will be watching the news. My feet barely touch the ground. The air is tart and fresh in my face. Perhaps some of my colour will return to my cheeks before my mother opens her front door. Will she tilt her head to the side gently when she looks at me? Following my nose miraculously works. There in front of me is a small stone cottage. Outside the roses are in bloom. There is a wonderful yellow rose bush. I bend to sniff one of the flowers. I always knew she would like yellow roses. I stare at the front door. It is painted plain white. Standing quietly next to the front door are two bottles of milk. I open the silver lid of one of them and drink, knocking it back on the doorstep. It is sour. It is lumpy. I test the other one. It is sour as well. I look into my mother's house through the letterbox. It is dark. I can't see a single thing.

PAOLO

Tim Parks

'*Pronto*?' I lift the phone in our bedroom.

'My name is Paolo Baldassarre and I wish to speak to the writer Mr Timothy Parks.'

It's a breathless, urgent, demanding voice that drags me back ten years and more. 'Paolo!'

I knew they'd recently allowed him access to a phone, so I should have been ready for a call.

'I'll get Rita,' I tell him; his younger sister, my wife.

But he insists he wants to speak to me.

'Next week we'll be seeing each other,' he says.

'That's right. I'm looking forward to it.'

'I want you to know I've changed. I'm very sorry about what happened.'

My last glimpse of Paolo was on the platform at Verona station when I pointed him out to the police. He had announced he was coming to Verona, where I live, to kill me. Shabby, frantic, and obese, he waved three or four bunches of keys as they took him away; he had slipped one round each finger to form a sort of gothic knuckleduster. Shortly afterwards we received a visit from the Digos, Italy's elite anti-terrorist police. At first I thought they were Jehovah's Witnesses, but then two men in plain clothes showed me their IDs and guns. Paolo had written to tell them I was working with Mossad to eliminate Palestinians in Italy. Now, a decade on, I assure him there are no hard feelings. I knew he was going through a bad patch.

'I'd like you to help get the Anglo-American sanctions against me lifted,' he says. 'In time for my release, the year after next.'

He begins to explain that he needs to purchase an academic book called *Symbolic Logic*. He has to read it at once. Only the American publisher is demanding £600 for a hardback edition. This is because of the sanctions against him. He can pay, of course, but would like me to negotiate the deal for him and bring the book personally, otherwise it will be confiscated by the post office. He must complete his education before leaving the institute. That is imperative. 'As you know my father never let me study,' he announces. 'He poisoned my orange juice.'

I mildly suggest that all this is bullshit. 'I bet I can get you a hefty discount on that book, Paolo.' From the other end of the line comes a nervous chuckle, the same one my son uses when he's been caught out telling a tall story. Except that my son is fourteen and Paolo forty-seven. Daunted by my bluntness, he changes tack. He begins to ask entirely sensible questions about our new house, the children, what we're doing for our holidays and so on. For five minutes we enjoy a completely normal brother-in-law conversation. '*A presto*,' I sign off.

Paolo was diagnosed as a paranoid schizophrenic some twenty-five years ago when both he and Rita were studying in the States, she at UMass Amherst, he at the University of Albany. The previous semester Paolo had written home asking if his mother would come to live with him. Then at a certain point he had stopped responding to either letters or phone calls. This had gone on for months. Finally Rita took the bus to Albany. She found her brother barricaded in his room in a supposedly supervised dorm, ankle-deep in filth, delirious and hallucinating. Nobody had noticed anything.

It is a curiosity of schizophrenia that while psychiatrists seem able to recognize and diagnose the condition with a certain rapidity (often a single interview is considered sufficient) it nevertheless remains extremely difficult to define or even describe. DSM-IV, the manual of diagnostic criteria prepared in 1994 by the American Psychiatric Association, is able to offer only a loose set of guidelines which at first glance seems to encompass an enormous range of possible disorders. Basically, for a diagnosis of schizophrenia, the manual demands that the patient exhibit at least two of the following symptoms: delusions, hallucinations, disorganized speech, grossly disorganized or catatonic behaviour, a 'flattening' of emotive responses, a loss of volition. These must be present for at least one month, although, somewhat enigmatically, 'continual signs of the disturbance' must be present for at least six months. In what way present, one wonders, if the 'symptoms' need be there only for a month?

When it comes to functional criteria, the manual becomes even vaguer, requiring that there be a noticeable impairment in the patient's ability to function in at least one of the following areas: work, personal relationships and self-care, and this 'for a significant portion of time since the onset of the disturbance'. What is 'a significant portion of time'? Aren't these areas in which many people, in certain periods of their lives, find it difficult to function?

But it is in its so-called 'exclusion criteria' that the manual is revealing of the psychiatric profession's embarrassment with this most perplexing of conditions. For although most psychiatrists are convinced that the cause of schizophrenia is in some way biological – not that it is the result of stress or particular social conditions – all the same DSM-IV explicitly rules out a diagnosis of schizophrenia in the event of a patient's problems being attributable to the physiological effects of a specific medical problem. The reason for this exclusion criterion, no doubt, is that over the last century all attempts to demonstrate a direct causative link between a biological malfunction and the disorder have proved vain. More mysterious than either cancer or Aids, schizophrenia becomes that organic illness for which, by definition of the psychiatric profession's diagnostic manual, there can be no organic cause.

Despite these problems of description, to read a series of case histories, or to talk with schizophrenics themselves, is to sense at once that the syndrome does have a character all its own, even if it's hard to pin it down to any one symptom. My brother-in-law Paolo's case is typical. Sent back from Albany to his family, then living in Ecuador, he began a long series of fruitless, short-lived therapies in Quito, Rome, Khartoum, Algiers and finally, when his father retired, Italy again. He seemed abnormally attached to and at the same time extremely antagonistic towards his parents. Incapable of forming relationships with girls he mailed pornography to his sister and myself. From time to time he disappeared and lived as a bum, practised various kinds of self-mutilation, attempted to buy an Algerian prostitute as a bride, 'ran rings', as he boasts, round a number of analysts, and read some of the most advanced books on quantum physics ever published. Or at least, those books were purchased for him, often at considerable expense.

In this way he was for many years a considerable financial burden, emotional strain and even potential physical danger to his parents. When violent he could be forced to stay in hospital and take the neuroleptic drugs that calmed him down. But then the law required he be released and being well aware of the long-term negative side effects of the drugs (drowsiness, obesity and, ultimately, impaired movement) he stopped taking them. Very soon the paranoid delusions and agitation would begin again. In the end it was only after he had committed a serious crime that he could be imprisoned and forced to take a sophisticated cocktail of medicine on a regular basis for a long period of time.

This happened seven years ago. Paolo held his mother at knifepoint, then smashed up the family home with a sledgehammer. Since then his parents have visited him fortnightly, first in high-security jails, then in the less restrictive mental institutions. We were told he didn't want to see other members of the family and so lost touch. But on New Year's Day 1999 my father-in-law died. Now his wife – we both call her Mamma – who never learned to drive, needs someone else to take her to where Paolo is presently based, way up in the rugged highlands between Genoa and Savona, a place apparently unreachable by public transport.

My mother-in-law arrives in Verona on the train from the family home in Pescara some 300 miles to the south on the Adriatic coast. Going to bed at nine she tells us we must be up at the crack of dawn to set off on the drive west to Genoa. She is irritated when Rita and I refuse to start before seven-thirty. Next morning, no sooner are we on the turnpike than we run into a big tailback. There's been an accident. 'Setting off early, Adelmo and I never had these problems,' Mamma announces.

In the car there's my mother-in-law, my wife, myself and Lucia, our five-year-old daughter. But the presence of little children was never an obstacle to adult conversation in the Baldassarre family. As we sit and simmer, waiting for the turnpike to clear, the old lady begins to talk about her husband's bones. Adelmo was buried in the earth, but in Italy the authorities remove the remains after fifteen years in order to recycle the space. 'Under no circumstances,' Mamma says heatedly, 'are those bones ever to be moved into my family tomb. Do you understand that, Rita? I will not have that whoremonger's bones in my family tomb.'

My father-in-law, I reflect, may have been willing to start early for every trip, but he had few other virtues in his wife's vision of things. Theirs was an embattled marriage. Towards the end they lived in separate apartments on the same decaying family property. Struck by a massive heart attack, having no phone in his apartment, Adelmo staggered over to knock on her windows in the middle of the night. She called an ambulance and went back to bed, believing he had overeaten again. In hospital he didn't wish to see her and she made no attempt to visit. Three days later he was dead.

My wife objects that Babbo – Dad – didn't want to be put in Mamma's family tomb, otherwise he wouldn't have insisted on being buried in the earth, would he? Being buried in the earth is often considered a little low-class in Italy. 'He'll be happy with the common ossuary,' Rita says. Then she steers the conversation to Mamma's favourite subject: the possibility that now, after seven years' imprisonment, Paolo will be allowed out of the institution for a week in order to come down to visit her in Pescara. 'Roberto can drive him down,' Mamma decides. Roberto is one of Rita's two younger brothers. Paolo was the firstborn. 'We can all be together for a week!' For some time she becomes extremely cheerful and excited thinking about this, as if such a visit could somehow cancel out all the terrible things that have happened. There is even a catch in her voice, as of someone looking forward to a week's pure evasion, with a lover perhaps, in any event a bliss beyond which life need never resume again.

Around one o'clock, an hour behind schedule, we finally get off the turnpike south of Alessandria and Mamma instructs me to take a first right up into the hills. But the map shows that there's a much shorter route starting from further down the valley. 'It'll be quicker,' I tell her. Mamma gets anxious. 'Adelmo always said there was only one road. It takes about an hour and a half.' After a brisk argument, I get my way and we reach our destination in just thirty-five minutes. Yet my father-in-law was no fool, I reflect. He must have known about this other road. And as I drive I realize that, either to spite Mamma, or because he was in no hurry to see his schizophrenic son, Babbo deliberately took the longer route. My father-in-law was a man who would always have chosen not to arrive at his destination if he could avoid it. He frequently said the happiest times with Mamma were in the car, he driving while she slept, his most enjoyable meals in the restaurants of turnpike service stations.

Three thousand feet above sea level, the mental institute is housed in a converted hotel. This is a region of thickly wooded but not dramatic or especially beautiful hills. Once travel became easier, people from the nearby towns who had used the area as a holiday destination started to go further afield for their fresh air. So amid the general atmosphere of decay and lost enterprise that characterizes the tiny villages along the way, it does not seem inappropriate that an erstwhile hotel should now house forty or so men and women who seem emblematic of all that is run-down and futureless, shuffling vacantly from room to room or standing catatonic in corners, trapped in a vacation that will never end. 'Then if they try to escape,' Mamma says, gesturing to the uninhabited landscape, 'it's easy for the police to find them before they reach the nearest town.'

In the porch, by the reception desk, an unshaven man standing in the attitude of one who has shat in his pants asks all and sundry for cigarettes. The receptionist gets on the phone to track down Paolo and after a few minutes he appears. To my immense relief, apart from the hollow, hunted eyes, the hunched shoulders, and the fact that on a hot day he is wearing at least five layers of shirts, jumpers and jackets, he seems pretty normal. We exchange friendly greetings and even a hug. The truth is, I had not fully understood, despite my wife's warnings, that the difficult person to deal with during this encounter would not be Paolo, but Mamma. 'Look at the make-up she's put on for him,' Rita had whispered that morning, but I'd thought nothing of it.

Immediately Mamma is kissing her son, almost on the lips. She disengages, but only to throw out her arms and embrace him again, kiss again. Seconds later she's adjusting the collar of one of his shirts. It's not straight. It's not clean. And his hair's too long. He hasn't been eating enough. Has he eaten? She apologizes that we didn't arrive at ten, as she promised. I had no idea she had promised such an impossible thing. 'There was a four-hour tailback,' she announces, exaggerating wildly. 'A terrible accident! Horrendous! We would have been here hours ago.' Paolo merely nods amiably, informing us that he's already had his lunch, but that he'll be happy to sit beside us while we eat at our hotel. So we climb back in the car and drive a further half mile to the place where we are to spend the night.

Some thirty years ago, in the crazy Sixties, a group of psychotherapists added to the confusion of those heady times by concluding that many mental disorders, including schizophrenia, might in some way be related to the family relationships surrounding the sufferers. In part the movement can be seen as a backlash against traditional psychiatry and its failure, as some perceived it, to go beyond the development of more and more sophisticated tranquillizers. In part, it came out of a frustration with Freudian psychoanalysis. In any event, a form of therapy was developed which involved getting the whole family together and trying to change the way people behaved with each other. Some successes were scored, particularly with anorexia, but any number of sensibilities were offended too. Who wants to hear that they are even indirectly responsible for anything? The feminists ran to the defence of the mothers who were being made scapegoats. Parents' associations complained about public money being spent on such mad ideas. Add to all this that with schizophrenia, particularly chronic schizophrenia, the results of this kind of therapy were disappointing, and it's hardly surprising that by the mid-Eighties the game was up. The medical profession settled back into its traditional vision that schizophrenia is basically the result of a biological disorder.

So today, if you consult the latest literature, you'll be told that the disorder is partly genetic (though how big a part they can't say), or that it may be due to an abnormally large right brain hemisphere (though many schizophrenics don't have this and many who aren't do), or that it's the result of an unidentified virus contracted in the mother's womb but mysteriously clicking in not, as you'd think, when they're cutting the umbilical cord, but twenty years later when most of us have our scissors out to deal with the apron strings.

Observe us, then, as we sit down to lunch, a perfectly 'normal' family except that twenty-five years ago one member sadly succumbed to this hypothetical organic anomaly, or gene defect, or virus . . .

The hotel restaurant is empty but the pleasant proprietress offers to rustle up what is the standard fare of Italian holiday hotels: tagliatelle and ragout followed by a steak. I had been warned that on a previous such visit Paolo drank two litres of Coke and suffered an attack of diarrhoea in the car afterwards, but so far his behaviour is exemplary. For some years now he has been receiving all the state-of-the-art neuroleptic tranquillizers, and one has to admit they are having a positive effect. Of course they are not designed to deal with the cause of this disease. They are not curing him. He is still completely crazy, already bothering Rita with the story of the hugely expensive *Symbolic Logic*, plus various other books he must order and read before his fantasized release in two years' time, not to mention the international sanctions against him that have still to be lifted. But he is calm and pleasant. 'No, no tagliatelle fqr me,' he tells the waitress cheerfully. 'I've already had an excellent lunch, thanks.'

'Bring a plate for him as well,' his mother says.

'Mamma,' Rita protests. 'He says he's eaten! Just the steak for me,' she tells the waitress. 'No pasta, thanks.'

'Bring a plate for my son,' the old lady orders.

'Mamma, no, I've had enough.'

'You're thin,' she accuses.

Proudly, Paolo begins to explain that over the last two months he's managed to lose ten pounds. The waitress is hovering.

'Bring tagliatelle for him as well!'

'Mamma, for Christ's sake!' I wade in. 'The guy's an adult. He knows whether he wants to eat or not!'

'You understand nothing!' she yells at me. 'Nothing! He's starving himself.'

'You're hopeless,' Rita tells her mother.

But exactly as we gang up against Mamma, Paolo turns his head to the waitress and says, 'Yes, do bring me a plate. I'll be happy to have the tagliatelle.' Then immediately he embraces his mother. He begins to caress her wrists and neck and face. One hand has slipped inside the arm of her short-sleeved dress. She is kissing him. *'Mammina,'* he says. *'Mammina.* You're all I have left now. There's only us two. Just a few years together,' he whimpers. *'Povero, povero,'* she says with immense satisfaction at our expense. But as he pulls away from her, he demands: 'So, have you brought the money? I want my money.'

One of the purposes of these trips is to bring Paolo his monthly spending money.

'We'll have to talk about that later,' Mamma says.

'But you can't not give me my money,' he whines. He uses the diminutive word, '*soldini*' – which is to say, small change, or pocket money. But there's a threat in his voice. In fact what we are talking about is the equivalent of £150 for his regular allowance plus £200 he has somehow managed to run up in debts since the last visit.

'We'll talk later,' Mamma says, patting his hand, and then the tagliatelle arrive in a great heap on a long metal dish. And she begins to serve.

Photos of Rita around the age of eleven or twelve show a pretty girl who is distinctly overweight. It wasn't until fifteen or sixteen that she got control over her own food intake. Now there is no question of anybody insisting that she touch the tagliatelle, while Paolo, who has already eaten, faces a considerable pile. When Mamma begins to insist on seconds, I ape her gestures of maternal insistence with Lucia. '*Povera cara ciccia*,' I wheedle, 'you really do need a secondy helpingy, don't you? You can't say no!'

Lucy laughs, belches and pushes her plate away. She doesn't want. Paolo breaks out into a huge grin. He understands perfectly. All the same the whole miserable rigmarole of his being persuaded to eat is repeated when the steaks arrive. First he surreptitiously slips his meat on to Rita's plate. Complicitous with his rebellion, she starts to eat it. But as soon as Mamma sees what's happened, she raises her hand in the air. 'Waitress! Waitress! Another steak!' Instinctively, Rita and I protest. Immediately, and one feels with deliberate perversity, Paolo capitulates, then turns to embrace her. '*Mammina, Mammina!*' Then: 'You will give me the *soldini*,' he demands.

Watching mother and son, I see with belated insight that the odd dynamic between them, something they are both equally involved in and responsible for, is forcing me to take on the role of my dead father-in-law. Except that this was probably the moment when the old man gave Paolo a soda or promised him money to counter these disturbing embraces and reassert his role as head of the house. Babbo always held all the purse strings. 'I understand money,' I remember him telling me once, 'but not women.'

Babbo, however, is no longer with us. This gambit in the family repertoire can no longer be played. Perhaps that explains the extreme anxiety now apparent on Paolo's face as he demands his cash. He's not quite sure he's going to get it. After all, one of the jollier talking points in the Baldassarre family is Mamma's extraordinary parsimoniousness, to the extent of using the same bowl of water for the dishes breakfast, lunch and dinner and then emptying it on the vegetable garden. And the bidet water too! Babbo, as Paolo well understood and learned to exploit, threw money around to annoy her.

After lunch there's a break while Paolo returns to the institute for his 'therapy'. We hang about in the lounge where there are ping-pong and pool tables, but the few inmates present are all smoking in front of the TV.

'Tell me about the therapy,' I ask when we're back in the car. It seems the ritual of these visits is to drive down to the nearest town thirty tortuous miles away, spend half an hour there, then drive back. This will exhaust the rest of the day.

'Just pills,' he says. He names an impressive list of drugs, mostly dopamine-blockers. He clearly relishes his expertise in this field. 'We're all schizophrenics,' he says candidly, 'all nuts, so we need these things, otherwise we'd smash the place up. Sometimes people do smash the place up, then they get a big injection right off.'

Sitting next to him now, in the front of the car, with the opportunity to talk quietly between ourselves, I begin to notice that Paolo's conversation is mostly normal so long as you don't touch on two key subjects: the reasons for his illness or 'failure in life', and the possibilities for his future. If this is the effect of a virus, it sure is an odd one.

Driving along he gives excellent directions, warns me of tough hairpins, gives information on the countryside, on some Roman ruins. He tells me how useless the dance therapy classes are, though the teacher is attractive, explains that cigarettes can be had extremely cheaply from a machine in the institute – 'Yes, about sixty per cent off the regular price! They hope we'll die of cancer.' He laughs. He's one of the very few who don't smoke. Mamma is proud of his not smoking. Sometimes an inmate wants a prostitute and smashes up his room when he can't get one. 'Basically people deal with each other through threats, violence and wheedling,' he explains. This seems all too recognizable a scenario.

But then I ask him if they ever try to reduce the amount of drugs they're giving him, to see if he still needs them. He says yes. 'And how is it?' 'Fine.' 'So why don't they reduce them some more?' 'They can't,' he says, 'because the levels were stipulated in the sentence that condemned me to my imprisonment.' 'I bet that's not true,' I tell him.

'They don't stipulate drug levels in court rulings.' He mutters something under his breath. 'What?' He grins. 'Come on, Paolo, what did you say?' 'I'm a *migliorillo*,' he laughs.

How can I translate this word? He's invented it. It must mean something like, 'I'm a bettersome boy'. 'I try to get better,' he says, 'so that I'll be ready to come out in two years' time.' I say nothing, because we all know that there is no limit to the ruling that forced him to live in an institute. He can only come out when a psychiatrist decides he's well enough.

We drive on. I find myself going very slowly, as if in memory of my father-in-law, one of the world's slowest drivers. And as I speak to Paolo, I can't help but feel he's engaging me in a sort of teasing game, inviting me to discuss serious questions, then suddenly retreating into fantasy when I poke my nose where I shouldn't. In each case these fantasies have to do with things that blocked him in the past or are preventing him from having any future now. In the past there was his father's perfidy, ordering that he couldn't study, couldn't marry and putting poison in his food. Now there is the court ruling about his level of drug treatment and the Anglo-American conspiracy to stop him reading by denying him books, or demanding he pay thousands of dollars for them.

'I used to shout a lot when I was in the States,' he says. 'That's why they threw me out. The acoustic insulation in the dorm was very poor. People heard me shouting. It's better nowadays.' He begins to discuss the technicalities of modern insulation about which he is surprisingly well informed.

'So if they'd had better insulation back in the Seventies, none of this would have happened and they wouldn't be trying to stop you from reading American books?'

He nods, faintly smiling.

'But Rita tells me you used to have a copy of this book *Symbolic Logic*. So they did let you have it for a while.'

'That's right.' Paolo admits that he himself tore the book up. One day he walked into his room and a voice from outside screamed, 'ZEOAM!'

'Which means?'

'Down with the Americans!' So he tore up all his American books. 'I only study in English. The Americans are a great nation.' He then begins a perfectly sane account of how one goes about destroying a book, first removing the cover from the pages, then separating out sections of pages thin enough to be reduced to shreds.

I interrupt. 'So it's not a conspiracy stopping you reading, but yourself. Something to do with being sent to America to study, maybe. After all, Babbo did pay for you to go to university.'

'Bullets,' he says.

'What?'

'You're preparing bullets for the lethal blow.'

'Only a suggestion,' I say.

'You shouldn't prepare bullets.'

'Just having a chat, it's been so many years.'

Under his breath, he mutters, 'Rita, Francesca Valentina.'

'I beg your pardon?'

He repeats, grinning. 'Rita, Francesca Valentina.'

'And what does that mean?'

'It means Rita has two degrees, one in French, Francesca, one in English, Valentina. But I don't have any.'

'But how could I have understood that?'

'*Francesca*, French, is easy. *Valentina* from "*valore*" [value] and "*ina*" *inglese* – English.'

'I could never have guessed that.'

He agrees, laughing. Despite the bullets, he seems to be enjoying himself. It's as if he'd found a willing sparring partner at a satisfactorily inferior level.

'So how can you expect people to understand you when you speak in code? Or would it help if we read *Symbolic Logic*?'

He pauses. Solemnly he announces: 'Everybody understands me according to his or her own ability.' He repeats. 'Each according to his ability.'

'And Mamma, how much does Mamma understand you?'

He turns brusquely in his seat. '*Mammina, Mammina*. You're the only one who cares for me.'

Mamma smiles and begins to talk about his possible visit to Pescara. Roberto will drive him down. 'That would be wonderful,' he agrees. 'So nice. I can see my old room. You will give me the money, won't you, *Mammina*?'

*

The following morning, waking in the early hours from a weird dream, some strange business where an old school friend was giving a lecture on how to keep the minutes of legal hearings while I was in a panic about the eyebrows sprouting over my nose, it occurs to me that yesterday's conversation with Paolo had a dreamlike process about it. There was the same bizarre meandering, the same explosion of odd images when something important seemed to be at stake. Perhaps the difference between those who believe schizophrenia is a disorder that at least partly comes out of the structural trauma of family relationships, and those who believe it is entirely organic, is not unlike the difference between those who believe that dreams have meaning, if only you could decode them, and those who are convinced they are completely random.

The plan is that we stay the morning with Paolo, see his doctor, lunch together, then drive Mamma directly down to Pescara where we can spend a few days by the sea. So immediately after breakfast we hurry over to the institute again, where two big surprises are in store . . .

The first is a bus stopping right outside. People get on and off. And where does that bus come from? From Savona. So it would be possible, after all, for Mamma to take the train to Savona and then the bus to the institute! It would be a tough journey for an old lady, but in the end no tougher than first coming up to Verona and then crossing Italy in the car.

'So you see, you can visit him when we're away in August,' Rita tells her mother.

Waiting for our interview with his psychiatrist, we discuss the situation. Paolo is extremely sensible. 'Why on earth come so often, Mamma?' he asks, 'especially when it's so hot. Wait till October.'

But Mamma has always insisted that she must visit him once a month if possible, once every two months at least, even though a number of doctors have suggested that these visits have a negative effect on Paolo.

'You can send the money by post,' he suggests.

She says she'll think about it. But as soon as Paolo goes off to the bathroom for a moment, she hisses, 'What on earth am I supposed to do with him if I come without a car? What am I going to say to him all day?'

Briefly I imagine lovers who don't share the same language and who have been forbidden to embrace. What can they do but, as we did yesterday, drive around all day while others do the talking? That is why Rita and I are here, not because Mamma needed transport. We are chaperones to their mad mismatch.

When Paolo returns Mamma is very businesslike and says it's time to sort out the money. Reluctantly, she gives him what he wants.

The second surprise comes when the psychiatrist finally ushers us into his office, forty minutes late for our appointment. I'd thought Mamma was going to ask whether Paolo could be granted leave to go down to Pescara. Instead she starts complaining about some detail related to her son's disabled person's pension, something that clearly has to do with an administrator not a psychiatrist. She rails about the tangles of Italian bureaucracy. The doctor agrees and in a matter of seconds seems to think the interview is over.

'But what about the visit to Pescara?' I ask. Mamma leans over to whisper, 'He'll never grant it. I asked last time.' She gets up to go. But I feel that if we don't ask about this visit, the interview will have been wasted.

'We've been wondering,' I say, 'if Paolo is well enough to spend a few days with the family in Pescara.'

Just as I speak the phone rings. With astonishing rudeness, the doctor becomes engaged in ten minutes of very jocular conversation about some barbecue he is planning. When finally he puts down the receiver I have to remind him of the question.

'What do you think, Paolo?' he asks.

Paolo is clearly unhappy to be exposed like this.

'I'd like to go,' he hesitates, 'so long as no one touches my room here. I'm very happy here.'

'Of course nobody will touch it,' the doctor says. 'That's fine then. Let's say, in three or four months' time, shall we? In the autumn.'

Suddenly I see that the doctor knows perfectly well that this visit will never happen because neither Mamma nor Paolo wants it. When autumn comes round no one will mention it. So his words are completely empty. Vaguely he grants what they vaguely ask. He isn't interested in discussing the contradiction of their dreaming about something they don't, when it comes to it, really want. Thus he integrates himself perfectly in the way they operate together. They can fantasize about it, without needing to clinch anything. In any event, the interview is over now. The doctor offers a limp hand over his handsome desk.

As soon as we're out Mamma is again very businesslike. No mention is made of the Pescara trip. 'You've got to have a haircut,' she tells Paolo. 'I don't want one,' he says. Mamma turns to us. 'You must drive him to the nearest village to get a haircut.' 'Paolo?' Rita asks. 'I don't want one,' he says. I say, 'But the moment we attack Mamma you'll start hugging her, right?' He grins.

So the haircut it is.

Then over our farewell lunch, Rita asks: 'Paolo, did they ever suggest you have some therapy with the family?'

Actually, I know she knows the answer to this. We discussed it with her father once.

Paolo nods. He's very matter-of-fact. He did two sessions with Babbo, he says, but Mamma wouldn't come.

'That's not true,' she exclaims.

'Yes it is,' Paolo is mild and matter-of-fact, completely convincing, 'I remember you said you didn't want to come.'

Mamma is furious. 'Do you think I wouldn't have come if it could have been useful for you? I can't believe this!'

Immediately he withdraws and we're back to the *Mammina* routine. Apparently it is impossible for him to comment openly on his mother's contradictory behaviour, her strange mixture of love and recalcitrance. Or could it be that he actually wants things this way, encourages this behaviour? Certainly there's no question here of any one person's being solely to blame, it's more the way each person's behaviour complements the other's that seems so unhealthy.

As we prepare to say goodbye, Paolo and I are left alone a moment while the others are in the bathroom. Standing outside the hotel, he suddenly stumbles rather strangely and bangs his nose on the top of the car.

'Paolo, what happened?'

'Some people produce a strong neuroperfume,' he explains, wiping away a bead of blood. 'It makes me fall over.'

I can only presume the 'some people' is myself. But then he hugs me. 'It's been lovely to see each other again.' 'Next time we'll come on

our own,' I tell him. 'Mamma and Babbo had told us you didn't want
to see us.' 'Not at all,' he says. 'Not at all.'

The drive down to Pescara is a long one. Seven hours. We start talking
about the building work that must be done on the family property. But
this only leads Mamma to attack Babbo again. He deliberately kept it
in a poor state of maintenance to spite her because it was originally
her family's not his. He always spited her. She starts to get wound up,
once again rehearsing the tension and betrayals of fifty years of
marriage. It's a litany we're all too familiar with, if only because the
policy of both parents was to tell you unpleasant stories about their
partner, only to side with each other if you ever said anything openly
to their faces.

'So why did your father marry me?' Mamma suddenly demands, 'if
all he wanted was his whores and sluts?' Fortunately little Lucia is
asleep. 'Why? We were engaged for years, the whole war, he had time
to say no. Then the very day after the wedding, the very day, I knew
it was a mistake! I knew he didn't love me!'

'Why didn't you leave him then?' Rita rehearses. It's an ancient
conversation. Once it gets going, no one seems able to stop it.

'Well, why didn't he leave me, if he didn't want me? If he'd just said,
"I don't want you," do you think I would have stayed? Anyway,' she
suddenly reflects, 'I couldn't upset my parents, could I? It would have
been the death of them if our marriage had failed, just like that. They
couldn't have borne it.' On other occasions, however, Mamma will tell
you almost proudly that her father also had endless 'little sluts', only
he was sufficiently respectful to do it far from home. 'Your father never
respected me,' she insists to Rita.

'It's true he was always making promises he never kept,' my wife
acknowledges. But this only introduces another area of family myth:
how Babbo was always just about to visit, or to treat, or to take his
children on a trip, but never quite got round to it. As always, various
incidents are remembered, half with amusement, half in pain. 'There
was the time,' Rita laughs, 'when not turning up from Algeria he sent
a telegram that simply said: LETTER FOLLOWING. Which of course it never
did.'

'Well, anyway, thank God both your old folks died without having
to think you'd separated,' I remark.

Mamma sees no irony in what I've said. '*Grazie al cielo*,' she says. 'It would have been the death of them.'

As evening draws on, speeding along this turnpike that my parents-in-law drove up and down so many times, it comes to me that in this family to talk about anything always means to talk about everything, because nothing has ever been resolved between them. The whole family is somehow marooned in the ambiguous behaviour of my father-in-law exactly fifty years ago when he married a woman without apparently wanting to, yet at the same time forever promising that one day everything would sort itself out, one day there would be the dreamt-of resolution, the whole family together and happy by the sea in Pescara.

It's a mentality that fits perfectly with the contemporary and strictly organic approach to schizophrenia. For the time being the patient can be tranquillized on what are truly very sophisticated drugs. If one has to be marooned somewhere, it's as well to keep the anguish levels low. Anyhow, nothing else can be done and it's certainly no one's fault – unless, that is, we're going to be so primitive as to believe that people can really drive each other mad. In the twenty-five years of Paolo's illness no one has suggested to Mamma that she might look for different ways of behaving with her son. No one has suggested that her weirdly intense relationship with him might have anything to do with the unhappy prevarications of her husband. But then, why bother? In the future, when medical research finally gets there, the whole disorder will be cleared up with an appropriate medicine and everybody can go on behaving exactly as they please.

THE UMBRELLA

Hanif Kureishi

The minute they arrived at the adventure playground, Roger's two sons charged up a long ramp and soon were clinging to the steel netting that hung from a high beam. Satisfied that it would take them some time to extract themselves, Roger sat on a bench and turned to the sports section of his newspaper. He had always found it relaxing to read reports of football matches he had not seen. Then it started to rain.

His sons, aged four and five and a half, had refused to put on their coats when he picked them up from the au pair half an hour before. Coats made them look 'fat', they claimed, and Roger had had to carry the coats under his arm. The older boy was dressed in a thin tight-fitting green outfit and a cardboard cap with a feather in it: he was either Robin Hood or Peter Pan. The younger wore a plastic belt with holsters containing two silver guns, a plastic dagger and a sword, blue wellington boots, jeans with the fly open, and a chequered neckerchief which he pulled over his mouth. 'Cowboys don't wear raincoats,' he said through a mouthful of cloth. The boys frequently refused Roger's commands, though he could not say that their stubbornness and pluck annoyed him. It did, however, cause him trouble with his wife, from whom he had separated a year previously. Only that morning she had said on the phone, 'You are a weak and inadequate disciplinarian. You only want their favour.'

For as long as he could, Roger pretended it was not raining, but when his newspaper began to go soggy and everyone else left the playground, he called the boys over.

'Damn this rain,' he said as he hustled them into their yellow hooded raincoats.

'Don't swear,' said the younger. 'Women think it's naughty.'

'Sorry.' Roger laughed. 'I was thinking I should have got a raincoat as well as the suit.'

'You do need a lovely raincoat, Daddy,' said Oliver, the eldest.

'My friend would have given me a raincoat, but I liked the suit more.'

He had picked up the chocolate-coloured suit from the shop that morning. Since that most extravagant of periods, the early Seventies, Roger had fancied himself as a restrained but amateur dandy. One of his best friends was a clothes designer with shops in Europe and Japan. A few years ago this friend, amused by Roger's interest in his business, had invited Roger, during a fashion show in the British Embassy in Paris, to parade on the catwalk in front of the fashion press, alongside men taller and younger than him. Roger's friend had given him the chocolate suit for his fortieth birthday, and had insisted he wear it with a blue silk shirt. Roger's sons liked to sleep in their newly acquired clothes, and he understood their enthusiasm. He would not normally wear a suit for the park, but that evening he was going to a publishing party, and on to his third date with a woman he had been introduced to at a friend's house, a woman he liked.

Roger took the boys' hands and pulled them along.

'We'd better go to the tea house,' he said. 'I hope I don't ruin my shoes.'

'They're beautiful,' said Oliver.

Eddie stopped to bend down and rub his father's loafers. 'I'll put my hands over your shoes while you walk,' he said.

'That might slow us down a little,' Roger said. 'Run for it, mates!'

He picked Eddie up, holding him flat in his arms like a baby, with his muddy boots pointing away from him. The three of them hurried across the darkening park.

The tea house was a wide, low-ceilinged shed, warm, brightly lit and decorated in the black-and-white colours and flags of Newcastle United. The coffee was good and they had all the newspapers. The place was crowded but Roger spotted a table and sent Oliver over to sit at it.

Roger recognized the mother of a boy in Eddie's nursery, as well as several nannies and au pairs, who seemed to congregate in some part of this park on most days. Three or four of them had come often to his house with their charges when he lived with his wife. If they seemed reticent with him, he doubted whether this was because they were young and simple, but rather that they saw him as an employer, as the boss. He was aware that he was the only man in the tea house. The men he ran into with children were either younger than him, or older, on their second families. He wished his children were older, and understood more; he should have had them earlier. He'd both enjoyed and wasted the years before they were born; it had been a long dissatisfied ease.

A girl in the queue turned to him.

'Thinking again?' she said.

He recognized her voice but had not brought his glasses. 'Hello,' he said at last. He called to Eddie, 'Hey, it's Lindy.' Eddie covered his face with both hands. 'You remember her giving you a bath and washing your hair.'

'Hey cowboy,' she said.

Lindy had looked after both children when Eddie was born, and lived in the house until precipitately deciding to leave. She had told them she wanted to do something else but, instead, had gone to work for a couple nearby. She bent over and kissed Oliver, as she used to, and he put his arms around her. The last time Roger had run into Lindy, he had overheard her imitating his sons' accents and laughing. They were 'posh'. He had been shocked by how early these notions of 'class' started.

'Haven't seen you for a while,' she said.

'I've been travelling.'

'Where to?'

'Belfast, Cape Town, Sarajevo.'

'Lovely,' she said.

'I'm off to the States next week,' he said.

'Doing what?'

'Lecturing on human rights. On the development of the notion of the individual – of the idea of the separate self.' He wanted to say something about Shakespeare and Montaigne here, as he had been thinking about them, but realized she would refuse to be curious about the subject. 'And on the idea of human rights in the post-war period. All of that kind of thing. I hope there's going to be a TV series.'

She said, 'I came back from the pub and turned on the TV last week, and there you were, criticising some clever book or other. I didn't understand it.'

'Right.'

He had always been polite to her, even when he had been unable to wake her up because she had been drinking the previous night. She had seen him unshaven, and in his pyjamas at four in the morning; she had opened doors and found him and his wife abusing one another behind them; she had been at their rented villa in Assisi when his wife tore the cloth from the table with four bowls of pasta on it. She must have heard energetic reconciliations.

'I hope it goes well,' she said.

'Thank you.'

The boys ordered big doughnuts and juice. The juice spilled over the table and the doughnuts were smeared round their mouths. Roger had to hold his cappuccino out in front of him to stop the boys sticking their grimy fingers in the froth and sucking the chocolate from them. To his relief they joined Lindy's child.

Roger began a conversation with a woman at the next table who had complimented him on his sons. She told him she wanted to write a newspaper article on how difficult some people found it to say 'no' to children. You could not charm them, she maintained, as you could people at a cocktail party; they had to know what the limits were. He did not like the idea that she shouted at her child, but he decided to ask for her phone number before he left. For more than a year he had not gone out socially, fearing that people would see his anguish.

He was extracting his notebook and pen when Lindy called him. He turned round. His sons were at the far end of the tea house, rolling on top of another, larger, boy, who was wailing, 'He's biting me!'

Eddie did bite; he kicked too.

'Boys!' Roger called.

He hurried them into their coats again, whispering furiously at them to shut up. He said goodbye to the woman without getting her phone number. He did not want to appear lecherous. He had always been timid, and proud of the idea that he was a good man who treated people fairly. He did not want to impose himself. The world would be a better place if people considered their actions. Perhaps he had put himself on a pedestal. 'You have a high reputation–with yourself!' a friend had said. Everyone was entitled to some pride and vanity. However, this whole business with his wife had stripped him of his moral certainties. There was no just or objective way to resolve competing claims: those of freedom – his freedom – to live and develop as he liked, against the right of his family to have his dependable presence. But no amount of conscience or morality would make him go back. He had not missed his wife for a moment.

As they were leaving the park, Eddie tore some daffodils from a flower bed and stuffed them in his pocket. 'For Mummy,' he explained.

The house was a ten-minute walk away. Holding hands, they ran home through the rain. His wife would be back soon, and he would be off.

It was not until he had taken out his key that he remembered his wife had changed the lock last week. What she had done was illegal; he owned the house, but he had laughed at the idea that she thought he would intrude, when he wanted to be as far away as possible.

He told the boys they would have to wait. They sheltered in the little porch where water dripped on their heads. The boys soon tired of standing with him and refused to sing the songs he started. They pulled their hoods down and chased one another up and down the path.

It was dark. People were coming home from work.

The next-door neighbour passed by. 'Locked out?' he said.

''Fraid so.'

Oliver said, 'Daddy, why can't we go in and watch the cartoons?'

'It's only me she's locked out,' he said. 'Not you. But you are, of course, with me.'

'Why has she locked us out?'

'Why don't you ask her?' he said.

His wife confused and frightened him. But he would greet her civilly, send the children into the house and say goodbye. It was, however, difficult to get cabs in the area; impossible at this time and in this weather. It was a twenty-minute walk to the tube station, across a dripping park where alcoholics and junkies gathered under the trees. His shoes, already wet, would be filthy. At the party he would have to try and remove the worst of the mud in the toilet.

After the violence of separation he had expected a diminishment of interest and of loathing, on her part. He himself had survived the worst of it and anticipated a quietness. Kind indifference had come to seem an important blessing. But as well as refusing to divorce him, she sent him lawyer's letters about the most trivial matters. One letter, he recalled, was entirely about a cheese sandwich he had made for himself when visiting the children. He was ordered to bring his own food in future. He thought of his wife years ago, laughing and putting out her tongue with his semen on it.

'Hey there,' she said, coming up the path.

'Mummy!' they called.

'Look at them,' he said. 'They're soaked through.'

'Oh dear.'

She unlocked the door and the children ran into the hall. She nodded at him. 'You're going out.'

'Sorry?'

'You've got a suit on.'

He stepped into the hall. 'Yes. A little party.'

He glanced into his former study where his books were packed in boxes on the floor. He had, as yet, nowhere to take them. Beside them were a pair of men's black shoes he had not seen before.

She said to the children, 'I'll get your tea.' To him she said, 'You haven't given them anything to eat, have you?'

'Doughnuts,' said Eddie. 'I had chocolate.'

'I had jam,' said Oliver.

She said, 'You let them eat that rubbish?'

Eddie pushed the crushed flowers at her. 'There you are, Mummy.'

'You must not take flowers from the park,' she said. 'They are for everyone.'

'Fuck, fuck, fuck,' said Eddie suddenly, with his hand over his mouth.

'Shut up! People don't like it!' said Oliver, and hit Eddie, who started to cry.

'Listen to him,' she said to Roger. 'You've taught them to use filthy language. You are really hopeless.'

'So are you,' he said.

In the past few months, preparing his lectures, he had visited some disorderly and murderous places. The hatred he witnessed puzzled him still. It was atavistic but abstract; mostly the people did not know one another. It had made him aware of how people clung to their antipathies, and used them to maintain an important distance, but in the end he failed to understand why this was. After all the political analysis and talk of rights, he had concluded that people had to grasp the necessity of loving one another; and if that was too much, they had to let one another alone. When this still seemed inadequate and banal, he suspected he was on the wrong path, that he was trying to say something about his own difficulties in the guise of intellectual discourse. Why could he not find a more direct method? He had, in fact, considered writing a novel. He had plenty to say, but could not afford the time, unpaid.

He looked out at the street. 'It's raining quite hard.'

'It's not too bad now.'

He said, 'You haven't got an umbrella, have you?'

'An umbrella?'

He was becoming impatient. 'Yes. An umbrella. You know, you hold it over your head.'

She sighed and went back into the house. He presumed she was opening the door to the airing cupboard in the bathroom.

He was standing in the porch, ready to go. After a while she returned empty-handed.

'No. No umbrella,' she said.

He said, 'There were three there last week.'

'Maybe there were.'

'Are there not still three umbrellas there?'

'Maybe there are,' she said.

'Give me one.'

'No.'

'Sorry?'

'I'm not giving you one,' she said. 'If there were a thousand umbrellas there I would not give you one.'

He had noticed how persistent his children were; they asked, pleaded, threatened and screamed, until he yielded.

He said, 'They are my umbrellas.'

'No,' she repeated.

'How petty you've become.'

'Didn't I give you everything?'

He cleared his throat. 'Everything but love.'

'I did give you that, actually.' She said, 'I've rung my friend. He's on his way.'

He said, 'I don't care. Just give me an umbrella.'

She shook her head. She went to shut the door. He put his foot out and she banged the door against his leg. He wanted to rub his shin but could not give her the pleasure.

He said, 'Let's try and be rational.'

He had hated before, his parents and brother, at certain times. But it was a fury, not a deep intellectual and emotional hatred like this. He had had psychotherapy; he took tranquillizers, but still he wanted to pulverize his wife. None of the ideas he had about life would make this feeling go away. A friend had suggested it would be no bad thing if he lost the 'good' idea of himself, seeing himself as more complicated and passionate. But he could not understand the advantage of seeing himself as unhinged.

'You used to find the rain "refreshing",' she said with a sneer.

'It has come to this,' he said.

'Here we are then,' she said. 'Don't start crying about it.'

He pushed the door. 'I'll get the umbrella.'

She pushed the door back at him. 'You cannot come in.'

'It is my house.'

'Not without prior arrangement.'

'We arranged it,' he said.

'The arrangement's off.'

He pushed her.

'Are you assaulting me?' she said.

He looked outside. An alcoholic woman he had had to remove from the front step on several occasions was standing at the end of the path holding a can of lager.

'I'm watching you,' she shouted. 'If you touch her you are reported!'

'Watch on!' he shouted back.

He pushed into the house. He placed his hand on his wife's chest and forced her against the wall. She cried out. She did bang her head, but it was, in football jargon, a 'dive'. The children ran at his legs. He pushed them away. He went to the airing cupboard, seized an umbrella and made his way to the front door.

As he passed her she snatched it. Her strength surprised him, but he yanked the umbrella back and went to move away. She raised her hand. He thought she would slap him. It would be the first time. But she made a fist. As she punched him in the face she continued to look at him. He had not been hit since he left school. He had forgotten the physical shock and then the disbelief, the shattering of the belief that the world was a safe place.

The boys had started to scream. He had dropped the umbrella. His mouth throbbed; his lip was bleeding. He must have staggered and lost his balance for she was able to push him outside.

He heard the door slam behind him. He could hear the children crying. He walked away, past the alcoholic woman still standing at the end of the path. He turned to look at the lighted house. When they had calmed down, the children would have their bath and get ready for bed. They liked being read to. It was a part of the day he had always enjoyed.

He turned his collar up but knew he would get soaked. He wiped his mouth with his hand. She had landed him quite a hit. He would not be able to find out until later whether it would show.

Justine Picardie, aged six, and her sister
Ruth, aged four, 1967

IF I DREAM I HAVE YOU

Justine Picardie

> The savage, it is said, fails to distinguish the visions of sleep from the realities of waking life, and, accordingly, when he has dreamed of his dead friends he necessarily concludes that they have not wholly perished, but that their spirits continue to exist in some place and some form, though in the ordinary course of events they elude the perceptions of his senses.
>
> *The Golden Bough* Book II, James George Frazer

Good Friday in the year 2000, Jesus is dead and so is my sister, and I'm running on a treadmill at the gym, watching MTV with no sound on. If my sister were still alive she would be thirty-six in ten days' time. But she died when she was thirty-three, the same age as Jesus. Obviously, I know she wasn't nearly as famous as Jesus was at the age of thirty-three – I'm not *that* crazy, nor even inclined to blasphemy under normal circumstances – but Ruth is a bit famous, because when she was diagnosed with terminal breast cancer in 1997, I asked her to write a column for the London *Observer*'s magazine section, which I was editing at the time. The section was called 'Life' and her column about death came on the final page. She only wrote a handful of columns before she died, but many thousands of readers responded to her pieces, which were later collected, together with her emails and letters, in a book called *Before I Say Goodbye*, published after her death. Thus she has a kind of public afterlife – she rose again, in the best-seller lists at least, which is both a blessing and a curse for those who loved her.

When I think about her now, which is most of the time, it's as if I'm rewinding a silent film in my head. I see the crucial scenes in our lives together: holding her hand while her twins were born in an emergency Caesarean; holding her hand when she kissed them goodbye just before she died two years later. But what I can't hear is her voice in my head, and that silence is driving me crazy. The treadmill is supposed to be good therapy, and sometimes it works, but not today, because Good Friday is the saddest day of the year. I've tried everything since my sister died, in the manner of the sophisticated consumer that I am supposed to be: bereavement counselling, psychotherapy, antidepressants, Valium, sleeping pills, homeopathic remedies, the gym. Prozac is sufficiently numbing to make the silence matter less, though I'm trying to stop taking it because I've begun to wonder if I've been missing something, whether the impermeable layer it provides is now necessary. But still nothing speaks to me.

I didn't expect silence. We had always talked so much. She was my best friend as well as my sister: a little less than three years younger than me, the child I needed to protect when I was still a child myself (and my parents scarcely grown-ups themselves). When we knew she was going to die, because the tumours had spread to her lungs and liver, we talked about how we would always talk to each other, even after her death. Neither of us had grown up believing in a conventional Christian afterlife (and anyway, I'd given up on that unkind God after his failure to answer my prayers); but even so, it seemed impossible that my sister and I would ever be separated by silence, that our voices were contained only in our flesh and blood.

Yet in the weeks after her death, I heard nothing. At night there were just my own muffled screams in the pillow, or the memory (more difficult to bear) of her agonized breathing on her last night, as she gasped for all that remained of life. I could say nothing to her except 'I love you, I love you, I love you'. 'I love you too,' she whispered, before she disappeared to a place where I could not follow her.

Since then there have been times when I have longed to go after her. But today, after I've finished at the gym, I walk back home and back upstairs to the computer in the attic. I'm almost expecting to find an email from Ruth ('message waiting') but there is nothing, just my half-reflected face on the blank screen. I wonder if she is on the other side, looking back at me looking in. I wonder if I could smash a hole in the screen and put my hand through to reach her. I often dream about being with Ruth in a wood. She is a little girl, lost in the wood, and I am on the other side of a glass screen watching her. In my dream I shatter it with my fists and reach through, cutting my wrists as I do so, on the broken glass. When I was a child I saw a television adaptation of *Wuthering Heights*, and Cathy's ghost came to a dark window; she was on the outside, and she smashed her way in, with bleeding wrists and knuckles. Or maybe – though I can't quite remember, maybe I dreamt this – it was a little girl in the house who closed the window against Cathy's ghost, slamming the window down on her dead fingers as they reached inside.

Do I need a therapist to explain this? No. I need only turn to Iona Opie's very useful *Dictionary of Superstitions*, page 117. 'DEATH: Opening locks/doors and windows frees spirit; 1891 *Church Times* 23 Jan. "Yesterday, at Willey, in Warwickshire, I buried a little boy three years old. It was snowing hard, yet the parents (of the labouring class) would have both front and back doors of their cottage wide open all the time of the funeral."'

So much for communication, then.

When I dream about my sister, which I do almost every night, she doesn't say very much. Just before dawn on Easter Sunday, at about the time that Jesus is doubtless rising again, I dream that I meet Ruth at a party.

'I thought you were dead!' I say.

'No, I just went to America,' she replies, looking evasive.

'But I saw your dead body! I went to the funeral and saw the coffin. You were cremated.'

'Hmm,' she says, infuriatingly.

'And what about the children?' I ask her. 'How could you just go to America and leave Lola and Joe? They've missed you so much! And I've missed you so much! How could you do that?'

She turns away.

'Ruth, listen to me,' I say. 'Your husband's got a girlfriend. They've just moved into a new house together, with the twins. Don't you care? Are you even listening to me?'

She still says nothing. I look at her more closely, at her cropped hair which has been dyed red, and then I realize that it is a stranger, someone pretending to be Ruth.

'You're not my sister,' I say.

'You *bitch*,' she replies, not very originally.

After this dream, I think maybe I need some help. A few months ago, a friend gave me the telephone number for a man – a medium, in fact – called Arthur Molinary, who works at the College of Psychic Studies. I liked his name – it made me smile – and I quite liked the idea of going to the strange-sounding place. But I'd stuffed the number in a drawer. I didn't feel the need to ring him then. Now, though, I couldn't think of what else to do.

Wednesday 26 April I ring the College of Psychic Studies from work. This is a very peculiar phone call to make in an open-plan office, so I try to whisper into the phone.

'I'd like to make an appointment to see Arthur Molinary.'

'Mr Molinary is fully booked until six-fifteen p.m. on the eighth of June,' says a businesslike woman at the other end. 'Would you like to take that appointment?'

'Yes,' I hiss quietly, 'but isn't there anything sooner?'

She pauses for a few seconds, as if she were scanning the appointment book of a popular doctor's surgery. Then: 'You could come in and see our Junior Sensitive on the sixteenth of May at six-thirty. We've been getting very good results from him.'

'I'll take both appointments,' I say, feeling excited, suddenly feeling Ruth. I can see her in my mind's eye, wearing her favourite lavender-coloured skirt from a shop called Ghost.

'See you then,' says the receptionist. 'And we need twenty-four hours' notice if you're going to cancel.'

'I won't cancel,' I say. (Later, when I tell my husband, who is a rationalist, about this conversation, he raises an eyebrow and says, 'You'd think the College of Psychic Studies would *know* if you were going to cancel.')

Monday 1 May It's Ruth's birthday. I've lost my good spirits and sunk back into an angry silence. Both my parents have spent the night at our house (sleeping in separate bedrooms because they are divorced). In the morning we make small talk between slices of toast. I wonder whether to tell them about my appointments at the College of Psychic Studies. My father used to be an Oxford don; my mother is a therapist. I can't see spiritualism going down well with either of them, though as it happens, my paternal grandfather developed an interest in seances after his parents died. This is a rarely spoken of family embarrassment: poor, sad, silly Louis, who was named Lazar (for Lazarus) but changed his name after he was reborn into evangelical Christianity, joined Jews for Jesus, and started listening out for rappings on the table and voices from beyond.

'Dad,' I say. 'Why don't you ever talk about Louis and the spiritualists?'

'Oh, that dreadful *rubbish*,' says my father. 'How absurd, how truly *ridiculous* can you get!'

My father had the first of several nervous breakdowns just after his mother died. I must have been seven or eight when he was taken to a mental hospital near Oxford, where he was given electric shock treatment. Since then, he has had years of therapy and brutal doses of medication that have left him rather frail and shaky. My grandfather's experiences with spiritualism were, possibly, a gentler way of dealing with grief than my father's own psychiatric treatment; but my father would almost certainly disagree with this observation.

As for my mother, she was raised in the rituals of Anglo-Catholicism by her mother, who had been sent away by her parents to a convent boarding school at the age of four. One of her ancestors, Henry Garnett, was a Catholic priest who had been beheaded after the Gunpowder Plot and later canonized by virtue of the image of Christ which was seen in a drop of his blood. As a teenager, my mother had thoughts of becoming a nun, but she decided against it; rather than marrying God, she met my Jewish father and discovered communism and her own cleverness instead. Their marriage failed. My father suffered from depression, and I grew up associating Easter and other holidays with his corresponding bouts of silence and melancholy (cause and effect might be explained by a recent email from him which observed, gnomically: 'There were pogroms in the Tsarist Empire at about Easter time, usually orchestrated by the Russian police themselves and fuelled by the Catholic priests, to blame the Christ-killers who would be accused of murdering Christian children for their blood to make matzos at Passover.') Recently, my father has found some consolation in the rituals of Judaism which he had previously rejected; while my mother returned to the Church with her second husband, who was a doctor – a blood specialist – and also a haemophiliac. When he died from Aids, she discovered a different kind of solace in the apparent science of psychotherapy.

After Ruth's death, I seemed to my mother to be silent and closed; in need of therapy, no doubt. But my own experiences with therapists have not been very successful. The first bereavement counsellor I saw made me irritable, partly because of his twinkly New Age language ('You need a safe place to be held'); and also because he sent me notes on blue paper decorated with pastel bunnies. The second therapist was far better, but we got stuck on my recollection of Ruth's blood phobia (she felt faint – and sometimes fainted, even fitted – at the sight of her own blood). This therapist seemed to suggest that perhaps my sister and I had repressed the memory of our father's suicide attempt: could there have been slit wrists or something? But as I kept telling the therapist, my father had only taken a minor overdose of pills, though during (or maybe because of) this period of therapy, I was haunted by the unasked-for image of him hanging in our living room in Oxford.

This delving into my subconscious soon got to be far too uncomfortable and exhausting. Prozac is so much easier, and anyway, I'm bored of myself; bored of grief; bored of hearing my own voice talking drearily, pointlessly, when what I really want is Ruth's voice.

And if not her voice, then maybe that of a medium who can hear her when I can't? That's what I try to tell my mother on the morning of Ruth's birthday. She looks at me quizzically. Somewhere in her measured response I hear the word 'internalized', but not much else. Then she tells me that she, too, dreams about Ruth.

'Once she was on the other side of a river, waving to me, but I couldn't cross the river,' says my mother. 'Another time, I dreamt I was driving very fast down a motorway, and I saw Ruth flash past in the opposite direction, in another car.'

'But do you ever feel her presence when you're awake?'

'Only in my memory and my sense of loss,' my mother says quietly.

I am silent. She wants me to love her more, but sometimes my love for her is pushed aside by my grief for Ruth. So she leaves without my telling her that I do love her, I do; even though my sister is dead. Then my husband drives my father, me and our two children south across London, over Blackfriars Bridge, the bridge that I crossed so many times, to and from the hospice that housed my sister in her last weeks, to the other side of the Thames. We park at the end of the bridge and walk alongside the grey river, past little bays of rubbish washed up on to the dirty sand. It is May Day. I think that my husband is angry with me for being sad on this spring holiday ('That's pure projection, and you know it,' says the voice of an imaginary therapist, which sometimes comes into my head when I least want to hear it). I walk ahead with the children, who are uncomplicated in their conversation, leaving my husband and my father in our wake.

Finally, we get to the Hayward Gallery, to an exhibition which has been curated by our neighbour, David Toop, whose wife, my friend Kimberley, killed herself five years ago. (Kimberley half believed in spiritualism, and in her despair hoped that death would free her soul from darkness, but that is another story.) The exhibition is called 'Sonic Boom', and is about sound, present and absent. I stand in front of a work called *A Procession of Ghosts*, made of graceful wires scratching on a huge, smooth white page. Nothing is there to read, and yet there is the faint sound of something being written. I stare at the blank space and try to imagine Ruth's words on her birthday. But the page stays empty, while the scratching of what might be a pen continues.

Ten days later. I'm sitting in a plane on my way to Hollywood to interview a clutch of film stars for *Vogue*. I look out of the window, in search of Ruth, as ever. The first time I flew after she died, I cried because of the sky's emptiness. This time, it's easier. I think, couldn't she be here in the cabin with me, her spirit flying from her children's pillows at dawn?

'Are you there?' I whisper, mouthing the words.

'I'm here,' says the voice in my head.

I close my eyes and hear her voice as mine.

'Ruth?'

'Yes.'

'I miss you.'

'I miss you, too. But I'm here you know.'

'Can't you just give me a sign?'

'You don't need one.'

'What's heaven?'

'Heaven is a state of mind.'

'And hell?'

'Hell is your unhappiness.'

'What's it like for you now?'

'Blue and fast and silver.'

'So where do you spend your time?'

'With the twins, and you, and by myself.'

'Can you remember the dream I had? The week after you died? We were in the gardens, at night, at the Trinity Hospice, and you were lying on a kind of mat as if you were sleeping. And then you sat up and said to me that you were spending all your time with strangers. I thought of you, like a lost ghost crossing Blackfriars Bridge, to and fro, over and over again.'

'That was before I found myself. I'm better now.'

I open my eyes and I'm crying, 36,000 feet up in the sky, wondering if my dead sister is sitting in the empty seat beside me.

'Of course I am, stupid,' her voice says.

'I feel stupid,' I say. 'I'm not as clever as you.'

'Yes you are,' she says to me. 'You are me.'

Tuesday 16 May My appointment with the Junior Sensitive at the College of Psychic Studies. It's a grand building in South Kensington, just around the corner from the Natural History Museum. Beyond the entrance hall is the library that doubles as a waiting room, with faded rows of Victorian books, and a brochure setting out the college's principles. ('Founded in 1884, the College is an educational charity. We seek to promote spiritual values and a greater understanding of the wider areas of human consciousness, welcoming the truths of all spiritual traditions and, equally, each and every individual . . .') I wait, browsing through the list of forthcoming lectures. Tomorrow night Dr Edgar Mitchell, who walked on the moon in 1971, will be delivering his thoughts on 'The Quantam Hologram: Nature's Mind', with special reference to 'intuitive, psychic and mystical experiences'. I don't get any further before my name is called.

'Room Four,' says the receptionist. She points up the stairs, past the oil paintings of former presidents and luminaries of the College, past the lecture theatre, to the second floor.

The Junior Sensitive is a middle-aged man, small and balding and nervous in a carefully ironed shirt and respectable trousers.

'Do you mind if I draw the curtains?' he says, in a soft northern accent. 'It's so light outside, it's blinding.'

'Go ahead,' I say, and we both sit down.

He closes his eyes. 'I definitely feel something,' he says. 'I felt it as soon as you came into the room. My nose is itching and my throat, my throat is sore.' He clutches his neck, his eyes still closed.

'There's a very high pollen count outside,' I say, unkindly. 'Maybe you've got hay fever?'

He opens his eyes and looks at me. 'You could be right,' he says. 'It could be hay fever.'

He closes his eyes again and starts waving his hands in the air, paddling them through the twilight in this hot, still room.

'You must remember to breathe deeply,' he says, breathing deeply himself by way of demonstration. 'In, out, in, out. And swim. When you're stressed, go swimming . . . and you need to drink plenty of water. Lots and lots of water.'

This doesn't seem to me to be particularly helpful advice, nor does it seem to have anything to do with my sister, so I remain silent.

'Clarissa!' he says suddenly. 'Clarissa! Does the name mean anything to you?'

'No,' I reply, wanting to leave now.

'Hmm, well, store that name away for the future.' He breathes deeply again, as if to reassure himself. His brow is furrowed and his nose wrinkles like the White Rabbit in *Alice in Wonderland*.

I gaze at the ceiling, feeling furious and silly and disappointed. What on earth am I doing here? Why would Ruth talk to me in this ridiculous place, through the guise of this peculiar man?

'I see someone who looks like you and talks like you,' he continues, undeterred. 'Do you have someone in your family who has passed on?'

'My sister.' I say this reluctantly.

'She died of cancer,' he says. His hands move to his stomach. 'I can feel her nausea.'

I feel like punching him on the nose, but I'm too polite to leave. I listen to his comments on my dead grandparents. ('They like this time of year. I see them eating ice cream. Did they like ice cream? I'm trying to find some proof for you, here. Did one of them have their tonsils removed, perhaps?')

Finally, I can go.

'Goodbye,' I say. 'Thank you.'

'Goodbye,' he says gently. 'Sometimes the spirits don't tell you what you want to hear.'

I walk down the stairs, past the portraits of Victorian mediums and the posters advertising next weekend's workshop on the path of the soul, and then out of the big front door, where suddenly I find myself laughing, looking up into an early summer sky where the pollen swirls like heaven's dust.

The next day I find in the morning post at work a book and a letter written on lavender notepaper. 'Dear Ms Picardie,' it begins,

I read your article in the *Daily Telegraph*, September 25th 1999, understanding exactly how you feel about your sister Ruth's death two years ago. Your remark about your longing for 'her advice and unique understanding of our shared past' is especially poignant.

Your story struck such a chord with me that I decided to send you my book, *Voices From Paradise*. I feel it can help you not only by expressing shared experience, but in a practical way too.

Please read it and if you feel it adds up, unbelievable though it all may seem at first, perhaps you'll recommend it in whatever way you feel is appropriate.

With kindest regards,
Judith Chisholm

The subtitle of the book is 'How the Dead Speak to Us', and despite my disappointing experience with the Junior Sensitive, I take it home and read it. It proves so absorbing that I miss *ER*, which is my favourite thing on television (and was also Ruth's: the unreal blood seemed not to disturb her, when we watched it every Wednesday night together before she became ill, and afterwards, and not long before she died, lying side by side on her hospital bed, though by then her brain tumour prevented her from following the dialogue – 'What are they talking about?' she complained. 'What are their voices *saying*?').

Judith Chisholm is a former *Sunday Times* journalist (the paper where I learned to be a reporter, though she left years before I arrived), whose son died unexpectedly at the age of thirty-six. The book begins as an account of her grief, moves on to her experiences with mediums and seances, and culminates in a detailed exposition of her belief in what she calls the 'electronic voice phenomenon', or EVP; a means of recording the voices of the dead. In support of this belief she cites Sir Oliver Lodge, the inventor of the spark plug, a former principal of Birmingham University, and president of the Society for Psychical Research from 1901 to 1903. ('The dead live in etheric wavelengths which operate at much higher frequencies than ours,' Lodge wrote in *The Outline of Science*. 'Our physical world is working on vibrations that are up to the speed of light. The etheric world operates at frequencies far in excess of the speed of of light.') She also quotes Thomas Edison, who, after inventing the light bulb and the phonograph, wrote at the age of seventy-three that he was 'inclined to believe that our personality hereafter will be able to affect matter' and that 'if we can evolve an instrument so delicate as to be affected or moved or manipulated by our personality as it survives in the next life, such an instrument when made available ought to record something'.

Judith Chisholm's book concludes with instructions on how to record the voices of the dead. 'You need: *a tape recorder* (variable speed is useful as some of the voices are very fast and need slowing down); *a new tape; a remote microphone*, if your tape recorder will take one, which should be hung up for maximum efficiency (a remote mike helps cut down background hiss); a quiet room and, very important, *a positive, expectant, cheerful, loving attitude of mind*.' She also recommends recording after sunset on the night of a full moon, preferably during a thunderstorm, because of the increased amounts of electricity and magnetism and what she calls 'gravitational effect'.

Thursday 18 May The children are asleep upstairs. There is a full moon, and a thunderstorm has just passed. 'Have you got a tape recorder and a microphone?' I ask my husband.

'Why?' he says. I don't answer, but he knows what I'm thinking, and looks at me with disbelief and exasperation. But he fetches the tape recorder and the microphone and a blank cassette and sets them up for me on the kitchen table. 'I'm going upstairs,' he says. 'Call me if you need me.'

I light a candle and switch off the lights. I turn on the tape recorder and whisper into it, in case anyone hears me. But then I remember that I want to be heard. I want Ruth to hear me, and Kimberley, and Oscar and Adam and Simon and Jon, all my friends who have died in the last few years. I speak up. 'Um, is anybody there? I would very much like to talk to somebody. I feel like so many people have died recently, it would make more sense to conduct my social life in the spirit world.'

Silence. I leave a gap on the tape, as instructed in the book. ('With the open-mike method, you will not hear any discarnate voices at the time of recording, only on playback. Leave gaps in your own speech for a response on the other side . . .')

Silence. I believe in this. I do. I have a positive, expectant, cheerful, loving attitude of mind. There is a full moon outside. There has been lightning and therefore masses of electricity. My sister is going to talk to me. She is going to leave me a message on my tape. I know this to be true.

I switch the tape off, rewind it, play it back.

I hear my voice on the tape . . . and nothing else. But there must be something. I rewind it and play it again. Silence. I consult the book. 'Play your tape back. Listen very carefully. At first it's hard to distinguish anything other than the background hiss of the tape recorder, which you can never completely eliminate, and the sound of your own voice. As the discarnate voices usually imprint at a level below that at which we expect to hear them you have to try to listen to all levels on the tape – listen through it. This is extremely hard at first, but becomes automatic later on. The voices can be whispered. At first they usually are. They are sometimes very fast, often curt, often seemingly banal in their utterances. There is great economy of words yet what is said usually has more than one meaning. Sometimes prepositions and auxiliary verbs are left out. Usually one to three words are imprinted at first. If you hear something that may be an 'extra' voice, run the tape back and listen again – and again.'

I run the tape back. I listen again, and again. Still nothing. I go upstairs and get my husband to listen to the tape. He puts on some headphones and I watch him listening. His eyes fill with tears, but he says nothing.

'Did you hear something?' I ask.

'Only your voice,' he says. 'There's only you. You know that, don't you? It's only you.'

Monday 22 May I rang Judith Chisholm after the failure of my experiment in EVP and now I am driving through the fading light to her house in east London. 'Are you cracking up?' asks a poster for the Samaritans behind the glass of a bus shelter. No, I'm not cracking up. I feel calm. Judith Chisholm lives in a long, narrow street which ends at the Hackney Marshes, the kind of place, I think to myself, where ghosts would live, if ghosts were to live anywhere. She lets me in. She is probably the same age as my mother, though my mother's hair is fading to a gentle grey, whereas Judith's is dyed the colour of thick blood. She shows me into her front room. It is painted dark green. There are crucifixes on the wall and containers of home-made wine on a side table. The house smells of damp cats or city roses in the rain. Her youngest son – her surviving son – comes into the room. His name is Vic. He is very thin and very pale. He works as an electrician. He's been expecting me.

'It's so amazing,' he says. 'You lost your younger sister. I lost my older brother. That's not a coincidence. That's a one-in-a-million chance.'

I don't reply. I feel silenced by this house. Judith brings me a cup of tea, and halfway through drinking it I lurch into a question. 'Do you believe in heaven?' I ask her, trying to concentrate on looking at her, rather than Christ hanging on the cross on the opposite wall.

'Spirits go through stages,' she says, not answering the question directly. 'I think some of them go to purgatory. And purgatory is . . .'

'Like a waiting room,' Vic cuts in. 'Or at least that's what I heard, anyway.'

'Vic, please, go and play with your computer,' his mother says. 'Two people can't do this. We can't both talk to Justine.'

'OK,' Vic says mildly. He looks at me and holds out a hand, which I take, briefly. 'I'm sure we'll meet again.'

Judith tells me about her EVP experiments. She has been engaged in them for seven years, at first in search of her dead son, who said a little, though now he can't get a word in edgeways because the voice that fills her tapes is that of a man called Jack Hallam. She used to work with Jack at the *Sunday Times*. He was the picture editor. He believed in ghosts and wrote books, collecting and editing other people's ghost stories. He died in 1986.

'Time is a curious thing,' Judith says. 'I've heard remarks that suggest that spirits are aware of the passage of time. I heard Jack say "It's a long time since I heard from Chisholm" – that's what he calls me, Chisholm. But I don't think he's aware that fourteen years have passed since his death.'

'Do you think he's in heaven?'

'I think that he's in purgatory. The evidence seems to point to that.'

Her evidence is on her tapes of Jack's voice. She has hours and hours of them, and she has listened to every minute of tape twenty or thirty times over. She says it's exhausting, so exhausting that often her head hurts. Yet now I am here, at last, an independent witness to these endeavours, and she is going to play me some of these tapes; but I will need to read her transcript, too. 'It's not like ordinary speech,' she says. 'You need to accustom your hearing. You may not even hear it. I have an extraordinarily wide range of hearing. I can hear things that other people can't.'

We go upstairs to the first floor, to her study, where she keeps her cassette player and her notes and her Dictaphone: her little door to the other world, where Jack Hallam is always waiting. Once Jack found Judith, it seems he couldn't be silenced.

She plays me the first recording she made of Jack Hallam's voice, on what was then a brand new Dictaphone, which, she tells me, cost eighty-nine pounds, much to her dismay. I hear a whispery, scratchy sound through the speakers – the sound of an empty pen on paper, or shallow gasps, or rats in the attic, a tap at the window; a ghost in the machine.

'Can you hear him?' she says urgently.

'I don't know,' I say.

'Listen,' she says, and rewinds the tape. But I still can't hear the words. So she rewinds it again. This time I ask her to tell me what he is saying. And I think, maybe . . . I think maybe I hear a voice. I read her transcript while I listen to the tape. It says:

OCTOBER 13TH 1999. KEY: SP = SPIRIT.

Sp: Hallam knows

Me: Having just recently bought this [a new tape recorder]

Sp: Yes

Me: I don't actually like it . . .

Sp: We do like it

Me: But is it useful to you? Can you come through on this and would you like me to keep it? I'm just going to leave this next bit of tape empty so you can perhaps speak on it

Sp: Now, Hallam's content. Hallam can progress. We need Hallam to know. Hallam needs someone who can help him. Tell him! Go and find Hallam! Go and get Hallam!

She plays me other tapes, and shows me other transcripts. In one, she asks Jack Hallam why he has been sent to communicate with her; could he please explain 'the plan'. 'There is no plan,' he replies. She wonders if she is missing something, because sometimes, despite her experience in these matters, even she finds it hard to understand all the words. And sometimes they frighten her. Her notes of an EVP session that took place on 12 January this year state that she can't tell if the spirit voice is saying 'let's kill her' or 'let's keep her happy' or maybe 'let's keep Hallam' or 'let's kill Hallam'.

She plays the tape to me. 'What can you hear?'

'I don't know,' I say.

She is obviously hoping for a better response from me, but I am unwilling to engage with what is happening here. She scrabbles around her study to find other tapes, searching for them with her glasses perched on the end of her nose like a storybook academic – the Professor Higgins of the psychic world, whose own perfect enunciation contrasts with the mumblings of these recalcitrant ghosts.

But as she plays me snippets of other tapes, I think I can hear the word 'Hallam', though it sounds as if it comes in a dream. Cheered by this, Judith suggests we make a recording together. She turns on the Dictaphone and speaks into it. She gives the date and says she is here with me to make a recording. 'I hope you're not angry with me for . . . I don't know what for, but I hope you're not angry with me anyway,' she says to Jack. 'Have you got anything you would like to say to us?'

She leaves a gap which is filled by silence. Then she asks me if I would like to say something.

I take a deep breath. 'I wonder if Ruth, my sister, is with you and could . . . speak to me.'

There is another silence. 'I hesitate to cut in,' Judith says politely. 'I hope I'm not cutting across what's being said, but as we don't really know where you are, Jack, if it is Jack who's speaking, we're not sure whether Ruth is there as well.'

After five minutes or so, she turns the machine off. She rewinds the tape and plays it back. This time I hear the voices. I know I hear them.

I can't make out what they are saying, but I hear them, faint, like moths fluttering against a light bulb. I can't hear Ruth's voice, but I do hear a man's voice – Jack Hallam! – saying, hoarsely, 'Ruth!'

Judith is excited. 'That's Jack!' she says. 'It's definitely Jack! I recognize everything about him! He always hogs the recorder! He's so stroppy ... But if he's there, they're all there. It stands to reason, doesn't it? It proves that there is life after death.

'You needn't worry about your sister any more,' she continues. 'She's OK. That's an amazing thought, isn't it?'

But I can't hear *her*. I hear Judith but I can't hear Ruth. I suddenly feel dog-tired, as if I'm swimming against the tide. Judith wants to replay the tape, over and over again, but I'm too exhausted to listen. She wants to make a transcript, now, with me, but I say no, it's late, I have to go home. So she makes me a copy of the tape, and we say goodbye.

At home, I take my tape into the kitchen, where Neill is sitting at the table.

'How was it?' he asks.

'Listen to this,' I say, 'just listen to this. I *heard* the voices.'

I play the tape out loud to him. But there is nothing to hear, apart from Judith's voice and mine.

'There's nothing here,' Neill says.

'There is,' I say. 'Well, there was. It must be a bad copy.'

I play it again. I play him the bit where Jack Hallam says 'Ruth!' But it doesn't sound like her name any more. 'That's the sound of a chair moving,' Neill says, 'or the click of the components in the machine, or your breathing. It's just your breathing.'

My face isn't moving but he looks at me as if I'm crying.

'You need to get some sleep,' he says. 'You've got to get some rest now. You'll feel better in the morning.'

Thursday 1 June I dream that I am cycling over Blackfriars Bridge to visit Ruth's children and her husband and his girlfriend. They have just moved into a new house and it takes me forever to get there, and when I arrive I'm hot and cross. I can't find anywhere to leave my bicycle, and Lola, Ruth's daughter, looks sad and Matt, Ruth's husband, looks anxious and where, exactly, am I supposed to sit? Then, in my dream, I see Ruth – and for the first time since her death, I see her not as sick

Ruth, dying Ruth, but Ruth as full of life as ever. I know that she is dead, that nobody other than me can see her ghost, but she looks happy and spirited, and she flashes her brilliant smile at me and tosses her pre-cancer halo of dark curls. She says nothing, and I am silent too, but it doesn't matter. I have seen my sister. My sister has seen me.

Thursday 8 June After my dream of Ruth, the date with Arthur Molinary seems less pressing; but now it is here, after all this waiting, and why waste the appointment? This time I feel no excitement as I climb the stairs to the second floor of the College of Psychic Studies. Inside Room Four, Arthur Molinary is waiting for me, a glass of water on the table in front of him, the sun shining through an open window. He gestures me to a chair opposite him, and looks at me through his pebble spectacles, head cocked to one side like a magpie. And then he begins to speak, and at first all I hear is the echoes of other voices in his voice: Yiddish, Italian, Spanish, northern English, merging and separating. I say nothing. He pauses, as if listening to the silence, and then starts talking again. 'You have someone here with you who is very close to you. She's your sister, your best friend, and she loves you very much. She knows that you love her. But she says, why are you unhappy? She is happy now and she wants you to be happy. She comes to you every night when you fall asleep. She is with you . . .'

'What does she want me to do?'

'She wants you to be happy,' Arthur Molinary says, with a small shrug of his shoulders in his buttercup cotton shirt.

He tells me other things: things I already know ('She had two lumps in her breast, and then her brain was troubled . . . she was confused and her legs grew weak, she couldn't walk . . . and when she died, she couldn't breathe, her lungs filled up . . . she died in the night and in the morning you sat and held her body').

Then he asks me a question. 'Your sister says, why don't you believe in God?'

'Well, *she* never used to,' I say, evasively.

'She does now,' he says, with another slight shrug of his shoulders, a quick blink behind his glasses. This somehow seems to me unlikely, though I do not say so out loud.

And just who is talking anyway? Is it Arthur Molinary, or my silent voice, or my sister's that he is listening to? Can he hear my thoughts, or is he stating the obvious here? And does it matter, anyway, because now I realize that I am her, and she is me, and my sister lives on inside my head and courses through my blood like life itself.

At home that night, I listen to the tape that Arthur Molinary made for me of our session. A lot of it is quite wonderfully true of Ruth, and some of it just as wonderfully banal. (My grandmother on the other side wants me to eat more Marmite, for the vitamins.)

Mostly, though, he is sensitive. He is a very senior sensitive, after all. As I listen to the tape, my faith in what he's telling me ebbs and flows. But I love my sister. And my sister loved me. And now I know, that after all this, in the end there is a beginning, there is life after death, because I am still living . . . Or that is what I seem to know, and I tell that to my husband as we lie in bed at the end of the long day.

He listens to me and then says, 'Have I ever told you about my friend, Tony King, who killed himself? He walked into the River Thames and drowned. It was after the death of his mother, but also he heard voices in his head. He was schizophrenic.'

'Well, I'm not mad,' I say, 'if that's what you're suggesting.'

'I'm not suggesting anything,' he says evenly. 'I'm just telling you about Tony . . . I'm sure I've told you this before – his mother died of a bee sting, and on my mother's birthday, he gave her a glass jar with three Roman nails in it that he had found on the shore of the Thames. He loved the river.'

'How did he know they were Roman nails?' I sound as if we're in court, not bed. 'That's too symbolic, like they were the ones used to nail Christ to the cross or something.'

'I don't know if they actually were Roman,' Neill says, 'but that's what he believed them to be. Anyhow, a couple of years after he died you and I played on a Ouija board one night with some friends.'

'That doesn't sound like you,' I say, 'the great sceptic, and I can't remember anything like that.'

'It was our first New Year's Eve together,' he says – and then I do recall the scene, but only that: no words, no story.

'I still felt guilty about Tony, I suppose, and I missed him. Anyway, I asked him where he was and the board spelled "home". I said, "Where's home?" And he said, "The sea".'

'So you do believe in something,' I say, point scoring while missing the point, trying to keep a small triumph out of my voice.

'I don't believe in one thing or the other,' he says. 'It made me feel better, that's all.'

'I'm feeling better now,' I say.

'I know,' he says. 'I'm glad.'

11 June Pentecostal Sunday in the year 2000. The voice on the radio at breakfast this morning tells me that this is the day of the coming of Jesus's spirit: fifty days after he ascended to heaven, his spirit returned to his disciples on earth, just in the nick of time, just as they were sinking into despair as they waited for a sign in an upstairs room.

In my own upstairs an email has arrived from my father. He composed it yesterday as an early birthday present for me; a reconsideration of his father, written at my request. 'Your grandfather Louis was evangelized into an inspirational form of Christianity by a highly unorthodox class teacher when he was about nine or ten,' my father has written. 'He wept at the account of the crucifixion . . . He was soft and sentimental, easily moved to tears. Later, people pitied me for having such a naive father and didn't blame me as much as him for my "meshugassen" – madnesses . . . As well as going to seances he went in for aura-seeing, through violet-tinted motorcycle glasses,' my father continues crossly, though maybe he was smiling, as I do now, grateful for these fragile threads of memory that bind us together. 'I was shown the invisible aura of myself and others at the age of about eleven, and I knew from then on that my father belonged to the World of strange cults which gave him the sense of belonging . . . Of course he despised Freudian insights into his very evident mechanisms of denial and projection of his deep cultural unease.'

There is more, but it's enough for now – I don't want to stay in with God on the radio or Christ on the computer (or Freud, which is where I know my father's birthday message is heading). So I send him a quick email back, telling him that I love him. Then we go out into the park, my husband and my children and some neighbours. The boys play football together, while I go for a walk with my dead friend Kimberley's daughter, Juliette, who is my elder son's best friend. The local churches have congregated on the dried grass of the old bowling green for a Pentecostal celebration; Juliette and I stay on the outskirts of the crowd, unwilling, or maybe just unable to join in the hymns because we don't know the words.

A woman walks towards us, smiling. She hands me a hymn sheet and the order of service, HOLY SPIRIT WHO ARE YOU? is printed at the top of the page, and then the words to the hymn 'Shine, Jesus, Shine'. I can see the choir and the congregation singing, but their voices are lost in the open air. I can't hear the words so I read them instead. 'Lord, I come to Your awesome presence/from the shadows into Your radiance/by the blood may I enter Your brightness . . .' But God doesn't speak to me, again, and all I feel is slightly embarrassed, as if I'm intruding. I look down at Juliette, though she's not looking at me, she's looking at all the people around us, watching quietly without saying a word.

'Shall we go?' I ask her.

'I don't mind,' she says, and then meets my eyes and smiles. We walk away, across the park, while the voices of the congregation drift into nothing behind us, into the wide, empty sky, where the silence reaches to the end of everything, where the dead wait, and speak in the beat of our hearts.

> So, if I dream I have you, I have you,
> For all our joys are but fantastical.

'Elegy 10: The Dream', John Donne

FAMOUS PEOPLE

Orhan Pamuk

Life is dull if there's no story to listen to or nothing to watch. When I was a child, if we weren't staring out of the window at the street and the passers-by, or into the apartments of the building opposite, we were listening to the radio, on top of which a small porcelain dog perpetually slept. Back then, in 1958, there was no television in Turkey. But we'd never admit to not having it. We'd optimistically say, just like we said about one of the legendary Hollywood movies which took some years to reach Istanbul: 'It hasn't come yet.'

Staring out of the window was such an essential habit that when television finally did arrive, people started watching it as if they were still looking outside. My father, my uncle and my grandmother talked and argued in front of the television without looking at one another, and described what they saw, as they used to do when gazing out of the window.

'At this rate, the snow will be really thick,' my aunt would say, for example, watching the snow that had been falling since morning.

'That halva-seller's come to Nishantashi again!' I'd say, peering through the other window at the tramlines.

On Sundays, we would go upstairs to my grandmother's apartment for lunch along with my aunts and uncles who, like us, lived on the building's lower floors. I'd wait for the food to be brought in, staring out of the window. I'd be so excited to be among this noisy gathering of relatives that the living room – dimly lit by the crystal chandelier hanging over the dining table – would brighten before my eyes.

My grandmother's living room was always in semi-darkness, like those on the other floors, but to me it seemed even gloomier. Maybe this was because of the net curtains and heavy drapes that hung in terrifying shadows at the edges of the balcony doors that were always kept closed. Or maybe it seemed that way to me because of the stuffy, cluttered rooms that smelled of dust and were filled with old worn wooden chests, screens inlaid with mother-of-pearl, colossal oak tables with elegant claw feet and a baby grand piano whose lid was covered with framed photographs.

After lunch one Sunday, my uncle, who was smoking a cigarette in one of the dark rooms that opened off the dining room, announced: 'I have two tickets for the football match, but I'm not going. Why doesn't your father take both of you.'

'Yes! Take us to the game, Dad!' said my older brother from the other room.

'It will give the boys some fresh air,' my mother said.

'Why don't *you* take them out,' said my father.

'I'm going to visit my mother,' my mother said.

'We don't *want* to go to Grandma's,' said my brother.

'You can take the car,' said my uncle.

'Come on, Dad, please,' said my brother.

There was a long, awkward silence, as if my father could sense what everyone in the room was thinking about him.

'Give me the keys, then,' my father said to my uncle.

Later, downstairs on our floor, my father smoked and paced the long hallway while my mother dressed us in thick patterned wool socks and made us put on two sweaters each. My uncle's elegant cream-coloured 1952 Dodge was parked in front of the Teshvikiye Mosque. My father agreed to let us both sit in the front seat. The engine started at the first turn of the key.

There wasn't a queue at the stadium entrance. 'This ticket is for both of them,' my father said to the man at the turnstile. 'One is eight, the other is ten.' Afraid to catch the ticket-man's eyes, we walked inside. There were plenty of empty seats in the stands. We sat down.

The teams were already on the muddy field and I liked seeing the players running back and forth in their white shorts warming up. 'Look, that's Little Mehmet,' my brother pointed out. 'He was called up from the junior team.'

'I know that, thanks.'

Sometime after the game began, when the entire stadium had grown mysteriously quiet, I stopped concentrating on the players and my mind began to wander: Why do footballers all wear the same strip but keep their own names? I watched the names as they ran around. Their shorts were gradually getting muddier. Later, I saw the slow-moving funnel of a ship passing behind the bleachers as it made its way through the Bosporus. There was no score at half time, and my father bought us a paper cone of roasted chickpeas and a pitta bread with melted cheese.

'Dad, I can't finish all of my pitta,' I said, showing him what was left in my hand.

'Just put it down,' he said. 'No one will notice.'

At half time we stood up and moved around, trying to keep warm along with everybody else. Just like my father, my brother and I put our hands in our trouser pockets and turned our backs to the field. We were watching the other spectators when a man in the crowd called out to my father. My father cupped his hand to his ear, gesturing that he couldn't hear over the din.

'I can't come now,' he said, pointing to us. 'I'm with the kids.'

The man in the crowd wore a purple scarf. He came down the rows, stepping over the backs of seats, pushing and prodding people out of his way, to sit beside us.

'Are they yours?' he asked after they had embraced and he had kissed my father on both cheeks. 'They're so grown-up. It's unbelievable.'

My father didn't reply.

'How did you manage it?' the man said, looking at us in disbelief. 'Did you get married straight after school?'

'Yes,' said my father without looking at him. They talked some more. The man with the purple scarf placed a single unshelled peanut in each of our palms. After he left, my father sat in silence.

The teams were back on the field wearing clean shorts when my father said, 'Come on, let's get back home. You two are cold.'

'I'm not cold,' my brother said.

'No, you boys are cold,' my father insisted. 'Ali's cold. Come on, let's see you get up.'

As we left, bumping knees and treading on toes, we trod on the cheese pitta I'd dropped on the ground. Walking down the stairs, we heard the referee's whistle signalling the start of the second half. 'Are you cold?' my brother asked me. 'Why didn't you say you weren't cold?'

I didn't answer.

'You idiot,' my brother said.

'You can listen to the second half on the radio at home,' said my father.

'It isn't on the radio,' my brother said.

'Hush,' my father said. 'On the way back I'll take you through Taksim Square.'

We were silent. After passing the square, our father parked the car by the off-track betting window, as we'd guessed he would. 'Don't open the doors for anyone,' he said. 'I'll be right back.'

He got out. Before he could lock the doors from the outside, we pushed down the locks from the inside, but my father didn't go to the betting window. He ran down the cobbled street and crossed to the other side where he went into a shop with posters of ships, large plastic model planes, and pictures of beaches in the window.

'Where's Dad going?' I said.

'When we get home, do you want to play Tops or Bottoms?' my brother asked.

When my father came back, my brother was playing with the gear lever. We quickly drove to Nishantashi. He parked the car in front of the mosque again. As we passed Aladdin's, the cut-price shop, my father said, 'Why don't I buy you two something? But not that Famous People series again.'

'Oh, please, Dad, please!' we said jumping up and down.

My father bought us ten pieces each of the gum that came with pictures of famous people folded up with it. Back home in the lift I thought I'd pee out of excitement. It was warm in the apartment and our mother hadn't come back yet. We unwrapped the gum quickly and dropped the wrappers on the floor. I ended up with two Marshal Fevzi Çakmaks, one Chaplin, one of the wrestler Hamit Kaplan, a Gandhi, a Mozart, a De Gaulle, two Atatürks, and a number 21, Greta Garbo, which my brother didn't have. My total was 173 famous people, but I was still twenty-seven short of a complete set. My brother ended up with four Marshal Fevzi Çakmaks, five Atatürks, and an Edison. We each tossed a piece of gum into our mouths and began reading the captions on the back of the pictures:

Marshal Fevzi Çakmak
Commanding Officer, Turkish War of Independence
(1876–1950)
Mambo Candy & Gum Co.
A leather football will be awarded to the lucky person
who collects all 100 Famous People

My brother held the 165 pictures he'd collected in a stack in his hand. 'Let's play Tops or Bottoms,' he said.

'No.'

'I'll give you twelve of my Marshal Çakmaks for one Greta Garbo,' he said. 'Then you'll have a total of 184.'

'Nope.'

'But you have two Greta Garbos.'

I didn't say anything.

'When they give us our inoculations tomorrow at school, you'll be in a lot of pain,' he said. 'So don't come crying to me, all right?'

'I won't.'

After we'd had dinner in silence, we listened to the Sports World programme and found out that the game had ended in a two–all draw. When my mother came into our room to put us to bed and my brother was sorting out his school bag, I ran into the living room. My father was gazing out into the street.

'I don't want to go to school tomorrow, Dad,' I said.

'How come?'

'We're going to have our jabs,' I said. 'They make my temperature go up, and then I have a hard time breathing. Mum knows about it.'

He didn't answer, but just looked at me. I ran and got him a pen and paper from the drawer.

'Are you sure your mother knows?' he asked as he placed the paper on top of the Kierkegaard he was always reading but never finished. 'You'll go to school, but you won't get the jabs,' he said. 'That's what I'm writing.'

He signed the note. I blew on the ink, folded it up and put it into my pocket. I rushed back into our bedroom, put the note into my bag, then climbed on to my bed and started jumping up and down.

'Behave yourself,' my mother said. 'Go to sleep, now.'

*

At school, right after lunch, the whole class assembled in two columns and we headed back down to the foul-smelling cafeteria to be inoculated. Some of us were crying, others were in a state of frightened anticipation. When I caught a whiff of the iodine coming up from below, my heart quickened. I left the line and went to the teacher at the top of the stairs. The class clattered past us making a tremendous commotion.

'Yes,' said the teacher. 'What is it?'

I took the note my father had written from my pocket and handed it to the teacher. She read it with a frown. 'But your father isn't a doctor,' she said. She thought for a moment. 'Go upstairs. Wait in 2A,' she said.

Upstairs in 2A there were six or seven other excused children like myself. One was staring in terror out of the window. From the corridor came an endless din of crying and turmoil. A fat kid with glasses was eating sunflower seeds and reading a Kinova cartoon book. The door opened and Seyfi Bey, the skeletal assistant principal, entered.

'No offence to you students who are perhaps genuinely sick,' he said. 'This is for those of you who are faking. One day, you'll all be called on to serve your country, maybe even die for it. If those of you who have avoided your shots today don't have a proper excuse then, you'll have committed an act of treason. Shame on you!'

We were silent. Glancing at Atatürk's picture, my eyes began to water.

Later we went back quietly to our classrooms. The ones who had been inoculated were long-faced. Some had their sleeves rolled up, others had tears in their eyes, and they were pushing and bumping into each other.

'Those of you who live nearby can go home,' said the teacher. 'Those of you who need someone to accompany you will wait here until the last bell. Don't hit each other in the arm like that! School is cancelled tomorrow.'

We cheered. Downstairs at the main gate some of the students who were leaving rolled up their sleeves and showed off their iodine stains to the doorman, Hilmi Effendi.

As soon as I was outside on the street with my bag in my hand I began to run. A horse-drawn cart was blocking the pavement in front of Karabet's butcher's shop. Running between the cars, I crossed to our side of the street. I ran past Hayri's fabric shop and Salih's flower shop. Our doorman, Hazim Effendi, let me in.

'What are you doing home at this hour?' he said.

'They gave us our jabs,' I said. 'Then they let us out of school.'

'Where's your brother? Did you walk back alone?'

'I crossed the tramlines by myself. There's no school tomorrow.'

'Your mother isn't home,' he said. 'Why don't you go up to your grandmother's.'

'I'm sick,' I said. 'I want to go to our floor. Let me in.'

He took the key from the hook on the wall and we went into the lift. In the time it took to go upstairs, the lift was filled with his cigarette smoke, which burned my eyes. He let me into the apartment. 'Don't fiddle with the lights,' he said, closing the door behind him as he left.

Though there was nobody there, I shouted, 'Is anybody home? I'm home, I'm home!' I dropped my bag, pulled open my brother's desk drawer and began to examine the film-ticket collection he'd never show me. After that I became so engrossed in the scrapbook where he pasted newspaper clippings of football games that I panicked when I heard the front door being unlocked. I knew it wasn't my mother by the sound of the steps. It was my father. I carefully replaced my brother's tickets and scrapbook so he couldn't tell I'd disturbed them.

My father walked into his bedroom, opened his wardrobe, and looked inside.

'Oh, you're at home?'

'No, I'm in Paris,' I said, the way they did at school.

'Didn't you go to school today?'

'Today was inoculation day.'

'Where's your brother? All right then, let's see you go and sit quietly in your room.'

I did as he said. Resting my forehead on the windowpane, I looked outside. From the sounds he made, I realized that he was taking down one of the suitcases from the hall cupboard. He went back into his room. He took his sports jackets and trousers out of the wardrobe; I recognized the hangers by their tinny sound. He opened and closed the drawers where he kept his shirts and socks. I heard him put them all into his suitcase. He went in and out of the bathroom. He shut the suitcase and locked the metallic clasps with a perfect click. He came to find me in my room.

'What are you doing in here?'

'Staring out of the window.'

'Come over here,' he said.

He pulled me on to his lap and together we looked outside. The tips of the tall cypress trees between us and the opposite apartment building began to sway slowly in a gentle breeze. I liked the way my dad smelled.

'I'm going far away,' he said. He kissed me. 'Don't tell your mother anything. I'll tell her later.'

'By plane?'

'Yes,' he said, 'to Paris. Don't say anything to anyone.' He took out a large two-and-a-half lira note and gave it to me. 'Don't mention this to anyone, either,' he added, and kissed me again. 'Or that you saw me here . . .'

I immediately pocketed the money. When he lowered me from his lap and picked up his suitcase, I said, 'Don't go, Dad.'

He kissed me again and left.

I watched him from the window. He walked towards Aladdin's store, then hailed a passing taxi. Before he bent down to get into the car, he glanced back at the apartment building and waved to me. I waved back and he disappeared.

I stared at the empty street. A tram went by and then the water-seller's cart pulled by its plodding horse. I rang the bell, calling for Hazim Effendi.

'Did you ring the bell?' he asked when he arrived. 'Don't play with the bell.'

'Take this two-and-a-half lira!' I said. 'Go to Aladdin's and buy me ten pieces of the Famous People gum. And don't forget to bring back the fifty kurus change.'

'Did your father give you the money?' he asked. 'Your mother won't be angry, will she?'

I didn't answer. From the window, I watched him go into the store. A few minutes later he came out and on his way back he ran into the doorman of the Marmara apartments on the opposite side of the street. They chatted.

When he came back he gave me the change. I unwrapped the gum straight away: three more Marshal Fevzi Çakmaks, one Atatürk, one each of Lindbergh, Leonardo da Vinci, Sultan Süleyman the Magnificent, Churchill and General Franco, and another number 21, Greta Garbo, which my brother didn't have. My total now was 183. But I was still missing twenty-six cards for a complete set.

While I was admiring the number 91 Lindbergh photo for the first time, taken in front of the plane he'd flown across the Atlantic, I heard someone unlocking the door. My mother! I quickly threw away the gum wrappers that had dropped on the floor.

'We had our jabs. I came back early,' I said, 'You know, typhoid, typhus, tetanus.'

'Where's your brother?'

'His class hasn't been inoculated yet,' I said. 'They sent us home. I crossed the street by myself.'

'Does it hurt?'

I didn't say anything.

Before long, my brother came home. He was in pain, and he lay on the bed on his right side frowning as he fell asleep. By the time he woke up it was almost dark outside. 'Mum, it really hurts,' he said.

'You'll have a fever by evening,' said my mother from the living room as she ironed.

'Ali, does yours hurt as well? Lie down and be still.'

We lay motionless, resting. After a nap, my brother sat up and read the sports section of the paper and told me that we'd missed seeing four goals yesterday because of me.

'If we hadn't left, they might not have scored any goals,' I said.

'What?'

After another nap my brother offered to trade me six Marshal Çakmaks, four Atatürks, and three other pictures I already had for one Greta Garbo.

I refused.

'Do you want to play Tops or Bottoms?' he asked then.

'OK, let's play.'

The game went like this: you sandwiched a stack of Famous People pictures between your palms and asked 'tops or bottoms?' If the other person said 'bottoms' you took out the picture at the bottom of the stack, let's say it was a number 78, Rita Hayworth, for example. Say number 18, the poet Dante, was on top. Then bottoms would win the round because it had the higher number and you'd have to give up one of your least favourite pictures. We traded pictures of Marshal Fevzi Çakmak until evening. At dinner time my mother said, 'One of you go up and take a look, maybe your father's come home.'

We both went upstairs. My father wasn't there. My uncle and my grandmother were smoking. We listened to the news on the radio and read the sports section. When my grandmother and uncle sat down to dinner, we went back downstairs.

'Where have you been?' my mother said. 'You didn't eat anything upstairs, did you? I'd better give you your lentil soup now. You can eat it slowly until your father arrives.'

'Isn't there any toast?' my brother said.

My mother watched us as we silently ate our soup. I could tell she was listening for the lift by the way she cocked her head and avoided our eyes. When we'd finished, she looked into the pot and said, 'Do you want any more? I should probably have mine before it gets cold.' But instead, she walked to the window that overlooked Nishantashi Square and gazed down in silence. She came back to the table and started eating her soup. My brother and I were talking about yesterday's game when suddenly she said, 'Shush! Isn't that the lift?'

We listened carefully. It wasn't the lift. A tram went by, faintly jiggling the table and the water in the glasses and the jug. As we were eating our oranges, we actually did hear the lift. It came nearer and nearer, but passed us on the way to my grandmother's on the top floor. 'It went upstairs,' my mother said.

When dinner was over, she said, 'Take your plates into the kitchen, but leave your father's place.' We cleared the table. Our father's empty dinner plate remained on the table.

My mother walked to the window facing the police station and gazed outside. As if she had suddenly come to a decision, she cleared away my father's plate, his knife, fork and spoon, and took them into the kitchen. She didn't wash the dishes. 'I'm going up to your grandmother's,' she said. 'Don't fight.'

My brother and I began a round of Tops or Bottoms.

'Tops,' I said, starting off.

He showed me the picture at the top of his stack first: 'The world-renowned wrestler Yusuf the Giant, number 34,' he said. Then he looked at the bottom of the stack, 'Atatürk, number 50,' he said. 'You lose. Hand one over.'

The more we played, the more he won. He quickly took nineteen number 21 Marshal Fevzi Çakmaks and two Atatürks from me.

'I quit,' I said angrily. 'I'm going upstairs with Mum.'

'She'll be mad.'

'You're just afraid of staying here by yourself, chicken!'

The door to my grandmother's apartment was open as usual. They'd finished dinner. The cook, Bekir, was washing the dishes and my uncle and grandmother sat facing each other. My mother was standing at the window overlooking Nishantashi Square.

'Come here,' she said, without moving her gaze from the window. I quickly squeezed into the space between my mother's body and the window, the space that seemed to be reserved just for me. I leaned my body against hers and, like her, began to stare out at Nishantashi Square. My mother put her hand on my forehead and stroked my hair.

'I know your father came home, and you saw him around noon,' she whispered.

'Yes.'

'Did he tell you where he was going, my love?'

'No,' I said, 'he gave me a two-and-a-half lira bill.'

The darkened shop fronts on the street below us, the car headlights, the absence of the traffic policeman from his usual spot, the wet cobblestones, the letters that made up the advertisements hanging from the trees, they were all so very lonely and sad. When it started to rain, my mother was still slowly stroking my hair.

I realized that the radio which always sat between my uncle and grandmother, the radio that was always on, was silent, and this frightened me.

'Don't just stand there, my dear girl,' said my grandmother after a while. 'Come here, please, and sit down.'

Meanwhile, my brother had also come upstairs.

'Go into the kitchen, you two,' my uncle said. 'Bekir,' he called. 'Make a ball for them, so they can play football in the hall.'

In the kitchen, Bekir had finished the dishes: 'Have a seat,' he said. He began to crumple and shape a ball from the newspapers he had fetched from the small glassed-in balcony off my grandmother's room. 'How's this?' he asked, when the ball was about the size of his fist.

'A bit bigger,' said my brother.

Bekir wrapped a few more sheets of newspaper round the growing wad. Through the half-open door, I noticed that my mother had sat down across from my grandmother and uncle. Bekir wound the string he had taken from the drawer tighter and tighter round the newspaper ball, making it perfectly round, and then tied a knot. To smooth out the remaining jutting corners of newspaper, he dampened the ball with a wet rag. Unable to contain himself, my brother grabbed it.

'Oh, man, it's hard as a rock.'

'Put your finger there,' said Bekir.

My brother carefully put his finger on the place where the string had been knotted and Bekir finished the ball off by tying one final knot. He tossed it into the air and we began kicking it.

'Out in the hallway,' said Bekir. 'You'll break everything here.'

We played furiously for a long time. I imagined I was Lefter of Fenerbahçe and could dodge my opponents like he could. Making wall passes, I ran into my brother's sore arm. He hit me, too, but I felt nothing. We were covered in sweat and the ball was coming apart. I was beating him five–three when I really laid into his arm. He fell to the ground and began crying. 'When this stops hurting, I'll kill you,' he said from where he lay.

I ducked into the living room. My grandmother, my mother and uncle had moved into the den. My grandmother was on the phone, dialling.

'Hello, dear,' she said in the same distant tone she adopted when she said 'my dear girl' to my mother. 'Is this the Yeshilkoy airport terminal? Yes, dear, we want to ask after a passenger on one of today's flights to Europe.' She gave my father's name and waited, winding the telephone cord around her finger. 'Go and get me my cigarettes,' she said to my uncle. When he left the room, my grandmother lifted the receiver away from her ear slightly.

'My dear girl, please,' she said to my mother, 'you would know, is there another woman involved?'

I couldn't hear my mother's reply. My grandmother regarded her as if she hadn't said anything at all. The person on the other end spoke and my grandmother said angrily to my uncle, who had returned with cigarettes and an ashtray in his hand, 'They're not giving me an answer.'

My mother must have been alerted to my presence by the expression on my uncle's face. She grabbed me by the arm and dragged me out into the hall. Sliding her hand from the nape of my neck down my back, she could feel how much I was sweating, but she didn't seem to care that I might catch a chill.

'Mum, my arm hurts,' said my brother.

'We'll go downstairs now, and I'll put you to bed.'

Downstairs, on our floor, the three of us moved silently. Before going to bed, I went into the kitchen in my pyjamas for a drink of water then walked into the living room. My mother was in front of the window, smoking.

'You'll catch a cold walking about in your bare feet,' she said when she heard me.

'Has your brother gone to sleep?'

'He's asleep. Mum, I want to tell you something.' I waited to position my body between my mother and the window. When my mother moved, creating that perfect space, I squeezed in. 'Dad's gone to Paris,' I said, 'and do you know which suitcase he took?'

She didn't say a thing. In the stillness of the night we watched the rainy street.

My maternal grandmother's house stood directly across from the Shishli Mosque, on the last tram stop before the station yard. Today, Shishli Square is filled with bus and minibus stands, multi-storey department stores covered in an orgy of signs, tall ugly buildings riddled with offices and armies of sandwich-carrying employees who flood the pavements like ants during the lunch hour. Back then it was a large, peaceful cobbled square, a fifteen-minute walk from our home. Walking under mulberry and linden trees, holding my mother's hands, it seemed as if we had reached the very edges of the city.

One side of my grandmother's four-storey stone house, which was shaped like a matchbox standing on end, faced west, towards old Istanbul; the other side faced east, towards the mulberry orchards and the first hills of Asia across the Bosporus. After her husband died and after she had married off her three daughters, my grandmother took to living in just one room of this house, which was packed from top to bottom with tables, armoires, pianos and piles of worn-out furniture. One of my aunts, my mother's oldest sister, would have meals prepared for my grandmother and bring them to the house herself or send them in containers with a driver. My grandmother wouldn't even venture into the other rooms, which were covered in a thick layer of dust and silky spider's webs, to tidy up, let alone go downstairs two flights to make herself something to eat. Just like her own mother, who had spent the last years of her life alone in a large wooden mansion, my grandmother wouldn't allow a caretaker, a housekeeper, or a maid to enter the house after she'd been stricken by this mysterious plague of loneliness.

Whenever we came to visit, my mother would ring the bell for a long time and bang on the heavy door, until finally my grandmother opened the rusty shutters of the second-storey window facing the mosque and peered down at us. Because she couldn't rely on her failing eyesight, she had us call to her and wave.

'Move away from the door, boys, so your grandmother can see you,' my mother would say. She'd walk to the middle of the pavement with us, waving and shouting, 'Mother, it's me and the boys, it's us, can you hear us?'

We'd know that our grandmother had seen and recognized us from the sweet smile that would light up her face. She'd turn quickly back inside, walk into her room, remove the large key she kept under her pillow and, after wrapping it in newspaper, toss it out of the window to us. My brother and I would jostle each other to be the one to catch it.

This time, since my brother's arm was still hurting him, he didn't try for the key and I ran and grabbed it off the pavement and handed it to my mother. She turned it inside the lock with difficulty. The large iron door opened slowly as we applied our combined weight to it, and from the darkness within came the stagnant smell of mould, age, and stuffiness – a smell I have never encountered anywhere else. On a coat stand next to the door hung my grandfather's fur-collared coat and felt hat that my grandmother had put there to scare away thieves, and off to one side rested his boots, which always frightened me.

We saw our grandmother in the distance, standing at the top of the dark wooden staircase that went straight up two flights. In the whitish light filtering through the frosted art-deco glass, she stood, cane in hand, not moving, a ghost in the shadows.

As she climbed the creaking stairs, my mother didn't say a word to her mother. ('How are you, Mother darling?' she'd say on other visits. 'I've missed you, Mother darling.' 'The weather's so very cold, Mother darling!') At the top of the stairs, I kissed my grandmother's hand and brought it to my forehead, as we used to do then, trying not to look at her, or at the large protruding mole on her wrist. Once again we were frightened by the sight of her single remaining tooth, her long chin and the hairs on her face, and as we entered her room, we stuck close to my mother and sat on either side of her. My grandmother climbed back into the large bed where she spent the majority of her day, wearing her long nightgown and thick woollen vest, and smiled at us with an expectant look that said, 'Go on, then, entertain me!'

'Your stove isn't working so well, Mother,' said my mother. She picked up the tongs and stoked the wood in the stove.

My grandmother waited a moment. 'Leave it right now,' she said. 'Tell me some news. What's going on in the world?'

'Nothing at all!' my mother said.

'Don't you have anything to tell me?'

After we were silent for a time, my grandmother asked, 'Haven't you seen anyone?'

'Not really, Mother,' said my mother.

'For the sake of Allah, isn't there any news?'

There was a pause.

'Grandma,' I said, 'we had our jabs.'

'*Did* you?' said my grandmother, opening her blue eyes wide. 'And did it hurt?'

'My arm's sore,' said my brother.

'Oh my goodness!' said my grandmother, smiling.

Another long silence. My brother and I stood and looked out of the window at the distant hilltops, the mulberry trees and the old empty chicken coop in the backyard.

'Don't you have a story for me?' my grandmother asked my mother, imploringly. 'You must go up to your mother-in-law's floor. Doesn't anyone drop in there?'

'Lady Dilruba came to visit yesterday afternoon,' my mother said. 'She played bezique with the children's grandmother.'

Delighted by this, my grandmother said what we knew she would say: '*She* was raised in the palace!'

Of course, by 'palace' we understood her to mean Dolmabahçe

Palace, not the colourful Western palaces that I'd read about for years in storybooks and newspapers. It was much later that I realized my grandmother's belittling implication that Lady Dilruba had been a *cariye*, a lady slave in the sultan's harem, not only demeaned Lady Dilruba, who had spent her youth in the harem and was later made to marry a businessman, but also my father's mother, who was her friend. Next they moved on to the subject that was guaranteed for discussion on each visit: once a week my grandmother lunched alone at Aptullah Effendi's famous and expensive restaurant in the Beyoglu district, after which she'd complain at length about everything she'd eaten. The third regular topic of conversation was introduced by my grandmother's sudden question: 'Boys, does your grandmother give you parsley to eat?'

As our mother had prompted us beforehand, we said in unison: 'No, Grandma, she doesn't.'

As usual, my grandmother explained how she had seen a cat urinating on parsley in a garden, adding that in all probability that very parsley, without being properly washed, had been served in who knows what idiot's meal, and she further explained how she squabbled with the greengrocers of Nishantashi and Shishli who still sold parsley, trying to convince them they should stop.

'Mother,' said my mother, 'the children are restless, they want to explore. Why don't I unlock the room across the hall?'

To prevent a thief getting into the house, my grandmother kept every door locked. My mother opened up the large, cold room which looked out over the tramlines and for a moment we all stood surveying the armchairs and divans covered in white sheets, the rusting dusty lamps, the chests, the yellowed stacks of newspaper, and the drooping handlebars and worn-out seat of a girl's bicycle which leaned forlornly in a corner. But this time she didn't happily pull something out of the chests to show us, as she would do when she was in better spirits. ('Your mother used to wear these sandals when she was little, my darlings.' 'Look, here's your aunt's school frock!' 'Do you want to see the piggy bank your mother had when she was small, my darlings?')

'If it gets too cold, come back into the other room,' she said as she left.

My brother and I ran to the window and looked out at the mosque across the road and at the deserted tram stop in the square. Then we read about old football matches in the papers. 'I'm bored,' I said a bit later. 'Do you want to play Tops or Bottoms?'

'Do you want to lose again?' my brother said without lifting his head from the paper.

'I'm reading now.'

After last night's game, we'd played again in the morning and my brother had continued to beat me.

'Please.'

'On one condition. If I win you give me two pictures, if you win, you get one.'

'No.'

'Then I'm not playing,' said my brother. 'As you can see, I'm reading the paper.'

He ostentatiously held his newspaper the same way the English detective had in the black-and-white film we'd seen recently at the Angel Theatre. After gazing out of the window for some time, I decided to accept my brother's rules. We took our Famous People stacks out of our pockets and began the game. I was winning at first, then I lost seventeen more pictures.

'I always lose this way,' I said. 'If we don't play like we used to, I'm giving up.'

'OK,' said my brother, imitating the detective. 'I was going to read the papers anyway.'

I went to the window and carefully counted my pictures: I had 121 left. Yesterday, after my dad had gone, there were 183! Why should I go on feeling so fed up? I accepted his terms.

At the beginning, I won some, then he began to beat me. As he added the pictures he'd taken from me to his pile, he tried to stop himself from smiling so I wouldn't get angry.

'If you want we can play by different rules,' he said a bit later. 'Whoever wins takes one picture. If I win I get to choose the picture, because I don't have some of the ones you do and you never give those up.'

I accepted, thinking I'd start to win. I don't know how it happened: I lost three times in a row and before I knew it, I'd given up two of my number 21 Greta Garbos and a number 78 King Farouk, which my brother already had. I wanted to win them all back at once so I upped the stakes. That's how I rapidly lost, in two rounds, my number 63

Einstein – which he didn't have – number 3 Rumi, number 100 Sarkis Nazaryan – the founder of the Mambo Gum and Candy Company – and number 51 Cleopatra.

I couldn't even swallow. Afraid I was going to cry, I ran to the window and looked outside. Five minutes ago, everything was so beautiful: the tram approaching its stop, the distant apartment buildings between the autumn chestnut trees with their falling leaves, the dog lying on the cobblestones lazily scratching itself. If only time would stop. If only I could go back five squares like in the horseracing game we played with dice, I'd never play Tops or Bottoms with my brother again.

'Let's play once more,' I said without taking my forehead off the windowpane.

'I'm not playing,' he said. 'You'll cry.'

'I *swear* I won't cry, Jevat,' I said earnestly, walking up to him. 'Only, let's play fair, like we did at first.'

'I'm reading the paper.'

'All right,' I said. I shuffled my dwindling stack of pictures. 'With the rules we last played by,' I said, 'tops or bottoms?'

'No crying allowed,' he said. 'All right then, tops.'

I won and he handed me a Marshal Fevzi Çakmak. I refused it. 'Please give me number 78 King Farouk.'

'No,' he said. 'That's not what we said.'

We played two more rounds and I lost. I shouldn't have played a third round: I surrendered my number 49, Napoleon, my hand trembling.

'I quit,' he said.

I begged him. We played twice more. When I lost, instead of giving him the pictures he wanted, I tossed the rest of my pile over his head. All of those number 28 Mae Wests and number 82 Jules Vernes, number 7 Sultan Mehmed the Conquerors and number 70 Queen Elizabeths, number 41 the journalist Celal Saliks and number 42 Voltaires that I had thought about one by one, painstakingly hidden and carefully collected every day for two-and-a-half months, flew into the air like butterflies and fell hopelessly to the ground.

If only I had a completely different life somewhere else. I headed towards my grandmother's room, then turned and quietly went down the creaky stairs thinking about our distant relative, an insurance salesman, who had killed himself. My father's mother had explained to me that people who commit suicide were condemned to a dark place underground and couldn't go to heaven. When I was almost at the bottom of the stairs, I stopped and stood in the darkness. Then I turned round again and went back upstairs and sat on the top step by my grandmother's room.

'I'm not well off like your mother-in-law,' I heard my grandmother say. 'You'll just have to take care of your children and wait.'

'But I'm asking you again, Mother, I want to move back in here with the children,' my mother said.

'You can't stay here in this dusty, haunted, thief-ridden house with two boys,' said my grandmother.

'But don't you remember, Mother, in the last years of Father's life, after my sisters married and left, how happy the three of us were living here together!'

'Mebrure, my dear, you'd only flip through your father's old magazines all day,' my grandmother said.

'I'd get the large stove downstairs lit and the whole house would warm up in two days.'

'I warned you about him before you got married,' said my grandmother.

'It would only take a couple of days to get rid of all the dust and dirt in the house, with the help of a maid.'

'I won't allow any pilfering maids to enter this house,' said my grandmother.

'Besides, it would take you six months to clean this place and get rid of all the spiders. In the meantime your wayward husband will have returned.'

'Is that your last word?' said my mother.

'Mebrure, my love, if you and the children move in here, how would we get by, the two of us?'

'But Mother, how many times have I asked you, begged you, to sell the property in Bebek before the government expropriates it?'

'I can't bring myself to go to the Land Registrar's office, sign my name, and give my photograph to those disgusting men.'

'But Mother, we sent you a lawyer, just so you wouldn't have to deal with that,' my mother said, her voice rising.

'I didn't trust that lawyer at all, not at all,' said my grandmother.

'You could tell from his face he was a swindler, I'm not even sure he was a real lawyer. And don't raise your voice at me.'

'Fine. I won't say anything else,' said my mother. She called to us, 'Children! Get ready, hurry, we're leaving.'

'Wait, where are you going?' said my grandmother. 'We haven't talked about anything yet.'

'You don't want us,' my mother whispered.

'Take this, buy the kids some sweets.'

'They shouldn't have any before lunch,' my mother said and went behind me into the room across the hall. 'Who scattered these pictures about? Pick them up right away. And you help him,' she said to my brother.

As we quietly picked up the Famous People pictures, my mother opened the old chests and looked at her childhood dresses, her ballet costumes, her angel costumes and everything else that was packed inside. The dust under the black skeleton of the pedal sewing machine filled my nostrils, making my eyes water.

As we washed our hands in the small closet, my grandmother said in her gentle imploring voice, 'Mebrure, why don't you take this teapot you're so fond of? It's rightfully yours. My grandfather – he was such a fine man – bought it for my mother when he was the governor of Damascus. It came all the way from China. Take it, please.'

'I don't want anything from you, Mother darling,' my mother said. 'Put it back in your cupboard, you'll break it. Come on, children, kiss your grandmother's hand.'

'But Mebrure, dearest, please don't even think of being angry at your poor mother,' my grandmother said as she held her hand out for us to kiss. 'Please, I beg of you, don't leave me here all alone without a visit.'

We quickly went down the stairs and the three of us pulled open the iron door. The glorious sunlight dazzled our eyes and the fresh air filled our lungs.

'Make sure you close the door properly!' my grandmother called out from the top of the stairs. 'Mebrure, stop by again this week, OK?'

We walked away in silence, holding our mother's hands. In the tram we sat quietly listening to the coughs of the other passengers until the tram left. When it set off, my brother and I moved up a row with the excuse that we wanted to sit in a seat where we could see the conductor, and began playing Tops or Bottoms. I won back some of the pictures I'd lost. In the confidence of winning, I upped the stakes and quickly began to lose again. At the Osmanbey stop, my brother changed the stakes, 'If I win I get the rest of your pile, if I lose, you get fifteen of your choice.'

We played. I lost. Secretly keeping two of the pictures, I gave the entire stack to him. I moved back a row and sat next to my mother. I didn't cry. Like my mother, I stared sadly out of the window as the tram gathered speed, moaning softly as it went, at the passing of all those people and places that no longer exist – the dressmakers' shops overflowing with spools of coloured thread and fabrics imported from Europe; the sun-faded, rain-tattered awnings of the pudding shops with their steamed-up windows, the bakeries with loaves of fresh bread neatly lining their shelves, the gloomy lobby of the Tan Film Theatre, where we saw films about ancient Rome full of slave girls more beautiful than goddesses, the street children selling used comic books in front of the cinema, the barber with the sharp moustache and scissors who always frightened me, and the half-naked local madman who always stood by the barber-shop door.

We left the tram at the Harbiye stop. As we walked home, my brother's smug silence drove me mad. I took the Lindbergh picture out of my pocket where I'd hidden it.

It was the first time he'd ever seen it. 'Number 91, Lindbergh,' he read with awe.

'With the plane he flew across the Atlantic! Where did you get that?'

'I didn't have my jabs yesterday,' I said. 'I came home from school early and saw Dad before he left. Dad bought it for me.'

'That means half of it is mine,' he said. 'Besides, in the last round we played for all your pictures.' He tried to snatch the picture out of my hand, but he wasn't fast enough. He grabbed my wrist and twisted it. I kicked him in the leg. We began fighting.

'Stop it!' my mother shouted. 'Stop it, you two! We're in the middle of the street!'

We stopped. A man in a suit and tie and a woman wearing a gigantic hat went past. I was embarrassed that we'd fought in public. My brother took two steps forward and then stumbled to his knees. 'It really hurts,' he said, holding his leg.

'Get up,' hissed my mother. 'Get up right now. Everyone's staring.'

My brother stood up and began limping like a wounded hero in a war movie. I was worried that maybe he really was hurt, but I was also satisfied to see him in that condition. After walking on in silence for a while, he said, 'You're going to get it when we get home.' He turned to my mother and said, 'Mum, Ali didn't get his jabs.'

'I did too, Mum.'

'Hush!' she shouted.

We'd reached the point across from our apartment. We waited for the tram coming from Maçka to pass before crossing the road. Immediately afterwards, a truck followed by the Beshiktash bus and then a light purple DeSoto went by. That's when I realized my uncle was peering through the window into the street. He hadn't noticed us; he was staring at the passing cars. I watched him intently for a while.

The road had long since cleared of traffic. When I turned to my mother to see why she hadn't taken our hands and led us across the street, I noticed she was weeping quietly.

Translated from the Turkish by Erdağ Göknar

ALIVE, ALIVE-OH!

Diana Athill

She thought of herself as a rational woman, but while she could sleep alone in an empty house for night after night without worrying, there were other nights when her nerves twitched like a rabbit's at the least sound. On the many good nights and the few bad the chances of a burglar's breaking in were exactly the same: the difference was within herself and signified nothing which she could identify. And she had always been like that over the possibility of pregnancy.

For several months it would not occur to her to worry, and in another she would be convinced, perhaps as much as a fortnight before the month's end, that this time it had happened. The anxiety seemed in itself an indication: why this sudden fret if there were no reason? She would start working out how to find the money for an abortion, or whether she was capable of bringing up a child single-handed, and when the anxiety proved groundless she would feel foolish as well as relieved.

This last month had been an easy-minded one. She happened, for once, to know the date on which, in this sense, it should have ended, having filled an idle moment by marking little crosses in her diary some way ahead; but although she was often a few days early and never late, she was so far from worrying that she hardly noticed when the day came and went. Six more days passed before she said to herself: 'Hadn't you better start acknowledging this? The curse is six days overdue and your breasts are hurting.'

Rational? How did she square that with the fact that in spite of the fluctuations in anxiety she had taken no precautions against pregnancy for almost two years? From time to time, at the end of an anxious month, she had thought of it: 'If I'm let off this time I'll never be such a fool again.' But she never did anything about it. 'Not today', 'Not this week', 'Another time', or even, 'What's the point? I'll only put the damned things in a drawer and forget to use them.' The mere thought of it seemed too tedious to bear. Although she had twice become pregnant in the past, that was now such a long time ago and surely she had reached an age when it was less likely? After all, month after month had gone by to confirm her optimism.

If anyone had said to her: 'There can be only one reason for an unmarried woman in her early forties to ignore good sense so stubbornly: she does it not from an optimistic belief that she will not conceive, but because of an exactly opposite subconscious optimism; deep inside herself she wants a child,' she would have answered, 'Of course she does. I do know that, really. I suppose I must have been choosing to ignore it.' But although she had not been able to prevent her subconscious from undermining her reason, she saw nothing against putting it in its place. She had overruled it twice before and had felt no ill effects. 'All right, so you want a baby. Who doesn't? But as things are you can't have one – I'm sorry but there it is, too bad for you.' Neither time had it put up any fight. It had accepted its frustration placidly – and placidly it had resumed its scheming.

She had once met a man who had been persuaded to consult an analyst about, of all things, his constipation. He had found the experience interesting and beneficial, and summed it up in words that delighted her: 'It is fascinating to learn what an old juggins one's subconscious is.' That was what she now felt: what an old juggins! What a touching and in some ways admirable old juggins! She saw her subconscious plodding along, pig-headed, single-minded, an old tortoise lumbering through undergrowth, heaving itself over fallen branches, subsiding into holes full of dead leaves. Sometimes, no doubt, the obstacles had been almost too much for him and he had lain panting slightly, staring up at the sky and blinking in apparent bewilderment, but then a blunt foreleg would begin to grope again, his toes would scratch for purchase and on he would go. The question was this: did she slap her subconscious down again by finding the necessary cash and the obliging doctor from the past (if he was still taking such risks), or did she capitulate and have this child?

The reasons against it were these: she was unmarried, forty-three years old and had no private income. She lived comfortably on what she earned, and could do things she enjoyed, such as travelling, with the extra money she had recently begun to earn by writing which, at present, was well within her energies. She would like to preserve these conditions.

The reasons for it were these: if she did not have a child now she would never have one, and she loved its father.

This child's father was married – well married, to an admirable woman who had done him no wrong and to whom he owed much. He had begun an affair simply because he had been married for seven years, was no longer romantically in love with his wife, and was polygamous by nature. He had come to take the affair seriously because the two of them suited each other in every way, one of their strongest bonds being that neither of them was possessive. He might have been described as sitting pretty, married to a good, dependable wife without whom he could not imagine himself, and in love with a good, dependable mistress to whom he could turn whenever he wished. But it was more complex than that. She was nine years older than he which, together with her nature, had given her a certain authority over the situation. He saw her as having *chosen* this form of relationship rather than having been persuaded or manoeuvred into it, and he was right: there was no reason why he should develop a sense of responsibility towards her except in their own terms of honesty and tenderness. It was a perfect situation for him, since he had no money and was trying to live by writing; but that one partner is well suited does not necessarily mean that the other is ill-used. She herself might have condemned some other woman's lover in a similar situation, but she knew him and herself too well to condemn him. He was what he was: the person with whom, *being as he was*, she was most at home. What, then, would be the point of wishing him otherwise?

And could she make him otherwise, if she wanted to? No. And she didn't mind that because she was perfectly willing to accept that they, as they both were, were each other's unexpected bonus from life. It was this that had established so much ease and sweetness between them. If, when she told him she was pregnant, he were to offer to leave his wife and come to her, she would be quite as anxious as she would be happy. She would not, whatever she decided, try to make him do that. Perhaps this was cowardice – a fear of actually facing a lack of success which she thought she could envisage with equanimity. Or perhaps it was vanity – a desire to go on representing freedom, pleasure, stimulation, all the joys of love rather than its burdens. Or perhaps it was really what she would like it to be: the kind of respect for another person's being that she would wish to have paid to her own. But there was no doubt that, if she was pregnant, life would be a great deal easier if her lover and her love were otherwise than they were.

So it would be sensible to have an abortion. In her experience it was not a profoundly disagreeable thing to have. The worst part of the operation, performed under a local anaesthetic, was the grotesque position into which one is trussed on the table. The last time she found that she could see a tiny but clear reflection of herself in the globe of the lampshade above her, and at that she almost lost grip but screwed her eyes shut instead. There is this humiliating ugliness, and there are sounds, and for a few moments there is a dim sensation of pain. If the doctor is businesslike and kind, treating one (as hers had done) like an ordinary patient, there is no sinister or shaming atmosphere to contend with. One is simply having a quick little operation for a sensible reason . . . So it was odd that she should start to shiver slightly as she thought about it. No, she did not feel that murder is committed during that operation. She would go so far as to say that she was sure it was not: no separate existence, at that stage, was being ended, any more than when a sperm was prevented from meeting an egg. But that old juggins, the pinheaded, pig-headed tortoise behind her reason: he was tough, he was good at recovering from setbacks, but at the prospect of yet another of them he was showing signs of turning into a porcupine. He wanted her to have this child.

Having acknowledged the situation, she found herself no nearer a decision, only slightly more aware of reluctance towards either course. It was still early. She could have an abortion, if she so decided, at any time within the next three months. So the best thing to do seemed to her to be nothing: go blank, drift for a week or so, think about it as little as possible and see what happened. Perhaps she would wake up one morning knowing what she wanted to do.

The next two weeks dragged. She managed to keep her mind on other things for much of the time, but the fact of pregnancy was always there,

lying in wait for any unoccupied moment. It seemed common sense not
to begin worrying again at least until she had missed her second period,
but long before that date came she felt that her condition had endured
for months. Each morning, when she awoke, she would lie still for a
minute or two trying to overhear her state of mind, but all she picked up
was irritation and depression at being in this quandary. About ten days
after the start of her 'truce' she spent a weekend in the country with her
mother, and the depression increased: supposing she had the child, how
appalling the family explanations would be, how impossible it was to
imagine the degree of consternation such a decision would raise in her
mother and the rest of the family. In the train on the way back to London
she looked up from her book and bumped, as usual, into 'What am I
going to do?' Oh god, she thought, I do wish *it would all go away*.

Well, she thought next morning, if that's the best I can do I suppose
I had better *make* it go away: get the money in, anyway. There was a sum
waiting for her in New York, where she had planned soon to spend a
holiday. If she used half of that, would there be enough left for the
holiday? Probably not. Resentment and disappointment were added to
the depression, but she told her agent a story of unexpected bills as a
result of moving house, and he cabled her the money at once. That done,
she had only to call the doctor – his number, on a grubby scrap of paper,
discreetly minus his name, still lurked at the back of a drawer in her
dressing table after all those years. 'I'll do it soon,' she thought. 'Next
week, perhaps. I've got the money and that's the main thing.' She spent
a couple of days in a rage at missing her first chance to visit New York,
and a couple more arguing that she needn't miss it after all: if she spent
only three weeks there instead of four, and lived very cheaply, she could
manage. If that were so she was not only being sensible, but was not
going to suffer for it, so there was nothing to be depressed about any
more.

It was on the fifth morning after the arrival of the money – a morning in
April – that she awoke congratulating herself on living in her new flat
and opening her eyes in her new bedroom. It was the top floor of a house
which might almost be in the country, the last house in a short street
which projected like a little promontory into a park. All the windows
looked on to trees and grass, and her bedroom window had gardens as
well, the long range of gardens behind the houses of the street at right

angles to hers. Cherry and pear trees were in flower, and a fine Magnolia; daffodils and narcissi twinkled in the grass. Soon the lilacs would be out, and the hawthorns, and the irises – it was a galloping spring after a mild winter. The sun shone into her bedroom window, and the birds were singing so loudly that they had woken her before her alarm clock went off: each garden seemed to have its own blackbird. She got out of bed to lean out of the window and sniff the green smells, and found herself saying, 'What a morning for birds and bees and buds and babies.'

This sentence was still humming in her mind as she walked to the bus stop, past the walls of more gardens, not high enough to conceal the trees and shrubs behind them. During the previous winter, before moving into the flat, she had thought as she walked this way: 'This will soon be my part of London – I shall see that pear, that crab apple tree in flower, and then heavy with dusty summer green, and then with hard little London fruit on their branches – they will be familiar landmarks.' And here they were, going into their spring performance with abandon against a brilliant blue sky, part of her daily walk to the bus. 'It is a lovely place to live,' she thought. 'I suppose I *am* going to have this baby after all.'

She was late, she had to run for a bus, those words evaporated and no thought of her predicament disturbed her morning's work. Then her business partner came into her room, to spring on her a discussion of long-term plans for the firm. Someone might be persuaded to join them and, if he did, shares would have to be reallocated, certain changes of status would have to be made. 'It concerns you, too,' he said, 'so you must think it over.' She had a slight sensation of breathlessness and could feel her face flushing, but she made no decision to say what in fact she did say: 'I don't know that it *will* concern me. I may not be here then. I'm going to have a baby.' And inside saying: 'Oh lord, now I've done it!' – but the dismay was a laughing dismay, not a horrified one.

Perhaps her mood would not have held if her news had been received differently. As it was, her partner, a very old friend, said, 'You mean you're pregnant *now*?'

'Yes.'

'Have you seen a doctor?'

'Not yet . . . of course it may be a mistake, but I'm sure it's not.'

'Well then, are you mad?' he said, sitting down on the radiator, frowning. 'How do you think you're going to support the child if you don't stay on here?'

'Oh somehow – people do manage. And I thought it might be a bit embarrassing in the office . . .'

'Good God! If anyone's embarrassed they can bloody well get out!'

Then, dropping his poker face, he asked if she had really thought he would expect her to leave, and she answered that of course she hadn't, but it had seemed that it would be such an imposition . . . each of them slightly awkward at being pitched so suddenly into full awareness of their long and usually taken-for-granted affection for each other, and she the more so for having to produce thoughts which she had not yet formed on the practical side of this pregnancy. Then he kissed her and said that he was happy for her, and she was left grinning across her desk like the Cheshire cat, established in her full glory as an Expectant Unmarried Mother.

After that she was happy. She was quite often frightened too, but on a level superficial compared with that of the happiness. The birth would be easy. She could take as much time off as she needed, drawing her salary all the while, and for so long as she could stay at home all would be simple. The house in which she had her flat was owned by a close friend who herself lived in the rest of it, and who, from the moment she knew of the pregnancy, was eager to help. Neither woman had much money – she herself had to let one of the rooms in her flat to help pay its modest rent – so she was anxious not to become a financial burden on her friend, but it was reassuring to know that if the worst came to the worst she would never be chased for the rent. But she could not take advantage of that reassurance for more than a short time, and didn't want to do even that. And in addition to her usual living expenses she would have to pay for someone to care for the child while she was working, and for its food and clothes, and for its education – no, it would go to a state school, of course, there was a good one near by – but for its bicycle and its roller skates and its holidays by the sea . . . Year after year of financial strain stretched ahead. Financial strain and, to start with at any rate, physical exhaustion: office all day, child for every other minute – would she ever again be free to write? Not for years, anyway.

And no less frightening was the thought of the gap in the child's life where a father ought to be. Material considerations could be smothered by 'I'll manage somehow – people do' – of course she would manage when she had to. But the argument advanced by her more sober-minded friends, and by her own mind as well, that one has no right to wish this lopsided upbringing on any child – that was less easy. Surely only an exceptional woman could reasonably expect to steer her child comfortably through the shoals of illegitimacy, and could she make any claim to be exceptional? To this question she could make no answer. She could only say: 'Whatever happens, whatever the child itself may one day say (and there probably *will* come a time when it will say "I never asked to be born"), I believe that it will prefer to exist rather than not.' But the real answer was not in those words, nor in any others that she might think up. It was simply that now it was beyond her to consider an abortion. When she tried to force herself to think about it she felt as though something physical happened in her skull, as though an actual shutter came down between the front part of her brain, just behind her eyes, where the thought began, and the back of her brain into which it would have to go if it were to be developed.

The biggest immediate worry was how to tell her mother whose outlook would make it very hard for her to accept such news. She veered between a desire to get the worst over by writing at once, and a longing to put it off for ever. Her lover advised her to put it off for a month or so, just in case something went wrong, and finally she agreed, though her itch to tell made her write in advance the letter she would send later, choosing a time to post it just before one of her visits home so that her mother could get over the worst of the shock before they discussed it. She enjoyed writing that letter: putting into words how much she wanted a child and how determined she had now become to have this one. She found her letter so convincing that she couldn't believe her mother would not agree.

The longing to tell everyone else was strong. She scolded herself, arguing that when she began to bulge would be soon enough; people *did* have miscarriages, and no discreet woman would announce a pregnancy before the fourth month. But as each day passed, discretion became less important, jubilation grew stronger, and she had soon told everyone with whom she was intimate and some with whom she was not. Almost all her friends appeared to be delighted for her, and their support gave her great pleasure. Sometimes they said she was brave, and she enjoyed that too, in spite of knowing that courage did not come into it. The interest and sympathy that seemed to surround her was like a good wine added to a delicious dinner.

The child's father was, in a detached way, pleased. The pregnancy made no difference to the form of their relationship, but it did deepen it: his tenderness and attention were a comfort and a pleasure. She wondered, sometimes, what would happen about that once the child was born: would an 'uncle' in its life instead of a father be a good thing or a bad one? They would have to see. She knew that if it proved a bad thing she would have to lose her lover – would lose him without hesitation however great the pain – but for the present having him there was a large, warm part of the happiness which carried the anxieties like driftwood on its broad tide.

She felt gloriously well, hungry, lively and pretty, without a single qualm of sickness and with only a shadow of extra fatigue at the end of a long day, from time to time. 'Well, *you* seem to be all right,' they said to her at the hospital clinic which she began to attend. During the long waits at this clinic she watched the other women and thought that none of them looked so well or so pleased as she did. At her first visit she kept quiet, half anxious and half amused as to how her spinsterhood would be treated by the nurses and doctors, but once she discovered that it was taken not only calmly but with extra kindness, she relaxed. One of the other expectant mothers, very young, was like herself in having suffered nothing in the way of sickness or discomfort, and the two of them made an almost guilty smug corner together. She contrived to read details about herself over the shoulder of a nurse who was filling in a form about her, and glowed with ridiculous pride at all the 'satisfactories' and at 'nipples: good'.

However simple and quick the examination itself, the clinic proved always to take between two and three hours, so she arranged to see her own doctor regularly instead. As she left the clinic for the last time she happened to be thinking about the problem of the child's care while she was at the office, when a man leaned out of the cab of a passing truck and shouted at her, 'That's right love – keep smiling!' She may have been worried, but there was still a smile on her face.

Those weeks of April and May were the only ones in her life when spring was wholly, fully beautiful. All other springs carried with them regret at their passing. If she thought, 'Today the white double cherries are at their most perfect' it summoned up the simultaneous awareness: 'Tomorrow the edges of their petals will begin to turn brown.' This time a particularly ebullient, sun-drenched spring simply existed for her. It was as though, instead of being a stationary object past which a current was flowing, she was flowing with it, in it, at the same rate. It was a happiness new to her, but it felt very ancient, and complete.

One Saturday, soon after her last clinic, the child's father came to see her at lunch-time. She had got up early and done a big shop, but not a heavy one, because a short time before she became pregnant she had bought a basket on wheels (was it coincidence that several of her purchases just before the pregnancy were of things suited to it: that basket, the slacks which were rather too loose round the waist, with the matching loose top?). She left the basket at the bottom of the stairs for him to bring up, because strong and well though she felt, she was taking no foolish risks. They ate a good lunch, both of them cheerful and relaxed. After it he was telling her a funny story when she interrupted with, 'Wait a minute, I must go to the loo – tell me when I get back,' and hurried out to have a pee, wanting to get back quickly for the end of the story. When she saw blood on the toilet paper her mind went, for a moment, quite literally blank.

So she got up and went slowly back into the sitting room, thinking, 'To press my fingers against my cheek like this must look absurdly over-dramatic.'

'I'm bleeding,' she said in a small voice.

He scrambled up from the floor, where he'd been lying, and said, 'What do you mean? Come and sit down. How badly?'

'Only a very little,' she said, and began to tremble.

He took her by the shoulders and pulled her against him, saying quieting things, saying, 'It's all right, we'll ring the doctor, it's probably nothing,' and although she didn't know she was going to start crying, she felt herself doing it. She had not yet been able to tell what she was feeling, but suddenly she was having to control herself hard in order not to scream. 'The important thing,' he said, 'is to find out.' He went to fetch the telephone directory and said, 'Come on now, ring the doctor.'

The telephone was near her chair, so she didn't have to move, which she felt was important. The doctor was off duty for the weekend, but a stand-in answered. Any pain? No. How much bleeding? She explained how little. Then there was nothing to be done but to go to bed at once and stay there for forty-eight hours. 'Does this necessarily mean a miscarriage?' she asked. No, certainly not. How would she know if it turned into one? It would seem like an exceptionally heavy period, with the passing of clots. If that happened she must telephone again, but otherwise just stay lying down.

Her lover ran out to buy her sanitary towels, alerting her friend downstairs as he went. During the few minutes she was alone she found herself crying again, flopped over the arm of her chair, tears streaming down her face, saying over and over again in a sort of whispered scream, 'I don't *want* to have a miscarriage, I don't *want* to have a miscarriage.' She knew it was a silly thing to be doing, and when her friend came she was relieved to find that she could pull herself together, sit up and talk.

They put her to bed, and there she lay, the bleeding almost imperceptible, feeling perfectly well. They reminded each other of women they knew about who had bled during pregnancy with no ill effect, and she soon became calm. During the next two days the bleeding became even less, but it did not quite stop, and over the phone her doctor repeated his colleague's words: no one could do anything, it was not necessarily going to be a miscarriage, she would know all right if it became one, and she must stay in bed until it stopped. She was comfortable in her pretty bedroom, reading Jane Austen almost non-stop for her calming quality (she reread the whole of *Mansfield Park*, *Northanger Abbey*, *Persuasion* and *The Watsons* in four days), listening to the radio and doing a little office work. By the fourth day her chief anxiety had become not the possibility of a miscarriage, but the fear that this slight bleeding might tie her to her bed not for days but for weeks. A bedridden pregnancy would be bad enough for anyone, but for her, entirely dependent as she was on friends who all had jobs or families . . . How could they possibly go on doing as much as they were doing now?

She was lucky in one way: anxiety, fear and certain kinds of misery always had an almost anaesthetic effect on her, making her mind and feelings sluggish. Under such stresses she shrank into the moment, just doing the next thing to be done, and sleeping a lot. So those four days passed in a state of suspended emotion rather than in unhappiness – suspended emotion stabbed every now and then with irritation at the absurdity of having to fear disaster when she was feeling as well as ever. It was ridiculous!

During the night of the fourth day she came slowly out of sleep at three in the morning to a vague feeling that something was amiss. It took her a minute or two of sleepy wondering before she identified it more exactly. Not since she was a girl had she suffered any pain during her period – she had almost forgotten what kind of pain it was – but now . . . yes. In a dim, shadowy way it was that old pain that was ebbing and flowing in her belly. When it ebbed she thought, 'Quick, go to sleep again, you were imagining it.' But it came back, its fluctuations confirming its nature. More numb than ever, barely awake, she got up, fetched a bucket from the kitchen and a newspaper to fold and use as a lid, and a big towel from the linen cupboard. She arranged all this beside her bed and went to sleep again.

When she woke an hour and a half later it was because blood was trickling over her thigh. 'This is it': dull resentment was what she felt. She hitched herself out of bed and over the bucket – and woke with a cold shock at the thudding gush, the sensation that a cork had blown. 'Oh god oh god,' she thought, 'I didn't know it would be like this.' Blood ran fast for about half a minute, then dwindled to a trickle. Swaddling herself in the towel, she lay back in the bed, telling herself that no doubt it had to be fairly gruesome to start with.

After that the warning trickle came every ten or fifteen minutes, out over the bucket she went, terrified that she might overturn it with a clumsy gesture as she removed and restored the newspaper lid. The gush was never as violent as the first one, but each time it was violent and it did not diminish. She tried not to see the dark, clotted contents of the bucket – it was only when she saw it that she almost began to cry. There was a peppery smell of blood, but if she turned her head in a certain way she could catch a whiff of fresh air from the window which lessened it. It was already light when she woke the second time, and soon after that the first blackbird began to sing. She lay still between the crises, watching the sun's first rays coming into the room and trying to make out how many blackbirds were singing behind the one in her own garden.

Her friend would be coming up to give her breakfast. She usually came at eight – but it might be later. 'If she doesn't come till late . . .' she thought, and became tearful. Then she decided to wait until seven-thirty, by which time the bleeding would surely be less, and telephone her – with the towel between her legs she would be able to get to the sitting room where the phone was. The thought of telephoning the doctor herself was too much because if his number were engaged or he were out she couldn't bear it, her friend must do it. Time was going very fast, she noticed, looking at the alarm clock on the corner of the chest of drawers. That was something anyway.

She had come out in a heavy sweat after the first flow, and at about six-thirty it happened again. The sweat streamed off her and she was icy cold, and – worse – she began to feel sick. The thought of having to complicate the horror by vomiting into that dreadful bucket put her in a panic, so when the sweating was over and the nausea had died away, immediately after another violent flow, she knew she must get to the telephone now. She huddled the towel between her legs, stood up, took two steps towards the door, felt herself swaying, thought quite clearly, 'They are wrong when they say everything goes black, it's not going black, it's disappearing. I must fall on to the bed.' Which she did.

The next hour was vague, but she managed to follow her routine: use bucket, put paper back, lie flat on bed, wrap dressing gown over belly. She began to feel much iller, with more sweating, more cold, more nausea. When she heard her lodger moving about in his room next door she knew she had to call him. He knew nothing of her pregnancy – thought she had been in bed with an upset stomach – and they were so far from being intimate that it had not entered her head to call him earlier. Perhaps she had even forgotten he was there. Now she tapped on the wall, and called his name, but he didn't hear. A little more time passed, and she heard him in the passage outside her door and called again. This time he heard, and answered, and she told him to go downstairs and fetch her friend. 'You mean now?' came his startled voice through the door. 'Yes, quickly.' Oh that was wonderful, the sound of his feet hurrying away, and only a minute or two later her door opened and in came her friend.

One look and she ran for the telephone without saying a word. She caught the doctor in his surgery, two minutes before he went out on a call. He arrived so soon that it seemed almost at once, looked into the bucket, felt her pulse, pulled down her eyelid and left the room quickly to call an ambulance and alert the hospital. She felt hurt that neither he nor her friend had spoken to her, but now her friend said could she drink a cup of tea and she felt it would be wonderful – but couldn't drink it when it appeared. The relief of not having to worry any more would have been exquisite, if it had not given her more time to realize how ill she was feeling. The ambulance men wrapped her in a beautiful big red blanket and said not to worry about bleeding all over it (so *that* was why ambulance blankets were usually red). The breath of fresh air as she was carried across the pavement made her feel splendidly alert after the dreadful dizziness of being carried downstairs, so she asked for a cigarette and they said it wasn't allowed in the ambulance but she could have one all the same and to put the ash in the sick bowl. One puff and she felt much worse, so that her friend had to wipe the sweat off her forehead with a paper handkerchief. There was a pattern by then: a slowly mounting pain, a gush of blood, the sweating and nausea following at once and getting worse every time, accompanied by a terrible feeling that was not identifiable as pain but simply as *illness*. It made her turn her head from side to side and moan, although it seemed wrong to moan without intolerable pain.

The men carried her into a cubicle in the casualty department, and she didn't want them to leave because they were so kind. As soon as she was there the nausea came again, stronger than ever so that this time she vomited, and was comforted because one of the men held her head and said, 'Never mind, dear.' A nurse said brusquely, while she was vomiting (trying to catch her unawares, she supposed), 'Did you have an injection to bring this on?' Her 'No' came out like a raucous scream, which made her feel apologetic so she had to gasp laboriously, 'I wanted most terribly to have this baby.' The man holding her head put his other hand on her arm and gave it a great squeeze, and that was the only time anyone questioned her.

Her head cleared a bit after she had been sick. She noticed that the nurse couldn't find her pulse, and that when the doctor who soon came was listening to her heart through his stethoscope he raised his eyebrows a fraction and pursed his lips, and then turned to look at her face, not as one looks at a face to communicate, but with close attention. She also noticed that they could never hear her answers to their questions although she thought she was speaking normally. 'They think I'm really bad,' she said to herself, but she didn't feel afraid. They would do whatever had to be done to make her better.

It went on being like that up in the ward, when they began to give her blood transfusions. Her consciousness was limited to the narrow oblong of her body on the stretcher, trolley or bed, and to the people doing things to it. Within those limits it was sharp, except during the recurring waves of horribleness, but it did not extend to speculation. When a nurse, being kind, said, 'You may not have lost the baby – one can lose a great deal of blood and the baby can still be all right,' she knew that was nonsense but felt nothing about it. When a doctor said to someone, 'Call them and tell him he must hurry with that blood – say that he must run,' she saw that things had gone further than she supposed but did not wonder whether he would run fast enough. When, a little later, they were discussing an injection and the same doctor said, 'She's very near collapse,' she thought perfectly clearly, 'Near collapse, indeed! If what I'm in now isn't collapse, it must be their euphemism for dying.' It did, then, swim dimly through her mind that she ought to think or feel something about this, but she hadn't the strength to produce any more than, 'Oh well, if I die, I die,' and that thought, once registered, did not set up any echoes. The things which were real were the sordidness of lying in a puddle of blood, and the oddness of not minding when they pushed needles into her.

She also wanted to impress the nurses and doctors. Not till afterwards did she understand that she had slipped back into infancy; that the total trust in these powerful people, and the wish to make them think, 'There's a good, clever girl,' belonged in the nursery. She wanted to ask them intelligent questions about what they were doing, and to make little jokes, provided she could do so in not more than four or five words, because more would be beyond her. It was annoying that they seemed not to hear her little mumblings, or else just said, 'Yes dear', looking at her face as they said it with that odd, examining expression. She made a brief contact with one of the doctors when he told them to do something 'to stop her from being agitated'. What she wanted to say was: 'Don't be silly, I can't wait for you to get me down to the theatre and start scraping,' but all that came out was a peevish 'Not agitated!' to which he replied politely, 'I'm sorry, of course you're not.' The only words she spoke from a deeper level than these feeble attempts at exhibitionism were when someone who was manipulating the blood bottle asked her if she was beginning to feel sleepy. It was during a wave of badness, and she heard her own voice replying hoarsely: 'I'm feeling *very ill*.'

She had always dreaded the kind of anaesthetic one breathes, because of a bad experience, but when she understood that they were about to give her that kind and began to attempt a protest, she suddenly realized that she didn't give a damn: let them hurry up, let them get that mask over her face and she would go with it willingly. This had been going on much, much too long and all she wanted was the end of it.

The operation must have been a quick one, under a light anaesthetic, because when she woke up to an awareness of hands manipulating her back into bed she was confused only for an instant, and only as to whether this was happening before or after the operation. That question was answered at once by the feeling in her belly: it was calm, she was no longer bleeding. She tried to move her hand down to touch herself in confirmation, and a nurse caught it and held it still – she hadn't realized that there was still a transfusion needle taped into the back of it. Having moved, she began to vomit. She had a deep-seated neurotic queasiness about vomiting, a horror of it, and until that moment she would never have believed that she could have been sick while lying flat on her back with the bowl so awkwardly placed under her chin that the sick went into her hair, and felt happy while doing it. But that was what was happening. An amazing glow of relief and joy was flowing up from her healed belly. 'I AM ALIVE.' It was enough. It was everything. It was filling her to the brim with pure and absolute joy, a feeling more intense than any she had known. And very soon after that she was wondering why they were bothering to set up a new bottle of plasma, because she could have told them that all she needed now was to rest.

So if she were pinned down to the question 'What did you feel on losing your child?' the only honest answer would be 'Nothing'. Nothing at all, while it was going on. What was happening was so bad – so nearly fatal – that it eclipsed its own significance. And during the four days she spent in hospital she felt very little; no more than a detached acknowledgement that it was sad. Hospital routine closed round her gently, isolating her in that odd, childish world where nurses in their early twenties are the 'grown-ups', and the exciting events are visiting time and being allowed to get up and walk to the lavatory. When it was time to go home she was afraid that she would hate her bedroom, expecting to have a horror of the blackbird's song and perhaps of some little rusty stain on the blue carpet, but friends took her home to an accompaniment of flowers, delicacies and cheerful talk, and she saw that it was still a pleasant room, her flat still a lovely place to live.

There was even relief: she would not now have to tell her mother anything, and she would not have to worry about money any more than usual. She could spend some on clothes for her holiday as soon as she liked, and she saw that she would enjoy the clothes and the holiday. It was this that was strange and sad, and made her think so often of how happy she had been while she was expecting the child (not of how unhappy she was now, because she wasn't). This was what sometimes gave her a dull ache, like a stomach-ache but not physical: that someone who didn't yet exist could have the power to create spring, and could then be gone, and that once he was gone (she had always thought of the child as a boy) he became, because he had never existed, so completely gone: that the only tears shed for him were those first, almost unconscious tears shed by her poor old tortoise of a subconscious rather than by her. 'I *don't want* to have a miscarriage.' Oh no, no, no, she hadn't wanted it, it was the thing she *didn't want* with all her heart. Yet now it had happened, and she was the same as she had always been . . . except that now she knew that, although if she had died during the miscarriage she would hardly, because of her physical state, have noticed it, the truth was that she loved being alive so much that not having died was more important to her by far than losing the child: more important than *anything*.

I lost that child forty years ago. Much has changed since then. Nowadays, if you want an abortion it is not necessary to know of a doctor willing to risk his career by breaking the law; and although the mother of a woman in her early forties would be unlikely to rejoice on learning that her unmarried daughter planned to have a child, she would be less shocked at such news than mothers used to be. The surroundings of the event would now be different. But the event itself – that would be the same.

After the miscarriage, I scribbled some notes to rid my mind of it and forgot all about them. Recently, when I was hunting for something in a rarely opened drawer, I found them under a pile of other old papers. My sense of recall as I read them was sharp, yet the woman to whom this happened, though not exactly a stranger – I knew her well – was no longer me. Retelling this experience in the third person is my way of acknowledging the difference between 'her' and me.

I think now that, if the child had been born, my lover would have been a devoted father; over the years I have seen how much he enjoys children. As for me, I suppose – I hope – that I would have loved the child wholeheartedly; but the truth is that in forty years I have hardly ever thought about it, and never with anything more poignant than painless speculation as to how it would have turned out.

Robyn Davidson, with some of Eddie's relatives by his grave, June 1998

MARRYING EDDIE

Robyn Davidson

Until I was in my twenties, I had never seen an Aborigine. Black Australians constituted one per cent of the population, and that one per cent was mostly located on reserves outside rural towns, or in outback government and mission settlements.

They were out of sight, though not always out of mind. Among my family photos is one of 'The Blacks' Camp'. It must have been taken at the turn of the century on one of the cattle properties settled by my forebears. Scattered through a stand of untidy gum trees are twenty or so 'humpies', shelters made of saplings and canvas sheeting. There are three black women dressed in Victorian skirts and high collars, a man in a stockman's outfit and a few children. They are all looking towards the camera, but from a hundred yards' distance. In spite of the familiar gum trees I could never escape the feeling that I was gazing into foreign territory. That hundred yards was a zone of separation between two worlds; worlds which shared the same space, but were entirely unconnected.

My first ever encounter with Aborigines occurred in the early Seventies, in Alice Springs, where I had gone to prepare for a journey west across the continent, alone, with camels. I had just got off the train from Sydney. I had a dog, six dollars, a small suitcase and one packet of tobacco.

As I was wandering about in a daze looking for a cheap place to stay, an old Aboriginal man stopped me and asked for a cigarette. I handed him the tobacco pouch, which he pocketed along with the papers and matches, thus demonstrating the shrewd adaptability of nomads everywhere, but hunter-gatherers in particular: the skilful milking of the natural environment – in this case, guilt-ridden whitefellas.

That long-ago Alice Springs did not quite reach one-horse standards. There were two pubs, a cafe – of the tea, white bread and mixed grill variety – and an Italian lunch joint called Sorrentino's. Or perhaps Sorrentino's came later. I remember that first year as if it is obscured by billowing dust: dry river beds, blacks' camps, river red gums, heat, barking dogs, corrugated iron, ugliness, loneliness, racial tension.

I found a place to stay a few miles out of town – an abandoned, roofless stone house, bound together by fig trees and alive with snakes. On the other side of the river bed was one of the several Aboriginal fringe camps that were situated on the outskirts of town. Its residents were the traditional owners of the country around and to the north of Alice. They lived under sheets of plastic and corrugated iron, or inside abandoned cars. They had no water tap.

I had made contact with some of them, and one in particular, old Ada Baxter, I counted as a friend. I would sometimes stay with her, watching as she drank herself into oblivion, or breaking up another fight with one of her succession of white, no-hoper boyfriends. Sometimes women would visit me from the camp, professing concern at my being alone and unprotected. I tolerated their company, was sometimes glad of it, but I didn't kid myself that I understood their world any more than I expected them to understand my pleasure in solitude.

Quite by chance I had arrived in the Alice just ahead of the first shock waves detonated by the Land Rights Act, under which untenanted stretches of desert in the Northern Territory could be claimed by Aboriginal clans, provided they could prove before a white tribunal that their 'ownership' was authentic. Suddenly the town was invaded by 'southern do-gooders' – young, urban, left-wing teachers, lawyers, doctors, anthropologists, linguists, artists, who had come to lend their skills to the Aboriginal cause. The Central Land Council, a little grass-roots organization, had been set up to administer the Act. Tiny bureaucracies began to form around specific issues – health, housing, education, communications. These were nominally led by Aborigines, but various kinds of expertise were needed and these were provided by the 'do-gooders'. The city had infiltrated the bush.

The backlash was predictable: 'Rights for Whites' graffiti and a pathetic little equivalent of the Ku Klux Klan. But the real battle was (as it still is) with the Northern Territory government, the Federal government, and the mining and pastoral lobbies.

Initially I kept my distance from this new group, which at the time numbered no more than twenty. I had come to the Alice for different reasons, and although my sympathies lay with them, my mind was on other things. But slowly they wore down my resistance until I came to depend upon them. These were friendships forged in extraordinary times, and destined to last. By the time I left on my journey, in March 1977, Alice was already transformed.

It is one of the great unsolved mysteries – why we are drawn to one individual more than another. When a shared language and shared sensibilities are involved, it is easier to explain. But why did I instantly respond to Eddie, like him, more than the people he was with?

I had been travelling west with my camels for about three months and had entered a drought area. The camels were thirsty. I arrived at a well to water them, but the well was dry. It was a week's walk to the next one. I was on Pitjantjatjara lands now, south-west of Ayers Rock, in the sand hills. The chances of coming across another human being were zero. The water drums were just about empty. I was very frightened. One night I heard a car in the distance, a clapped-out car without muffler or suspension – an Aboriginal car. The men in it had seen my fire and driven through the scrub to my camp. They were elders who had been to a land rights meeting and were on their way home to a tiny settlement – Wingelina.

Eddie is the only one who stands out in my memory of that night. He handed me some par-cooked rabbit, which I ate. His face got lost in wrinkles when he smiled. He was wearing a huge Adidas running shoe on one foot, and a woman's slipper on the other. He was a couple of inches shorter than me. He looked to be about seventy years old. He spoke no English and my Pitjantjatjara was rudimentary. I said my name was Robbie, which he pronounced 'Raaapie'.

In the morning, when I packed up to leave, it was Eddie who fell in beside me, announcing that he would escort me into Wingelina – two days' trudge away. I will never know why he chose to do that. I don't know whether the affinity I felt was reciprocated, or whether they had all discussed it when I was asleep and Eddie had got landed with the job; whether the escort was to protect me, or to protect the sacred places I might stumble into; or whether, on a whim, he felt like a walk – an unusual thing for these old nomads who now preferred to do their hunting in cars. Perhaps Eddie was, inside his own context, an unusual man.

He ended up staying with me for a month, escorting me several hundred miles beyond Wingelina into Western Australia. During that time we struggled to communicate with each other, were irritable with each other, resorted to laughter or eloquent silence. He gave me *pituri*, native tobacco, to chew so I wouldn't feel tired. My hunting skills broke his heart. Several times I missed kangaroo, but managed to shoot him some rabbits. He was half-blind with trachoma, so couldn't use the rifle himself, but he insisted on carrying it. He was solicitous and protective of me. At night he would build the wilcha, indicating where I should roll out my swag, and wake in the night to see if I was all right, building and stoking the fire. Or if by chance we came across a carload of strangers along a lonely track, Eddie, despite his size, displayed the rifle to maximum effect. He gave me two small pieces of stone, and to this day I have no idea if they were significant in any way. Often he broke into song as we walked along – singing up his country through which we were travelling. He tried to explain these ideas to me. He was dingo. This was where dingo had travelled, where dingo still is. He was singing dingo. I understood very little of Aboriginal philosophy then, but I certainly understood that when this old man talked of country, of his place, his whole being was transfused with something like joy. He was utterly at home. Often I would catch him looking at me sideways, trying to figure me out. I suppose that we posed the same questions to each other. Who are you? How do I make sense of you? How can I accommodate what you know?

Eddie probably saw his first whitefella when he was in his forties. Since then there would have been minimal contact – a missionary perhaps, an Afghan trader with his camel team, more recently a white lawyer or 'adviser'. Of course, even these remote Western desert cultures had been shaken by the tremors of invasion. They had already undergone rapid adaptation. But Eddie's consciousness had been formed by a tradition that stretched down into the very root of the continent, and that meant that his mind and mine were about as different as it is possible for minds to be. In the fundamentals – conceptions of time and space – we were mutually uninterpretable. My world was anchored in history, his in geography. His country – dingo – was 'conscious' and he, being a particle of that country, was therefore also conscious. He was not sundered from phenomena, as I was – an observer looking in at the world as if I were not quite of it. By the end of our journey together we had signally failed to understand each other, yet an unlikely, even unprecedented connection had formed.

Alice Springs 1988. Of the town I knew, bits remained like old stage props incorporated into a new play. There were now shopping malls, wide bitumen roads, a Woolworths, a Sheraton hotel, stop lights. Even the fringe camps had houses and ablution blocks. Aboriginal bureaucracies were housed in large buildings and employed large staffs. There was an Aboriginal radio station, Aboriginal rock bands, an Aboriginal women's refuge, a couple of cooperative galleries selling dot-dot paintings.

The subculture inhabited by my friends had changed, too. For a start, it had expanded. Within the group there was now room for variant ideologies, around which smaller subgroups had coalesced. There were a few more Communists, a new ghetto of lesbian feminists and a couple of my old friends had joined the New Age camp. Despite its internal divisions, the little community remained powerfully bound together – its ethos was founded in the Sixties and Seventies, and its raison d'être was still Aboriginal politics. Almost everyone, it seemed, had lucrative consultancies or well-paid jobs in Aboriginal organizations. 'Nigger farming', as the more cynical urbanized blacks termed it, was a flourishing industry.

But some things were unchanged: the beauty of the Macdonnell ranges in contrast to the vileness of the town; Aboriginal drunks in the Todd river bed, Aborigines in bandages, Aborigines cadging from tourists, or trying to sell paintings for cash with which to buy more grog, Aboriginal health statistics – among the worst in the world.

I went to visit my friends in the fringe camps. The redoubtable Ada was just the same, only the boyfriend had changed. Joanie, a young girl from across the creek, who had once said, 'What have I got to look forward to? Getting drunk and beaten up every night?' had been prescient, as it turned out. I visited her in the morning and she was already swigging from a flagon. Ten years before, she would dress up in my clothes and fantasize about being a model. Now there was scar tissue where her top lip used to be.

A week later I was in a tiny aeroplane bumping along the heat shimmer 7,000 feet above the desert. The pilot squinted at the horizon, looking for Ayers Rock. There it was – a blue bump – and to the right of it, Lake Amadeus, a sheet of frosted glass fractured into patterns of icier white. Round islands of orange sand in the middle of the lake were covered in stubble, and criss-crossing the salt-ice were stitchings of animal pads. The landscape was a dot-dot painting.

Half an hour later I saw a pinprick of light in that vast canvas – one small corrugated-iron roof at the end of a four-wheel-drive track leading back to vanishing point. It was an Aboriginal outstation. Outstations, we all believed, were one of the uncontestable successes of the whole land rights struggle. Having gained freehold title of their land – thousands of square miles of it – the Pitjantjatjara were involved in a reverse diaspora. Extended families were setting up their own little communities away from the pressures and corruptions of settlement life. They were going 'home'.

I was on my way to Eddie. I had no idea what my reception would be. I had brought him an enormous bowie knife with scabbard and belt, and a skirt and new billycan for his wife, Winkicha. I had also brought the customary load of fresh meat.

By the time I got to his wilcha it was dark. He and Winkicha were sitting on the ground behind the corrugated-iron windbreak, surrounded by old blankets and mangy dogs, cooking a hunk of roo over their fire. Eddie was naked and smeared in ash.

'*Nyuntu palya*, Eddie?' He leaped up, peered through those milky-blind eyes into the darkness, then dashed out from behind the windbreak. He squinted up into my face for a second to make sure it was really me, then grabbed my breasts and gave them a vigorous and heartfelt shake. '*Laarrrrraaa!*' he said. 'Raaaapie!'

The next morning, early, people began gathering at Eddie's camp. Old women came up to me, stroking my chest, indicating they wanted to paint me up for a ceremony. I had forgotten almost all my Pitjantjatjara but I knew that this big a welcome was . . . odd. Did Eddie seem nervous, or have I inserted that into my memory? He was certainly very proud of the bowie knife and passed it around for everyone to see. A younger man who could speak a little English said: 'That proper good knife that one. You proper good wife, eh.'

Anyone who enters an Aboriginal community for any length of time will be placed in a family category. You will be daughter, sister, daughter-in-law, mother, auntie and so on, and your relationship to everyone in the community will thus be formalized. I knew I would be claimed by Eddie as a valuable resource, useful not just for the bowie knives I might provide, but as a conduit to the white world – that bewildering cornucopia of Toyota trucks, government money, white advisers and bureaucrats. I suppose I had assumed Eddie would make me his daughter, though I had never given this more than a cursory thought. But wife? What did this astonishing bit of news portend? What was expected of me?

That evening I went to visit the whitefellas – a nurse and doctor living in a caravan – hoping to avoid the problem. Eddie's son (and therefore my 'son'), Lance, who was about five years my junior, escorted me. He showed me where I was to camp that night – a crumbling cement plinth surrounded by broken glass, plastic bags and a razor-wired cyclone fence. It stood next to a suppurating ablution block and near to Eddie's wilcha. The fence was to protect me from the dogs. I stayed with the whitefellas until late at night, then quietly made my way back to my swag.

The Aboriginal community was long asleep by now. But Eddie was standing by the fence with his dogs. My heart lurched into my throat. We whispered in Pitjantjatjara: 'Are you OK?'

'Yes, I'm OK. Are you OK?'

'Yes, I'm OK.' But he looked uneasy. Then I thought I understood. He must have boasted that during our journey together we had been lovers. And now he had to save face. We touched each other on the shoulder and started laughing in a suppressed sort of way. I brought him across to my swag. We sat there for a short time in affectionate and amused silence, the dogs slumped against us, and then he went back to his wilcha.

At dawn he woke me up, shaking me gently by the shoulder and grinning down into my face. 'Raaapie, Raaapie.' He had brought a chunk of cold, bloody, fly-encrusted meat and some damper. I put the billy on the fire and made tea. For the rest of that morning we sat on the cement plinth, under the shade of corrugated iron, sanded by a hot, gritty wind, receiving guests – old men and women, presumably my relatives.

I gleaned several things from Eddie's conversation. He wanted me to come back the following winter with my camels, a rifle, a new shirt and a jumper for him, and we would go walking into 'country'.

'I can't come back then, Eddie, but I will try to come back the winter after that.'

He laughed. 'But I'll be dead by then.' He lifted his shirt to show me a long scar down the front of his body. Something had been sung into him by an enemy near Perth. He, Eddie, was counter-singing this person, but there was no guarantee whose sorcery would prove the stronger. There was not a shred of anxiety displayed over the possibility of his imminent death. The personality known as Eddie would disappear, but the essence of the man, that fragment that had been extruded from his country, would return to it.

He expressed what I assumed was fatherly concern over my childlessness. '*Tsc tsc, nyaltajarra* [poor thing], Raaapie.' He surveyed my body, and then patted me on the stomach, breasts and thighs. No question about it now – this was erotic intent. There was nothing awkward about his approach. It was frank and straightforward. And full of tenderness. I was floored by it.

Later that afternoon, I found out from the medical team that Eddie had had an operation to remove a stomach tumour. The prognosis was about five years, they thought.

I went for a long walk by myself up into the hills. I had been so concerned with simply managing this weird event that I hadn't had time to think through my own responses to it. I perched on a rock and surveyed the land below. Plains of yellow grasses like wheat fields swept up to the foot of rocky chocolate-brown ranges, covered at the foot by pale-green spinifex and silvery bushes which gradually gave way to bare outcroppings at the top. Small washaways sheltered a filigree of trees, and here and there, a single, flame-coloured sand dune rose out of the yellow. Eagles, kites and crows carved up wind currents in a perennially cobalt sky. The space was empty of people yet saturated with human meaning. Just as paintings can gain in value until they become priceless, this place was so old that it had become timeless. As so often before in that landscape, I felt as if I belonged somewhere, that I was home.

In the years since Eddie and I travelled together, I had entered and taken up residence in many and various worlds, in many and various countries. I had never consciously articulated what drove me to do this – the desire to see things through others' eyes; to go beyond the confines of my prejudices and habits – but these impulses had undeniably given my life its shape. I had not just studied, but had tried to participate in other ways of life, not in order to bring them within the already existing boundaries of my own, but to break through those boundaries. But these explorations had left me oddly dislocated. I had learned that each world had its own coherence and validity. Each was logical to itself, a whole. And that meant that I no longer felt firmly fastened inside any version of the world. I was a stranger, now, wherever I was, with no reliable centre from which to judge or compare elsewhere.

It is as extraordinary to me now as it was terrifying to me then, that, while sitting on that rock, I seriously considered staying with Eddie. All it would take was a tiny act, as simple as opening a door. I was as close to immersion in another universe as that. Just opening a door, and stepping through. What, in ordinary life, was unthinkable – entering into a psychological and physical intimacy with an eighty-year-old traditional Aboriginal man – was not just thinkable, it was effortlessly doable, once you understood that there was no such thing as ordinary life. There was only the habit of sticking with what one knows – a version of how-things-really-are, which is as arbitrary, strange and illusory as anyone else's. Why not 'marry' Eddie? Why not?

I felt the appalling ease of it, the seduction of it, as vertigo; as if the fabric of the world had unravelled and I was falling through it. But a self-preserving cowardice acted as a parachute. I would most certainly not step through that door. Apart from anything else, there would be no way back. I left Wingelina the following day, with relief, yet in a state of intense and bewildering grief.

A few years later, when I was living in India, I received a formal letter from the community notifying me that Eddie had died.

It wasn't until 1999 that I felt ready to go back. I intended to drive down from the Alice to Wingelina, where Eddie was buried, past Ayers Rock, following my own tracks. Again, I had no idea what my reception would be. Would the family be angry that I hadn't come sooner? Would they care at all?

In the ten years I had been away, Aborigines had undergone something of a transformation in the national psyche. Previously, they had been on their way to extinction because social Darwinism said we were better than them. Now they had become – at least for the purposes of commerce, eco-tourism, international art markets and the spiritually destitute, that is to say, outside the realities of politics – better than us.

All down the Alice mall there was a barrage of photographs and advertisements suggesting that here, contact with 'natural man' could be bought. (A visitor could, for a certain sum, spend a morning out bush, hunting and gathering with bona fide blackfellas, though later she might bump into those same blackfellas buying sweets and grog at a supermarket.) Dot-dots in nauseating profusion covered everything – shop fronts, didgeridoos, tea towels, T-shirts, and, of course, the canvases that now sold for thousands of pounds.

Plus ça change.

And yet, there were the drunks in the Todd river bed, Aborigines in bandages, Aborigines cadging from tourists.

Plus c'est la même chose.

As always, those old friends who worked for Aboriginal organizations were on the verge of burnout. As always there was only one conversation in town – Aborigines – and although it was an endlessly fascinating one, I didn't feel I had much to contribute. I hadn't been involved in the day-to-day political struggles that defined life for my friends here. But it was pretty clear that very little had turned out as anyone had expected or hoped.

No one had believed the situation for Aborigines in Australia could get worse, but in many ways it had. There were patches of coherence and success, but they quickly faded. Did this mean that the liberal policies of the past twenty years had paved a way to hell, or did it mean that there had not yet been enough time for those policies to work? Had welfare crippled Aboriginal self-respect, or had too little money been thrown at their problems? These were not debates it was easy to have publicly – the old fear that admitting anomalies and failures only gave ammunition to 'the Right' effectively shut everyone up – though they certainly went on privately.

The Seventies had been a romantic and idealistic time. Now relations between town Aborigines and the do-gooders were more complicated, less innocent. Black bosses sometimes treated their white workers with a contempt and hostility that would be tolerated nowhere else. And where there is money and power to be gained, there will always be nepotism and corruption.

It was, therefore, in a somewhat disheartened state that I set out for Eddie's country, three days' drive away. On the way I called in at the outstation I had spotted from the plane over a decade before. It was all but abandoned – a straggle of people lived there, among them just one adolescent boy without companions. He stood outside the group, the epitome of hopelessness, uselessness and desolation. He had shot himself a few months before but the bullet had missed his heart. No one seemed to know what to do with him, perhaps even how to think about him. Suicide was apparently unknown in traditional Aboriginal society. Now there was an epidemic amongst the young – hangings, shootings, self-mutilations.

Previously boys would have been removed from their families and placed under the tutelage of older men, who would guide them through a series of initiations, gradually introducing them into the masculine 'mysteries'. Only when this education had been successfully completed would they be allowed to marry. All these structures have now collapsed.

I reached the settlement late on the third evening. It had grown – more tin houses, more rubbish, more rusted cars, abandoned Toyota trucks, dogs snuffling at used nappies, groups of staggering teenagers sniffing petrol, some boys playing basketball on a weedy court, their caps turned backwards, Harlem-style.

I found Lance, my son, the following morning. He was wearing the red headband of a fully initiated man, and he looked more like Eddie than ever. He invited me to his outstation, twenty miles away from the settlement, close to one of his Dreaming sites. His dogs jumped in the back of his truck, then we picked up his wife Linda, various other relatives and children and more dogs and headed for the hills.

The outstation consisted of a tin house with two rooms joined by a roofed cement veranda. Along one side of the cement platform there was a sink; inside the rooms, blankets and dogs; a loo and shower out the back. Stretching away from the house in all directions: desert, marked by one corrugated dirt track and a line of low hills formed by ancestral sisters as they danced their way across Australia.

My companions barely spoke English; only a few words of Pitjantjatjara floated up from the mud of my memory. Awkward silences punctuated the efforts to communicate on both sides. But what was genuine and palpable was their pleasure at my arrival, and my pleasure in being with them.

I had brought the customary gift of meat, but Lance went out to shoot some game – two bush turkeys – the very best he could find. The shyness passed, and we settled down to serious talk. He told me of a new mining venture trying to 'get in' down here; of the crooked black bureaucrats out to line their own pockets. He told me that a lot of Aborigines from the city were coming home to find the families they had been 'stolen' from. He mimed something knitting together. He told me that the problem in remote places like this was still poverty. Owning land was all very well, but if there was no work, no industry, what was the point of it. The old people were dying, and with them the old certainties. Young people were not so interested in ceremonial life. They fell into the twilight zone between the world of their elders and the world of European Australia. The traditional systems of sharing were breaking down. What money there was down here was absorbed by ten per cent of the families, while the others starved – an unheard-of state of affairs in the old days.

That night a sleeping place was cleared for me on the veranda. Linda washed down the cement floor with a broom, then the sink, then our tin cups with the same broom. I was covered in red sand because all afternoon I had been helping Lance plant fruit trees around the house. A fire was lit on the cement, and we all crowded around it, smoke stinging our eyes. First course was a tin of beef stew. The old man opposite me poured honey on slices of white bread, loaded beef stew on top and passed it over. As I ate, the dogs stared at my mouth, waiting for handouts. When I threw something, they snapped it in mid air, not six inches from my face. The bush turkeys, cooking all afternoon in the ground outside, were ready. The old lady next to me blew snot out of her nose with her hand, then with the same hand passed me the turkey leg. Few would understand how privileged I felt to be with these people who had managed to survive the apocalypse with their humanity, their generosity and capacity for laughter intact.

The next day we went to visit Eddie's grave. It had been Christianized by his grandchildren – plastic flowers and a plaque which read:

> MANTJAKURA EDDY. HE WAS A CHRISTIAN MAN
> HE ALWAYS CARRIED HIS BIBLE
> SO CARRY YOUR BIBLES WHERE
> EVER YOU GO

It was an odd epitaph for a man who had needed no gods because nothing he had been or done in his life could have affected the inevitability of his return to the spirit of place. But Eddie's world was ending, and no one could say yet what might evolve out of it.

A strange intimacy had existed between us, but it was across such a vast divide that we could never have come close to answering the questions we posed each other: who are you, how do I make sense of you, how can I accommodate what you know? But with Lance and his generation, the respect, amity and compassion were grounded in something closer to familiarity.

When we all piled back in the truck, I told Lance that a couple of weeks before I'd received the news of Eddie's death, I had dreamed of him for the first time I could remember.

'Oh yeah,' he said, without a twitch of surprise, 'that was 'im.'

OUR NICKY'S HEART

Graham Swift

Frank Randall had three sons: Michael, Eddy and Mark. That was fine by him. A farmer whose business is rearing livestock knows that the sums extend to his own offspring. Sons are a good investment. His wife couldn't argue. She'd married a farmer with her eyes open and knew the score. Three sons in nine years at almost exact three-year intervals, and that was that. But she could have done with a daughter to leaven the male dough. So when she became pregnant a fourth time, and a little unexpectedly, she set her hopes high. She even named her Sally secretly to herself. I know because she told me, years later.

When Sally turned out to be Nick she put a good face on her disappointment and never made a grudge of it. All the same, I think Nicky must have known he was meant to have been a girl because when he grew up all his emphasis was in the other direction. More than any of his brothers, he was the cocky, reckless young stud and, being such, was indulged like none of his brothers had been – his mother's favourite despite, or because of, not being a girl. She doted on him, I think, more than if he *had* been a girl, while to the males of the family he was always the baby and something of an amusement. Michael, nearly twelve when Nick was born, could almost have felt he could be Nick's father, though in practice the image hardly worked, since Michael seemed not to get around to women till he was past twenty, and then in no great rush.

By contrast, I can remember catching Nicky once in front of the bathroom mirror when he hadn't seen me, running a comb again and

again through his hair and giving himself a steady slow burn of a stare.
He was only sixteen but he had the looks and the way about him, and
he knew it. He wasn't a girl but he got them. As many at least as there
were to be had in our corner of the county.

He never saw me looking at him – too busy with himself. That comb
was like a knife with which he was sculpting the last touches to his
head, but he put it aside anyway to run a claw of a hand through the
results.

When men, or boys, look at themselves like this in a mirror, which
way round does it work? Do they see the girl in their own face in the
glass, or is the girl inside them, getting the stare and going weak-
kneed?

Sometimes it wasn't Nicky who ran that final rough hand through
his hair. It was Mum. She'd see him all slicked and preened and she'd
go and muss it up for him, just a bit. He got the habit from her.

I was the odd one out in my own way: Mark, the 'clever one', the
renegade – or the one with ambition and sense. Michael and Eddy
stuck to Dad and the farm, I went to veterinary college. As it turned
out, I never became a farmer's vet. I live in Exeter now and my practice
is mostly domestic pets. All this might have just earned me the family's
scorn – cats and dogs! Guinea pigs for God's sake! But, as things have
gone, they're in no position to mock.

At one time I might even have opted for general medicine. Vets will
always seem like thwarted doctors. It's not true of course, and anyway
it's different when animals were what you grew up with. I like my
practice, my cats and dogs. I like the attachment, the care their owners
have for them. It rests on simple affection, not on a way of life.

Besides, I have a link with human medicine. My wife is a theatre
sister at the Devon and Exeter.

All this – I mean remembering Nicky combing his hair in front of the
mirror – seems far off now, across a divide. If you'd said to my father
even then – it's only sixteen years ago – that one day meat and stock
prices would plunge, that one day there'd be talk of 'mad cows', one
day he'd only be punishing himself, bringing bull calves into the world
just to send them to slaughter, he'd have laughed in your face, looked
round at the yard and called you an idiot.

If you'd said to him that one day, soon, what had always been a
given, the way a farmer works not just for himself but for what he

hands on, wouldn't seem like a given at all but like something teetering on its edge, he'd have called you more than a fool. And if you'd said it wouldn't be so rare for a farmer at the end of the twentieth century to go into his barn with a shotgun and never walk out . . . Well, you wouldn't have said that, even if you'd known.

I didn't know. I couldn't read the future. I just went my own way. What happened to Nicky clinched it. Now it seems, of course, except to my mother, that I was the traitor, the deserter, making my escape safe, leaving a sinking ship.

Nicky was no girl. When he was seventeen he somehow scraped together the cash to buy a six-year-old Yamaha on which he careered round the lanes and burned up and down the main roads, discovering, I think, that for all its throb and roar – what could you expect with the money he'd paid? – the thing was pretty short on power. Michael and Eddy would never have been allowed to do this, nor would I, if I'd wanted, but with Nicky it was somehow all right. Somehow it went with Nicky. Mum would have hated stopping him having his own way – he could twist her round his finger. All the same, I could see her dreading the worst, and it happened.

As far as we know, he tried to overtake a lorry and cut in before the bend, but he didn't judge the speed, or didn't have it, and the wet road was against him. After the accident it was a matter of less than two days before he was dead, but those days were like months, they were like a shift into a different time, a different world, one in which the farm and all that sure sense it could give you of how things lived and died, safe in the bosom of the land, didn't count for a thing. Nicky was in his own little lost bubble of a world, held there by tubes and drips and wires, and the man who was in charge of Nicky and was seeing us now was carefully trying to explain that, because of the brain injury, Nicky would never regain consciousness again.

There was only one decision to be made.

They found us somewhere to sit, to think it through. It was three o'clock in the morning. As if we could think. There are times when a family has to cling together but those same times can make a family seem like a pretty clumsy piece of apparatus. The tubes going into Nicky seemed more efficient. Dad looked at me as if maybe I should pronounce – as if being in my final year at vet college gave me an authority in situations like this. Anyhow, hadn't I always been so keen to show it? That I was the one with the brains in the family? He started to shake his head slowly and mechanically from side to side.

Then Mum, who was drawing every breath like some long, deep adventure, took Dad's hand, squeezed it and they got up. They asked me to go with them – as if I should be some kind of interpreter – and I saw Michael and Eddy shoot me looks I'd never seen them shoot me before but that I realized they must have been giving me all my life behind my back. I'll never know what they said to each other, left by themselves.

Back with the doctor, Dad looked at Mum first, then he cleared his throat and said that we understood. I never heard him say anything further from the truth.

And that should have been the end of it. But the doctor said there was another doctor who wanted to speak to us, he was on his way. He glanced at his watch.

At that moment, I remember, a sudden light came into my mother's face and I realized later that she must have thought for a few wild seconds that this other doctor was some super-special specialist who had overruled the first doctor and was coming to tell us that, after all, Nicky could be saved. But the second doctor said that he understood what we must be going through but in these situations more than one decision had to be made. He had his own careful way of saying what he said next – it must have come from training and practice – but the gist was that Nicky was (he didn't say 'had been') a very healthy young man and we should consider whether his organs should be made available to others.

In particular, the heart.

In my memory of that night I try to keep to the essentials, to remove the daze of sheer shock and amazement in which everything occurred, the dither of secondary complications, like those looks from Michael and Eddy.

In such a situation – to speak like an outsider – there are two opposing arguments. First, that only the victim has authority over his own body and since the victim is beyond all power of intelligence, how do we know that he would have been willing? (I'm sure it never entered Nicky's mind.) On the other hand, how do we know, if we suppose the victim were able to judge his own situation, that he would *not* be willing?

Time, of course, was of the essence.

I remember looking at my parents and thinking there simply was no readiness for this. The one decision, or inevitable acceptance, was enough – too much. Now this. I remember too how they began to look suddenly like guilty, disobedient parties, placed more and more, as each moment passed by, in a position of blameworthy obstinacy, backsliders who wouldn't come round. They looked like they were under arrest.

And as more time passed, it changed into something worse. I could see the picture seeping into at least my mother's head (the second doctor hadn't painted it for her but perhaps it was part of his training to let it take shape) of some person, perhaps not very far away, perhaps just down a corridor in this very hospital, some person in a situation, in its way, not unlike Nicky's, some person, in fact, not unlike *Nicky*, a kind of second Nicky, and she was – we were – denying him life.

We ought to have discussed it with Michael and Eddy. Not sharing it with them might be a bad move, it might only store up permanent trouble. (It did.) But I said nothing and I could see that democratic debate was far from my mother's thoughts. If word had to be given and given quickly, it could only be given under the pressure of whatever imaginings were right then rushing through her head. *Her* head – since I could see that my father was simply going to defer to her. Twenty-five years of being in charge of 400 acres and all that lived on it, generations of Randalls ruling the roost, of which he was the latest heir, hadn't made him capable at that moment of being the one to step forward and speak.

My mother nodded. She said, 'Yes. OK.' The second doctor left a just measurable pause (that, also, might have been in the training), then nodded too, gave a squeeze to his mouth. There were forms that had to be signed.

First and foremost, they needed the heart.

My father walked out of that room a second-in-command, but he had the task, he knew it, of telling Michael and Eddy what had been decided upon without their knowing.

If you'd said to him, years back, that one day they'd be able to take out someone's heart and put it in someone else, he'd have thought you were crazy too.

*

In the subsequent days and weeks my mother's grief went through terrible lurches and swings. She was torn, I know, between the thought that she'd signed away the last living part of her son – what mother could do that? – and the knowledge that part of her son lived on, giving life to another. Wasn't that some small answer to grief? But then, if part of her son lived on in another, wasn't it just a new kind of agony not to know who or where? Wasn't it worse? She had only denied her grief its completion. It was like knowing someone was missing but never knowing, finally, that they were dead. Or knowing they were dead and never knowing the whereabouts of the remains.

As for my own grief, I kept it suppressed, even vaguely concealed, like something that had an edge of shame. My mother had taken on for herself a pitch of anguish that none of the men in her family could match.

The heart, what is it? It's a piece of muscle, a pump.

In more recent years, I've come to see my practice, my cats and dogs, as my principal cushion – a solace, a kind of immunization even – against the worst things life can bring. It sounds like mere softness, an evasion, I know. But I think we demean what they give us, the animals we choose to keep by our side, by calling them 'pets'. In those weeks after Nicky's death it wasn't the cows in the shed, with their own lot of doom, that either comforted or troubled me. It was our border collie, Ned, who knew there was a gap, an unclosable space. We all rubbed against each other strangely harshly and cruelly, but we were all of us more tender than we'd ever been with Ned.

It's a regular part of my job to put down animals, to 'send them to sleep'. I never take it lightly. I know that the brave or matter-of-fact face their owners put on things – their 'let's not be silly, it's only a dog' – isn't the whole story at all. Usually, the animal comes to me. Sometimes, because of the circumstances, I have to go to the house. I always take a heavy-duty black plastic sack. After the procedure is over I might be seen off with the same householderly mannerliness with which the man who's fixed the washing machine is shown on his way. But more than once, barely a pace or two down the front path, I've been stopped like a thief in my tracks by the sudden sob, wail even, of genuine grief coming from behind the closed door.

I think it was in those weeks after Nicky's death that I decided that when I became a vet, it wouldn't be of the kind that visits farms.

Nicky, after all – it's not to make light or soft, either – had been a kind of pet.

As for that space that my mother could never close, her not knowing where Nicky's heart had *gone*, it seemed to become more of an issue for her, not less, not a secondary thing but somehow the nub – I can't say the other word – of the matter.

She understood, of course, that there were strict rules about preserving the anonymity of the recipient – understood, but didn't understand, though I tried to explain some of the reasons. She wanted to know, at least – didn't she have the right? – what had happened to Nicky's heart during that first astonishing stage of disconnection, when it had been removed from Nicky and before it was lodged with its new owner.

I said that first (as if I really knew) you had to think of it from the other end. Someone – they might have been close or hundreds of miles away – would have received a phone call, been woken from sleep, perhaps in those same early hours in which we sat, sleepless and disbelieving, in the hospital. A phone call they had been given to understand could come at any time – soon or maybe years ahead (if they were still there to receive it), maybe never – a phone call they knew would allow them only seconds to agree and prepare.

They would have gone through an instant, perhaps, of wishing that this wished-for call *hadn't* come, that life as they'd known it, with all its risk and distress, might simply go on as it had and not be subject to this imminent, immense change. Then they would have swallowed that thought with the thought that this moment, this chance, might never come again.

They would have been told what to do, to pack the things needed for a stay in hospital, where and to whom to present themselves.

Amid everything else, they would know there was only one way, a necessary prior event, in which this could be happening.

Meanwhile, I said – as I went on it seemed more and more like some impossible fairy tale, like something I must be making up – Nicky's heart would have been placed in a container, a container perhaps a bit like a picnic cool-box, and then it would have been transported by special priority service, by a network of links that exists for such things. Who knows – it might even have been put on a plane? But almost certainly at some stage in the journey it would have been carried in the special pannier of a motorcycle – the quickest way through traffic. There were motorcyclists who volunteered for such tasks. And almost certainly (but I didn't offer this thought to my mother) it would occur to such motorcyclists that motorcyclists themselves formed a significant portion of the stock of organ donors. They tended to be young and fit. They had fatal accidents.

But it seemed my mother, even after months, would not give up her yearning. Surely, she had the right? To think that someone, somewhere, was walking around. A whole new person, with a whole new life. A lease of life. A deliverance.

In the end I did something irresponsible, foolish perhaps. By this time I knew Pauline, my future wife. She was only a junior nurse in those days, she didn't even work at the hospital where Nicky had died. She knew no more than I did, and if she was about to make clandestine enquiries it could be at the risk of her job. All she suggested – I could have come up with this myself – was that I phone up the office of Reynolds (that was the second doctor), hassle the secretary, play the distraught relative (but I was a distraught relative), see what might not, in a moment's exasperation, be let slip over the phone.

She said, 'But are you sure about this? It could all backfire.'

I made the call. I pleaded. The secretary insisted: she simply didn't have access, even if she could release it, to this information. In the end she went away, for some while, came back. 'All I can tell you,' she said, 'is that the recipient was female and forty-six.' She didn't say it as if she were whispering a secret that could get her dismissed. She said it as if it was meaningless knowledge: it hardly narrowed things down.

A female. I hadn't really thought it or imagined it, though of course it was always possible. Nicky's seventeen-year-old heart had ended up in the body of a forty-six-year-old woman. And of course that was a possibility too – the difference in age. That the organs of the young might be received by those older. Not the very old but, still, in this case, someone a lot older than Nicky.

But I didn't say this to my mother. This has been my one big lie, the biggest lie of my life. I said I'd found out something. I'd been 'ferreting around'. Contacts, I said, through vet college (as if there should have been any). I said there was absolutely nothing more to be found out, but I'd learned something: Nicky's heart had gone to a girl. 'A girl,' I said, 'a young woman. That's all I know.'

I said, 'Keep this between you and me.'

The biggest lie of my life. But it gave my mother something with which to close, almost completely, that gap. Something to content her with never knowing more. It was only a half lie too, of sorts, false only by a span of years. If I'd told my mother that Nicky's heart was inside the body of an older woman, a woman, in fact, not so far from my mother's age, I know what my mother would have thought from that moment on. I know what I'd spared her from.

If only, she would have thought, it had not been that other woman's fate to have the dicky ticker, if only it could have been herself. If only she had not been a strong, robust woman, a mother of four, doomed to carry on being strong and robust while a farm and all that it stood for seemed to crumble away around her, and the men on it, a husband and two sons, seemed to crumble too, so it seemed it was left to her to put things right, to change things back. As if she could do that, as if she could wave a wand.

If only she hadn't been that robust woman but a woman, in her middle years, with an incurable complaint of the heart. Then of course it wouldn't have been terrible or even difficult to have made that decision that night, it wouldn't have been the source for ever afterwards of confusion, mystery and remorse. They wouldn't even have needed motorcyclists. She would have said, yes, let them take out Nicky's heart and meanwhile cut her open and take out her iffy one, and then tuck Nicky's up safely inside her. Then everything would have been all right.

Bill Lanchester, *c.* 1968

EARLY RETIREMENT

John Lanchester

My father used to tell the story of a tutor at his university, a Viennese professor of something or other. There was a general conversation about what people would have, if they could have anything in the world. There were some surprising answers – a youngish woman don said she wanted an enormous wine cellar. When it came to the old Viennese, he sucked his pipe for a moment, and then said, 'Vell, if I could really have anything I wanted, anything at all, I think I would choose . . . permanent delusions of grandeur.'

Dad loved that story. He liked it because it was funny, but I also think he liked the idea of a permanent state of feeling that excluded difficulty or pain. For instance, he could never bring himself to discuss money. He could talk about it in the abstract, in relation to businesses in the news or tax policy. But he couldn't bear to talk about money in any personal context to do with his income or – and this was a particular issue – my pocket money. I wasn't allowed to ask for money or even to mention it. The subject caused Dad too much pain. It touched on things from his own childhood to do with the fact that his father had used money as a means of control and interference.

What was odd about this was that my father worked for a bank. Dealing with money was what he did all day, every day, for his entire working life. And yet he couldn't bear to speak of it at home. As a teenager I would resort to simply stealing money from his wallet rather than having to put him and me through the impossible ordeal of asking for it. I would steal it resentfully, too, from the wallet he left lying on the hall table, as if giving me permission to steal from it. I felt that I didn't want to steal but had no choice, and that the whole episode was showing both our characters in their least good light. I now see that the banking and the not-being-able-to-discuss-money were tightly linked: he had gone to work in a bank because his father had bullied him into doing a job which would keep him grounded in the real world – which, in his father's world-view, meant doing a job which was all about money. The memory of that, and all that it implied, was so painful for Dad that if I ever mentioned money to him, he was overpowered by flashbacks from his youth and sent into a gloom.

We lived in Hong Kong, where my father was working, first as deputy and then as manager, at the North Point branch of the Hongkong and Shanghai Bank. He must have felt that his best years in career terms were in front of him: he was serving a long apprenticeship as a relative junior, but that wasn't unusual for the bank in its colonial days. He would still have expected to start to rise and for big opportunities to open up. That might seem like a naive hope for someone who had already spent seventeen years working for the same company; but the pace of banking life, like that of other forms of work, was slower in those days. His chance might yet come.

When it did, in the late 1960s, it was in the form of a transfer to head office in Hong Kong: the bank's HQ at 1 Queen's Road Central. Today, that address is occupied by a famous building designed by Norman Foster – at the time it was built, the most expensive privately owned building in the world, and a highly ugly and impractical one too. In those days the bank was a chunky stone structure with a lovely central hall illustrated with a mural of striving workers; it was so low, relative to the Hong Kong of my childhood, that it was impossible to believe that when my grandparents were first in Hong Kong it was the tallest building in the city. This was where my father was to spend the rest of his working life. It's where I best remember him as a working man, when I used to drop in on him, semi-unannounced. I would either ring up to his secretary from the banking floor, or simply sneak into the staff lift and go up to his section before asking to be taken in by the 'boy' – a Cantonese man in his forties who was this section's administrative manager. Dad was always pleased to see me and I him, and there was something very reassuring about my father in his office in his shirtsleeves at the centre of all this bustle, a picture of me and my mother on his desk.

In his career, though, my father was a disappointed man. He climbed to the stair below the top one, in terms of the bank's hierarchy. He was a senior member of the overseas staff, well paid and as secure as any worker in the world, the beneficiary of a pension scheme which, as it happened, he helped design. But the next level up was that of the head honchos, the people who decided things and set the course, as opposed to running things and keeping them on course. He never got to that level. He had a platform with a perfect view of the personalities and political issues at the high levels of the bank, and he worked with three men who were eventually to run the organization, and oversee the process which took it from being a minor colonial bank to one of the biggest financial institutions in the world. One thing he told me I often remember: two of the chairmen he had known were, he said, diametrically opposite in their behaviour to colleagues. One would scream and shout and berate them, but he never sacked anybody. The other was mild-mannered and calm and never raised his voice, but was utterly ruthless and would sack and demote people without hesitation. I've kept that in mind ever since, and it's been borne out: in every organization I've ever seen at close range, the bosses tend to be either screamers or sackers. People have either a bark or a bite, almost never both.

The next level of promotion, however, did not come. There were one or two attempts by other senior bank figures to poach him to go and work for them – once, by a friend of my father's who was setting up a merchant bank to wheel and deal, in what was to be the far more buccaneering style of banking so prevalent in the 1980s and since. But my father's superior fought off the move, mainly, it seems, because he needed Dad to do all the work and run the department. My father saw this as a disappointment, and so it was, since the main thing in life isn't so much what happens to us as what we think happens to us. I do wonder, though. The cure for being a banker wasn't to be a more interesting kind of banker; it was, probably, not to be a banker at all. But it's hard to accept, once you have been doing a thing for so long, that you have been doing the wrong thing.

Duty was important for him. He was a good man, in his

unostentatious and shy way one of the best men I have known. He
grew up in a culture in which duty and reticence and honour and
privacy and lack of ostentation were all regarded as forms of goodness
and public-spiritedness. Plenty of people still believe in all these things,
but they have vanished from our public culture, or at least from our
publicized culture, and no one celebrates them any more, or even
admits that they were once seen, and not so long ago, as virtues. One
aspect of this was the good deeds he did, and another was that he
never spoke about them. I knew that he was appointed to sit on the
Hong Kong rent tribunal, overseeing arguments between landlords
and tenants – a highly sensitive position in a place where there is no
freehold land, and a tribute to his reputation for fair-mindedness. It
was also a tribute to the fact that he had taken the time to go to night
classes and learn functional Cantonese, something few expatriates
bothered to do, not least because it is so difficult. But there were things
I did not know. In our latter years in Hong Kong, from the early 1970s
onwards, we came to know a group of Catholic nuns who were lively
and funny and did a variety of demanding jobs, mostly linked to
poverty relief – one was a surgeon, another the private secretary to
Cardinal Wu; others we met later were involved in medical aid work
in Guangzhou. They had the unusual virtue in Hong Kong of being
equal-opportunity sceptics, as unillusioned about the Communist
Chinese as about Britain and the self-serving billionaires and big shots
of the Hong Kong business community. I had always assumed that we
met them through my mother's Irish contacts in what my father
always called 'the Murphia'. Much later I found out that we knew
them because my father served unpaid as the treasurer of one of the
local hospitals, where some of the nuns worked. I had had no idea: he
never mentioned it in front of me. That is how you are supposed to do
charity, with the left hand not knowing what the right is doing, and it
is the best side of my father's reticence.

My awareness of my father's unhappiness at work was not a vivid
thing. He did not complain at length, only in muted asides. He felt that
he was brighter and more able than the people he worked for. As for
his work, he hardly every spoke about it, and only once showed me
papers he had brought home when there was a choice between three
candidates applying for a senior job. He spread out the papers,
explained who the men were, and then said that although one of them

was obviously the best and brightest he wouldn't get the job because he was too spiky and cocky and wouldn't necessarily fit in. That, he explained, is how things often worked. People want to have a quiet time and don't like to be disrupted, even if it is by someone who in other ways is the best man for the job.

The defining event of all these years happened in 1974, when my father had a serious heart attack while in the office. Until this point he had, in twenty-five years of employment, not missed a single day's work through illness, something of which he was very proud, especially because he had so often been sickly in his childhood. He was forty-seven years old and a smoker, getting through a pack of Benson & Hedges Gold a day, but apart from being overweight – not obese, but overweight – and sedentary there were no warnings. Years afterwards he told me two things about his heart attack. One was that the first symptoms were like those of indigestion. At the time I didn't understand what a glimpse this was into a world of constant, tormenting anxiety. He also told me that at the moment of having the heart attack he felt himself falling over, losing his footing as he collapsed, so that whenever now he began to lose his balance, on something like a carpet that was slipping over a smooth floor underneath, he had a flashback to the moment of losing consciousness during the heart attack. Again, I didn't understand how terrible the ensuing anxiety and sense of apprehension must have been. The main thing I saw was the physical caution which never left my father afterwards, and the regular angina attacks he used to suffer when out walking, which would cause him to pause and catch his breath with his fists resting on his hips – a syndrome called 'window shopper's angina'. He kept his nitroglycerine pills on him at all times, and latterly we had an oxygen cabinet in the coat cupboard. He gave up smoking, began to take regular exercise in the form of walking, and never ate so much as a mouthful of butter or bacon again.

My father had had difficulties with phobias and anxieties in the past. Wide open spaces triggered moments of irrational fear, and so did moving from dark places into sunlight suddenly; he once said to me he thought the feeling might be linked to traumatic hidden memories about being born. He dreaded social situations that he couldn't get out of, and had a particular fear of restaurants; he would have to walk up and down outside them for a while, summoning the nerve to go in.

These anxieties were taken to a different level by the heart attack, since he now had reason to worry that he might overtax his heart by panicking and suffer another infarct. In other words, the anxiety gave him a powerful legitimate reason to feel more anxious.

I don't want to make my father's life sound unrelievedly grim. He was a popular colleague and people were quick to like him: he was unpompous in a time and a place when that wasn't a common trait in men. He was gentle, funny, intelligent, kind, and also had the rare quality of actually listening to what people said. Women liked him. He had very few close friends and, I sometimes think, no intimate ones. He almost never spoke of his deepest feelings; I think I might be the only person apart from my mother to whom he did. But that did not make him seem a closed or secretive man, merely a private one.

The material comfort he provided for his family was a source of pride to him. He once told me, 'I like the feeling that if I wanted to go down to London and stay at the Ritz for a night or two, you know, I could.' Not that he ever did, but I know what he meant: he liked the wiggle room, the psychic sense of space, that earning a good living brought. This sense of potential freedom came at the cost of mortgaging his life away – but at least in some sense he felt free. He was proud of the good education I was getting, and very proud when I got into Oxford, and then even more proud when I got a first in my moderations, the exams at the end of my first year. He saw this, with reason, as a set of opportunities he had created. When my mother told me about my father's pride in these things, she would always use the same phrase: 'He opened the window and flung his chest out.'

In 1979, having spent thirty years with the same employer, my father had the option of taking early retirement. This might seem like a no-brainer: to have got to the age of fifty-three and now to be free of a job you are bored by, on a comfortable pension, free to do anything you wanted with the rest of your life. What's not to like? It was difficult for my father, though, because it meant accepting that he wasn't going to get any further at the bank and therefore that his career ambition had failed. So taking retirement involved facing and accepting the fact that he was disappointed. He decided to do it anyway, and 1979 was our last year in Hong Kong. Rather than take a summer holiday in

England he worked through and left the territory forever in September. I went back to boarding school in England to start my A-level year, and my parents took the long, slow trip home which they had been discussing ever since he decided to stop working: Thailand, Cyprus, and then Sweden to buy a new Saab and drive it home across northern Europe. At school I received a sequence of postcards. And then my parents arrived in Norfolk, some time in early November, and the open-ended years of retirement began.

This was at Alderfen, a house he and my mother bought in 1972. There was no connection of any sort with Norfolk other than the fact that my mother's sister lived in Norwich. In many ways it was an unfortunate choice. Village life proved to be unfriendly even by the standards of English village life – read: very unfriendly indeed. There was next to no culture and no ready-made social life. The site was windy and bleak; the house itself was an unlovely 'chalet bungalow' of recent construction. But my father loved the idea of owning his property, with no street address beyond that one word, 'Alderfen'. It had nineteen acres of land, most of it unusable, indeed unwalkable, marsh; but beautiful nonetheless. It felt like he owned a piece of somewhere. For someone who felt like he didn't belong anywhere and who had lived all his life in property belonging to other people, that was a novel and consoling feeling.

I recently went back to the village and the thought that hit me with great force was: what were they thinking? My father went to a Norfolk village from a highly structured work environment with long hours and a built-in social life in a city where he had lived for most of his life. To go from living in the Tropics, mostly in one of the world's great metropolises, to a sleepy, isolated, insular, cold piece of nowhere – how could it possibly work?

The fact is that my father was entirely unprepared for retirement. As a lively-minded man with many interests, he no doubt thought he would be free of the intellectual underemployment which can blight life after work; he had lived mostly in his head for many years, and probably thought retirement would be more of the same. He began to study electronics on a two-year course at Norwich Technical College, pursuing an interest he had had for years and, characteristically, wanting to find things out from the ground up. (The other mature student doing the course was twenty-four.) When he bought a BBC

Microcomputer, one of the first affordable consumer models in the UK, he wanted to know how to program it, and how it worked, software and hardware, from the bare machine-code upwards. I said, 'But what can it do? Who cares how it works?' He shrugged. 'Difference of approach,' he said.

In the summer holiday of 1983, I took him out on the canoe that was my great source of happiness at Alderfen – a neighbour and I would spend hours and hours on the small dykes, the river and the local Broad, the most excitingly wild and natural place I, a city boy, had ever known. On some days we would see a kingfisher that lived near where I kept the canoe: the electric-blue flash of his wings, so startlingly vivid amid all the greens and greys, would, whenever I saw it, be the high spot of my day. I had not known before that a natural phenomenon could be the high spot of a day. At the end of our narrow, overhung mooring, you could turn right and head down to the Broad, or left and explore the narrow, shallow, shifting waterways which were impassable to even a rowing boat. There was never a soul there, except the one day we rescued a man who had got lost (we were in the garage playing darts when we heard him shouting for help – a trick of marsh acoustics, since, when we eventually got to him, he was well over a mile away).

My father didn't often come out in the canoe. Looking back, I think he was worried that the exertion of paddling would overtax his heart. That day, though, it was clear and warm and I managed to get him to come out with me. Instead of heading for the Broad we went down the narrow dyke that ran by the edge of our property – the only way of getting there, since the marsh was too boggy and treacherous to walk. It could have been about 400 yards from our house, no more. The low, overshadowed dyke had been transformed into a broad water avenue, and it only took a moment to see why: about a dozen of the trees on our side of the bank had been cut down. I was surprised and curious, but my father was aghast. We cancelled the day out and went quickly home. A few days later I was back at university. Very soon after that I heard that my parents had put our house on the market and were planning to move.

What had happened was that a few locals had cut the trees down to provide access to the Broad for a mooring down past our property. They knew the trees belonged to us but had done it without asking for the straightforward reason that if they had asked my father might have said no. Quite a few people knew what was happening, but no one thought to tell him. After all he had had the house for only eleven years and had only been living there full-time for three.

The resulting feeling of betrayal was, for my father, very sharp. People he was on nodding and chatting terms with had, he felt, done something behind his back. He had a deep sense of insecurity about the untrustworthiness of the locals; he felt a lack of goodwill. So he sold the house and moved to Norwich.

At the time of my next holiday from university, at Christmas, my mother had gone to Ireland for a week so my father and I had a few days alone together. I had gone home in some triumph, having just won a university prize exam, and Dad was very proud and happy – his own finals result had been, by his own account, the worst day of his life. He was very glad to be in the city. 'It was only when we got here that I realized that I had been so fucking bored,' he said. 'Here you can go out for a drink, you can go for a coffee, you can go to see a film. In the countryside there's just nothing to do.' We went to see Peter Weir's film *The Year of Living Dangerously*, and he said it was uncanny how it caught what Indonesia had been like in the 1950s and 60s. We had dinner together on Wednesday night. On Thursday, my mother came back from Ireland and my girlfriend came to stay for a few days. On Friday my parents went out for a drink after dinner and came back at about nine o'clock. My girlfriend and I were watching Roman Polanski's film *Repulsion* when my father went out of the room. He was gone for about half an hour. My mother went to see what he was doing. She screamed my name. I ran upstairs and saw her standing over my father. 'I think he's died,' she said. My first feeling was a great surge of tenderness for her: I felt so sad for her. Not him, not me – her. I knelt down beside her. She was right. My father was already, not cold, but not live-warm. He had had a massive heart attack.

We buried my father a few days later. The turnout was sparse, since he had so few connections with Norwich. In Hong Kong we could have filled a big church, perhaps even a cathedral. I can remember those days with a terrible clarity. As far as I could tell, I felt nothing, nothing at all. This wasn't denial so much as the fact that I simply couldn't locate my feelings. I just didn't know where they were. And there was so much to do. There were phone calls to make, letters to write, probate to arrange, my mother to look after. I wasn't prepared for anything about death, and one of the things I wasn't prepared for was the sheer workload.

This was the first time I was ever impressed by my mother's religious faith. Her reaction the night my father died was one of pure shock: 'What am I going to do? What will become of me?' she kept saying. But by the next day she was deeply, passionately grieving. She told me that she had always thought it would be her who died first. She was able to feel the loss in a way I simply couldn't, and at the same time I felt it was somehow connected to her ability to see something beyond the loss, a context or meaning, provided by her faith. Somehow, because she could see beyond it, she could also see it – that was how it seemed. As for me, partly because the loss of my father seemed so random, so meaningless other than as pure loss, I couldn't even acknowledge it, much less cope with any of the feelings it brought up. Because I had no way of describing to myself what had happened, it was on some level as if nothing had happened. It was as if I couldn't find my keys; or rather, that I knew I had a pair of keys somewhere, and knew that they would be in some way useful, but couldn't find them. No: it was as if somebody had told me that there was something called a 'key', and that these things called 'keys' were essential, and that I would surely be able to find them if I looked, but I had no idea where they were or what they looked like or even, really, what they were for – just that somewhere, somehow, there were these things I probably needed.

Anthony Powell says somewhere that there's nothing quite like having a father go bankrupt to force a man to think for himself. My father's early death was a version of that. His life was not inherently tragic: he wasn't inherently a sad man. If he had lived to be alive today, aged seventy, he would have had about twenty years of comfortable retirement to balance the years spent doing his boring job. He would, perhaps, have found things he wanted to do – the move into Norwich was a good start. He might have made a new life for himself, or even have just resigned himself to the fact that he was going to potter about enjoying his hobbies. But none of that happened. He didn't have that long balanced life, with years of drudgery evened out by years of suiting himself; he had a truncated life, with years of drudgery followed by an untimely death. That made me determined not to do what he did. Whatever else I did with my working life I wasn't going to spend it doing something I hated.

Delilah Mae White, *c.* 1930

THE MERRY WIDOW

Edmund White

My mother was born Delilah Mae Teddlie in Texas at the beginning of the last century. Her father, Jim Teddlie, was a railroad johnny, one of those men who repaired track or laid it. He died when my mother was seven or eight. She used to say he died of malaria while working in the swamps around Houston, but she had a postcard from him which he'd sent from a hospital in Colorado; perhaps he had tuberculosis. Was TB a more shameful disease than malaria? Was it the Aids of its day?

Mother always thought the loss of her father when she was still a child had instilled in her a floating, but permanent, dread of being abandoned by a man, a crucial man, or just by men, men in general. She had a very posed photo of her straight-nosed, square-jawed, wavy-haired father, looking no more than twenty-seven, in a rocking chair, while her full-faced ageless mother, Willie Lulu, hovered behind him in clean, copious laces, her glossy hair pulled back in a bun. She was standing and he sitting, the reverse of the usual positions for men and women in that day and age. My mother's brother, Jack, stood off to one side in short pants, with freckles and anger written all over his face. Beside him in a blur was my tiny mother as a five year old with a big, vague, white bow in her hair; the blur seemed to have been generated by the intensity of her feelings – or by a sudden movement. I'm sure that even then she never stood still.

She met my father in Texas and then they moved north, where I was born in Cincinnati. They were married twenty-two years – and then my father left my mother for his secretary. After the divorce, Mother moved my sister and me first to Evanston, Illinois, then to Dallas. She wanted to be near her folks in Texas and their town of Ranger was just a half-day's drive away. I can still picture Lila Mae standing in front of her mother and stepfather in Ranger with a scarily bright smile on her face as she explained how wonderfully everything was going to turn out. She worked (in Evanston, then in Dallas, later in Rockford, Illinois) as a state psychologist. For a small salary she drove long distances from one primary school to another, testing all the children, on the lookout for those who were 'exceptional' (very bright or very slow) or handicapped in some way and in need of special training. She carried with her her testing materials in a brown leather attaché case. At night, she'd perch her reading glasses on the tip of her nose and grade dozens and dozens of IQ tests and personality tests.

Her mother had married again, to a Mr Snider, and the couple lived in a small, three-room house with a double bed in the living room. Mr Snider would sit in his big upholstered chair with the fan trained on his heavy body. Willie Lulu, constantly shaking almost as if sitting were a penance and she needed to stay in perpetual motion to remain in working order, would sit on the edge of their double bed. Every time she tried to get up to fetch more iced tea or bring out the peach ice cream she'd been churning all afternoon, Lila Mae would stop her. 'Mother,' she'd say, 'now you just sit still because I have something very, very important to tell you.'

Then Lila Mae would stand in her absurdly fashionable and expensive clothes she'd bought at Neiman-Marcus, stiff and brocaded and sweat-stained under the arms, her short, squat body bedecked one season in the New Look with its ballooning, crinolined skirts, the next season in the Trapeze Look, cut on the bias. These Paris couture styles looked as unlikely as kabuki costumes in the hot, humble Ranger house – beside Mr Snider with his collarless blue-and-white-striped shirt unbuttoned sufficiently to reveal his undershirt, his unbending wooden leg propped up on an ottoman and Willie in her loose housedress and carpet slippers, the baggy sleeves of her dress revealing her jiggly arms, fidgeting on the bed. Lila Mae would be wearing her high heels and nylons, attached under her skirt to the garters that dangled from her fat-crushing girdle. She owned no casual clothes – no shorts or halter tops, no trousers or T-shirts, no denim. Nothing except these costumes as costly and constricting as ceremonial kimonos. Though she was just five feet tall she weighed 160 or even 170 pounds, which her dramatic dresses emphasized. She'd been given a quick make-up course by a salesgirl at Neiman's and now she wore her eyebrows plucked and pencilled brown. Her cheeks were clown red, her eyelids smudged a faint blue. Above the right corner of her mouth was a large white mole that she thought of as a beauty mark. When Mother was in her twenties, a doctor had burned this mole but instead of dropping off it had just faded from its original black.

She'd say to Willie Lulu, 'Please, Mother, listen to my plan, because I'm going to go places in this world. I always try to present the best appearance possible, I never let myself just go, I've got my fine new Packard and brother!' – Here she shook her fists and let her face go radiant –'Just watch me go!'

'That's right, Sister, I always did say you're going to go places,' Willie said, smiling to herself, almost embarrassed that she'd taken the floor, though she meant to be nothing more than the Greek chorus to Lila Mae's protagonist. She called her own daughter 'Sister' and Jack 'Brother', just as our mother called my sister Margaret and me 'Sister' and 'Brother'. I guess it was a Southern custom but I imagined it derived from all those years Willie had lived alone with her children before her second marriage, just as my sister and I were our mother's only companions – siblings more than children.

People back then didn't have friends. They surrounded themselves with the families they'd been born into or had acquired through marriage. They knew many professional acquaintances, of course, and entertained them lavishly, but though they might become boozily chummy during an out-of-town convention, they never confided in one another and they did nothing to intensify these relationships. Mother would befriend people she met through her work but she always referred to them as 'the little people'. She'd say, 'I'm always very warm and open with the little people but I have to keep my distance or else they'd eat me alive.' She'd say with serene, unreflecting complacency, 'The little people just love me. No wonder. I'm so nice to them. It's not often they get to meet a fine lady like me.'

Mother was full of contradictions. She admired rich people and the few she knew she'd describe as constituting 'a lovely family', or they were 'fine people', as if material success and moral superiority naturally coincided. She didn't pursue the rich, however, occasionally dismissing them as 'spoiled' and 'idle', especially non-working wives. She admired scientists and doctors most of all, since they contributed to the advancement of humanity. Research was the highest good and Mother would have ranked a poor medical researcher over a rich real estate agent, but she was not given to setting up such clarifying contrasts in her mind. She didn't torment herself over moral quandaries; for her, everything coexisted in a general beige haze.

Not that she couldn't come down hard on cheating or stealing or cursing ('I don't like ugly talk,' she'd say). Nor did she approve of criticizing other people ('When did you become so high and mighty?' she'd ask my sister, who had a nasty satirical streak). Mother was more likely to pity people than ridicule them. Although she believed in medicine and eventually worked in a free medical clinic for the retarded and brain damaged at Cook County Hospital in Chicago, nevertheless, in her inconsistent way, she continued all her life to read Mary Baker Eddy's texts as well as a magazine published by the Christian Scientists. What she liked about the Scientists was their uplift, especially their certitude that evil was only a form of ignorance that could be banished by wisdom. Mother described herself as 'bouncy'. The Ford she owned when I was an infant she named Bouncer. She longed to go on the Arthur Godfrey show as a good-time gal who was also a mysterious femme fatale. She thought her name, Delilah, was so alluring that it made her a natural for a talk show.

She also read Emerson, not for his uncomfortable questions but for his reassuring answers. She liked his Yankee individuality, joined to German idealism and Hindu passivity, though she was not one to ferret out the contradictory sources of his thinking. She was a pantheist. She liked to believe we were all waves in a single big sea, that for a moment we rose as individuals before we crashed and were reabsorbed into the swelling mass. Sometimes we were all mirrors reflecting the sun, just slightly different glimpses of the same Oversoul. Even at an early age I found Mother's pantheism attractive but unconvincing. I never liked God in any form, even at his most universal. To me he was like Santa Claus – a grown-up conspiracy perpetrated on children to humiliate them. Too good to be true. Was I unconvinced by God because he was a man, an adult, white, authoritative male, and his son seemed an unfamiliar type to me back then in the 1940s and 1950s: bearded, long-haired, liquid-eyed, compassionate to the point of morbidity? Mother loved the Christ of the Sermon on the Mount but her God she took in two incompatible forms – diffused through nature and concentrated in one kindly, attentive, all-forgiving grandfather. Christ himself she thought of as a wise man, nothing more, the Emerson of his day. Certainly not as God. She rejected Jesus the personal saviour whom her niece (Jack's daughter) embraced so fervently. After Mother died, I surmised that her niece believed she was writhing in hell; all Mother's good works, her daily prayers to God, counted for nothing since she'd not been born again, she'd not been washed in the blood of the Lamb.

As I was growing up, Mother and I would go on long car trips. After we started living in Evanston outside Chicago we'd drive down to Texas in two or three long days. My sister must have been in the back seat but I can't remember her. Along the way Mother liked me to read to her, hopeful, deep books that would sometimes cause her to look dreamy ('Read that again – we must remember that') or that would make her drum her hands with glee on the steering wheel and bounce up and down with the sheer excitement of absorbing beautiful words and inspiring ideas. Sometimes she'd forgo Emerson and Eddy in favour of something meaty like Bruno Bettelheim's thoughts about death camp survivors or childhood schizophrenia.

For everything she did was oriented to her career. Her reading (or rather her listening, since she'd decided that audition was her natural 'modality' and she was more an aural than a visual learner) gave her ideas or strength for her work, and often I would read aloud articles about retardation from a professional journal. Even her inspirational reading was destined to give her the fortitude and compassion necessary for her draining work.

She had no hobbies, though she could sew and cook. She never minded sewing a button back on or taking tiny neat stitches to repair a tear and I can still see her sitting on the couch, her short legs dangling, her reading glasses weirdly enlarging my view of her eyes, as she performed the humble task with admirable calm and efficiency, often still wearing her fancy work clothes instead of her nightgown. She'd stop everything, wherever she was, and do the bit of sewing required. She would never have wasted her time gardening or playing the piano – or playing cards or even going for a walk. She collected nothing for herself though she bought me a music box for every birthday, all 'improving' in that they played a Chopin waltz or something from Gounod's *Faust*. Everyone she spoke to during the day was a patient or parent, colleague or volunteer, or some sort of 'professional contact'. She worked a full day – at first in the schools, later in her Chicago clinic – and often filled up her evenings doing private testing and consultations.

She had no interest in therapy or purely psychological problems. For her, all mental torment was ultimately due to chemical imbalance, genetic deficits or brain traumas, usually sustained during birth. Her own suffering alone was due to genuine distress, usually caused by men's cruelty. For all the rest of us, she was convinced that birth was so hard on the infant that he or she invariably sustained some form of brain damage. To Mother, everyone alive was brain damaged, a condition obvious if important functions had been disturbed such as speech or hand-eye coordination, less apparent if a subtler form of agnosia had been triggered (the interpretation of visual signals, for instance). When I had trouble learning to drive from a brusque, untalkative instructor who would demonstrate the right moves but never describe them, Mother assured me I would make progress only if I'd switch to a college student who'd talk me through everything and show me nothing. She was right. My birth, apparently, was so long and difficult that her obstetrician had made her promise she would have no more babies. I had several convulsions in my first few weeks. 'He told me to close the store,' she said, laughing one of her laughs, a low, vulgar, humourless, even menacing, chuckle. It strikes me only now that her decision to close the store was timed with (and may have caused) the beginning of Daddy's affair with Kay.

If my sister or I ever spoke of general apathy, a broken heart, listlessness, anxiety, Mother would say, 'I think we should run an electroencephalogram on you,' or 'Maybe you need a good neurological work-up. After all, you had those convulsions . . .' Quite rightly, she saw deviance and neurosis as an unsoundable swamp and preferred a diagnosis of previously undetected petit mal seizures to one of philosophical despair or psychogenic angst.

She was a hard worker: up at six, at the clinic by seven-thirty, not home till seven or eight, at which time she often saw private cases, as she also did on the weekends. She loved the once-a-week open clinic every Wednesday morning at the hospital when doctors of all different specialties would pool their expertise; she would take notes and write up the final report. She'd describe pitiful, grotesque children as 'a beautiful case of hydrocephalia' or 'a classic example of Down's syndrome'. She'd refer to sickle-cell anaemia or phenylketonuria. As a Southerner she was convinced she could communicate more effectively with blacks than could the Yankee (or Indian or Chinese) doctors. If the doctor would ask if the child 'drooled', Delilah would translate: 'Mother, does your baby pule?'

Like my father, who bragged that he'd never gone bankrupt or killed a man, my mother would also stress the basics. They were children of the frontier. She admired someone like her own mother, who rose early, made her bed, cleaned her house and cooked at least one hot meal a day for herself and Mr Snider. 'When I'm alone in the house,' Mother would say, 'I set myself a place and even put a flower in a bud vase.'

She and Willie Lulu wrote each other one-page letters every day. Sometimes just two or three sentences scrawled in pencil: 'Hot here in the nineties. Need a good rain. Mr Snider still got his summer cold.' Sometimes Grandma would add, ungrammatically, 'Tell Eddie never to smoke nor drank.'

My mother wanted to give me the blanket approval that Willie Lulu had bestowed on her. But Willie had led such a circumscribed life, seldom travelling out of Texas or even Ranger, that she never doubted for a moment what she thought about something. Either it was a part of her familiar, over-observed world, or it was utterly foreign and she said, 'Well, I declare, will wonders never cease,' and she conceded it was beyond her intellectual means.

But Lila Mae had taken on whole new worlds for which she'd not been prepared. Not just the miracles of technology (men walking on the moon) – for those innovations were precisely the ones she could take in her stride since she had been programmed to believe in progress. No, what made her uncertain were the proper boundaries between children and adults, love and sex, work and play. And what bewildered her were her children – their strange, mocking sense of humour, their self-hatred, their duplicity or at least doubleness. Mother couldn't tolerate or even fathom our inexplicable suffering. 'I don't see what you're complaining about,' she'd say. 'You're not deformed, you're well housed and well fed, you attend good schools, your health is excellent, you're both intelligent, in the top percentile of the population, you're of normal height and average weight, you're good-looking kids, you weren't born in Armenia or Mongolia but in the greatest country on earth in a century of splendid medical care –' She'd look offended and tired when Margaret and I laughed at her chirpiness. My sister didn't like me much (I was too obviously an egghead and nerd and pansy) but as teenagers we did share a bitter sense of humour. Our mother's kind of *statistical* reassurance struck us as grotesque since we didn't want to be of average weight or normal height – we wanted to be exceptionally beautiful and lovable. Whereas in fact we were each obsessed by our own flaws. I knew that I had a huge black mole growing between my shoulder blades, that I threw a ball like a faggot, that my big black glasses made me look like a creep. Margaret hated her teeth, which had gaps between them because our mother had been too cheap to pay for braces. She'd rather buy herself a mink coat and a matching mink hat – 'I *need* it,' she'd wail. 'A good appearance is half of professional success. And I get cold in the winter going down to that ugly old Cook County Hospital when it's still dark outside in sub-zero weather. I'm with welfare mothers all day long and babies who are no more than monsters and I need a bit of luxury in my life. Your teeth look fine, Margaret Anne. It's all just your imagination. Why can't you accentuate the positive the way I do?'

But Mother, too, had something she was ashamed of: fat. The ninety pounds she'd once weighed still seemed to her her rightful, God-given size. That she now weighed seventy pounds more struck her as a horrible but temporary aberration. I had no sympathy for her; being overweight seemed to me to be a form of adult carelessness, even moral failure. She was always wrestling with her size.

Her girdle was a medieval device called the Merry Widow that simultaneously cinched in her waist (and made it hard for her to breathe) and pushed up her breasts with half cups that barely came up to the nipples. The Widow moulded her ass into one seamless, rounded sphere, a mono-ass in which no crack was detectable under her skirt. The girdle, which was French, was laced up the back. That was my job. First I'd thread the laces around the outer, easier vertical line of grommets. Once they were in place Mother would inhale deeply and suck in her stomach, and like a professional torturer I'd shift the laces to the inner line of grommets, one by one. She would groan from the pain but stoically order me to go on pulling them as tight as I could. Her hair was wild, as brittle and blown-up as a tumbleweed from years and years of sitting under the dryer, her pale face not yet made up, featureless and shiny, her height minuscule since she wasn't wearing her high heels, to which she'd become so habituated that her calf muscles had shrunk and now she couldn't walk more than a few paces without stretching them painfully. Once she was strapped into the Merry Widow she could clip her nylons in place, apply her make-up, brush and spray her hair into shape, slip on her dress (which I'd have to zip up), put on her woven white-and-yellow-gold bracelet and matching brooch and her black oval ring with the carved intaglio of Athena's head in profile, finally step into her immaculately polished high heels and douse herself with perfume, grab a purse that matched her shoes and shrug into the three-quarter-length mink cape she'd had her full-length coat reduced to on the theory that people would think she'd been able to afford a new fur at the newly fashionable length.

There was no provision for wearing panties under the girdle. Maybe some women did but Mother would have been too obese to bend over and pull them down to urinate, which she had to do frequently during the day. Because she was pantyless her black bush was visible just below the bottom of her girdle when she was not wearing a dress. Margaret thought this situation repulsive and unhygienic and wouldn't help Mother into her foundation garment. 'Oh, God,' she'd moan to me, 'it's so yucky. Somebody could look up her skirt and see *everything*, and she wears that damn girdle every day – it's not even clean! Most women wear big baggy panties over the girdle – why can't she? Is she a pervert?' Although even young slender women were expected to wear girdles under fitted suits and evening dresses, Margaret categorically refused. She'd been plump as a ten- and eleven-year-old, but as a teen she'd become lean and athletic and she knew she didn't have to compress her hips and stomach into a rubberized tube. When I was a high school freshman I slow-danced at a school party with a famous local beauty. Under the chiffon I could feel the unyielding bones and webbing of the girdle. Girls were revealing their bare shoulders and arms to admiring men, but mothers made sure their daughters' bodies, the important parts at least, were armoured inside strong, protective foundations.

The minute our mother would come home she'd say, 'Get me out of this girdle!' She'd throw off her dress and I would unlace her as quickly as possible, keeping my eyes away from the glossy bush below. Her extremely white skin was inflamed and waffled as it emerged out of the Widow. Mother visibly sagged into a bigger, rounder, shorter shape. She'd throw on her nightgown even if it was only five in the evening. She used cold cream to remove her elaborate make-up. She believed that a woman should never wash her face. In fact, water must never touch the skin. No, she must thoroughly slather it in cold cream then wipe it off with cotton balls. To this daily ritual she attributed her glowing, unwrinkled complexion – a claim she'd make loudly and clearly to anyone present, despite the incontrovertible evidence that her face was covered with a mass of tiny wrinkles around her mouth and eyes and two deep creases across her forehead.

Once her face was stripped of paint she'd make herself her first highball of the evening. 'Ooh-eeh, I need a drink, brother!' she'd say, the barnyard exclamation an echo of her mother, though Willie had never sipped a drink in her life. Mother diluted her inch of scotch with a tall glassful of water and ice; she kept a highball going throughout the evening. She'd write up reports in her neat, round hand, which her secretary at the clinic would type the next day. She didn't approve of television though she liked it ('I don't see how you can watch that dumb stuff') just as she enjoyed popular music but usually only let herself listen to Mozart's 'Jupiter' symphony or Beethoven's 'Moonlight' sonata. 'I like fine music,' she'd say, 'beautiful, deep music meant for the ages.' I would laugh at her cruelly, mockingly, though I agreed with her completely.

Somewhere along the line my sister and I had decided our mother was a character, a caricature like Tennessee Williams's Blanche DuBois or Amanda Wingfield. Lila Mae's baseless optimism, her coquetry, her insistence that she was 'an old-fashioned gal' and 'one hundred per cent feminine' made us grin like gargoyles. Adolescents are wretchedly conventional as they tiptoe nervously into the great crowded ballroom of adulthood. Margaret and I were ashamed that our mother was a divorcee – a 'gay divorcee' as she put it, to our minds as dubious as a 'Merry Widow'. In Evanston in the 1950s, during the Eisenhower years, a divorcee was just a step away from a prostitute. Our mother said she left Cincinnati because she needed 'a big stage, a big world, I need to think big and be with big people who have big ideas.' But if she'd stayed put she would have been humiliated every day since there were no single men or women in their world in Cincinnati and all the couples they had known would have sided – *did* side! – with Daddy and Kay. A divorcee was seen as a potential husband stealer and home wrecker.

When we lived in Dallas Mother was not allowed to sit at the bar or dine alone in the restaurant at the Baker hotel: no unaccompanied women was their policy. When we moved back to Illinois, Mother made up for lost time. She became a habitué of Chicago's supper clubs and piano bars. Her favourite place was Ricardo's, an Italian restaurant and bar in the Rush Street area of nightclubs near the Chicago River down behind the Wrigley Building. The lighting was low, the creamy pasta dishes comforting, the waiters friendly. Mrs White was a good tipper and a real lady (she'd tell you so herself). Short and fat and girdled, smiling and drunk and fearless, Delilah would clamber with some difficulty up on a stool and eat her noodles Alfredo at the demilune bar behind which were illuminated full-length paintings of the vices and virtues, abstractions that struck a Christian Scientist as theatrical and unreal. I can remember one naked man transfixed in a pitiless shaft of light. Another canvas by Ivan Albright, Chicago's best-known artist, showed a hag covered with sores and cellulite; we were told that Albright had worked on it for ten years. I also recall a scaly, infected-looking painting by him with a long portentous title; it was no accident that Albright had painted the picture of Dorian Gray for the movie, both the bland Before and the oozing, scary After.

When I accompanied my mother to Ricardo's we'd be seated at a corner table within hailing distance of the bar. We never had enough money to order without thinking; Mother would split a green salad with me and then split a pasta dish. She claimed she ate like a bird and probably most of her calories did come from whisky. An accordionist – always the same little, deferential man – would come by our table and serenade us, his mouth producing a sad smile and his head cocked to one side.

One evening at our corner table, where Mother always kept the highballs coming, she turned her unfocused smile on the extremely tall businessman at the bar who kept glancing over. 'Roberto,' she whispered to her favourite waiter, 'do you know anything about that very tall man – don't look now! – that tall man at the bar?'

'Oh, that's Abe, Mrs White. I don't know his last name, big tipper, owns a yacht that he keeps down on the marina here. Lives somewhere nearby on the Gold Coast, I think he said.'

'That's interesting,' Mother said with a smile. 'That's *very* interesting.'

Maybe Abe noticed them conferring about him, because Roberto came over a moment later with a new highball and a ginger ale for me. 'Compliments of Abe,' he whispered. Rather than exclaiming with excitement as I would have predicted, Mother merely smiled with boozy serenity and raised her glass to toast Abe, her head tilted slightly to one side. Her smile was pursed as if to reproach him tenderly for an extravagance. A minute later he was standing at our table.

'May I join you?' he asked.

Mother smiled enigmatically and nodded and he slipped into the booth beside her and reached over to shake my hand. 'Abe Silverstein,' he said. It all seemed so easy to me and I wondered if Mother was sober enough not to ruin this chance. For it did appear a remarkable opportunity since I knew that Mother sat beside the silent phone night after night, anxious and depressed, because none of the men she'd given her number to at Ricardo's or at the Miller Steak House ever called her. At age fourteen I had replicated within myself all of her doubts about herself – was she too old, too fat, too short, too drunk to attract this tall slender man in his forties with the unseasonable tan and the shiny dome circled by a monk's tonsure of dark curls, with the well tailored suit that gave him staggeringly wide shoulders and exposed an elegant quarter inch of white shirt cuffs, this man with the bright smile and the one winningly chipped tooth, with the big warm dry hand (I could imagine his hands trying to unlace the complicated genetic code of the Merry Widow's double helix)? I felt anxiety building up inside of me. Should I say something remarkable that would win Abe over? That would lure him into a relationship with Mother, with us?

Mother spoke too much about herself, about her work with the retarded, and I squirmed with irritation at her ineptness. Didn't she know that men needed to be drawn out, made to feel important? 'I love my work,' she said, 'because I feel I'm making a real contribution to retardation.' She's retarded herself, I thought.

But Abe wasn't put off. 'That's just great, Delilah,' he said. 'I didn't think I'd be meeting someone classy like you in a place like this.'

'Like me?' Mother asked disingenuously. 'Whatever do you mean?'

She wanted him to elaborate on how unexpectedly important and admirable she was, but he didn't pick up on his cue and instead started rambling on about other interesting men and women he'd met at Ricardo's. Naturally, Mother didn't want to hear about them. She didn't want to be placed in a context, no matter how flattering. She wanted to hear that she was unique. Her smile faded from the goodwill she'd radiated when she'd been talking about herself into a drunken fragment of resentment and impatience. If I'd been in her pumps I would have produced all the appropriate little nods and murmurs of assent, but she went inert and heavy with frustration. I'd learned to make myself extremely agreeable to the two or three handsome guys my age I knew at Evanston High (in a year I'd be sent off to prep school). I admitted they'd never sleep with me but I wanted them to enjoy themselves so much in my company that they'd gravitate to me almost unconsciously. Mother had perfected none of my dark arts.

She could always fall back on Mr Hamilton, a newspaperman who liked nothing more than to have Mother prepare him a hot buttery meal. Then they'd watch a variety show on television. He was half blind and couldn't drive, which removed any reason for his going easy on the bourbons and branch water. He had been in the newspaper business for nearly forty years but he exhibited no interest in current events or office gossip and relayed no anecdotes of interest. I think he made up the pages, chose which stories would run where and for how many inches. His conversation was all boilerplate, the odd bits of information used to fill up columns. In some ways he was Mother's version of Mr Snider – a big soft man who was companionable. Mother kept hoping for someone better and when she thought things were working out with Abe she'd dismiss the thought of Mr Hamilton with scorn. 'I need a real man,' she'd say. 'Someone who's got some oomph.' But when better prospects would vanish she'd go back to preparing homey dinners for Mr Hamilton or let him invite her out for a big, sizzling steak at Miller's and a baked potato engorged with sour cream and chives.

As I grew older I became more and more difficult with my mother just as she was becoming sadder and lonelier. When I turned fifteen she was fifty-three; she was finding fewer and fewer men to ask her out, she was nearly as wide as she was tall and she was constantly out of breath. When I'd let myself in at midnight after a date she'd want to know every detail about my evening. She'd be lying awake in bed in her darkened room just beside the front hallway. I knew she couldn't sleep until I came home and I resented this form of emotional blackmail. Nor did she suffer in silence. 'Remember,' she'd say, 'I won't be able to sleep a wink until you're safely back here, and I've got a killing schedule at the clinic tomorrow. Please don't keep me up all night, honey.'

When I'd stand in her doorway at midnight she'd want me to sit on the edge of her bed and rub her back; sometimes she'd turn on a light and ask me to press out the blackheads. Her skin felt clammy. I could smell the whisky seeping from her pores; in a kittenish way she called it 'wicky'.

'Was she cute, that Helen of yours?' she'd ask.

I felt trapped, compromised by her nosiness, revolted by the touch of her skin which, however, was terribly familiar. I didn't want to discuss girls with her. I had bought a latch for my bedroom door and installed it myself so I'd have a little privacy, but she was always tapping at the door. If I didn't respond she'd say, 'Now Eddie, you either open this door for your mother or I'm going to break it down.' And I knew she would and could. If I stayed in the bath too long

she'd shout through the locked door, 'You've washed it long
enough.'

As a little boy I'd lived for her. I'd suffered when she wept over the
divorce (which we referred to as the 'XA', a term I'd made up out of a
superstitious fear of naming it). I had read to her the beautiful words
of Emerson and felt the same glow of admiration as she did, for such
depth, such wisdom. I would sometimes cry hysterically when I was
unable to console her. In my fantasies (and in my responses to the ink-
blot tests she was administering to me) I saw empty royal palaces and
objects – jewels and graveyards – just as when I built castles of sand in
the summer or of snow in the winter I peopled them with lonely, tragic
tsarinas floating through crumbling wings of the Old Palace that had
long since been abandoned.

But as I grew older I resented my mother's dependence.

When she'd say, 'You and I are exactly alike,' I would reply, 'Oh
no we're not. You like to lump everything together. You prefer
resemblance to difference – that's why you like the Baha'i Temple in
Glencoe, because they claim all the nine great religions of the world are
really the same. But they're not! You have to make distinctions and not
lump things together. That's your biggest mistake.'

Her 'mistakes' were legion to my eyes. She was unafraid of the
obvious. I lorded over her my more extensive reading, my better
memory, my more critical approach to life, forgetting that if I had
respect for the mind it was due to her. I attacked her for not keeping
her distance, for not respecting my autonomy; I could make her cry but
if I was nice to her, even for a moment, she'd be all smiles and forgive
my trespasses against her. I felt she loved me without understanding
me, just as her mother loved us all but knew little about us. Mother
saw me as a sort of philosopher king, something like her secular vision
of Christ. In her view, I was eager to make my 'contribution' in order
to reduce the sum total of human suffering. When she finally accepted
that I was a gay writer, she'd say, 'You've truly become a spokesman
for your people.' Gays were my tribe and I was leading them into the
Promised Land. I knew I was selfish and egotistical and too afraid of
failure, obscurity and poverty to be able to afford the luxury of 'helping
my people'.

In the late 1970s, when I was approaching forty and she seventy,
she was drinking so much that she could scarcely walk to the corner.

Her belly was a swollen watermelon under her girdle, her face resembled that of a squalling infant – creased, nearly toothless, red. She'd been forced into retirement when the clinic she headed at Cook County Hospital closed its doors. It had been a private clinic, if in a public hospital, and it had been financed by rich Jewish benefactors, friends of Abraham Levinson, the doctor who'd established the foundation after his son's early death and named it in his honour. Now Dr Levinson was dead, too, as were most of his friends. Whereas the clinic (and my mother) had been pioneers in the diagnosis and treatment of retarded and brain damaged children, now, thirty years later, better care had become common and there was no need for the Julius D. Levinson Foundation. My mother was forced into retirement with no pension and no savings; she had nothing but the pitiful monthly sums she received from Social Security.

And the money I gave her. I sent her a cheque every month for the next twenty years; in that way I had replaced my father, who was now dead, and his alimony, which had run out. I maintained my mother in her fancy Gold Coast apartment with its doorman and view of Lake Michigan. I paid her dress bills at Neiman's and Saks Fifth Avenue. Actually, she economized so skilfully – she who had always been recklessly extravagant – that she was able to afford her little luxuries even on the small sums I was able to spare.

At the same time as my mother lost her job she had a second mastectomy. Her latest and much younger boyfriend found a job in California, took his leave and was never heard from again. He'd been a self-serving drip, but Mother had loved him and losing him was a terrible blow for her. Mother felt he couldn't endure the loss of her second breast (not to mention her colostomy, for altogether she suffered from three primary cancers, poor battered thing). As if these trials had not been harsh enough, she couldn't keep up the payments on her modest summer house and had to sell it. Jobless, loveless, breastless and homeless, she began drinking so heavily that one night, driving home to the house she was about to vacate, she crashed into the garage door then staggered inside and fell in the bathroom. She cracked a rib and was unable to get up. No one knew she was there and no one came looking for her. One day went by, then a second. By now thoroughly sober but in terrible pain and still immobilized, she began to worry about a new complication. She was too weak to irrigate her colostomy and her peristalsis seemed to have shut down. She knew that soon she'd be poisoned by her backed-up faeces.

It was then she made her strange bargain with God. She told him that if he'd unplug her colostomy she'd never touch another drink. No sooner had she made this deal with the deity than the shit began to shoot out of her side. And she honoured her promise of abstinence ever after.

Once she stopped drinking she succumbed to the most terrible delusions. My sister and I failed to see that she had the DTs, though her symptoms were classic. She boarded a plane for Amarillo where she descended on her brother Jack's daughter. Two days later my cousin was on the phone: 'Eddie, you've got to come down here and get Aunt Lila Mae. She's gone crazy. You know those little bugs we have down here we call millers? Well, there were just three or four millers flying around the ceiling light last night but your mother saw *thousands*, revolving like devils at the mouth of hell. Now you know, Eddie, I keep a nice clean house, a Christian house. Your poor mother is out of control. I don't know anything about her business, but I kind of suspect she's not a rich, rich woman?'

'Not at all,' I said.

'Well, she's offering money, even very large sums, to just about everyone she meets. She's not at all nasty. She's as sweet as sweet can be. But she never draws a breath; I hear her in her room talking to herself, very excited and bubbly, like a little girl. You know I've always thought Aunt Lila Mae is a very special person. I love her to bits. She's believed in me all my life when my own mother did nothing but criticize me and tear me down. I owe your mother so much but I just don't know what to do now.'

I flew down to Amarillo and Mother was at the airport in a funny little costume she'd cobbled together, with pompoms in her hands. She'd decided she was a cheerleader. Her eyes wouldn't meet mine, her smile was a manic blur and she was singing a little pep song of her own devising: 'Go, Eddie, go, go, go.'

At this time my sister and I grew closer as it dawned on us that we were no longer neglected children but newly needed if not officially designated guardians to our mother. She had been too unhappy, too obsessed with her work and men, too alcoholic to be the serene, all-giving, nothing-taking goddess for whom our society reserves the label 'Good Mother'. But she'd given herself to us entirely, we were the brats who rattled behind her like cans tied to a cat's tail and we were the excess baggage who'd prevented any man from ever proposing to her after the divorce, or so she firmly believed.

Although she'd rocked us and hugged us and wept as she did so when we were small, later my sister and I wouldn't let her touch us. We were repelled by her body – so fat, so corseted; I am certain this distaste was inspired by her own self-loathing and her drunken, coquettish demands for massages.

I have replicated too many of her traits to be entitled to judge her. I alternate thin decades with fat decades; the thin periods have always been hard-won through medically supervised dieting, exercise and even surgery. Like her I am always pursuing one man or another, though unlike her I've usually lived with my lovers for an average of five years at a time. Recently when a lover left me, I sobbed for two months just as my mother had when one of her boyfriends left her. Like her I'm work-obsessed, but I've certainly never put in the long, hard days she relished and bemoaned. Like her I've had my problems with alcohol and had to stop drinking altogether. Like her I alternate between low self-esteem and a prickly sense of my own importance.

Eventually my mother straightened herself out. As her DTs subsided she hid out in a Michigan hotel, scribbling away at her memoirs, just as I'm doing now. She discovered the only effective cure for mental illness: room service. She was able to summon another living human being – a handsome young waiter – whenever she wanted him. And since she was in small-town mid-America she could engage him in conversation as long as she liked. Whenever she felt threatened by his presence she could dismiss him with a smile and a large tip. Whenever he appeared he brought her warm, nourishing food. No hospital or clinic or doctor can provide this precise winning formula.

My father's death left my mother nonplussed. In her own mind she'd been involved year after year in the most dramatic communication with him, a dialogue constructed out of silent replies, some silences short, others heavy with irony or protest, still others

staccato and excited and overlapping. Now all that artful combative
silence had ended, replaced by the senseless low telephone buzz of
death. What she'd always believed to be a heavily meaningful
rupture in communication she now understood had long since gone
dead for him and perhaps had never been interesting enough for him
to notice. He didn't give a damn about her, never had.

She was so incapable of grasping that her long years of work as a
psychologist were over that she rented a one-room office at the top of
her building – the 'crow's nest', as she called it – and filled it with
metal filing cabinets containing hundreds and hundreds of case
histories. These were documents. They were official. They must be
preserved. She might be held accountable, possibly before the law.
She might be called on as an expert witness.

She teamed up with her grandson Keith, my sister's son. He and
his mother were on the outs for the moment so his grandmother
moved him into the crow's nest – which gave her a graceful excuse
for no longer going up to her desk and files and staring dumbly at the
yellowing folders and the names of retarded children who were now
forty or fifty years old if still alive. My nephew was her new project.
Mother would make him supper and then he'd read to her out loud,
no longer from Bruno Bettelheim's but from my books. Yes, I'd
replaced Mary Baker Eddy and all those wise men; no matter that my
pages were too ironic to read comfortably, too descriptive and dirty
to be uplifting. In a different way my nephew had replaced me, the
young male person who could stimulate Delilah's reveries, plunge
her into a serene ecstasy; no matter that he wasn't a worshipful
seven-year-old sissy but, rather, an unhappy young adult who was
laughing at his cracked granny half the time. She could thicken her
skin wilfully to signs of mockery so long as she could obtain a rough
simulacrum of her old familiar rituals.

She'd turn down the lights and listen to Pavarotti singing Puccini.
My nephew liked Bach or Morrissey but sentimental Italian warbling
wasn't his demitasse of espresso. Yet he was tolerant. And how hard
was it, to listen to his old granny praising his 'genius' (as a writer, as
a guitarist and songwriter, as a student of literature)? She was certain
that he, too, would make an important contribution, as his
grandmother had done, working with the retarded, as his mother
was doing as a social worker and therapist, as his Uncle Eddie was

doing liberating his homosexual tribe. She beamed with joy at the swooning beauty of 'Nessun dorma' and drummed her tiny fists against the invisible gong suspended just before her in the air – gleaming, the metal mottled, the surface immense.

THE GRIEF OF STRANGERS

Chimamanda Ngozi Adichie

Chinechelum said little as her mother drove her to the airport. She looked out of the window, at the trees whose leaves had turned the colour of a ripe banana, or a berry-red, and others that had shed all their leaves and stood with their naked branches sticking up. It was one of the things she liked to talk about: fall in New England, how it looked like the flowers had lent their colours to the leaves. She liked to talk about summer, too, how the sun lingered and flirted until late. Or winter, how there was something primal about the stillness of snow and the cold needles at the tips of her ears. 'Please,' her mother would say. 'Please, *nne*, try and talk about something real.' Her mother said it always in that pleading-pitying tone, as if to say she knew Chinechelum had to be handled with care but it still had to be said. Before they left for the airport that morning, her mother had said in that same tone, 'When you get to London, *biko*, try and talk normally to Odin.' And she had wanted to tell her mother that she had talked to Odin on the phone, hadn't she? Odin had seemed to find her conversation normal enough, too, because he had invited her to visit, hadn't he? But she said, 'Mama, I will.'

She would try and talk normally, although she was not sure what normally was. Was it the self-indulgence people lapped up from one another these days, the mutual navel-gazing that went on at the recent faculty holiday party, for example? She had listened to a string of self-reflexives, the things that the 'I' would do or had done or wished to do with, or to, the 'me'. Nobody talked about things outside of themselves, and if they did, it became about the relationship of those things to the 'me' or the 'I'. But maybe it was the way conversation had always been. Maybe she had been away from life for too long and she didn't recognize the rules any more. Nine years was a long time. That holiday party was her first party, indeed her first social function, in so long. And maybe it was what had finally made her give in to the idea of her mother and Aunty Ngolika 'connecting' her to a husband, a Nigerian man. *Connect*. That word had amused her, still amused her now.

She rolled the window down a little because the car heater was turned on high, and recalled the first few Nigerian men she'd been 'connected' to, whom she had talked to on the phone, who had faked American accents and littered their conversation with clunky mentions of BMWs and suburban houses. But Odin had been different, perhaps because he had said little about himself when they talked, had come across as self-confident without needing anything to prop him up. Or so she thought. It was Aunty Ngolika who found him. 'The only thing is that he does not live in the US, he lives in London,' Aunty Ngolika had said, in an almost conspiratorial whisper. 'But you can easily relocate, it shouldn't be a problem.' Chinechelum had wanted to ask her aunt why the man – she hadn't been told his name was Odin then – could not relocate. But she didn't ask, because she didn't want to come across as the old Chinechelum, the one her mother said was distant and faraway, the one her mother had worried so much about. She wanted to be the new one who was willing to live again.

When they got to the airport, her mother hugged her and held her face between hands that were scrubbed weekly in the Korean-owned nail studio and said, 'I am praying, *nnem*, it will work out.' Chinechelum nodded, looking at her mother's anxious face with its thin-shaved eyebrows. She wished she had her mother's enthusiasm and her mother's serious hope. She wished that she felt something, anything, rather than the numbness that still wrapped itself around her, that had wrapped itself around her for nine years.

Before she boarded her flight, she saw a woman hugging her children and husband. The woman had unsightly jerry-curl hair. Her heavy make-up streaked as she cried. Her children were crying. Her husband was looking away with a false braveness. Chinechelum watched them for a while and then started to cry. She had discovered that she had the uncanny ability to participate in the grief of strangers, and so she felt the acute pain of that family, crying at the airport, at their looming separation.

Chinechelum liked the claustrophobic feel of London, the way everything seemed to be too small, too tight. She liked the tiny room in her cousin Amara's cramped flat and the concrete neighbourhood with no trees and the scarred brick walls of the apartment building. Amara had been talking to her non-stop since they hugged at the Arrivals in Heathrow, and now Amara's nine-year-old son was shouting as he played a video game in front of the TV. Amara's voice, her son's shouting, the sounds from the TV, irritated Chinechelum, made her feel a throbbing tightness at her temples.

'These West Indian women are taking our men and our men are stupid enough to follow them. Next thing, they will have a baby and they don't want the men to marry them oh, they just want child support,' Amara was saying when Jonathan screamed, his eyes now glued to the TV screen.

'Turn down the volume, Jonathan,' Amara said.

'Mum!'

'Turn down the volume right now!'

'Mum! I can't hear!'

He didn't turn down the volume and Amara didn't say anything else to him; instead she turned to Chinechelum to continue talking.

'You know,' Chinechelum said, wrapping her arms around herself, 'It's interesting how much we forgive our children because they have foreign accents.'

'What do you mean?'

'Back home in Nigeria, Jonathan would be punished.'

Amara looked away. 'I'm going to take that game away from him soon oh.'

But Chinechelum knew she would not, because Jonathan was her son from her broken marriage and his father was rich and he came back from his weekends at his father's house with new toys and the least Amara imagined she could do to maintain her son's respect was to let him do whatever he wanted.

Amara was talking again. 'I met this man recently. He is kind oh, but he is so bush. He grew up in Onitsha and so you can imagine what kind of bush accent he has. He mixes up *ch* and *sh*. I want to go to the *ch*opping centre. Sit down on a *sh*eer. Anyway, he told me he was willing to marry me and adopt Jonathan. Willing! As if he was doing charity work. Willing! Imagine that. But it's not his fault, it's because we are in London, after all, and water never finds its different levels here. He is the kind of man I would never even look at in Nigeria, not to talk of going out with. But you know London is a leveller.'

Chinechelum thought about what Amara had just said – London is a leveller. It amused her. It amused her the way Nigerians in the diaspora complained that the class lines blurred outside Nigeria, that upstarts rose to take places that they would never even dream about in Nigeria. London is a leveller.

'Are you all right, Chelum?' Amara asked. 'You look distant.'

Chinechelum stretched out her legs, still hugging herself. She and Amara had grown up together in Enugu, shared dolls as children, gone to Queens' College Lagos and graduated the same year, before the coup happened and Amara's family moved to England and her own family moved to the United States. Now, she watched Amara, thirty-eight with bleached brownish-yellow hair and vermilion coloured talons. 'Are *you* okay, Amara?' she asked mildly. 'You look like a bad fake of some sort of doll.'

The minute she said it, she wished she hadn't, because it was very much like the old Chinechelum, the one who her mother said had forgotten the delicate rules of living. But Amara did not look offended. And Chinechelum knew that it was because Amara – her whole extended family in fact – had devised a means of dealing with her, a strategy she liked to call Containment. She thought of a letter her mother had once written to the whole family; it had been written nine years ago but she had read it again recently, the weekend she visited her mother and started to go through her mother's drawers. Her mother had kept a copy; she was a meticulous record keeper. *Chinechelum has not been herself since Ikeadi's tragedy*, her mother's loopy handwriting said. *Don't take anything she tells you personal. Don't react to anything. She will get over it with time but she will need our patience.*

Now, she wondered if Amara was thinking about that letter and choosing not to be offended. Amara had always been incredibly even-tempered, anyway. Too-nice, some had said she was, when they were in secondary school. And perhaps that too-nice person still existed underneath the angst of the Divorced and Unsatisfied and Almost-forty.

'I'm sorry, Amara,' Chinechelum said. 'I didn't mean it like that.'

'It's all right,' Amara said, adding after a pause, 'So what of Ikeadi? Have there been any changes? I mean, will he never, well, be normal again?'

'Who's to say?' Chinechelum replied. 'Miracles happen, don't they? So who's to say?'

'Those goats,' Amara muttered. But Chinechelum knew that Amara was saying that for her, because Amara imagined it was what she wanted to hear. What had happened to Ikeadi was too long ago for Amara, too long for everyone but her. The collective anger of her family and friends had become diluted with time, even though none of them would ever admit it. And now in Amara's eyes she saw that pity that was reserved for people who were not even aware that they deserved pity.

'I think I'll go out for a while,' she said. 'I'll get a day's travelcard and explore.'

Amara looked doubtful. 'Do you want me to come with you? Will you be okay?'

'I'll be fine.'

'Will you do some shopping? Do you have something to wear to your date with Odin?'

'I didn't realize I had to shop for something to wear.'

'Oh, but Chelum, you used to like shopping. You used to walk around all over the centre of London and in the end you would tell me everything was cheaper in the outlet malls in America and you would buy from there instead,' Amara said, and the wistfulness in her voice, in her eyes, amused Chinechelum. She used to like bargain shopping, in her old life with Ikeadi, used to know all the outlet malls in the tri-state area, even befriended the managers so they called her when there was a sale. Her taste had reflected Ikeadi, too: sometimes she'd searched for hours for discounted shirts that made a political statement but had a designer label. Still, she felt no nostalgia for that life, even now that she was walking towards living again.

A blue-grey dusk was settling over London when Chinechelum walked into the Starbucks near Embankment tube station and sat down to a mocha and a blueberry muffin. The soles of her feet ached pleasantly. It was not very cold here – nothing compared to chilly Connecticut for sure – and she had been sweating in her wool pea coat which now hung on the back of her chair. Somebody had left a *New Statesman* on the table and she started to read it. She felt comfortable, cosy even, and was warming quickly to an article about Byron in the books section when a Pakistani woman and a little boy came up to ask if they could share her table. She did not realize how quickly the cafe had filled up.

'Of course,' she said, and shifted her bag, even though it had not been on the side of the table that they would use.

The woman was wearing a nose ring, a tiny glass-like thing that glittered as she moved her head this way and that. Her son looked eight or nine years old, wearing a Mickey Mouse sweater and clutching a blue Gameboy. It took Chinechelum a little while to realize that he was flirting with her. First, he asked if the narrow wooden sticks next to the packets of sugar were for stirring. She said that they were. Then he asked if she had enough room for her magazine – if she wanted him to move his chair. Then he snapped at his mother and said, 'I'm not a baby!' when she wanted to cut his muffin.

He had a delightful chubby face and spoke elegant English with what she assumed to be the accent of the Privileged Pakistani. She imagined a huge house in Karachi, their cars and servants, and his mother with the nose ring struggling to make him grow up responsible and unspoiled amid it all.

'Do you live in London?' he leaned over to ask. And before she could respond, his mother cut in quickly in a smooth language and he glared at her.

'I'm sorry,' his mother said, turning to Chinechelum. 'He talks too much.'

'It's all right,' Chinechelum said. She closed the *New Statesman* to signal that she was open to make conversation.

'His father passed away last year,' his mother whispered. 'This is our first vacation in London without him. We used to do it every year before Christmas.' The woman nodded continuously as she spoke and the boy looked annoyed, as if he had not wanted Chinechelum to know that.

'Oh,' Chinechelum said.

'We went to the Tate,' the boy said.

'Did you like it?' she asked.

He scowled, and she knew he imagined that he looked older doing that. 'It was boring.'

His mother rose. 'We should go. We're going to the theatre later.' She turned to her son and added, 'You're not taking that Gameboy in, you know that.'

The boy ignored her, said 'bye' to Chinechelum, and turned towards the door. Chinechelum knew he wanted to linger, and that it was the reason he had hardly touched his muffin. She watched them leave. She wished so much that she had asked him his name and that she had asked his mother a little about her late husband.

A freezing drizzle was falling when she left the café. She walked to the tube station, feeling the tiny raindrops splatter on her coat, and when she got there, she was absorbed by how many frothy blobs of spit were on the stairs. She was thinking that there might be a poem somewhere here – perhaps a free verse, a ramble on the chaos and spit and style of London – when her train came. Later, she sat on the stained seat of the noisy train holding the *New Statesman* in her hand and thought about the Pakistani woman, and the little boy, and their grief that was so lacquered by activities and muffins and arguments. Quietly, she started to cry.

Odin was handsome; she knew that already from the photo he'd sent her as an email attachment. But seeing him, face-to-face, she saw the cragginess glossed over by the photo finish, and she thought it made him even more attractive. She didn't know another man who smiled so much, showing a flash of very white teeth that she was certain he bleached.

They sat in the dim basement of a French restaurant in Soho, a glowing candle between them as they both ate a goat's cheese salad. She had ordered first and then he'd said he would have the same. She wondered what he would say if she told him that she had not sat in a restaurant with a man in nine years. Would he consider her strange, like her Aunty Ngolika had said? 'Don't tell him about Ikeadi yet, or he might think you a little strange. Wait until you get close,' Aunty Ngolika had suggested. It had amused Chinechelum because she hadn't even imagined telling Odin about Ikeadi.

'You're so beautiful,' Odin said. 'I'm surprised some man hasn't carried you off since.'

She stabbed a piece of lettuce on her plate, slightly alarmed. Were there no rules to this game? Was marriage alluded to so soon? 'You're not too bad yourself,' she said. Her mother would like her saying that. It sounded normal. She'd heard it at the faculty party last year. The Eighteenth Century Literature woman two offices from hers had lurched up to the department head and said, 'You are a fucking amazing writer,' and he replied, 'You're not too bad yourself,' and everybody around them laughed until they staggered. Chinechelum had wondered if it was just their drunkenness, but it seemed not, because Odin was laughing now.

'You're so unusual,' he said. 'You have this look on your face, as if you are detached from everything and yet you're not. It's fascinating.'

She drank some water, not sure what to say.

'So what is it really like living in New England?' Odin asked.

Chinechelum launched into a poetic vignette about New England in the fall, about the blushing sun and nature's different shades of gold and crisp winds chasing carrot-coloured leaves. Odin looked taken aback. Finally he said, 'Mm, that's interesting. You know, whenever I hear New England, I see Connecticut and Maine and places like that and I imagine it's just full of white people.'

'Well, there is some diversity. The student body in my classes is about ten per cent black.' Chinechelum shrugged, and hoped it looked natural. 'The food is very good,' she added, looking down at her plate.

They ate in silence for a while, a silence that she was too aware of. She was too conscious of the movements of the fork in her hand from plate to mouth, of the movements of his jaw.

'So,' he said, putting his fork down. 'How is it going?'

She was not sure what he meant. During one of their telephone conversations, she had mentioned that she had just received a grant and taken a sabbatical to try and complete her book of poetry. Did he mean the poetry? Or did he mean right now, their meal, their meeting? 'How is what going?' she asked.

He laughed. 'I don't know. Just wanted to engage you. You seemed to be faraway.'

'Oh no, I'm here,' she said and sat up straighter.

While they had dessert – they shared a tiramisu – he talked about the attitudes some Nigerian men in the diaspora had about women. They think they can sleep around and it's okay but the woman can't. They sit and watch TV while the woman cooks even though they both work the same hours. He said all of this, shaking his head in a way that meant he thought these men should know better. And she realized, touched, that he was trying to tell her what he was like, or perhaps what he wanted to be like.

He was holding her hand now, both hands clasped on the table. 'I'm so glad we met,' he said. It struck her then that there was something generic about the scene; it could have been any other woman with him, any other educated Nigerian woman, resident abroad, thirty years and above, looking for a man. It didn't have to be her.

Her mother and Aunty Ngolika called two-way, and she listened to two strained voices ask how the dinner had gone, and gasp when she said she wasn't seeing him until Friday. 'Hei! But that's three days away! Was it your suggestion or his?'

It was her suggestion, of course, since Odin had asked her to have lunch with him the next day; in fact he had asked her to come home with him that night.

'It was Odin's idea. He is very busy at work,' she said.

'Mh, that is not a good sign.' She was not sure who had said that, because her mother and aunt sounded alike. Then her mother asked, hesitantly, 'Did you talk normally, *nne*?' And Chinechelum said, calmly, 'Yes, Mama, I did.'

After she hung up, Amara said there was a party in somebody's house in Bayswater, a Yoruba friend, and she thought it would be good for Chinechelum to go.

Chinechelum said she would rather stay at home and read, that she had not finished the *New Statesman*, that the least she could do with a magazine she had not paid for was finish reading it. Amara gave her a long patient look but said nothing. After Amara left, Chinechelum imagined what the party would be like. She had gone to a few with Ikeadi; it didn't matter if they were Christmas or engagement or birthday parties because they were all the same, steeped in jollof rice and jealousy, pepper soup and whispers of who had bought a new flat in Chelsea or a house in suburban Chicago and who had had an autistic baby and whose wife had packed her things and left and who had still not got his legal stay or his green card and who was involved in dirty credit card fraud money and whose husband went back to Nigeria to sleep around with young-young girls. It – the party in Bayswater – was what her mother would consider normal.

Chinechelum ran into Neville Lipton the next day. She had met him before; Amara had introduced them, and later muttered to Chinechelum that the neighbours called him the Overbearing Oxbridge Octogenarian. But Amara liked him, as did the other neighbours in the block of flats, because he gave their children presents and opportunities. Half of Jonathan's library was made of books from Neville Lipton. Jonathan had gone on trips to museums and galleries sponsored by Neville Lipton. Jonathan placed a mark of authenticity on anything by saying, 'Mr Lipton says.'

'He has no business living in this neighbourhood,' Amara had told Chinechelum. 'I think he's doing it to make a political statement.'

'If he is, then that's extremely paternalistic,' Chinechelum had said. Or had she? She wasn't sure now what her response had been. She did recall being both vaguely fascinated and repulsed by how much Neville Lipton seemed to know about Nigeria, rattling off the history with dates during their brief conversation. And so when she ran into him on the street, on her way to explore London once again, he remembered her and kissed both her cheeks and noticed that she had cut her hair since the last time he saw her.

'Let's have lunch together, shall we? Come with me,' he said, already moving and expecting her to follow. Chinechelum did. This was what living life again was about, after all, giving in to impulse, embracing spontaneity. Going off to lunch with Amara's elderly neighbour whom she hardly knew. This was *life*.

'I'll take you to the Traveller's Club. That's a lovely jacket you have on, so we won't have any difficulty being let in. They have a quite annoying dress code, you see.'

'Really,' Chinechelum said, surprised that he thought her old jacket was lovely, and later as they were led into the ornate interior of the Traveller's Club, she looked around at the men seated at the tables to see what they were wearing. She had expected to see bow ties. But she saw mostly suits that seemed staid next to Neville Lipton's well-tailored jacket lined in bright orange-and-green kente print. It was clear that Neville Lipton was different from the men here and that he embraced his being different. She imagined him, in another life, going off to explore Africa and returning with triumphant skins, with stories of surprisingly articulate natives.

'It's so stuffy in here,' she said after they had been seated. She meant it figuratively and he understood and laughed.

'You have such a lovely voice,' he said, leaning closer. 'If only you didn't have that American inflection to your speech.' He was staring at her. His eyes were so blue they looked painted-on and his hair was a startling white, receding from a finely wrinkled face. As they waited for their orders, he gave her a brief history of the Traveller's Club, a monologue on the necessity of the monarchy, a scathing attack on the misguided asses who wanted to outlaw fox hunting. He called her 'dear one' and 'darling girl' and used the adverb 'iniquitously'. He made her laugh when he said 'fuck' with the old-world Englishness of an Oxbridge octogenarian. He seemed determined to introduce her to everyone that passed, even the waiters, and after he had said her name in a quick, indistinguishable mumble, he added, always, 'She's Nigerian.'

Right after their orders came, a man with hair sticking out of his nose came up to them, glanced at Chinechelum and asked Neville, 'Who's the dusky beauty with you?'

Neville introduced her, told the man that she was Nigerian and added that she was a poet and an assistant professor in America.

'How do you do?' the man asked her.

Chinechelum said nothing. The man was smiling.

'It's a pleasure meeting you,' the man said, raising his voice slightly, as if he imagined she might not have heard him the first time. Still, Chinechelum said nothing. The silence stretched out. She felt the tension, revelled in the awkwardness. This was the old Chinechelum and she was comfortable with it. The man muttered something to Neville and then moved on.

'Dear girl!' Neville said, in a theatrical whisper. 'Whatever did you do that for?'

'*Dusky beauty*.'

'Well. He was complimenting *you*.'

'No, he was complimenting you. Like one would compliment somebody who had a good racehorse.'

'The old chap meant no harm, in fact he would give anything to be sitting in my place.' Neville chuckled and Chinechelum felt the urge to throw her glass of water in his face. She ran a finger over the rim of her glass instead and said, pleasantly, 'You know, Mr Lipton, I think all of you here are tight-assed old men.'

Neville stared at her for a moment before he burst out laughing. 'Goodness, Chichilum . . .'

'What did you call me?'

He looked at her as if he was not sure what she had said.

'My name is Chinechelum, Mr Lipton. *Chi-ne-che-lum.*'

He repeated her name a few times, with the earnest expression of one eager to get it right although he mauled it each time. Then he asked, 'What does it mean, by the way?'

'God Thinks For Me.'

'Does it? I have a friend from Zimbabwe, a Shona, whose name means The Fire of God. Interesting. I did wonder if God possessing fire was desirable or not.' He sipped his water. 'God Thinks For Me. It doesn't suit you much, does it?'

'Why?'

'Why? Darling one, it does suggest passivity, doesn't it, and there is nothing passive about you. My goodness, you don't have one deferential bone in your body.'

He sounded surprised. She examined the coffee-coloured age spots on his face for a while. And then she said, 'You sound as if I should.'

Was it her imagination or did he blush, this hard-boiled worldly old man? 'You're terribly touchy, aren't you, on the subject of race? Africans aren't, unless of course they've lived in America.'

'You seem to know everything about Africans.'

He reached out and took her hand. 'Don't be like that, darling one.'

And she didn't know why, but she started talking about Ikeadi. Perhaps it was to tell Neville Lipton that he had no right to tell her how to be, about race, or about anything else. Perhaps there was no reason to it, only that the words came out of her, chased one another past her lips.

First, before she told him about the night Ikeadi was shot, she told him what Ikeadi used to say. That he and she were destined. That if somebody drained the streams of both their ancestral villages, their names would be written on the riverbed, intertwined. After he was shot, she had wanted to go back to Nigeria, to his hometown of Umunnachi and her hometown of Abba, and she wanted to jump into the streams at both places and drain them somehow and see what was written there, see if Ikeadi's name would now appear in crippled letters. She told Neville Lipton about Ikeadi's temper, that he broke beer bottles when he was angry; about Ikeadi's idealism, that he joined causes and marched and picketed, that his father owned an often-empty home in West Hartford but he chose to live in a minuscule apartment in East Hartford, which he paid for himself, and that he was in front of that apartment building, about to unlock his door when the police cars arrived. Three men. Three white men. Later, during the trial, they said they thought he was pulling a gun. And she sat in the courtroom and cried because the vestibule in front of his apartment door was so narrow and it was inconceivable how he had evaded so many of those forty bullets. And even later she had wished that Ikeadi was the Haitian man who was all over the news for a while, the one who had only been sodomized with a dirty broom handle by a policeman. At least that man, the Haitian, had been left whole.

Finally, she told Neville Lipton, 'When Ikeadi lost the use of his body, it was the end of fall, and two days later it was snowing and weeks later spring came and it rained and the seasons kept changing, as if nothing had happened to Ikeadi. I kept waiting for something to happen. You know? I just kept waiting.'

She put her fork down, angry that she had talked to this undeserving man about Ikeadi, angry that Ikeadi was there right now in the nursing home in Hartford, paralysed, and now so clinically depressed he could no longer blink when she arrived. Or he chose to no longer blink.

But she was also exhilarated that she had finally talked about Ikeadi, that she could talk to an acquaintance she wasn't even sure she liked about the man for whom she had kept her life on hold for nine years.

Odin had spoken so highly of the restaurant he took her to the next day that Chinechelum was determined to like it no matter what. It was very modern-chic, with chrome decor and wide gleaming spaces and a menu carved on to thin metal sheets.

'This decor is art, isn't it? But it's a different art from yours, from your poetry,' Odin said.

'I suppose so,' she murmured. There was something different about Odin today, or was it – whatever it was – there the last time she saw him only that she hadn't looked closely enough to notice? She didn't want to talk about her art, the expression 'your art' was troubling enough, and so she said, 'Odin doesn't sound like an Igbo name.'

'It's Odinchezo, but I made it shorter, you know, it's easier for these people.'

'Oh,' Chinechelum said and looked down at her food, strips of grilled fish so painstakingly arranged she felt bad having to disrupt the pattern by eating them. She remembered how she and Ikeadi used to criticize her Aunty Ngolika for calling her son 'Bob' although his name was Nnaemeka, and then saying it was because of 'these people'. 'What people?' she wanted to ask Odin. You didn't have to deny your heritage and then blame some phantom people for a choice that you had made.

'How's the fish?' Odin asked. He looked nervous, that was it. Nervous.

'It tastes as interesting as it looks,' she said.

Odin placed his fork down. 'There is something I haven't told you. Something you should know.'

'Yes?'

Odin cleared his throat loudly. 'I have a son. He's six. His mother has custody but I see him every other week.'

There was a short stretch of silence between them; even the people at other tables seemed to stop speaking. 'I didn't want to tell you earlier,' Odin said. 'I didn't want to tell you anything that would make you back off too early.' He was avoiding her eyes: looking above her head and then swiftly back to focus on his food. She thought he suddenly looked so much younger, so much more vulnerable. And she wanted to tell him that it was okay, that we all are allowed, should be allowed, to put down our load, to untie the baggage we carry, only when we want to. Only when we are ready to.

'It's all right,' she said.

'I just knew you were different.' Odin leaned closer towards her, across the table. 'I think lately I've been wondering where my life has gone. I think you being in my life can help me find a balance.'

She held her fork in wonder. How could he possibly know that? How could he possibly know that it was *her*, just *her*, who would make him happy?

She felt the urge to tell him about Ikeadi, to let him know that she, too, had something she hadn't told him. But she didn't. She didn't have to. It was freeing to realize that he didn't have to know, and even more freeing to realize, sitting there and looking at his clean jaw and his deep-brown eyes, that it would never work between them, that he would eventually be connected to another Nigerian woman unburdened by a new desire for life. A woman who, unlike her, would not long for *spontaneity*, for *realness*, for a connection that was unchoreographed, such as meeting strangers in a Starbucks café.

Back in Connecticut, she took a taxi from the airport, huddled in the back because the heater was taking too long. The air was still; the sides of the road were covered with piles of snow and the piercing whiteness hurt her eyes. On the news, she heard that some children had been killed in Massachusetts, that they were playing on a frozen lake when the surface broke and they sank in. They drowned in sub-zero water: three little boys aged between seven and nine.

Chinechelum closed her eyes, but she didn't cry.

Hilda Smith, with Sheila and Graham, Redcar sands, 1948

ALBERT SMITH

Graham Smith

My dad, George Albert Newton Smith, was born into a family whose culture, work and class were rooted deep in the heavy industry of ironmaking. In hope of a better life, his great grandfather left the ironstone mines at Rosedale during the middle of the nineteenth century to look for work in the fast-growing industrial town of Middlesbrough. He was the first of four generations to work for the powerful ironmasters who, with their vision of an iron and steel metropolis, built so many blast furnaces along the River Tees that it was said one man could not count them all in one day. There was a job for any man who had the strength to work and the will to give loyalty for life to the company. As a young boy older than his years my dad knew that when his days at school ended, by tradition he would follow his own dad into the Cargo Fleet Iron Company. Working together under the structure of three formidable blast furnaces, they repaired the large steam cranes used for moving ironstone and slag. His older brother Bill worked as a front man at the foot of one of those blast furnaces, but some years later was crushed to death when the ageing furnace, under too much pressure, exploded.

Cargo Fleet was about one mile from where the family lived in South Bank. Opposite their house in North Street, just over a high slagstone wall, was an industrial landscape that followed the river as far as they could see. On days with no wind, polluted air glittered with metallic dust from furnaces producing iron day and night, coke ovens and slag tips leaked their stench of sulphurous gas, and the continual clatter of wagons echoed off a vast complex of railway lines, veins feeding every part of the industry. Somewhere on that ironworks land my dad worked an allotment and kept hens. With money made from selling eggs he bought a double format box camera, taught himself how to develop film and make contact prints from negatives. A year later the war started. Taking photographs in public places was prohibited, film was almost impossible to get and he exposed only a few rolls in that first year of owning a camera.

Three months after the war ended he met Hilda Cheesbrough, my mother. She was on her twenty-first birthday night out in the Albion pub down Dock Street in Middlesbrough. My dad was there as captain of the visiting darts team from the Princess Alice, South Bank. She was a good-looking woman. He bought her that drink.

The pleasures of youth, love, children, and a secure job in the ironworks: it was a good time for both of them. They were starting a life together and despite recurring poverty, my dad's photographs confirm how much they were celebrating that life, the love they had for each other and their children. There is a photograph of my mother on the sands at Redcar taken at the beginning of those years, wearing a blouse and skirt she lovingly embroidered with floral hearts.

Those years passed. Three growing children, debt, my mother's late night job as a barmaid and the routine grind for my dad working all the overtime hours he could get, turned their life into one they had no time or desire to continue celebrating. What few photographs my dad was motivated to take of the family became weaker as domestic friction infected their lives with bitterness. Drink was no medicine for the pain they suffered. My mam and dad struggled to keep their heads above water, and life together gradually became one of survival with little comfort from love. Good times still surprised us all, but not often and not for long.

At about the age of eight I made a mousetrap from my dad's box camera. In my child's mind the mousetrap had a use. His neglected camera, which was almost beyond reach on the top shelf of our pantry, was never replaced. The photographs stopped.

Four or five bad years later, the County Court issued an Order of Legal Separation against my dad for mental cruelty towards his children. An unfair ruling by a judge blind to the provocation from a woman my dad never stopped loving. The judge also ordered that he had just forty-eight hours to pack up and get out of his home for good.

Apart from his tools and a suit of clothes my dad had no personal belongings that I can remember, no books, not even the box camera he brought into the marriage, only his negatives and a small family photo album, half full. During those forty eight hours and for a long time after, he was in a state of shock, his sense of purpose lost in despair. I can still remember the day he came home from work looking tired as if he had just finished a double shift under the furnaces. No words were spoken, it was hard to look at him or be in the same room, he was offered nothing to eat and what bits of food we had in the pantry were hidden away. We even burned off what was left of a shilling's worth of gas in the coin meter just in case he tried to make a cup of tea. He washed in silence, packed a small case, filled a brown paper carrier bag with dirty work clothes, and without looking up to say goodbye, left his home, wife and three children. On that sunny evening, I followed a man walking slowly through our alley on to Keith Road and, hiding in the shadows of our neighbour's privet hedge, watched him disappear down the road towards the bus stop. He never again set foot inside the house that was his home. Although he found lodgings only a few miles away in South Bank, I didn't see my dad again for what turned out to be eight disturbing years. Remnants he left behind were gathered up by my mother and triumphantly thrown away. Our bin was kept outside the back door and that week it was full. Next to the bin among a heap of worn out work clothes, old boots and some unfinished wooden toys I found the cardboard shoebox full of my dad's carefully cut single negatives. Although each one was scratched and many bent or sticky with jam from the years we had played with those mysterious pictures, they were a part of my life. But whatever hope that box full of better days gave me it was empty for those two very special people on that awful and final day we were a family. One of the rare times I knew without doubt that I had done something right was on bin men day when, before leaving for school, I salvaged the box of negatives and hid them in a dark corner on the top shelf of our pantry, well away from the nerves of my mother.

Most of the negatives were moments from the best years of both my mam and dad's long life, going back to the night down Dock Street when he bought her that drink, up to a time when his last photograph of family life found a place in the shoe box.

Only forty-four years old and a proud man, my dad accepted that his marriage was over. He was also a strong man and once talked of street fighting outside the Princess Alice with any drinker who matched his challenge of a ten-shilling note put on the bar. Although it was a tough way for a young man to get extra beer money, the eviction from his home and family later in life hit him much harder. The only way he knew how to live with the grief was to work. There were exceptions but eventually he worked every twelve-hour shift he could get, seven days a week year after year. He no longer considered such endless hours as overtime. Hard work was in his blood, it earned him respect and gave some purpose to the rest of his life.

For more than twenty years, my dad went back to an empty house at the end of a long day's work. With the urgency of closing time on his mind, he fed the cats, cooked himself something from a tin, washed, and dressed in a smart suit that lifted his mood. He depended on pubs for his social life and enjoyed a good drink. The warning bell followed by those sharp words from a barmaid 'last orders please' were an unsettling reminder that good times end. Always the last to leave the pub, three more pints and ten minutes drinking-up time closed down most of his days. His open face, warm smile and sense of humour were well known and well liked. Albert's company was looked for in whichever local pub kept the best pint of beer. He embraced strangers, particularly women, yet my mother was to be the only woman in his life. Although his experience of love became confused with feelings of anger and hate, I found two small racing diaries after his death, each with a photograph of her inside the plastic cover. These two photographs, treasured but painful reminders of the love they once shared, were pulled from the family album knowing at the time that life would never be as it was at the end of his next day's shift. Our dad did not come home from work again. Many years later I got to know a little of who my dad was, and I think the love and belonging he left behind in that shoebox full of negatives were all he ever wanted from life.

Living on his own for so long my dad eventually felt the need to keep a diary. Over ten years he filled two exercise books and started a third, recording important information and events in his life. His last entry noted the weather getting colder, that he'd finished making a garden bench and cleared tomato plants from the greenhouse, that there was too much cigarette smoke in local pubs, and, 'Health getting worse this week, difficulty in breathing after any exertion'. That same week he also left two self portraits in his camera, pictures of a man with a brave smile and eyes lost for a moment somewhere far beyond the walls of his living room. To leave loved ones such a gift was how much he valued photography. He used it well. It was a sad and unexpected phone call. My dad's heart suffered from the stress of too much overtime and stopped working. He died getting into his old car outside the bookies on Middlesbrough Road, only two streets away from where he was born. No betting slip was found, so either he was collecting winnings or, after studying the form, didn't fancy his chances that day.

EARLY ONE MORNING

Helen Simpson

Sometimes they were quiet in the car and sometimes they talked.

'Mum.'

'Yes?'

'Can I swear one time in the day? If I don't swear in the others?'

'Why?'

'In the morning. When you come and wake me. Can I say, Bollocks?'

'No.'

He's the only person in the world who listens to me and does what I tell him (thought Zoe). That morning when she had gone to wake him he had groaned, unconscious, spontaneous – 'Already?' Then he had reached up from his pillow to put strong sleepy arms round her neck.

For these years of her life she was spending more time alone with her boy, side by side in the car, than with anybody else, certainly far more than with her husband, thirty times more, unless you counted the hours asleep. There was the daily business of showing herself to him and to no one else; thinking aloud, urging each other on in the hunt for swimming things, car keys, maths books; yawning like cats, as they had to leave soon after seven if they were going to get to school on time. Then they might tell each other the remains of a dream during the first twenty-five minutes on the way to Freda's house, or they might sit in comfortable silence, or sometimes they would talk.

This morning when she had pointed out the sun rising in the east to hit the windscreen and blind them with its flood of flashy light, her nine-year-old boy had scoffed at her and said the earth twizzled on its axis and went round the sun, and how she, his mother, was as bad as the ancient Egyptians, how they sacrificed someone to Ra if the sun went in and finished off everybody when there was an eclipse. It's running out, this hidden time (thought Zoe). You're on your own at eleven, goes the current unwritten transport protocol, but until then you need a minder. Less than two years to go.

'I remember when I was at school,' she'd said that morning while they waited for the Caedmon Hill lights. 'It seemed to go on forever. Time goes by slowly at school. Slowly. Slowly. Then, after you're about thirty, it goes faster and faster.'

'Why?' asked George.

'I don't know,' she said. 'Maybe it's because after that you somehow know there'll be a moment for you when there isn't any more.'

'Ooh-ah!' Then he looked at a passing cyclist and commented, 'Big arse.'

'George!' she said, shocked.

'It just slipped out,' he said, apologetic, adult. 'You know, like when that man in the white van wouldn't let you in and you said, Bastard.'

Sometimes this daily struggle and inching along through filthy air thick with the thwarted rage of 10,000 drivers gave her, Zoe, pause. It took forty-five minutes to travel the two and three-quarter miles to George's school (Sacred Heart thanks to his father's faith springing anew, rather than Hereward the Wake half a mile along), and forty-five minutes for her to come back alone in the empty car. In the afternoons it was the same, but the other way round of course, setting off a little after two-thirty and arriving back well after four. There was no train. To do the journey by bus, they would have had to catch a 63A then change and wait for a 119 at Sollers Junction. They had tried this, and it had doubled the journey time. Why couldn't there be school buses for everyone as there were in America, the mothers asked each other. Nobody knew why not, but apparently there couldn't. They were just about able to walk it in the same time as it took in the car, and they had tried this too, carrying rucksacks of homework and packed lunch and sports equipment through the soup of fumes pumped out by crawling cars. Add wind and rain, and the whole idea of pavement travel looked positively quixotic.

'I'll get it, Mum,' said George, as her mobile beeped its receipt of a text.

It was from her friend Stella, whose husband had recently left her for one of his students.

– If I say anything, he gets very angry (Stella had told her on their last phone call); he doesn't allow me to be angry.

– But he was the one to leave you.

– Yes. But now he's furious with me, he hates me.

– Do you still love him?

– I don't recognize him. I can't believe this man I ate with and slept beside for fifteen years is capable of being so cold and so, yes, cruel.

Is it true, then, that women can take grief as grief (thought Zoe), but men refuse to do that, they have to convert it into diesel in order to deal with it, all the loss and pain converted into rage?

Her husband had looked around and said, 'Why don't you do like Sally and Chitra and Mo, organize an au pair, pay for a few driving lessons if necessary, hand it over to someone who'll be glad of the job.' She, Zoe, had thought about this, but she'd already been through it all once before, with Joe and Theresa, who were both now at secondary school. She'd done the sums, gone through the interviews in imagination, considered the no-claims bonus; she'd counted the years for which her work time would be cut in half, she'd set off the loss of potential income against the cost of childcare, and she'd bitten the bullet. 'It's your choice,' said Patrick. And it was.

'You're a loser, Mum,' her daughter Theresa had told her on her return from a recent careers convention. But she wasn't. She'd done it all now – she'd been through the whole process of hanging on to her old self, carving out patches of time, not relinquishing her work, then partly letting go in order to be more with the children, his work taking precedence over hers as generally seemed to be the case when the parents were still together. Unless the woman earned more, which opened up a whole new can of modern worms. Those long-forgotten hours and days were now like nourishing leaf mould round their roots. Let the past go (sang Zoe beneath her breath), time to move on; her own built-in obsolescence could make her feel lively rather than sad. And perhaps the shape of life would be like an hourglass, clear and wide to begin with, narrowing down to the tunnel of the middle years, then flaring wide again before the sands ran out.

'Mum, can you test me on my words?' asked George. He was doing a French taster term, taking it seriously because he wanted to outstrip his friend Mick who was better than him at maths.

'Well I'm not supposed to,' said Zoe. 'But we're not moving. Here, put it on my lap and keep your eye open for when the car in front starts to move.'

When I was starting out, leaving babies till after thirty was seen as leaving it late (thought Zoe). Over thirty was the time of fade for women, loss of bloom and all that. Now you're expected to be still a girl at forty-two – slim, active, up for it. But if I hadn't done it, had Joe at twenty-six and Theresa at twenty-eight, hammered away at work and sweated blood in pursuit of good childminders, nurseries, au pairs, you name it, and finally, five years later when George came along, slowed down for a while at least; then I wouldn't know why so many women are the way they are. Stymied at some point; silenced somewhere. Stalled. Or, merely delayed?

'It's who, when, where, how and all that sort of thing,' said George. 'I'll tell you how I remember *quand*. I think of the Sorcerer's Apprentice because you know he had a WAND, rhymes with quand, and then he goes away with all those buckets of water and then WHEN he comes back . . . Get it? WHEN he comes back! That's how it stays in my mind. And *qui* is the KEY in a door and you answer it and who is there? WHO! I thought of all that myself, yeah. Course. And *ou* is monkeys in the rainforest. Oo oo oo. Hey look, it's moving.'

They crawled forward, even getting into second gear for a few seconds, then settled again into stasis.

'Why the rainforest?' asked Zoe. 'Monkeys in the rainforest?'

'Because, where are they?' he asked. 'Where *are* they, the trees in the rainforest. That's what the monkeys want to know, oo oo oo. 'Cos they aren't there any more, the trees in the rainforest.'

'You remember everything they teach you at school, don't you,' said Zoe admiringly.

'Just about,' said George with a pleased smile. 'Mum, I don't want you to die until I'm grown up.'

There was a pause.

'But I don't want to die *before* you,' he added.

'No, I don't want that either,' said Zoe.

This boy remembers every detail of every unremarkable day (thought Zoe), he's not been alive that long and he's got acres of lovely empty space in his memory bank. Whereas I've been alive for ages and it's got to the point where my mind is saying it already has enough on its shelves, it just can't be bothered to store something new unless it's really worth remembering.

I climb the stairs and forget what I'm looking for. I forgot to pick up Natasha last week when I'd promised her mother, and I had to do a three-point turn in the middle of Ivanhoe Avenue and go back for her and just hope that none of the children already in the car would snitch on me. But that's nothing new. I can't remember a thing about the last decade or so, she told other mothers, and they agreed, it was a blur, a blank, they had photographs to prove it had happened but they couldn't remember it themselves. She, Zoe, saw her memory banks as having shrivelled for lack of sleep's welcome rain; she brooded over the return of those refreshing showers and the rehydration of her pot-noodle bundles of memories, and how (one day) the past would plump into action, swelling with import, newly alive. When she was old and free and in her second adolescence, she would sleep in royally, till midday or one. Yet old people cannot revisit that country, they report; they wake and listen to the dawn chorus after four or five threadbare hours, and long for the old three-ply youth-giving slumber.

They had reached Freda's house, and Zoe stopped the car to let George out. He went off to ring the bell and wait while Freda and also Harry, who was in on this lift, gathered their bags and shoes and coats. It was too narrow a road to hover in, or rather Zoe did not have the nerve to make other people queue behind her while she waited for her passengers to arrive. This morning she shoehorned the car into a minute space 300 yards away, proudly parking on a sixpence.

What's truly radical now though (thought Zoe, rereading the text from Stella as she waited) is to imagine a man and woman having children and living happily together, justice and love prevailing, self-respect on both sides, each making sure the other flourishes as well as the children. The windscreen blurred as it started to rain. If not constantly, she modified, then taking turns. Where *are* they?

But this wave of divorces (she thought), the couples who'd had ten or fifteen years or more of being together, her feeling was that often it wasn't as corny as it seemed to be in Stella's case – being left for youth. When she, Zoe, looked closely, it was more to do with the mercurial resentment quotient present in every marriage having risen to the top of the thermometer. It was more to do with how the marriage had turned out, now it was this far down the line. Was one of the couple thriving and satisfied, with the other restless or foundering? Or perhaps the years had spawned a marital Black Dog, where one of them dragged the other down with endless gloom or bad temper or censoriousness and refused to be comforted, ever, and also held the other responsible for their misery.

There had been a scattering of bust-ups during the first two or three years of having babies, and then things seemed to settle down. This was the second wave, a decade or so on, a wild tsunami of divorce as children reached adolescence and parents left youth behind. The third big wave was set to come when the children left home. She, Zoe, had grown familiar with the process simply by listening. First came the shock, the vulnerability and hurt; then the nastiness (particularly about money) with accompanying baffled incredulity; down on to indignation at the exposure of unsuspected talents for treachery, secretiveness, two-faced liardom; falling last of all into scalding grief or adamantine hatred. Only last week her next-door neighbour, forced to put the house on the market, had hissed at her over the fence, 'I hope he gets cancer and dies.' Though when it came to showing round prospective purchasers, the estate agents always murmured the word amicable as reassurance; purchasers wanted to hear it was amicable rather than that other divorce word, acrimonious.

She peered into the driver's mirror and saw them trudging towards the car with their usual heaps of school luggage. It was still well before eight and, judging herself more bleached and craggy than usual, she added some colour just as they got to the car.

'Lipstick, hey,' said George, taking the front seat. The other two shuffled themselves and their bags into the back.

'I used to wear make-up,' said Zoe. 'Well, a bit. When I was younger. I really enjoyed it.'

'Why don't you now?' asked Freda. Freda's mother did, of course. Her mother was thirty-eight rather than forty-two. It made a difference, this slide over to the other side, reflected Zoe, and also one was tireder.

'Well, I still do if I feel like it,' she said, starting the car and indicating. She waited for a removal van to lumber along and shave past. 'But I don't do it every day like brushing my teeth. It's just another thing.' Also, nobody but you lot is going to see me so why would I, she added silently, churlishly.

She was aware of the children thinking, What? *Why* not? Women *should* wear make-up. Freda in particular would be on the side of glamour and looking one's best at all times.

'We had a Mexican student staying with us once,' she told them, edging on to the main road. 'And at first she would spend ages looking after her long glossy hair, and more ages brushing make-up on to her eyelids and applying that gorgeous glassy lipgloss. But after a while she stopped, and she looked just like the rest of us – she said to me, it was a lovely holiday after Mexico City, where she really couldn't go outside without the full works or everybody would stare at her. So she kept it for parties or times when she felt like putting it on, after that.'

'Women look better with make-up,' commented Harry from the back. Harry's au pair dropped him off at Freda's on Tuesday and Thursday mornings, and in the spirit of hawk-eyed reciprocity on which the whole fragile school-run ecosystem was founded, Zoe collected George from Harry's house on Monday and Wednesday afternoons, which cut *that* journey in half.

'Well I'm always going to wear make-up when I'm older,' said Freda.

'Women used to set their alarm clocks an hour early so they could put on their false eyelashes and lid liner and all that,' said Zoe. 'Imagine being frightened of your husband seeing your bare face!'

There was silence as they considered this; grudging assent, even. But the old advice was still doing the rounds, Zoe had noticed, for women to listen admiringly to men and not to laugh at them if they wanted to snare one of their very own. Give a man respect for being higher caste than you, freer, more powerful. And men, what was it men wanted? Was it true they only wanted a cipher? That a woman should not expect admiration from a man for any other qualities than physical beauty or selflessness? Surely not. If this were the case, why live with such a poor sap if you could scrape your own living?

'Do you like Alex?' asked Harry. 'I don't. I hate Alex, he whines and he's mean and he cries and he whinges all the time. But I pretend I like him, because I want him to like me.'

There was no comment from the other three. They were sunk in early morning torpor, staring at the static traffic around them.

'I despite him,' said Harry.

'You can't say that,' said Freda. 'It's despise.'

'That's what I said,' said Harry.

George snorted.

It was nothing short of dangerous and misguided (thought Zoe) not to keep earning, even if it wasn't very much and you were doing all the domestic and emotional work as well, for the sake of keeping the marital Black Dog at bay. Otherwise if you spoke up it would be like biting the hand that fed you. Yes you wanted to be around (thought Zoe), to be an armoire, to make them safe as houses. But surrendering your autonomy for too long, subsumption without promise of future release, those weren't good for the health.

'I hate that feeling in the playground when I've bullied someone and then they start crying,' said Harry with candour.

'I don't like it if someone cries because of something I've said,' said Freda.

'I don't like it when there's a group of people and they're making someone cry,' said George over his shoulder. 'That makes me feel bad.'

'Oh I don't mind that,' said Harry. 'If it wasn't me that made them cry. If it was other people, that's nothing to do with me.'

'No, but don't you feel bad when you see one person like that,' replied George, 'And everyone picking on them, if you don't, like, say something?'

'No,' said Harry. 'I don't care. As long as I'm not being nasty to them I don't feel bad at what's happening.'

'Oh,' said George, considering. 'I do.'

'Look at that car's number plate,' said Freda. 'The letters say XAN. XAN! XAN!'

'FWMMM!' joined in Harry. 'FWMMFWMM! FWMM FWMM-FWMM!'

'BGA,' growled George. 'BGA. Can you touch your nose with your tongue?'

Zoe stared out from the static car at the line of people waiting in the rain at a bus stop, and studied their faces. Time sinks into flesh (she mused), gradually sinks it. A look of distant bruising arrives, and also for some reason asymmetry. One eye sits higher than the other and the mouth looks crooked. We start to look like cartoons or caricatures of ourselves. On cold days like today the effect can be quite trollish.

'Who would you choose to push off a cliff or send to prison or give a big hug?' George threw over his shoulder. 'Out of three – Peter Vallings –'

'Ugh, not Peter Vallings!' shrieked Freda in an ecstasy of disgust.

'Mrs Campbell. And – Mr Starling!'

'Mr Starling! Oh my God, Mr Starling,' said Harry, caught between spasms of distaste and delight. 'Yesterday he was wearing this top, yeah, he lets you see how many ripples he's got.'

Your skin won't stay with your flesh as it used to (thought Zoe), it won't move and follow muscle the way it did before. You turn, and there is a fan of creases however trim you are; yet once you were one of these young things at the bus stop, these over-eleven secondary school pupils. Why do we smile at adolescent boys, so unfinished, so lumpy (she wondered), but feel disturbed by this early beauty of the girls, who gleam with benefit, their hair smooth as glass or in rich ringlets, smiling big smiles and speaking up and nobody these days saying, 'Who do you think you are?' or 'You look like a prostitute.' It's not as if the boys won't catch up with a vengeance.

'I love my dog,' said Harry fiercely.

'Yes, he's a nice dog,' agreed Freda.

'I love my dog so much,' continued Harry, 'I would rather die than see my dog die.'

'*You* would rather die than your *dog*?' said George in disbelief.

'Yes! I love my dog! Don't you love *your* dog?'

'Yes. But . . .'

'You don't really love your dog. If you wouldn't die instead of him.'

Zoe bit her tongue. Her rule was, never join in. That way they could pretend she wasn't there. The sort of internal monologue she enjoyed these days came from being around older children, at their disposal but silent. She was able to dip in and out of her thoughts now with the freedom of a bird. Whereas it was true enough that no thought could take wing around the under-fives; what they needed was too constant and minute and demanding, you had to be out of the room in order to think and they needed you in the room.

When George walked beside her he liked to hold on to what he called her elbow flab. He pinched it till it held a separate shape. He was going to be tall. As high as my heart, she used to say last year, but he had grown since then; he came up to her shoulder now, this nine-year-old.

'Teenagers!' he'd said to her not long ago. 'When I turn thirteen I'll be horrible in one night. Covered in spots and rude to you and not talking. Jus' grunting.'

Where did he get all that from? The most difficult age for girls was fourteen, they now claimed, the parenting experts; while for boys it was nineteen. Ten more years then. Good.

'Would you like to be tall?' she'd asked him that time.

'Not very,' he'd said decisively. 'But I wouldn't like just to be five eight or something. I'd want to be taller than my wife.'

His *wife*! Some way down the corridor of the years, she saw his wife against the fading sun, her face in shade. Would his wife mind if she, Zoe, hugged him when they met? She might, she might well. More than the father giving away his daughter, the mother must hand over her son. Perhaps his *wife* would only allow them to shake hands. When he was little his hands had been like velvet, without knuckles or veins; he used to put his small warm hands up her cardigan sleeves when he was wheedling for something.

They were inching their way down Mordred Hill, some sort of delay having been caused by a juggernaut trying to back into an eighteenth-century alley centimetres too narrow for it. Zoe sighed with disbelief, then practised her deep breathing. Nothing you could do about it, no point in road rage, the country was stuffed to the gills with cars and that was all there was to it. She had taken the Civil Service exams after college and one of the questions had been, How would you arrange the transport system of this country? At the time, being utterly wrapped up in cliometrics and dendrochronology, she had been quite unable to answer; but now, a couple of decades down the line, she felt fully qualified to write several thousand impassioned words, if not a thesis, on the subject.

But then if you believe in wives and steadfastness and heroic monogamy (thought Zoe, as the lorry cleared the space and the traffic began to flow again), how can you admit change? Her sister Valerie had described how she was making her husband read aloud each night in bed from *How to Rescue a Relationship*. When he protested, she pointed out that it was instead of going to a marriage guidance counsellor. Whoever wants to live must forget, Valerie had told her drily; that was the gist of it. She, Zoe, wasn't sure that she would be able to take marriage guidance counselling seriously either, as she suspected it was probably done mainly by women who were no longer needed on the school run. It all seemed to be about women needed and wanted, then not needed and not wanted. She moved off in second gear.

No wonder there were gaggles of mothers sitting over milky lattes all over the place from 8.40 a.m. They were recovering from driving exclusively in the first two gears for the last hour; they had met the school deadline and now wanted some pleasure on the return run. Zoe preferred her own company at this time of the morning, and also did not relish the conversation of such groups, which tended to be fault-finding sessions on how Miss Scantlebury taught long division or post-mortems on reported classroom injustices, bubblings-up of indignation and the urge to interfere, still to be the main moving force in their child's day. She needed a coffee though – a double macchiato, to be precise – and she liked the café sensation of being alone but in company, surrounded by tables of huddled intimacies each hived off from the other, scraps of conversation drifting in the air. Yesterday, she remembered, there had been those two women in baggy velour tracksuits at the table nearest to her, very solemn.

'I feel rather protective towards him. The girls are very provocative the way they dress now. He's thirteen.'

'Especially when you're surrounded by all these images. Everywhere you go.'

'It's not a very nice culture.'

'No, it's not.'

And all around there had been that steady self-justificatory hum of women telling each other the latest version of themselves, their lives, punctuated with the occasional righteous cry as yet another patch of moral high ground was claimed. That's a real weakness (she thought, shaking her head), and an enemy of, of – whatever it is we're after. Amity, would you call it?

'Last year when we were in Cornwall we went out in a boat and we saw sharks,' said Harry.

'Sharks!' scoffed George. 'Ho yes. In Cornwall.'

'No, really,' insisted Harry.

'It's eels as well,' said Freda. 'I don't like them either.'

'Ooh no,' Harry agreed, shuddering.

'What about sea snakes,' said George. 'They can swim into any hole in your body.'

The car fell silent as they absorbed this information.

'Where did you hear this?' asked Zoe suspiciously; she had her own reservations about Mr Starling.

'Mr Starling told us,' smirked George. 'If it goes in at your ear, you're dead because it sneaks into your brain. But if it goes up your . . .'

'What happens if it gets in up there?' asked Harry.

'If it gets in there, up inside you,' said George, 'You don't die but they have to take you to hospital and cut you open and pull it out.'

The talk progressed naturally from here to tapeworms.

'They hang on to you by hooks all the way down,' said Harry. 'You have to poison them, by giving the person enough to kill the worm but not them. Then the worm dies and the hooks get loose and the worm comes out. Either out of your bottom or somehow they pull it through your mouth.'

'That's enough of that,' said Zoe at last. 'It's too early in the morning.'

They reached the road where the school was with five minutes to spare, and Zoe drew in to the kerb some way off while they decanted their bags and shoes and morning selves. Would George kiss her? She only got a kiss when they arrived if none of the boys in his class was around. He knew she wanted a kiss, and gave her a warning look. No, there was Sean McIlroy; no chance today.

They were gone. The car was suddenly empty, she sat unkissed, redundant, cast off like an old boot. 'Boohoo,' she murmured, her eyes blurring for a moment, and carefully adjusted her wing mirror for something to do.

Then George reappeared, tapping at the window, looking stern and furtive.

'I said I'd forgotten my maths book,' he muttered when she opened the car door and, leaning across as though to pick up something from the seat beside her, smudged her cheek with a hurried – but (thought Zoe) unsurpassable – kiss.

Norman Hecht in the late 1940s

LIKE AN EPISODE OF *LA LAW*

A. M. Homes

Deposition – a curious word meaning to remove from office or a position of power and/or testimony under oath – a written statement by a witness for use in court in his absence.

Deposition: I think of suing my father to prove that he is my father and just the phrasing – suing my father to prove that he is my father – has the equally surreal echo of the moment my mother told me that my mother was dead.

I am adopted – I grew up knowing that I was the mistress's daughter, that my mother had been young and unmarried and my father was older and married with a family of his own. In 1992 my biological parents resurfaced, and at my first meeting with my father he proposed the idea of a DNA test, saying that his wife wanted and needed him to prove that I was his child and that it would allow him to take me into his family.

The entire episode was sufficiently strange that it seemed smart to apply a bit of science, to bring fact into a situation that was otherwise entirely emotional and almost pathological in its peculiarity.

My father and I had our blood drawn, several months passed and my father called to tell me he had the results. 'The test says it's 99.9 per cent likely I'm your father,' he said. 'So what are my responsibilities?'

I said nothing. There was nothing to say.

He never managed to take me into his family; his other children found out about my existence only accidentally – after a letter I'd sent to my father was opened by mistake by his youngest son.

I never asked for a copy of the DNA test – never questioned it – and my relationship to my biological parents ended rather abruptly; in 1998 my biological mother died at sixty years old, alone on her sofa in Atlantic City, New Jersey. My biological father knew she was ill; she had asked him to speak to me about donating a kidney and he refused, saying they couldn't ask me for anything considering how they'd never done anything for me. My father and I had one final conversation after my mother died. I told him that I'd had enough, that I couldn't do this again – that I didn't want to one day get a call summoning me to another church, where I'd stand in the back, unwelcome, and witness friends and family mourning the passing of a man I never really knew but was somehow a part of.

'I understand,' he said. 'Call me. Call me in the car. My wife isn't in the car very often – we can talk.'

'I'm not your mistress. I'm your daughter. And I'm not calling you in your car,' I said.

'Fine thing,' he replied.

Several years later, as part of a quest to know more about my background, I asked a lawyer to call my father and request a copy of the DNA test. Naively I assumed he would provide it. My father refused. I had the lawyer ask again, pointing out that legally I was most likely entitled to the information. My father again refused and this time asked the lawyer not to call him any more. I brought in more lawyers, who together pondered what might be done to compel my father to produce the document; could we sue for paternity, for breach of contract, unfair use of the results?

Suing my father – I picture the papers being filed, a summons served telling him to appear at a certain place at a certain time. I imagine there being a man, a stranger to both of us, someone hired to do the job, to ask the questions.

Mr Hecht, before we begin I would like to remind you that the length of a deposition is limited to seven hours a day, over the course of however many days it takes to do the kind of call and response, asking of questions related to the actions and activities of the last forty-four years – that's how old she is now, the infant in question.

Rules of Civil Procedure. Rule 26 – Discovery. We will be asking you, the deposed, to provide a copy of your birth certificate and a copy of the DNA test which you and Ms Homes jointly participated in. Given that a potential witness is anyone who has information relevant to the issues of a lawsuit or who has information that may lead to relevant information, we will also call your wife and your children. Unlike a trial, where a judge can rule on objections, at a deposition lawyers can ask irrelevant questions and enquire into hearsay.

Is all of this clear?

Have you ever had your deposition taken before?
Do you understand that you are under oath – sworn to tell the truth?
Are you prepared to answer my questions?
Is there anything about your physical state – are you taking any medications that will prevent you from giving me complete and truthful answers?
If you need to take a break at any time, let me know.

What is your full name?
Your place and date of birth?
Your parents' names and place and date of birth?

Mr Hecht, can you tell me why are we here today? Is there a particular issue? In 1993 you asked Ms Homes to participate in a DNA blood test which would genetically compare DNA samples from both you and Ms Homes to prove that in fact you are her father. And the result of that test showed that it was 99.9 per cent likely that you are her father, and recently when she requested a copy of that test from you, you declined to provide it – is that correct?

You asked Ms Homes to participate in the test, but you don't believe you should both have access to the results.
Why is that?
You participated equally?
You paid for the test, Mr Hecht – actually you had some trouble paying for the test, didn't you? You scheduled the appointment for the test in July of 1993, Ms Homes travelled from New York to Washington and met you at the lab, but you didn't have the right

kind of payment, the right kind of cheque – and you had to go back again the next day?

At the time you scheduled the test, Ms Homes offered to pay for the test as well or split the cost with you?

Now, if it is all about the money – the costs associated with this meeting here today are in excess of the charges for the test. So perhaps this is not about money?

How would you describe yourself, Mr Hecht?

Would you describe yourself as a family man?

Is there more to you than that – than just a retired businessman?

Are you close to your family?

Do you go to church?

You have a son and a nephew who share your name – what does the name mean to you?

What is your identity, Mr Hecht?

Did you always know who you were?

Have you ever been arrested?

Been charged with a crime?

For the record, can you tell us about any and all claims, lawsuits that you've been involved in over the years?

What was your age and place of first employment?

And your last – were you fired or asked to step down?

Did you feel any personal responsibility?

Do you think of yourself as someone who gets things done?

Has anyone ever called you a big shot?

Do you think you're an average man?

Same level of ambition as your peers?

Did you graduate from college?

Were you in the army?

Ever kill anyone?

Where did you grow up, Mr Hecht?

How would you describe your childhood?

Who raised you?

How was it that you lived with your grandparents – where were your mother and father?

How did your parents meet?

What did your father do for a living?
How would you describe your relationship with your father?
Were you close?
Did he love you?
Do you think it's true that boys are closer to their mothers and girls to their fathers?

Are you proud of your family history?
Involved in any lineage organizations?
What clubs are you a member of?
Have you ever wanted to join a club and not been allowed in?
What kind of name is Hecht?
Was your father Jewish?
Was he raised in a Jewish home?
Did your mother's family consider you Jewish?
Was your father's father a kosher butcher?
Why did your paternal grandmother carry a gun?

Would you describe yourself as charitable?
Do you give money to charities?
Do you give of your time and abilities?
Do you drink?
Did you ever use recreational drugs?
Ever smoke marijuana?
Ever take pills for energy?
Ever use cocaine?
Ever try Viagra?

Where did you meet your wife?
At what age were you married?
Did you engage in relations before the wedding?
Was she a virgin?
Were you?
Have you ever had a sexually transmitted disease?

When did you last have sex, Mr Hecht?
With whom?
Would you say that you and your wife had a good sex life?

Did you and your wife ever discuss open marriage?

So, initially she didn't know that you were having a sexual relationship with Ms Ballman?

Was Ms Ballman your first relationship outside of your marriage, or did someone precede her?

How did your wife find out about Ms Ballman?

Can you tell me the names of your children?

Do you know their birth dates?

Besides Ms Homes – did you have any other children outside of your marriage?

Is it possible, Mr Hecht, that there are others?

How many relationships did you have outside your marriage?

How long did they last?

Your wife was pregnant at the same time as Ms Ballman?

How old was Ms Ballman when you met her?

How would you describe her physically – her appearance?

Did you know that she was a minor?

What were the circumstances of that meeting?

Were you the owner of the Princess Shop?

How long did Ms Ballman work for you?

When did your sexual relationship begin?

What were the circumstances of that first encounter?

Was she a virgin?

Do you think your libido is average?

Was Ms Ballman a nymphomaniac?

Was she a lesbian?

Did you once tell Ms Homes that Ellen Ballman was a nymphomaniac and on another occasion that she was a lesbian?

Did your male friends also have girls on the side?

How many of them knew Ms Ballman?

Did you worry that Ms Ballman was sleeping with other men – your friends?

When your sexual relationship with Ms Ballman began how old was she?

What would prompt a teenage girl in the 1950s to leave her mother's good care and take up with a married man?

Did Ellen Ballman tell you that someone was molesting her?

You told Ms Homes that Ms Ballman told you something that would have indicated that something was happening in her mother's home and that you probably should have listened better.

Did you take advantage of Ms Ballman?

Did you use birth control?

Did Ms Ballman meet your family – your mother?

Your children?

Your wife?

How did it happen that your eldest son spent time with Ms Ballman?

When did you realize you were in love with Ms Ballman?

So, were you or were you not in love with Ms Ballman?

Did she believe you were in love with her?

On more than one occasion did you propose marriage?

Even though you were already married, Mr Hecht, you proposed to Ms Ballman when she was seventeen – you called her mother and asked for permission to marry her?

How did you think you would explain that to your wife?

Do you believe in polygamy, Mr Hecht?

How and when did your wife find out that you and Ms Ballman were having a relationship?

Did your wife know how old Ms Ballman was?

And what did you say to your wife? Again, I'd like to remind you that you are under oath and your wife will be answering the same question?

Did your wife contemplate divorcing you?

Is divorce in opposition to her faith?

Are you and your wife of the same faith?

Is adultery in opposition to your faith?

Are you a religious man, Mr Hecht?

Do you believe in heaven, Mr Hecht?

What was your nickname for Ms Ballman?

Was 'the Dragon Lady' one of them?

Where did that come from? Was it from something you shared?

Did Ms Ballman have you arrested for deserting her?

When Ms Ballman was pregnant you sent her to Florida to live and said you'd be joining her there – but you never showed up?

And your wife was pregnant at the same time as Ms Ballman?

You must have felt like an exceptionally fertile man?

Later in the pregnancy did you visit Ms Ballman at her mother's home?

Did you offer to take her shopping to buy things for the baby?

Did you have Ms Ballman meet with you and your lawyer and together discuss the fact that 'there are only so many slices of the pie?'

Did you ask either Ms Ballman or your wife to consider an abortion?

Can you swim, Mr Hecht?

I'm just wondering if at some point during all this you felt like you were going under. Drowning.

When was the last time you saw Ms Ballman pregnant? What month was that?

How did you hear about the birth of your child with Ms Ballman?

Were you ever asked to sign any legal documents relating to the child?

How long did your relationship with Ms Ballman last?

Did Ms Ballman ever marry?

Are you proud of your daughter, Mr Hecht?

Are you proud of Ms Homes?

Have you read her work?

Did you ask your daughter to meet you in hotels?

Why not coffee shops?

What is the nature of your thoughts about your daughter?

Did your wife know when and where you were meeting your daughter?

If you had been meeting one of your other children, would she have known?

Are you circumcised?

Is this common knowledge?

Does your other daughter know?

Why was this information that you shared with Ms Homes?

How did your other children find out that they had a sister?

And what was their reaction to discovering that information?

Do you think of yourself as a good father?

Let's backtrack a little bit . . .

In May of 1993 you read a review of Ms Homes's book in the *Washington Post* and called her in New York City?

What prompted you to call her on that day?

If Ms Homes were not a successful, well-known figure, would you have ever called her?

You made a plan to meet in Washington several days later?

Was anyone else at the meeting? Was the meeting taped or otherwise recorded or monitored by anyone?

What was your reaction to meeting Ms Homes?

When you met her were you surprised by the degree to which she looks like you?

Does she look more like you than your other children?

Despite the physical similarity at that meeting you asked Ms Homes if she would consent to a paternity test – saying that you had no question as to the likelihood that she was your child, but that your wife was insisting, and that you would need that in order to be able to take her into your family. Is that correct?

What made you question Ms Homes's paternity?

After the blood was drawn, as you were walking out with Ms Homes you told her you had something you wanted to give her – and yet you didn't give her anything?

What did you want to give her?

Was it something of your mother's? A family heirloom?

Several months later, you phoned Ms Homes to say you had the results of the test, and you asked Ms Homes to once again meet you in a hotel in Maryland?

At that meeting you told Ms Homes that you were in fact her father – that the DNA test said it was 99.9 per cent likely – and you asked, 'What are my responsibilities?'

What did you envision as your responsibilities? What were your intentions towards Ms Homes when you asked her to submit to the test?

Did you follow through by 'taking her into your family'?

Before you discussed the results with Ms Homes, did you discuss them with anyone else?

Did you discuss them with your wife?

Why did you not offer Ms Homes a copy of the test result?

What did you do with the test result?

When did you give a copy to your lawyer?

Did you keep a copy for yourself?

Do you typically give the one and only copy of an important document to your attorney?

Did you not put it in your safe deposit box because you didn't want your wife to discover it?

But didn't you tell Ms Homes that it was your wife who insisted on Ms Homes having the paternity test before you could 'take her into your family'?

Was the reason your wife wanted Ms Homes to have the DNA test because you had portrayed Ms Ballman to your wife as a floozy to make it seem like you were Ms Ballman's victim?

You arranged for your eldest son to meet Ms Homes?

How did that meeting go?

Was your son happy to have more information about something that had only been a dim memory from his childhood – the time he spent with Ms Ballman?

Was there a lot of tension in your home when your eldest son was a boy?

What was the occasion of your wife meeting Ms Homes?

Is there a reason why your wife wouldn't like Ms Homes?

Why did you say to Ms Homes later that she and your wife didn't hit it off?

Did Ms Homes ever ask you for anything?

Do you have concerns about Ms Homes making a claim on your estate?

Did she ever in any way indicate that she had any interest in your estate?

Did you have her take the paternity test in order that you might by name exclude her from your estate?

When did you last speak to Ms Ballman?

And what was the substance of that call?

Did you see Ms Ballman in the months before she died?

Did your wife know you were meeting her?

How did she look? Was she still attractive?

Did Ms Ballman ask you to ask Ms Homes if she would give her a kidney?

And what did you tell Ms Ballman?

Did you later tell Ms Ballman that in fact you had asked Ms Homes and that she said no?

Did it occur to you that this misinformation meant that Ms Homes did not know about Ms Ballman's condition, nor did she have a chance to say goodbye?

Did you go to your own personal doctor and enquire about donating a kidney to Ms Ballman?

Did you tell Ms Homes that you had done that?

And what would your wife have thought about that – would you have had the surgery without telling her?

Did you know that Ms Ballman was going to die?

How did you feel when you heard that Ms Ballman had passed?

And your last phone call with Ms Homes – several months after Ms Ballman's death – how did that go?

How did it end? Did you say, 'Call me anytime, call me in my car, my wife's not usually in the car'?

Why would Ms Homes need to call you in the car as opposed to in your home?

Is anyone harming you, confining you, not allowing you to make and receive calls and/or mail?

Are you angry with Ms Homes?

When Ms Homes's New York lawyer called you – the same man who called you to tell you that Ms Ballman had passed – and asked you for a copy of the DNA test, you told him never to call you again and referred him to your lawyer.

Mr Glick called your lawyer and was told by your lawyer that the DNA document had been misplaced and that you would not sign an affidavit of paternity.

Did you know that Mr Smith had misplaced the test results?

Are you concerned that other important documents may have been misplaced or mishandled?

Does it not seem a little too convenient that Ms Homes is asking for this document, and now it is missing?

You have children and now grandchildren? Do they look like you, Mr Hecht?

You have adopted grandchildren as well. Do they look like you also?

Do they have a right to know who they are – where they came from?

What is your understanding of why Ms Homes wants this document?

If Ms Homes is your biological relative, why should she not be treated in the same way that your other equally biological children are treated? Why should she have different, less than equal, rights?

Does that seem fair? Are you a fair man? A just man?

Could you please repeat for the record your name?

And Mr Hecht, could you please for the record state the names of all your children?

Jeremy Seabrook (left) and his twin brother, 1946

TWINS

Jeremy Seabrook

My twin brother and I were separated at birth, even though we lived in the same house, with the same mother, for the first eighteen years of our lives. The separation was total, psychological, emotional and social; and it lasted until his death early in 2005. I heard only indirectly that he had died, since there had been no communication between us since our mother's funeral, fifteen years earlier.

I can scarcely believe these words, even as I write them. How could we have grown up in such intense physical closeness, and yet behave towards each other as though we were strangers? It was worse than being strangers, for we had been familiar everyday figures in each other's life. There was a deep temperamental difference between us; but this was reinforced by the determination of a powerful woman, and by a social system that supported separation. Our mother had skilfully maintained the state of hostile indifference that kept us apart; and we lived together in a state of frozen kinship, our lives both turned towards our mother. Our relationship – or absence of one – was decided from the beginning.

Or maybe even before that. When our mother was already well into her thirties and still childless, she discovered that her husband had tertiary syphilis. He had always been a 'wanderer', a characteristic that referred as much to his sexual rovings as to his need for constant physical movement. My earliest memories of him are of watching as he shaved himself in readiness for an evening out, scraping his neck with a cut-throat razor and plastering his curly black hair with lard to make it shine. The symptoms of syphilis were attributed for a long time to an infection contracted while catching rabbits – he was also an accomplished poacher, and at one time kept a ferret in a hutch in the garden.

Our mother had already had a series of miscarriages. The treatment for syphilis in the late 1930s involved continuous injections of a mixture of mercury and arsenic, and there was little prospect that sexual relations between them would ever resume, and even less that they would have any children.

She was standing one day at the kitchen window which looked on to a piece of waste ground, when a man working on a nearby building site asked for a bucket of water. He came into the kitchen to collect it. She immediately saw that he was no ordinary workman: this was a time when the working class was full of earnest self-taught people, autodidacts, the intelligent uninstructed and people hungry for knowledge. Our town, Northampton, had its good share of them. Within a few minutes, he had promised to lend her some books – George Bernard Shaw's *The Intelligent Woman's Guide to Socialism*, William Morris's *News from Nowhere* and Robert Blatchford's *Merrie England*. I found them among her small treasures after her death.

She must have decided there and then that he would become the father of the child she so much wanted. She could scarcely believe her good fortune. He was everything her husband was not: clever, smart and in perfect health. Although he was married, he made it clear he had no intention of leaving his wife. They had no children. She was a semi-invalid. Discovery, he said, would destroy her. The relationship between them developed quickly. Within months she was pregnant.

Dealing with this was no simple matter. Appalled and elated by what she had done, she came to an accommodation with her husband. She was by then looking after the butcher's shop they had taken on a new housing estate, while nursing a man whose shaming illness would certainly have ruined the family livelihood if it had become known. It was wartime. She promised that she would look after him until he was fully recovered, and then she expected him to be gone. In the meantime, he would accept that the child she was carrying was his. He had no choice. When she was not serving in the shop, she was emptying zinc pails of waste discharged from his mouth and nose, which had been partly destroyed by the sickness. She always said that the stench remained with her for the rest of her life. She used quantities of bleach and disinfectant, which she travelled far afield to buy, lest anyone should wonder why she needed so much of a commodity which did not figure prominently in most people's weekly shopping list.

He fiercely resented his dependency, and there were frequent arguments. I remember standing at the top of the stairs early one morning and watching as he threw a cup of tea at her: it flew solid through the air before shattering in scalding drops on her face and shoulder. Frightened by what he had done, he burst into tears. He was in more urgent need of consolation than she was of medical attention, and she administered it, despite her injuries. Sometimes she would pretend to be hurt by his clumsy blows and would lie still on the floor. He would panic and try to revive her. I saw her often, prone, in a posture that prefigured my worst nightmare.

As it turned out, she was to have twins as a result of this encounter with a stranger. Here was a tangle of secrets to be concealed at all costs. Was it her own secretiveness that made her insist her children tell her everything, keep nothing back? Sometimes she would say, 'There's nothing I don't know,' and she turned upon us her grim grey eyes, in which we saw reflected our own guilt and shame. We yielded up to her everything she asked for, including a promise that we would never desert her as others had. She extracted from her children promises of constancy which the men in her life had withheld.

Her main concern was to keep the two men apart, and to ensure they would never meet. Our biological father, aggrieved at what he saw as her trickery, refused to contribute anything to our upkeep. Who can tell what menacing possibility she foresaw if her twin boys should combine or conspire against her, when one man had deserted her for a sexually transmitted disease and the other had abandoned her to the consequences of what he called her own lack of foresight?

I don't think any meeting between our joint fathers ever did occur; just as no significant encounter between their divided children ever took place. Later, as we grew up, our 'true' father occasionally made an appearance in our lives; unaccountably lachrymose and emotional, he questioned us closely about our ambitions and what we wanted to be when we grew up, a state so unimaginably distant at the time that it was difficult to formulate any answer at all. We resented his intrusive enquiries. It seems he was angered by her deception and, repelled by the role he had been selected to play, felt manipulated and abused: it had not been for his own sake that our mother had been attracted to him, but for the sake of as yet unknown others, her future children. He made it clear she could expect no material help; and even when she could scarcely make a living in the late 1940s, as the meat ration fell to the equivalent of 10d a person, she didn't ask him for anything. She was frugal and sparing, and spent nothing on herself, while we had what she emphatically called 'the best of everything'. Nothing was too good for us, except the one thing we might have valued above all else, the sweetness of uninhibited companionship.

As soon as her husband was well – by that time we were eight or nine – they were divorced. Divorce, despite being a rare occurrence, was the inevitable outcome of the one-sided bargain she had struck with him; and separation was an art in which she was already practised. Some virtuous people in the neighbourhood ostentatiously withdrew their ration books from the shop: who could be expected to deal with tradespeople who had flouted the sacrament of marriage? She accepted their judgement with dignity, thankful that nobody knew the whole story. At the same time, certain men propositioned her. They must have been discouraged by her response.

The effort and energy she spent on ensuring that my brother and I grew up as distant from each other as possible were relentless. She watched us all the time. One day, when we were about four, we were giggling in a corner over some trivial amusement. She parted us roughly. We were puzzled by her anger. Significantly, she told me to go and look at a book, and my brother to play with the dog.

The distribution of roles had already long been made. We were physically and psychically isolated. I was clever and he was beautiful: no more malign division could be imagined. It was decided that I would rise socially and he would break hearts. The emotional causes of my estrangement from my brother were woven into our mother's psychological fears; but they were also strengthened and reinforced by circumstances which, in the 1950s, made it possible for my brother and me to be assigned to different social classes, a fact which has continued to bewilder and pain me every day of my life, and never more so than now that he is dead.

The separation was made easier by the fact that our characters and temperaments could not have been less compatible. All we had in common was a shared introversion, and this made communication between us even more difficult.

He slept in a room of his own from the age of about six. I continued to share a room with my mother, frightened, as I was, of the dark, of shadows, of death. My mother's husband, the man we called our father, had been consigned to 'the spare room', a damp and prohibited chamber, which smelled of smoke and rancidity, the unspoken mingling of maleness with disease. It exercised its own fateful lure, and sometimes I would cast a fearful glance at the disorder within – the dingy bedclothes folded back to reveal the mysterious hollow in which his body slept, the blot of mildew on the damp wall, the smell of semen, all of which combined to furnish me with early fantasies of the stranger who represented the absent intimacy of fatherhood. I had erotic dreams about him, which induced a further, and wholly unnecessary, sense of guilt, since in the end he proved to have been no blood relation at all. All this led to a profound estrangement from my own gender.

Our mother rigorously policed the slow unfolding of our maleness, which she would have preferred us to abjure. One day, when I was about nine, undressing in front of the fire, where we had our night-time strip-down wash, she inspected my underpants. I had dribbled into them after peeing. She sniffed and looked up me suspiciously. 'What's this?' I was terrified. 'Wee-wee. What else could it be?' She examined the stained garment dubiously. 'What else could it be?' 'Never you mind.' I kept on asking – and wondering – what it could have signified. 'What else could it be?' This served as a premature and elliptical form of sex instruction: I concluded that other, and no doubt shameful discharges might in time be expected from my body. Our childhood was pervaded by her mute entreaty that, if time rendered adulthood inevitable, we should at least not grow up to be men. This had a seriously repressive effect on my brother, whose emotional and sexual development was delayed by her mute prohibitive power; whereas I tried to oblige, although the best I could do was to grow up gay.

There was no space for emotional attachment to my brother. Our mother whispered to each of us her dissatisfaction with the other, with the consequence that we viewed one another with distrust and a fierce defensiveness of our wronged parent.

Separation has been, perhaps, the single biggest determining influence in my life. The completeness of separation from my twin was accompanied by a morbid fear of separation from my mother. For the first few years of my life, I could not bear to lose sight of her; whenever she was swallowed up by the closing of a door or even by extinguishing the light, I howled until her presence was restored to me. It seems that the premature loss of my brother was accompanied by an excessive attachment to her: she was, as it were, the phantom of a kind of amputation of the twin who was always present but scarcely visible.

My dependency on our mother, and my terror of losing her, set up other pathologies. Her departure (or death, which seemed a more likely agent of her disappearance) seemed to me the most terrible thing that could happen; and I came early to the comfortless conclusion that it would be folly ever to permit myself the pain of any other relationship which would involve the same frightening abridgement. For this reason, all my feelings (and not only those of love) were locked up in the claustral relationship with her, and I was unwilling to form – or perhaps incapable of – any other close attachment, least of all with the brother whose extinguished presence remained as inert to me as that of the kitchen table or the contents of the broom cupboard.

For a long time, I did not recognize the origin of what later appeared to me an inability to feel for others. I took refuge in dwelling upon the suffering of humanity in general, the brevity of life, the certainty of death, but this was the only way I could express the stifled emotions of a dependency that had little to do with love, but everything to do with the fear of loss. I was well into my thirties before I knew the meaning of a reciprocal and loving relationship with another adult. I didn't reason it like this, but I felt that since irreparable loss is inscribed in every relationship, I should stay away from them. And I did.

I think my brother may have experienced something similar; indeed, it may well have been worse for him, since he did not so readily yield to our mother's demand for unconditional surrender to her will. I had the misfortune to resemble her. He didn't, and this is why he probably felt the exercise of her controlling power as violence. She could not tie him to herself as she had effortlessly bound me. As a result, she made greater efforts to attach him, which he found intolerably oppressive. This led him to believe that she cared more for me than for him, and only I knew that the opposite was the truth. I was a pushover, while he was a challenge. Her attempts to win him over were evidence of a preference which he could not, perhaps, have been expected to see. I was jealous of his difference, and of his ability to resist, which suggested an independence I wanted. I had little sympathy for him, and nothing remained in the depleted account of my feelings to spend on him.

I can now see the many ways in which I failed him, although at the time these remained opaque and mysterious to me. One day in primary school, he fell ill and had to be taken home. I begged that someone else might go with him, since I did not wish to miss the lesson. I remember feeling virtuous in making this request, and if the teacher gave me a strange look of pity and puzzlement, its meaning became clear to me only much later. On another occasion, walking home from school, he had what was politely called 'an accident': suffering from diarrhoea, he stood immobile on the path, his legs stained with shit. Appalled, I abandoned him and ran home to tell our mother what had happened. She closed the shop and went out to meet him. Gathering some dock leaves from the hedgerow, she wiped him down and brought him back, consoling him with the story that, although I had fled the scene of his embarrassment and shame, he could trust her never to do so.

I was convinced that my brother brought nothing but trouble and unhappiness to her. That, presumably, was why she never ceased worrying about him and chose me as her confidant. On the day her own mother died, in November 1948, I was in bed with one of the unnamed sicknesses that impaired my childhood. She came upstairs and leaned over the bed, her eyes dark and her cheeks smeared with tears. 'What's the matter?' I asked. 'Is it him?' To my brother, in order to explain her yielding to the constant demands I made on her, she used to say, 'Well, you know what he is', so that he also came to understand that I was the source of her constant suffering. She had developed a complicity with each of us against the other, and she betrayed us all the time, in order to prevent us from betraying her.

But all this careful engineering of our souls was moved by an overwhelming and expiatory love. She felt guilty that she had brought two illegitimate children into the world at a time when such children still bore the stigma of events over which they had not the slightest influence. Enough people were in on the secret for its inevitable disclosure at some point. The wounds were inflicted by the most tender hands, and these are always more painful than those delivered with the intention of hurting. The work of separation was not conscious, and if anyone had pointed out what she was doing, she would have been appalled. The most anyone ever said was, 'They are like chalk and cheese'; which of these substances each of us resembled was not spoken.

She needn't have taken quite so much trouble to keep us apart. The social arrangements which would assist her so ably in her work of separation were at hand. At eleven, he went to the secondary modern school, which was a scruffy holding centre for the wayward youngsters of an estate known as Windy Ridge, into which former town centre slum-dwellers had been transferred. I had gone prematurely, at the age of ten, to the grammar school. While he struggled in the C-stream (against teachers, the other kids and low expectations), I raced through my studies, and soon learned to ascribe to myself all the qualities which a new meritocracy claimed to have detected in me. My brother was said to be 'good with his hands'; but everyone knew that was a euphemism for not being a scholar, and was in fact a humiliating consolation prize. He came home with objects he had crafted – a wooden stool, a small chest of drawers – on which he had concentrated all his considerable creative powers; our mother kept the little chest beside her chair for the rest of her life. It became a small shrine to him; and when she died we found it contained some of his rare letters to her from his time in the army in Germany, his wedding photographs and pictures of his children as infants.

Largely self-taught, she retained a veneration for formal education; and my brother's inability to conform to her superstition, created one of the most significant rifts between us. She also sought, not very successfully, to cultivate in us a taste for the arts as she understood them, in her obscure yearning for a better life that went beyond the material. This meant being allowed to stay up late on Sunday evenings to listen to a concert of light classics on the radio, called *Grand Hotel*, which featured the singing voices of Margaret Eaves and Olive Groves, singing from *The Merry Widow* or *White Horse Inn*. She read to us from her favourite book, *Bleak House*. The first part about the fog was entrancing; but when it came to Lady Dedlock and the incessant rain in Lincolnshire, I was frightened: perhaps it evoked too sharply the narrow, oppressive horizons of our own lives. I wept so much that the readings had to be suspended. They never resumed.

My brother left school at fifteen to be apprenticed to a carpenter and joiner. He came home shedding pale wood shavings and the resinous scent of distant pine forests. He would go out of the house every morning on his bicycle, with a tin box of sandwiches and an apple, skidding in the icy February dawn, while I remained in bed, anticipating further adventures in the subjunctive of French verbs. He worked diligently and uncomplainingly, although once, when he had been detained for prolonged and unpaid overtime, our mother went up to the workshop and told his boss that if he thought he could exploit a boy because he had no father who would stand up for him, he had another think coming, because she was as capable as any man at defending him. In fact, she often said to us that she had had to be both father and mother to us, and I sometimes wondered at the effortless capacity with which she could pass in and out of genders, when I had such difficulty in establishing a security in just one of them.

In his spare time, my brother used to make model aeroplanes with balsa wood, covered with tissue paper and stuck together with a glue that smelled of molten bone, and which had the effect of inducing a euphoria which no one at that time could quite identify.

As an adolescent, he went out regularly for Sunday evening cycle rides with Uncle Alex, husband of my mother's eldest sister. He was a gaunt, taciturn man, dominated by his wastrel wife, whose fondness for whisky, melodrama and horse racing scandalized her family. He took my brother to visit country churches, admiring medieval misericords and vestigial wall paintings. They would drink lemonade outside pubs, to the melancholy accompaniment of church bells and acrid October bonfires. I was always incredulous at this unlikely friendship, which had so small a dependency on words; perhaps there was a tacit understanding that both were victims of the powerful women of our mother's family. I once came across Alex with our mother, she all flustered and blushing, he saying, 'You're the one I should have had.' It later emerged that he had worked his way through the sisters and had had a relationship with at least two of the others, excluding the one to whom he was officially wedded. It occurred to me that if he was so assiduous in seeking out the lustreless company of my brother, this was probably a pretext which would open up the way to our mother; and I felt obscurely comforted by the realization.

Once my brother tried to talk to me about sex. Although by then – we were about fifteen – I knew much about the mechanics of sex, I could not conceive of sharing with him either what I knew or what I suspected about myself. When I consider our time together, I am aware that during our childhood and youth he made a number of oblique pleas to me. If I rebuffed them, it was because I had no idea of what they were, and regarded them as trespass, or encroachment on the slender areas of autonomy remaining to me after our mother had, like some imperial power, annexed all the emotional territory around her, which she governed like the empress-queen herself.

At eighteen, he was 'called up' into the army; significant verb – he had been called up by others all his life. Indeed, our very birth had been a summons from our mother to relieve her of her own isolation and despair. He was posted to Germany, while I remained in the sixth form, acting with my friends in plays in the Co-op Hall, and discussing the iniquities of Suez and the Hungarian uprising against the Soviet Union. I took it as no more than due recognition that I would go to Cambridge, deferring indefinitely a military service which had been abolished by the time I had finished my prolonged and indispensable studies into the symbolism of the celestial rose in Dante's *Paradiso*.

I envied him his looks. My school friends found my brother fascinating, and were often attracted, in ways which they could not then satisfactorily explain to themselves, to his silent beauty. He exercised a mysterious power to draw people to him, which I certainly did not possess. This irritated me, since it suggested that my public proclaimed supremacy might be less significant than I imagined. If he coveted that which came to me so easily, I was bitterly resentful of that which he had never earned. How little we value what we do without effort or merit; and how we long for what is not granted to us! In any case, I was probably quite wrong to be jealous of my brother's attractiveness. Since a great deal of his charm lay in his artless unconsciousness of it, it was of no use to him, and he failed to employ it in the knowing way I would have done, had I been so favoured.

My own apparent good fortune was not without its problems. Life at the grammar school was frightening and I stayed away as much as

I could, even writing notes to the headmaster from our departed father, excusing my frequent truancies. One teacher, a lay preacher who had some notion of pastoral care of the pupils, visited our house one day to look into the reasons for my constant absences. When he saw my brother, he turned to me and said, 'Why didn't you tell me you had such a lovely brother?' and playfully let his hand roam over his thigh. I was outraged by his question: I was, after all, the object of his visit, and the question struck me as an accusation, as though I had locked my brother away or concealed his existence from those who would have been only too delighted to learn of it. Far from revealing the cause of my loathing of school, I clenched inside, determined that I would never disclose any feeling or thought to this insensitive man, with his wheedling tone and wandering hands.

There were rare occasions on which my brother and I went out together. I can recall a day one summer holiday, when we walked our aunt's dog through the fields on a thundery afternoon, when huge anvil clouds blotted the sun and the rain began to fall, scenting like caramel the burnt grasses. Nothing happened: only that I caught a glimpse of the companionability we might have had together, and of the confidences we might have shared. The day remains, saturated with rain and regret.

Later – I remember the date, August 1, 1958, a rare day of warmth in a cold, wet summer – we went to the theatre in London. It was a performance of an Australian play called *The Summer of the Seventeenth Doll*, about a group of people who met each summer to reaffirm their friendships and marriages; but in the seventeenth year of their celebration, everything went wrong and they quarrelled irretrievably. He was enchanted by it. Afterwards, we went for a meal in a dismal one-storey fish restaurant on Tottenham Court Road, where, after reading the menu, he asked for 'steak and chips'. I corrected him. 'He means skate and chips,' I told the waiter, as though I were the child of an immigrant, interpreting for a parent who had never mastered the language.

After national service, my brother worked in the construction industry, helping to reshape the face of our town, transforming its ornamental blood-red brick into pale geometric structures of concrete and glass. He worked for the local council as assistant supervisor on the building of the first multi-storey car park – a dazzling symbol of modernity, evidence that our town had indeed entered the modern era. At the same time, I was lamenting the passing of the streets which were being torn down with such exuberance – yet another curious division of labour between us. He represented the future, while I was drawn to the past. While he looked to the age of concrete and cars, I was organizing protests against the construction of an expressway, which would demolish almost a thousand houses, the 'little palaces', as people called the terraced houses they had bought and tended with such care. This further separation was to have fateful results: it was a direct contributor to his early death.

He was, of course, also called to get married. His marriage was arranged; not in the way that matchmakers and extended families in India make marriages, but through the more or less inevitable acceptance of decent people that this was the natural order of things, that they were made for each other, the silent handsome man and the homely and dutiful young woman who wrote to him every day while he was in Germany.

It proved to be a sad error, in which the naivety of the protagonists and the eagerness of the families combined to create a marriage which only kindled the smothered dissatisfactions and the deep inner misery that childhood and adolescence had deposited, tenacious as limescale, on the interior of his trusting and receptive soul. He once spoke, in one rare confessional moment, of being buried alive.

He went to work in Zambia, and there met the woman who was to become his second wife. It was only with her that he began to discover himself, and was able to determine who he was and what he needed. She gave him the confidence and strength he had never received from anyone in the long years of denial. He was already over thirty. His second marriage was a rebirth. Unhappily, this also meant the death of his former self, that inauthentic shell made up of duty, obedience and self-effacement, and of all who had been involved in its making. He detached himself from everyone and everything that had gone before, with the obduracy of those whose will has always been thwarted by others.

He literally remade himself, and in the process discarded his birth family and everyone connected with it. The rift which had run through our childhood, reinforced by our upbringing as effectively as if we had lived under some stringent laws of an emotional apartheid, became final. A few clumsy gestures at reconciliation, an occasional meeting full of suppressed anger and unspoken resentment, brought us to an intractable estrangement which nothing, it seemed, had the power to dissolve.

He came to our mother's funeral, although he had not seen her for some years. I held out my hand to him. He said, 'I'll shake your hand and that's it.' Those were the last words I heard him say. I knew I would never speak to him again. After that, I grieved for him. I woke in the night, unable to believe that this was how our sombre and unsparing childhood, gravid with secrets and sorrows which our mother had confided only when we were almost forty and the two men in her life were dead, would end. Adulthood is always full of mysterious secrets for children: when these are compounded with shame, guilt and remorse with no obvious cause, they can become virulently destructive. Children will inevitably assume that they are at the centre of what is being concealed; and in this case, we were not mistaken. Our mother thought she was sheltering us from harm; but she sought to protect us with her own hurt and wounded feelings – the very source of the damage from which she would have shielded us. Sometimes she could not prevent herself from saying, 'If only you knew.' 'If only we knew what, Mum?' 'Never you mind.' Or, 'You'll know one day.'

As the years passed, I thought about my brother less often; but there remained a dull ache, a sense of absence, the phantom limb of an amputee. When I received the news that he had died, it was like confirmation that the body of a missing person had been found after a long search. He had vanished fifteen years earlier, and the remains washed up on the shore of the time that divided us were identified as his.

There was another bitter irony in his death. He died of mesothelioma, an asbestos-related cancer. This was a consequence of his building work, which had produced multi-storey car parks and concrete office blocks in our town, and also, no doubt, in Lusaka and Windhoek, where he worked, supplied with the miracle substance that was to make them proof against fire. His early working-class occupation also determined his premature death. Although he had appeared as an emissary of the future, altering the aspect of Victorian and colonial towns and cities, the past was not to release him so readily.

Over time, the class destination of our early years was transformed. The separation ceased to be so clearly based on class and mutated, so that it later came to appear that the distance was culturally rather than class-determined. He was dedicated to his family and his work, was prosperous and certainly at peace in the life he led in a converted parsonage in the west of England. I had fulfilled my mother's ambition and become a writer, an occupation which my brother held in the greatest contempt. Our mother came to agree with him: it never pleased her that I wrote about poor people. Nobody, she predicted – quite correctly – wanted to know about that. Had she not sacrificed herself, so that we should be sheltered against the asperities of poverty? Why would I return to such things, if not out of perverseness, in order to humiliate her and mock all her efforts on our behalf? Nothing would come of it. She prided herself on her capacity for prophecy, and although she was shown to be conspicuously fallible in most of her forecasts, in this she was right.

The man we did not know was our father also contributed to the differences between us – a practical demonstration of the power of heredity, since neither of us had the faintest idea of his role in our lives until our mother's belated disclosure. He had been a craftsman, a builder, and a restorer of churches and historic buildings, and my brother had inherited his ability to mend and remake beautiful things. He had also been a vehement Leftist, and a member of the Communist Party, as some of his books remaining with our mother testified. From him, I received a hatred of the orthodoxies of the age, a compulsive dissent from all the revealed ideologies and received wisdom that seem to be indispensable for social cohesion.

George Eliot once wrote of Nature as 'a great tragic dramatist' that unites people by flesh and bone and then divides them by temperament and character. The sensibility that set me apart from my brother was supported by a social system that emphasized competitiveness, disunity and division; the dislocations of kinship were aggravated by social circumstances. That after an unhappy childhood and youth my brother found himself content at last is a consolation; that we were never able to reach out in reconciliation means that death has become one more, and final, aspect of the multiple injuries of separation that dominated our lives.

David and Ivor, Ruislip, 1968

DOING THE PAPERWORK

David Goldblatt

It just wasn't his strong suit. He hardly did it. He barely kept it, and as he got older he cared even less about the consequences of not doing his paperwork. It wasn't a form of learnt absent-mindedness or elderly decline. It wasn't a kind of shallow front or brittle bravado but a cussed indifference to authority, a refusal to live with fear of any kind. The old man really didn't give a fuck what happened. It became more pronounced as my mother, Bobby, was dying and the tedious bureaucracy of car ownership that had been her domain went untouched. The summonses and the fines began to mount up, but still no tax, MOT or insurance. In fact, a year after Bobby's death he had taken to sporting a beer mat in his tax disc holder. Why? He didn't need to. For years Ivor had had access to backdated tax discs, MOT certificates and insurance papers. Anyone unfortunate enough to be stopped by the police and asked to produce their documentation, anyone who had through no fault of their own overlooked their renewal, could remedy the situation for a small fee. Notices of fines from magistrates' courts across the south east of England kept rolling in for another three or four years. The total value of those fines – the interest on unpaid fines and the fines for not paying fines – peaked at around three grand. Then it stopped. Maybe he paid up, maybe they gave in? They probably did a deal where he agreed to pay twenty-five pence a week until the end of time and then he put the paperwork in the bin.

Although Ivor spent the last years of his life as a reasonably legal motorist, this did not mark a sea change in his personal administration. He made a will, but that was as far as it went. Among the many elements of his estate that I dealt with after his death were over four thousand pounds' worth of unpaid parking tickets, a wide variety of pending utility bills and a number of unresolved court cases involving motoring accidents and insurance claims. More impressively, he hadn't paid any council tax or made any mortgage payments for eight years and, despite running a considerable small business, he had not passed on a jot to the Inland Revenue or the VAT. He had, however, had a small but useful injection of cash from social security on the grounds of disability. In truth, for the first year after Bobby's death he was good for nothing. The other seven are harder to account for.

Sometimes, the bailiffs arrived, but his response was always the same. They would knock on the door and introduce themselves. He would then greet them, step out of the house, close the door behind him and walk out on to the neat green in front of his flat, ringed by six other mock-Tudor blocks, and shout at the top of his voice, 'This man is a bailiff. He wants to take my possessions away to pay for unpaid bills and unjust fines, but he will not be getting anything.' They never did.

For the most part my paperwork is in better shape than his. My car is legal and my tax records are so clean that, after a random going-over, the Inland Revenue decided they owed me money. I'm not neat, organized or obsessive about paperwork – I do the easy stuff first and then I procrastinate – but I do eventually get round to it. The boxes, however, remain unsorted. They contain what's left of his paperwork; the stuff that I took from his flat when we cleared it out and sold it, minus the choicest items, which were taken by the police and the lawyers. The boxes have been through various incarnations: thick plastic bags, taped-up grocery cartons, old book boxes. I think that they have, at last, taken their final form. In their current state, there are four. There used to be more, but over the seven years that I have carted them from one cupboard, shelf or attic to another, their contents appear to have contracted. Although I have unpacked and repacked the boxes, stopping along the way to dwell on the odd paper, I haven't really opened them. I'm always squinting, half shielding my eyes.

The paperwork first arrived in black plastic sacks and putting it into in some kind of order had helped. It felt like an act of salvage. That was the easy bit; then it stopped helping. My partner Sarah said to me, 'Are you sure you want to open the boxes? You know what happens when you open the boxes . . . I'm not saying don't open them, but you know what happens . . . and . . . I just wonder if it's helping any more.'

I knew what happened when I opened the boxes. I started crying. Not moist eye crying, or dabbing with tissues crying, or tears down the cheeks crying. I mean raging, head banging, animal noise crying. Crying that made my skull tighten and my head throb, crying that wouldn't stop. After she spoke, I was angry that she was on to me. Angry that she couldn't bear another night of standing by helpless as I wailed. Angry that I had so much bile to swallow. Angry because she was right. I'd done enough anger to know how addictive and self-satisfying the acid burn of rage can be and how it corrodes what's left of your love. When my brother broke the news to me, I said, 'I don't know what we are going to do, but we are not going to get angry.'

I made a choice. I chose not to be angry. I put the boxes away and I left my paperwork undone. If I was more like the old man, that would have been that. The boxes would have mouldered in the loft until my kids got their hands on them. Their contents would, I imagine, be all but incomprehensible to them. I worry that they are becoming incomprehensible to me. That's what happens if you don't do your paperwork: time comes round and takes your stories, characters flatten out into the two-dimensional shapes of comfortable family legend. But I'm not like the old man. I can't let it ride, I can't front the bailiffs, I can't put the paperwork in the bin.

When anyone is murdered the police want to take a look at their home. When they're murdered in that home, the police want to take a good long look. In Ivor's case they examined his flat for almost a month. They looked at him for just as long – time enough for three autopsies, one for the prosecution and one for each of the two defence cases. We got to see him for ten minutes in the Uxbridge morgue, a low brick building of studied anonymity. Unadorned, it is surrounded by stark beds of cracked earth and leggy municipal roses strewn with a thousand cigarette butts. Inside, it's suffused with seedy, thin yellow light, furnished like a cheapskate undertakers. We couldn't touch him or even be in the same room at the same time; he remained a piece of evidence. They let my brother and me into a viewing room with a gridded glass window through which you could see the broken corpse ruddy with smashed capillary beds, his battered jowls drooping heavily down his face, his eyes tiny black crosses sunk in his skull, his thick dark pelt still lush on his greying skin. When the police had finished inspecting his flat, there remained the matter of his blood; lots of it and all over his new pink carpet. We agreed it would be a good thing if the carpet was removed and if someone washed the woodwork. When I asked the police, for no reason in particular, who would be doing it, they replied, 'Rentokil'.

Early April, a blank white sky, and we're driving down the Westway, heading out of London towards Ruislip. In the car we are tight-lipped, wondering whether they really have taken out the carpet, whether they really did clean the woodwork, wondering what we'll do if we have to clean the flat before we clear it. I didn't think I would dare play it, but I slide in the cassette, a battered copy of AC/DC's Highway to Hell. *It's already wound to track eight: 'If You Want Blood (You've Got It)'. We pull off at the Polish War Memorial. I see his smile, not his wounds. I hear his laughter and swallow my horror.*

I see myself enter the house through the back door. The air in the flat is hard and still and cold. At the edge of my vision I can see strange but familiar landmarks: his collection of tannin-stained mugs, the deep-fat fryer and its crust of oil sludge and dust, the stacks of duty-free Rothmans cartons. But the coin jars have gone and so has most of the linoleum. It's been cut away and removed. He must have bled all over it as he lay slumped in the hallway. I look through into the hall. The carpet is gone. They've taken the lot, leaving dirty boards, copies of the local freebie, the sharp tips of the exposed runners, but no blood. I feel relieved and suddenly emboldened. Walking into his bedroom, it feels even staler: the curtains are drawn, dust hangs in the air. My parents' private space – their drawers, their papers, their clothes, their bed. I head straight for the top drawer on his side of the dresser. I am looking for a letter. I paw through lighters, hip flasks, old casino chips, scraps of paper with scribbled addresses, rotting Polaroids, cufflinks – and the letter. He wrote it twenty years ago, the first time they left James and me at home while they flew off on holiday somewhere. 'Only to be opened in the event of our demise,' he had said, theatrically but in earnest. We never opened it. It sat for a long weekend on the coffee table. They didn't die, they came back. I always supposed the letter would be in the drawer. It is handwritten, with an air of mock seriousness. He tells us that he and Bobby love us and are proud of us. We are

to go and see the solicitors, Cathcart and Co., which, of course, we've already
done. He tells us, 'David look after James. James help David.'

Now I'm crushed. I'm heady with my find. I am lost. I can hear a distant
rasp that is my sister-in-law vomiting: Rentokil scrubbed his blood up, but
they overlooked the steak he was going to cook that evening defrosting on the
draining board. She found it in a pool of stinking brown blood. We are
grabbing papers and folders and anything official: letters, postcards, photos,
paperwork. I'm opening Bobby's bedside cupboard. Sarah's talking to me, close
to my ear: 'We don't have to do it all today; we can and will come back.' He
hasn't touched it. He hasn't touched it for eight years. It's exactly as she left
it; the old exercise books, lip balms, her last handbag. I rub the dust from the
zip and open it. Inside there's an appointment card from Northwick Park
Hospital, bearing a date for two weeks after she died. There is a small orange
pill pot, with a single tiny capsule of diazepam left.

After that day, I put Bobby's handbag and her diazepam in the boxes.
I kept her letters and her books of poetry. I sorted the birth, death and
marriage certificates for three generations, immigration papers and
passports. I collected the cards that celebrated my birth and my
brother's, our bar mitzvahs, Bobby's twenty-first birthday and the
cards that consoled us when she died. I sifted what was left of her
schoolwork, and mine and James's, kids' artwork, holiday mementos:
this was treasure. But the old man's paperwork remained unsorted and
unexamined, still toxic to the touch. I shovelled it all in – bulging
folders and files, bundles of bills and summonses and judgements,
photos and fan mail, correspondence with lawyers, bank and business
papers wrapped in rubber bands – and put it away.

The boxes move slowly from loft to landing to study. I circle around
them, delaying. I read the letter. I hold the pill pot up to the light.
Finally, I begin to sort his paperwork, but I am not being thorough; I'm
jumping ahead of myself. Like the letter in his drawer, there are things
that I know are here and I am looking for them, and there are things I
want to overlook. I don't want to do our fights. I don't want to do how
he sent my brother all the wrong messages and fucked his head up. I
don't want to do all the shit he put Bobby through. I want to start with
the legend.

I've got his certificate from the Morris School of Hairdressing in
Piccadilly, which recalls his adventures as an apprentice hairdresser,

working for Raymond 'Mr Teasy Weasy' Bessone in his Knightsbridge salon. Ivor at work with a faux French hairdresser, the sought-after stylist to the debutantes and blue-bloods of west London and the star turn on a BBC variety show: a hint of camp, a swirl of cigarette smoke, a pencil-thin moustache. Ivor escaping from his suburban prison into the penumbra of the London set, louche cocktail parties and weekends in the country. I've got his discharge card from the RAF and the tale of how he reported sick for three months and got an honourable discharge three months later, how he never did drill or fired a gun or received a uniform that fitted him. I've got the transcript of a police interview with him in the embezzlement case he managed to escape scot-free, but for the cannabis plant they found in his office. I've got the betting slips and casino cheques and his days of low-rolling and high-rolling, card marking and cheating, betting coups and scams in private rooms at the back of west London gambling dens. This is the easy stuff. I know these stories and they're good ones. The stories of his first lives and selves: secure, fixed and funny. Shall I break the habit of a lifetime and do the difficult paperwork first? The stuff that's not settled? That's not funny? I pick up his notebook – I've only ever glanced through it before – and I start to read and I start to write.

Ivor is sitting on the sofa with the notebook. It's 1994, he is fifty-five and this is a low. Bobby has been dead for nine months: breast cancer that came and went and came back again and ate her liver and shrank her body to a husk before it snuffed her out. She was fifty-one. There had been plenty of cancer in the family and there's the luck of the draw, but the thought nags at me; he didn't do their paperwork. If the pressure of their life didn't kill her it made the fight too hard. Seven years earlier, Ivor and Bobby were running Robertero, a women's clothing shop in Ruislip Manor. It was a shoestring operation, but run with great charm and acumen. No one earned a fortune, but all the bills were paid without pain and that definitely constituted an advance. Of course, one of the reasons it went so well was that Ivor had learned a few lessons from previous brushes with commercial law and bookkeeping. Instead of not keeping any books, he kept two sets of books. In 1987 Customs and Excise showed up on the not entirely unreasonable grounds that the business had paid barely any VAT for the previous five years. The Inland Revenue was a bit perplexed by the numbers too. The ensuing bankruptcy proceedings would last six years. Bobby would get breast cancer and, although they did eventually clear all the debts, she was dead before the case was closed. The old man never did finalize the paperwork.

For the first time in my life I saw him helpless. James and I arranged Bobby's funeral. She had to be buried at Bushy cemetery, where everyone else in the family has ended up, but they had blown out the synagogue and the burial plans a decade ago, so that was £1,500 now and another £4,500 later. I gave the United Synagogue Burial Society the bounciest cheque you've ever seen and we put her in the ground and cancelled it.

A few days later, we told him and he was delighted; he rose from the sofa, put on a jacket and headed up to town, where he told the burial authorities that we weren't going to pay, we didn't want a headstone and they could make their own arrangements. He and Bobby's father had the row they'd been waiting to have for forty years and met only once again before they both died. The thin web of family networks and friends sustained by Bobby was either left to gather dust or sharply and deliberately broken. Ivor's gambling crew were *personae non gratae*; everyone was *persona non grata*. For maybe six months he sat on the sofa in impenetrable despair.

He has reduced the sagging golden sofa to a pulp of wood, springs and stuffing. He's been lying on this sofa a lot, but today he's sitting, probably cross-legged, slightly hunched over a pad of lined paper that lies on an old marble coffee table. Around him is a sea of ashtrays, mostly full, Rothmans packets, lighters, mobile phones, pens, toothpicks, business cards, Post-its, playing cards, torches and nail care equipment, glasses, spare glasses, a magnifying glass. There is at least one, but most likely more than one, very strong cup of tea stewing. The TV is on, a cable sports channel, probably with no sound and definitely with no subscription. He's smoking and carefully, methodically, he writes, making his points, then reading and rereading his notes. I have the notebook in front of me. Flipping through it I find his usual hieroglyphics and doodles, lists of things to do and bills to pay, names, numbers and addresses including my own, but they are all to come. On the opening pages, in capitalized script, is a list of complaints. It's odd to read through this moment of self-reflection. I never saw the old man on the wrong end of a power inequality before. I never heard him admit that slights had hurt or that he had ever tasted humiliation. I'd seen him grieve, but this was a part of his psyche that never went on public display. He blows out a long slow stream of acrid smoke and taps each point on the page with his biro.

Believing rumours and not checking with me (and not apologizing when proved wrong)
Making decisions without consulting me
Milking club funds for personal use or worse to help other groups
Making the newsletter a personal voice
Not helping me to clear my name
Not paying me the money I am owed

He stubs out his cigarette, drains the tea and turns the page.

Hitting Heidi in the face at Framfield
Watching experienced girls and ignoring novices
Telling members to strip girls off without consulting the girl
Interfering with members scenarios
Always jumping in at party's and in so doing preventing paying members getting their fair share of the action

Since Bobby died he hasn't picked up a playing card. He doesn't drink and the last time he smoked weed he got the whites. He's not interested in anything stronger that might dull the pain. Cigarettes and tea are his drugs of choice. They serve to mark the time, structuring his loneliness, helping pass the agonizing tedium of every day. It wasn't working. We have conversations on the phone where no one knows what to say and no one can tell who is trying to help whom. Ivor has crawled out of the wreckage of past lives and shed his skin a dozen times, but this time I really wonder if he has run out of conjuring tricks.

But he hasn't. In the depths of his grief, he has turned to his remaining obsession: spanking, in fact the full range of corporal punishment. It's a long-held peccadillo but now he thinks he's found a way not only to have fun but to make a living. He is in with Keith and Abi at the Posterity Club (like the hairdressing fraternity, fetish clubs are fond of a cheesy pun). They are operating out of deepest Berkshire, putting on afternoon spanking parties in detached houses for paying guests. Keith is the main man, he's been running the club for two years, but I can see Ivor is not happy. Not because he's not the boss – he knows he's still learning this game – but because he's not being respected, the girls are not being respected, the punters are not being respected. What should be a mutually satisfying and above all profitable affair is being run as an ego trip and at a loss.

I turn the pages: there's a bespoke scenario laid out for Mr Freddie Romero involving the silent treatment in a limousine followed by a trip to the dungeon; a party in Surbiton to be arranged, guests and girls to be paired; fragments of scripts for movies and routines for a cabaret club. And then there is the Red Stripe Club. He has two or three goes at writing his opening pitch and then he finds his voice:

> Thank you for writing to Red Stripe. We are the only hands-on spanking club in Great Britain and these are the reasons why. Red Stripe is run by people who are as enthusiastic about the spanking scene as you are. Because the girls who attend Red Stripe parties are truly submissive and really enjoy the spanking scene, and because we listen to the opinions of our members. So if you enjoy putting a cheeky schoolgirl over your knee, pulling down her knickers and giving her a thorough and well-deserved spanking then you will definitely enjoy a Red Stripe party. We haven't forgotten all the submissive gentlemen either. Our dominant ladies are just as enthusiastic as our submissive ladies and really understand what is required. If you would like to join Red Stripe, meet the girls and other like-minded men please send a cheque for £25. This is to cover the cost of post and the printing of our newsletter which will keep you informed of the monthly upcoming events for you to choose from.

A month later he splits from Keith and Abi. He puts a few ads in the back pages of the *Sunday Sport* and the specialist press and the cheques come rolling in. List after list of party guests and girls fill the final pages of the pad. For a time after this he went very quiet on the details of his life. His phone was suddenly always engaged, but who was he talking to? No, he couldn't come over because he had to go to Manchester. Manchester? This man wouldn't go to Uxbridge normally. The real giveaway, though, was the nine video machines in his sitting room, all wired up together and each showing a paused picture of a woman being caned. I made him tell me about it. It didn't come as much of a surprise: my brother and I had discovered his stash of spanking porn a long time ago and thought little more about it. Sure it was kind of weird, but he was kind of weird. Whatever it was all about, it wasn't turning us on. We had enough of our own stuff to sort out without trying to fathom the old man's fetishes. When we talked it over and he tried to explain what the turn-on was, we never got very far. In the end he didn't care, he just knew that he liked it. Self-reflection was no substitute for having fun.

Ivor never looked back. Seven years on the Red Stripe Club had 2,000 members, held four or five parties a month and made ten movies a year. The girls loved him because he was an old-fashioned gentleman. He made them feel safe and never failed to pay them on the day, generously. Some, as his pitch claimed, were enthusiasts, others less so; but he couldn't abide faking, believing it bad for both business and the soul. There was a queue round the block to audition. He set very clear rules of behaviour and enforced them assiduously; at the parties, encounters were carefully policed, with code words that girls could use at any time to terminate a session. There was as little nudity as was possible given the nature of the fetish, and there was absolutely no sex. The punters loved it because it was safe, suburban and regulated, and what turned Ivor on is what turned them on. The whole circus was conducted with an air of endless and effortless bonhomie.

Money, love, fame and fun were flooding into Ruislip Court. On a business trip to New York, Ivor was recognized in a fetish club as 'the Headmaster' – his alter ego, who appeared in the fabulously successful Red Stripe College Classic series of movies. He recalled with relish a high-pitched New Yorker in a leather cat suit and furry ears who exclaimed, 'It's the Headmaster! It's the Headmaster!' A buzz ran through the club and proceedings were halted to allow the Headmaster and his escort to take to the podium and give an impromptu master class in the finer points of using the cane and the paddle. I stopped worrying that he might top himself and started worrying that the tax man would come calling again.

In the mass of unopened post in his flat was a letter from Uxbridge Police. It read:

Dear Mr Goldblatt, We are sorry to hear that you have been a victim of crime.

In a world where Rentokil is hired to clean up homicide sites, this was surely a grotesque but routine response from the police to the recently murdered. It had, in fact, arrived two days before his death and he had been the victim of a crime a few weeks before that. The two were not unconnected. That's what I like about the letter: not its irony, but its prescience. When I read it I think about the question everyone asks – 'Why? Why him?' – and it reminds me of the only answer that makes sense. 'Why not?' Do the paperwork. Shuffle the files and stack the cards for long enough and you can make the inconceivable feel inevitable.

He'd lived with the sofa and the swirling orange carpet it had arrived with for thirty years and now they were all used up, threadbare and finished. Even he had had his money's worth, and just maybe it was time to start moving on from Bobby and that life. Suddenly a pair of white leather sofas and a pale pink deep-pile carpet filled his living room and hallway. Pale pink? What was he thinking? There had been method in the swirly orange carpet madness and a month later there were tea stains on the sofas and cigarette burns in the new carpet.

Ivor calls for a running repair and two men show up to fix the carpet. The small pale one is actually the carpet fitter. The big bearded one doesn't seem to do that much and mooches about. The old man barely notices as he waves them into the sitting room, the phone clamped to his head and Nigel from Loughborough or Gareth from Nuneaton bending his ear about some minor breach of party protocol at the switch do in Leicester last week. Or maybe it's Ken calling to say that he's finished recording the big video order; or he's counselling one of the girls on some issue in her life, money problems, boyfriend problems, housing problems; and all the time he's making very strong tea, smoking Rothmans and laughing. The carpet fitters must be taking a good look round. There would have been no effort to disguise what was going on. The Red Stripe show would certainly have been diverting, but much more interesting, I suspect, was Ivor's wallet and the five grand in cash that he invariably carried with him, secured by a very large, old-fashioned paper clip. They palm that as they finish the job and, as they go through the kitchen, the change bottles must have caught their eye. Three-litre plastic soft-drinks bottles with the tops cut off; ten to fifteen of them crammed on to the kitchen work surfaces between the toaster and the cooker, stacked around the bread bin and sitting on the open shelves, all overflowing with pound coins and fifty-pence pieces. Five hundred coins a bottle, ten bottles, another five grand at least. And where there's that much coinage and that much cash in a wallet, there's bound to be more.

He reported the theft to the police; he knew who had done it. He even had them round to investigate the crime. He cleared up a bit, but he wouldn't let them into the sitting room, where the carpet had been fixed and the crime committed. So what's anyone going to do? The police left it and wrote him a nice letter. He left it and never got the letter. At another time he might well have taken matters into his own hands, or pulled in a few favours from the wide range of heavies and knuckle merchants that he knew. But he didn't. He didn't really need the money back, he didn't need revenge, he didn't need the aggravation. The *News of the Screws*, with whom he had advertised in the past, had infiltrated the Red Stripe Christmas party. He was appalled at the photograph of him that they had used but he was unshakeable in his insouciance: 'It's the life I chose . . . Might even end up bringing in a few new punters.' Only once did he hint that his casualness might mask fear. He had told me just a few weeks earlier that he couldn't quite march on like he used to. Yes, he had felt something move across his heart.

A month later, March 1, 2001, the carpet fitters are in the pub in Hayes. It's lunchtime. They're drinking their second or third lager of the day and then they retreat to the toilets to do the last line of a very large bag of cocaine. The five grand is spent, the cupboard is bare and the party is coming to an end. Except it doesn't have to. Everyone around the table knows this; they know exactly where to go to refresh their funds. A friend drives them the twenty minutes from Hayes to Ruislip Court and, some time around two o'clock, they knock on the door. Ivor, alone, knows exactly who they are and what they want, but you can't play the kinds of games he played with the bailiffs with this lot. He's pushed back down the narrow hall and the door closes. After that, the precise details are a matter of conjecture but we know this much:

Ivor is stabbed twenty-six times with one of his own kitchen knives.

His lungs are punctured and there are deep wounds in his shoulders and his flanks. He receives a variety of other blows to his head, neck and arms. At 2.08 the emergency services receive a call from him. The carpet fitters are grabbing whatever they can and leaving. The conversation was recorded and it was played in court.

I faced almost everything. I watched them argue over the diagram of his knife wounds, I looked the carpet fitters in the eye, but I couldn't listen to the tape. What do you want: some justice or no justice, some truths or no truths, enough of the story or all the story? I reach the limit of my paperwork. I am told the tape is gentle and dignified. I'm told he didn't panic, but just explained the situation and waited for the ambulance to arrive. It came twelve minutes later. He was dead in a pool of his own blood, which was ebbing away into the deep pile of his new pink carpet.

I sifted the contents of his house for another five months. After the trial I finally felt strong enough to empty it: the furniture, his clothes, my mother's clothes, the nine video machines, the box of butt plugs, the bamboo canes and the leather paddles, the vaulting horse and the blackboard. Then I started stripping and cleaning. I told myself that it would help sell the flat. How could anyone think of buying it? But I also imagined that if I cleaned long enough and hard enough, the dull patina of dried blood that seemed to cling to every surface would finally go. I hoped that if I emptied the flat of its objects, and pared back its contents to nothing, I would uncover the place that I grew up in, before Ivor was the old man, before he was a legend. I couldn't find that place and I didn't think I would find it in the boxes and among the papers either.

I make a final trip. I know I'm going to say goodbye, but it feels like a hollow journey. There's nothing left to take, no scraps of memory remaining. I'm standing in the bathroom in front of the sink, looking at the light bending and breaking through the textured windows. The sink is still leaking. A patch of the rough, greasy brown carpet is wet. I look up at the waste water pipe and see that an old rag is wrapped around the leaking joint; an old grey fraying rag. Along its edge, woven into the fabric, are two lines of small navy rectangles. I bite on my own breath. The navy rectangles edge a huge white soft towel. My father is standing over the bath holding it up for me. I'm four. My brother has just been born and tonight, for the first night that I can remember, my father and I are alone and he is bathing me. He's bathing me and lifting me out of the bath in the rectangle-edged towel. I unwind the rag from the pipe and spread it out in my palms and I'm crying. The towel is huge and soft and enveloping. He dries me. There's the sweet smell of baby powder in the air. He brushes my short, tightly curled hair and dresses me in my finery: m12 available12y orange cords, my smart pink shirt, my orange braces. I'm holding the rag and I'm crying, but not because I can't stand the bloodstains and the gash in the linoleum. We eat, side by side, at the marble coffee table. He bathes and dresses and sings to me. I gather up biscuits for my new brother, knowing full well that I will eat them. He holds a gigantic, ostentatious bunch of roses for Bobby. I'm holding the rag and I'm crying, but not because the grime and the dust have obscured every moment of the everyday life I lived here. I'm crying because he's taking my hand and he's leading me out and we're walking down the hall and we're going to the hospital and I feel safe and warm and loved and tingling with anticipation.

LITTLE SISTER

Anne Enright

The year I'm talking about, the year my sister left (or whatever you choose to call it), I was twenty-one and she was seventeen. We had been keeping our proper distance, that is to say, for seventeen years. Four years apart – which is sometimes a long way apart, and sometimes closer than you think. Some years we liked each other and some years we didn't. But near or far, she was my sister. And I suppose I am trying to say what that meant.

Serena always thought she would overtake me some day, hence the under age drinking and the statutory sex. But even though she was getting into pubs and into trouble before I was in high heels, I knew deep down and weary that I was the older one – I always would be the older one, and the only way she would get to be older than me, is if I got dead.

And of course, I liked it too. It was fun having someone smaller than you. She always said I bossed her around, but I know we had fun. Because with Serena you were always asking yourself what went wrong, or even Where did I go wrong? But, believe me, I am just about done with all that – with shuffling through her life in my mind.

There was the time when she was six and I was ten. I used to take her to the bus at lunch time, because she still only had a half day at school. So I spent my break waiting at the bus stop with my little sister instead of playing German Jumps in the playground, which is not me complaining, it is me saying that she was cared for endlessly, by all of us. But there are just some things you cannot do for a child. There are some things you cannot help.

This particular day, we were walking out of the school lane and on to the main road when a girl sailed through the air and landed on the roof of a braking car. Serena said, 'Look!' and I pulled her along. It was far too serious. And as if she knew it was far too serious she came along with me without a fuss. A girl landed on the roof of a braking car. She turned in the air, as though she was doing a cartwheel. But it was a very slow cartwheel. There was a bicycle, if you thought hard about it, skidding away from the car, the pedal scraping the tarmac and spraying sparks. But you had to think hard to remember the bike. What you really remembered was this girl's white socks and the pleated fan of her gymslip following her through the air.

The next day there were rumours of an accident, and my mind tells me now that the girl died, but they didn't want to tell us in case we got upset. I don't know the truth of it. At the time there was just the two of us on an empty road, and a girl turning her slow cartwheel, and my hand finding Serena's little hand and pulling her silently by.

That was one incident. There was another incident when she was maybe eight and I was twelve when a man in plaid trousers said, 'Hello girls' and took his thing out of his fly. Maybe I should say he let his thing escape out of his fly, because it sort of jumped out and curled up, in a way that I now might recognize. At the time it looked like giblets, the same colour of old blood, dark and cooked, like that piece of the turkey our parents liked and called 'the Pope's nose'. So we ran home all excited and told my mother about the man in plaid trousers and the Pope's nose, and she laughed, which I think was the right thing to do. By the lights of the time. And we had three ordinary brothers, who went through their phases of this or that. Nothing abnormal – though the year Jim wouldn't wash was a bit of a trial. Look at me, I'm scraping the barrel here. We had a great childhood. And I'm fine, that's the bottom line of it. I'm fine and Serena is no longer alive.

But the year I am talking about, it was 1981 and I was finished at uni and starting a job. I had money and was buying clothes and I was completely delighted with myself. I even thought about leaving home, but my mother was lonely with us all growing up. She said she felt the creak of the world turning and she talked about getting old. She cried more; a general sort of weep, now and then – not about *her* life, but just about the way life goes.

I came home one day and Serena was in the doghouse, which was nothing new, because my mother smelled cigarettes off her, and also Something Else. I couldn't think what this something else might be – there was no whiff of drink – perhaps it was sperm, I wouldn't be surprised. It was three weeks before her final school exams and Serena was trashing our bedroom while my mother stood in the kitchen, wearing her coat, strangely enough, and chopping carrots. I went in and sat with Mam for a while, and when the silence upstairs finally settled, I went to check the damage. Clothes everywhere. One curtain ripped down. My alarm clock smashed. A bottle of perfume snapped at the neck – there was a pool of Chanel No. 5 soaking into the chest of drawers. I had a boyfriend at the time. The room stank. I didn't blow my top. I said, 'Clean yourself up, you stupid moron, Da's nearly home.'

None of us liked our father, except Serena, who was always a little flirt, even at the age of three. I don't think even my mother liked him – of course she said she 'loved' him, but that was only because you're supposed to when you marry someone and sleep with them. He had a fused knee from some childhood accident and always sat with his leg sticking out in front of him. He wasn't a bad man. But he sat looking at us shouting and laughing and fighting, like we were all an awful bore.

Or maybe I liked him then, but I don't like him since – because after Serena he got a job managing a pub and he started sleeping over the shop. So that's another one, now, who never comes home.

For three weeks the bedroom was thick with the smell of Chanel, we did not speak, and Serena did not eat. She fainted during her maths exam and had to be carried out, with a big crowd of people fanning her on the corridor floor. All of June she spent in the bathroom squeezing her spots, or she sat downstairs and did nothing and wouldn't say what she wanted to do next. And then, on July 14, she went out and did not come home.

We waited for ninety-one days. On Saturday, September 13, there was the sound of a key in the door and a child walked in – a sort of death-child. She was six and a half stone. Behind her was a guy carrying a suitcase. He said his name was Brian. He looked like he didn't know what to do.

We gave him a cup of tea, while Serena sat in a corner of the kitchen, glaring. As far as we could gather, she just turned up on his doorstep, and stayed. He was a nice guy. I don't know what he was doing with a girl just out of school, but then again, Serena always looked old for her age.

It is hard to remember what it was like in those days, but anorexia was just starting then, it was just getting trendy. We looked at her and thought she had cancer, we couldn't believe this was some sort of diet. Then trying to make her eat, the cooing and cajoling, the desperate silences, as Serena looked at her plate and picked up one green bean. They say anorexics are bright girls who try too hard and get tipped over the brink – but Serena sauntered up to the brink. She looked over her shoulder at the rest of us, as we stood and called to her, and then she turned and jumped. It is not too much to say that she enjoyed her death. I don't think it is too much to say that.

But I'm stuck with Brian in the kitchen, and Serena's eye sockets are huge, her eyes burning in the middle of them. Of course there were tears – my mother's tears, my tears. My father hit the door jamb, and then leaned his forehead against his clenched fist. Serena's own tears, when they came, looked hot, like she had very little liquid left. My mother put her to bed, so tenderly, like she was still a child, and we called the doctor while she slept. She woke to find his fingers on her pulse and she looked like she was going to start yelling again, but it was too late for all that. He went out to the phone in the hall and booked her into hospital on the spot.

Ninety-one days. And believe me, we lived them one by one. We lived those days one at a time. We went through each hour of them, and we didn't skip a single minute.

I met Brian from time to time in the hospital and we exchanged a few grim jokes about the ward. A row of little sticks in the beds, knitting, jigging, anything to burn the calories off. I opened the bathroom door one day and saw one of them checking herself in the mirror. She was standing on a toilet seat with the cubicle door open and her nightdress pulled up to her face. You could see all her bones. There was a mile of space between her legs, and her pubis stuck out, a bulging hammock of flesh, terribly split. She pulled the nightdress down when she heard the door open, so by the time I looked from her reflection to the cubicle, she was decent again. It was just a flash, like flicking the remote to find a sitcom and getting a shot of famine in the middle, or of porn.

Serena lay in a bed near the end of the row, a still shape in the fidgeting ward. She read books, and turned the pages slowly. I brought her wine gums and fruit pastilles, because when she was little she used to steal them from my stash. Serena was the kind of girl whose pocket money was gone by Tuesday, and spent the rest of the week in a whine. Now, it was a shower of things she might want, Jaffa Cakes, an ice-cream birthday cake, highlights in her hair, all of them utterly stupid and small. We were indulging a five-year-old child and nothing was enough and everything was too late.

Then there was the therapy. We all had to go, walking out the front door in our good coats like we were off to mass. We sat around on plastic chairs, my father with his leg stuck silently out, my mother in a welter of worry, scarcely listening, or jumping at some silly thing and hanging on to it for dear life. Serena sat there, looking bored. I couldn't help it, I lost my temper. I actually shouted at her. I said she should be ashamed of herself, the things she was putting Mam through. 'Look at her,' I said. 'Look!' I said I hoped she was pleased with herself now. She just sat through it all, and then she leaned forward to say, very deliberate, 'If I got knocked down by a bus, you'd say I was just looking for attention.' Which made me think about that car crash when she was small. Perhaps I should have mentioned it, but I didn't. Brian, as official boyfriend, sat in the middle of this family row with his legs set wide and his big hands dangling into the gap. At the end of the session he guided her out of the room with his palm on the small of her back, like he was her protector and not part of this at all.

It takes years for anorexics to die, that's the other thing. During the first course of therapy they decided it would be better if she moved out of home. Was there another family, they said, where she could stay for a while? As if. As if my parents had a bunch of cheerful friends with spare rooms, who wanted to clean up after Serena and hand over their bathroom while she locked herself in there for three hours at a time. We got her a bedsit in Rathmines, and I paid. It was either that or my mother going out to work part-time.

So Serena was living my life now. She had my flat and my freedom and my money. It sounds like an odd thing to say, but I didn't begrudge it at the time. I just wanted it to be over. I mean, I just wanted my mother to smile.

Five months later she was six stone and one ounce, and back in the ward after collapsing in the street. I expected to see Brian, but she had got rid of him, she said. I went to pick up some things from the flat for her, and found that it was full of empty packets of Paracetamol and used tissues that she didn't even bother to throw away. They were stuck together in little lumps. I don't know what was in them – cleanser? Maybe she spat into them, maybe her own spit was a nuisance to her. I had to buy a pair of rubber gloves to tackle them, and I never told anyone, not the therapist, not the doctor, not my mother. But I recognized something in her face now, like we had a secret we were forced to share.

I went through her life in my head. Every Tuesday night before the goddamn therapy, I sifted the moments: a cat that died, my grandmother's death, Santa Claus. I went through the caravan holidays and the time she cried halfway up Carantoohill and sat down and had to be carried to the top. I went through her first period and the time I bawled her out for stealing my mohair jumper. The time she used up a can of fly spray in an afternoon slaughter and the way she played horsey on my father's bocketty leg. It was all just bits. I really wanted it to add up to something, but it didn't.

They beefed her up a bit and let her go. A couple of months later we got a card from Amsterdam. I don't know where she got the money. The flat was all paid up till Christmas and I might have taken it myself, but one look at my mother was enough. I could not do a thing to hurt her more.

Then one day I saw a woman in the street who looked like my gran. I thought it was my gran for a minute, just before she died, out of the hospice somehow ten years later and walking towards St Stephen's Green. Actually, I thought she was dead and I was terrified – literally petrified – of what she had come back to say to me. Our eyes met, and hers were wicked with some joke or other. It was Serena, of course. And her teeth by now were yellow as butter.

I stopped her and tried to talk, but she came over all adult and suggested we go for coffee. She said Brian had followed her to Amsterdam. She looked over her shoulder. I think she was hallucinating by now. But there was something so fake about all this grown-up stuff, I was glad when we said, 'Goodbye, so.' When I looked after her in the street, there she was, my little sister, the toy walk of her, the way she held her neck – Serena running away from some stupid game at the age of seven, too proud to cry.

The phone call from the hospital came six weeks later. There was something wrong with her liver. After that it was kidneys. And after that she died. Her yellow teeth were falling out by the end, and for some reason she grew a bit of a moustache. All her beauty was gone – because, even though she was my sister, I have to say that Serena was truly, radiantly beautiful, in her day.

So, she died. There is no getting away from something like that. You can't recover. I didn't even try. The first year was a mess and after that our lives were just punctured, not even sad – just less, just never the same again.

But it is those ninety-one days I think about – when it was all ahead of us, and no one knew. The summer I was twenty-one and Serena was seventeen, I woke up in the morning and I had the room to myself. She was mysteriously gone from the bed across the room, she was absolutely gone from the downstairs sofa, and the bathroom was free for hours at a time. Gone. Not there. Vamoosed. My mother, especially, was infatuated by her absence. It is not enough to say she fought Serena's death, even then – she was absolutely intimate with it. To my mother, my sister's death was an enemy's embrace. They were locked together in her own sitting room, in the kitchen, in the hall. They met and talked, and bargained and wept. She might have been saying, 'Take me. Take me, instead.' But I think – you get that close to it, you bring it into your sitting room, everybody's going to lose.

So, it was no surprise to us when, after ninety-one days, Serena walked back into the house looking like she did. The only surprise was Brian, this mooching, ordinary, slightly bitter man, who watched her so helplessly, and answered our questions one by one.

I met him some time after the funeral in a nightclub and we ended up crying at a little round table in the corner, and shouting over the music. We both were a bit drunk, so I can't remember who made the first move. It was a tearful, astonishing kiss. All the sadness welled into my face and into my lips. We went out for a while, as though we hoped something good could come of it all – a little love. But it was a faded sort of romance, a sort of second thought. Two ordinary people, making do. Don't get me wrong, I didn't mind that he loved Serena, because of course I loved her too. And her ghost did not bother us: try as we might, it did not even appear. But I tell you, I have a child now and who does she look like? Serena. The same hungry, petulant look, and beautiful, too. So that is my penance I suppose, that is the thing I have to live with now.

I am trying to stop this story, but it just won't end. Because years later I saw a report in the newspaper about a man who murdered his wife. The police said he was worried she would find out about his financial problems, and so he torched the house when she was asleep. He made extraordinary preparations for the crime. He called out the Gas Board to complain about a non-existent leak and he started redecorating so there would be plenty of paint and white spirit in the hall. He even wrote a series of threatening letters to himself, on a typewriter that he later dumped in the canal. I read the article carefully, not just for the horror of it, but because his name was Brian Dempsey. The name of the broody, handsome man that I had slept with, and who had slept with my sister. Which sounds a bit frank, but that was the way it was.

Brian. I could not get those letters out of my head. He started writing them two whole months before he set the fire. I thought about those eight weeks he had spent with her, complaining about the dinner or his lack of clean shirts, annoyed with her because she did not, would not, realize that she was going to die. I even wanted to visit him in prison before the trial, just to look at him, just to say 'Brian'. When the case finally came to court, there was a picture in the paper, and I thought he looked old, and terribly fat. I looked and looked at the eyes, until they turned into newspaper dots. Then, when I read the report, I realized it was another Brian Dempsey altogether, a man originally from Athlone.

That was last month, but even now, I find myself holding my breath in empty rooms. Yesterday, I set a bottle of Chanel No. 5 on the dressing table and took the lid off for a while. I keep thinking, not about Brian, but about those ninety-one days, my mother half crazed, my father feigning boredom, and me, with my own bedroom for the first time since I was four years old. I remember the way we lived from one phone call to the next, the skipped meals, and each of us, some days, forgetting to dress. I think of Serena's absence, how astonishing it was, and all of us sitting looking at each other, until the door opened and she walked in, half dead, with an ordinary, living man in tow. And I think that we made her up somehow, that we imagined her. And him too, maybe. And I think that if I made her up now, if she walked into the room, I'd kill her all over again.

Ali and Donald Smith, 1971

FIVE THINGS BEGINNING
WITH MY FATHER

Ali Smith

My father left school at thirteen; his family needed the money. When I asked him what he'd like me to say in this piece, he said, 'Tell them I was in the Navy from 1942 to 1947, in four different invasions, in North Africa, France, Italy and I forget the other one.

Tell them I'm eighty-four and a half. Tell them I'm a good salmon fisherman and so's my daughter, who caught the third biggest fish of the year last month at Delphi in Ireland.' No I didn't, I said. It was the gillie. I just held the rod a bit. He laughed. 'Aye, but don't tell them that.'

My father put all five of us, my brothers and sisters and me, through university with a passion and foresight it took me decades to appreciate.

My father is English. Whenever people in the Highlands, where he's lived since he married my mother in 1949 (she died in 1990), comment on his Lincolnshire accent, he says, 'I came up to work on the Hydro dams and never had the train fare back again.' He was the main electrical contractor in Inverness and the Highlands in the Sixties and Seventies, until the coming of Thatcher, Dixons, Currys. 'Tell them I'm still Conservative after all these years,' he said. There's no way I'm telling them that, I said.

My father, one afternoon, sat at the dinette table, unscrewed my talking bear whose cord had broken, and screwed it back together.

It worked. 'When people are dead, graves aren't where to find them. They're in the wind, the grass.' That's the kind of thing he said. When I asked him what you do if you see something in the dark that frightens you, he said, 'What you do is, you go up to it, and touch it.' When things went wrong in the neighbourhood, people would come to my father for help. When we went to visit an old neighbour last autumn, in her eighties too, she called him Mr Smith. 'Call me Donald, now, Chrissie,' he said. She shook her head. 'You'll have another biscuit with your tea, Mr Smith,' she said.

My father, as a boy, was a champion footballer, boxer, ping-pong player. His handsomeness, as a young man, is legendary. Every time I left for university, he tucked twenty pounds and a folded sheet of stamps into my pocket. 'Write to your mother,' he said.

CONTRIBUTORS

Chimamanda Ngozi Adichie was born in Nigeria in 1977. She completed a master's degree in creative writing at Johns Hopkins University, Baltimore, and a master's degree in African Studies at Yale University. Her first novel, *Purple Hibiscus* (2003), was awarded the Commonwealth Writers' Prize for Best First Book. She was a Hodder fellow at Princeton University during the 2005–6 academic year. Her second novel, *Half of a Yellow Sun* (2006), set during the Nigerian–Biafran war in the late 1960s, won the 2007 Orange Prize for Fiction. She is a 2008 MacArthur Foundation fellow and currently divides her time between the United States and Nigeria. Her most recent book is a collection of short stories, *The Thing Around Your Neck* (2009).

Diana Athill was born in Norfolk, England in 1917. She graduated from Lady Margaret Hall, Oxford in 1939 and worked for the BBC throughout the Second World War. After the war she helped André Deutsch establish his publishing company, founded in 1951, and worked closely as an editor with many of his authors, including Philip Roth, Norman Mailer, John Updike, Simone de Beauvoir, Jean Rhys, V. S. Naipaul, Gitta Sereny and Brian Moore. Among her early books was a collection of short stories, *An Unavoidable Delay* (1962), and a memoir, *Instead of a Letter* (1963). *After a Funeral* (1987) won the J. R. Ackerley Prize for Autobiography. In 1993 she retired after more than fifty years in publishing. She subsequently wrote three further volumes of autobiography: *Stet* (2000), *Yesterday Morning: A Very English Childhood* (2002) and *Somewhere Towards the End* (2008). She was awarded an OBE in 2009.

Urvashi Butalia was born in Ambala, India in 1952. She worked as an editor at Oxford University Press in Delhi and in Oxford before joining Zed Books in 1982 where she helped to set up their Women and Gender list. Returning to Delhi she co-founded Kali for Women, India's first feminist publishing house, in 1984. Her books include *Making a Difference: Feminist Publishing in the South* (1995), *Women and Right Wing Movements: Indian Experiences* (1995) and *Speaking Peace: Women's Voices from Kashmir* (2002). *The Other Side of Silence: Voices from the Partition of India (1988)* has become one of the most influential books in recent South Asian studies. She is currently the director of Zubaan Books, which she founded in 2003, and which is an imprint of Kali.

Raymond Carver was born in Clatskanie, Oregon in 1938, and grew up in Yakima, Washington State, USA. He moved to California in 1958 and took up writing in the early 1960s. During the 1960s he worked as a textbook editor, lecturer and teacher and published several short stories. He established his reputation with his 1976 collection of stories *Will You Please Be Quiet, Please?*. In the late 1970s Carver was hospitalized for acute alcoholism. In 1981 he published a second acclaimed collection, *What We Talk About When We Talk About Love*. By the mid-1980s, he was sober, writing full-time and married to the poet Tess Gallagher, his second wife. He died in 1988 at the age of fifty from lung cancer. His last collection of stories, *Where I'm Calling From*, was published posthumously in 1989.

Robyn Davidson was born at Stanley Park, a cattle station in Miles, Queensland in 1950. Her mother committed suicide when she was eleven. She went to a girls' boarding school in Brisbane and was offered a music scholarship but did not take it up. In the 1970s she moved to Alice Springs and in 1977 she set off for the west coast of Australia with a dog and four camels. She wrote about the journey in her first book, *Tracks*, which won the 1980 Thomas Cook Travel Book Award and the Blind Society Award. She published a collection of essays, *Travelling Light*, in 1993. From 1990 to 1992 she travelled with nomads in India and wrote about it in *Desert Places* (1996). She edited *The Picador Book of Journeys* (2002) and her essay, *No Fixed Address: Nomads and the Fate of the Planet*, was published in the Australian journal *Quarterly Essay* in 2006. She lives in Sydney and shares a house in the Himalayas.

Anne Enright was born in Dublin in 1962 and lives in Bray, County Wicklow. She worked as a television producer and director for Radio Telefis Eireann (RTÉ) in Dublin for six years, then in children's programming for two years, doing her writing at the weekends. *The Portable Virgin*, her first collection of stories, was published in 1991 and won the Rooney Prize for Irish Literature. Her first novel, *The Wig My Father Wore* (1995), was followed by *What Are You Like?* (2000) and *The Pleasure of Eliza Lynch* (2002). *Making Babies: Stumbling into Motherhood* (2004) is a collection of humorous essays about childbirth and motherhood. Her fourth novel, *The Gathering* (2007), won the 2007 Man Booker Prize for Fiction and was the 2008 Irish Novel of the Year.

David Goldblatt was born in London in 1965 and now lives in Bristol. He has written for newspapers including the *Guardian*, the *Financial Times* and the *Independent on Sunday*, and for magazines such as the *New Statesman* and the *New Left Review*. He reviews books about sport for the *Independent* and the *Times Literary Supplement* and is the sports columnist for *Prospect* magazine. He has taught the sociology of sport at the University of Bristol and run literacy programmes at Bristol City and Bristol Rovers football clubs, as well as teaching sport, film and media at the Watershed arts cinema in Bristol. His most recent book is *The Ball is Round: A Global History of Football* (2006).

Linda Grant was born in Liverpool, England in 1951, the child of Russian and Polish Jewish immigrants. Her first novel, *The Cast Iron Shore* (1996), won the David Higham First Novel Award. Her piece in this anthology was an early section of *Remind Me Who I Am Again* (1999), an account of her mother's decline into dementia, and her novel *When I Lived in Modern Times* (2000) won that year's Orange Prize for Fiction. In *The People on the Street: A Writer's View of Israel* (2006) she described the lives of ordinary Israelis. Her most recent book, *The Thoughtful Dresser*, was published by Virago in spring 2009.

A. M. Homes (Amy M.) was born in Washington, D.C. in 1961. Her novels include *Jack* (1989), *In a Country of Mothers* (1993), *The End of Alice* (1996), *Music for Torching* (1999) and *This Book Will Save Your Life* (2006). She has published two short-story collections, *The Safety of Objects* (1990) and *Things You Should Know* (2002). She was writer/ producer of the hit US television show *The L Word* in 2004–5 and several of her books have been optioned for television and cinema. Her most recent book is a memoir, *The Mistress's Daughter* (2007), which tells the story of her being 'found' by her biological family.

Jackie Kay was born in Edinburgh, Scotland in 1961 to a Scottish mother and a Nigerian father. She was adopted at birth by a white couple and was brought up in Glasgow. Her first collection of poetry, *The Adoption Papers* (1991), won a Scottish Arts Council Book Award and the Saltire Society Scottish First Book of the Year Award. Her poetry collections include *Other Lovers* (1993) and *Off Colour* (1998). Her first novel, *Trumpet* (1998), won the *Guardian* Fiction Prize. It was followed by two short-story collections, *Why Don't You Stop Talking* (2002) and *Wish I Was Here* (2006). She has also published a children's novel, *Strawgirl* (2002), and a collection of poetry for children, *Red, Cherry Red* (2007). *Darling: New and Selected Poems* was published in 2007 and her dramatised poem, *The Lamplighter*, in 2008. She was awarded an MBE for services to literature in 2006.

A. L. Kennedy (Alison Louise) was born in Dundee, Scotland in 1965. She began writing dramatic monologues and short stories while still at university. Since 1989 she has worked for the arts and special needs charity Project Ability, first as Writer in Residence (1989–95), then as editor of *Outside Lines* magazine. She has been a judge for the Booker Prize for Fiction (1996) and the *Guardian* First Book Award (2001). In 1993 she was named as one of *Granta*'s twenty 'Best of Young British Novelists'. Her short-story collections include *Night Geometry and the Garscadden Trains* (1990), *Now That You're Back* (1994), *Original Bliss* (1997) and *Indelible Acts* (2002). Her novels include *Looking for the Possible Dance* (1993), *So I Am Glad* (1995) and *Everything You Need* (1999). In 2003 she was nominated for a second time as one of *Granta*'s twenty 'Best of Young British Novelists'. Her most recent book of stories is *What Becomes* (2009).

Hanif Kureishi was born in Bromley, Kent in 1954. His first play, *Soaking the Heat*, was performed at the Royal Court Theatre in London in 1976 and followed in 1980 by *The Mother Country*, for which he won the Thames TV Playwright Award. In 1982 he became Writer in Residence at the Royal Court. His screenplay for *My Beautiful Laundrette*, directed by Stephen Frears, was nominated for an Academy Award. He also wrote the screenplays for *Sammy and Rosie Get Laid* (1987) and *London Kills Me* (1991), which he directed. His first novel, *The Buddha of Suburbia* (1990) won the Whitbread First Novel Award and in 1993 was produced as a four-part series by the BBC. His second novel, *The Black Album* (1995), was followed by a collection of stories, *Love in a Blue Time* (1997). *Intimacy* (1998), a novella, was produced as a film in 2001. His most recent novel is *Something to Tell You* (2008).

John Lanchester was born in Hamburg in 1962. He grew up in the Far East, but was educated in England. His first novel, *The Debt to Pleasure* (1996), won the Whitbread First Novel Award, the Betty Trask Prize, the Hawthornden Prize and, in America, the Julia Child Award for literary food writing. His second novel was *Mr Phillips* (2000), and his third, *Fragrant Harbour* (2002), was shortlisted for the James Tait Black Memorial Prize. His most recent work is a memoir, *Family Romance* (2007). He is a member of the editorial board of the *London Review of Books*, to which he contributes. He also writes for the *New Yorker*, the *New York Review of Books* and the *Daily Telegraph*.

Hilary Mantel was born in Glossop, Derbyshire in 1952. She studied law, was employed as a social worker, and lived in Botswana for five years, followed by four years in Saudi Arabia, before returning to Britain in the mid-1980s. She was film critic of the *Spectator* from 1987 to 1991. Her novels include *Eight Months on Ghazzah Street* (1988), *A Change of Climate* (1994), *An Experiment in Love* (1995), which won the Hawthornden Prize, *Beyond Black* (2005), which was shortlisted for the Orange Prize and *Wolf Hall* (2009). *Giving Up the Ghost: A Memoir* was published in 2003. She was awarded a CBE in 2006.

John McGahern was born in Dublin in 1934 and grew up in the west of Ireland. He worked as a primary school teacher before turning to full-time writing. He is the author of six highly acclaimed novels and four collections of short stories, as well as a memoir, published in 2005. His second novel, *The Dark* (1965), was banned in Ireland because of its alleged pornographic content. His fifth novel, *Amongst Women* (1990), was shortlisted for the Booker Prize. He held various academic posts at universities in Britain, Ireland and America and received many awards for his work. He died in March 2006, aged seventy-one, and was buried in St Patrick's Church, Aughawillan, County Leitrim, alongside his mother.

Blake Morrison was born in Skipton, Yorkshire in 1950. He became Literary Editor of the *Observer* in 1981 and Literary Editor of the *Independent on Sunday* in 1989 before becoming a full-time writer in 1995. He has written fiction, poetry, journalism, literary criticism and works for the stage. His memoir *And When Did You Last See Your Father?* (1993) won the J. R. Ackerley Prize for Autobiography (1993) and a film based on it was released in 2007. *Bicycle Thieves*, the story included in this anthology, was made into a short feature film for Channel 4 in 1995. His most recent book is a novel, *South of the River* (2007). He has been Professor of Creative and Life Writing at Goldsmiths College since 2003.

Orhan Pamuk was born in Istanbul in 1952. He studied architecture before moving to the Institute of Journalism at the University of Istanbul, graduating in 1976. His early novels won critical praise in Turkey before *The White Castle* (1985, English translation 1990) won the *Independent* Award for Foreign Fiction in 1990. It was followed by *The Black Book* (1990, English translation 1994), and *The New Life* (1995, English translation 1997). In 1995, Pamuk was among a group of authors tried for writing essays that criticized Turkey's treatment of the Kurds. His book of essays, *Other Colours*, was published in 1999 (English translation 2007). His novel *My Name is Red* (2000, English translation 2001) won the IMPAC Award in 2003. After this came *Snow* (2002, English translation 2004) and *Istanbul – Memories and the City* (2003, English translation 2005). In 2005 in Turkey, a criminal case was opened against Pamuk after he made a statement in the Swiss journal *Das Magazin* about the mass killings of Armenians and Kurds in the Ottoman Empire. Rallies were held to burn his books. The charges were dropped in January 2006. In October 2006, Pamuk was awarded the 2006 Nobel Prize in literature. He is a professor of comparative literature at Columbia University, New York. His latest novel is *The Museum of Innocence* (2008, English translation 2009).

Tim Parks was born in Manchester, England in 1954, and studied at Cambridge and Harvard. In 1981 he moved to Verona in northern Italy where he lives today. He teaches literary translation at IULM University Milan and has written about provincial life in the Veneto in *Italian Neighbours* (1992) and *An Italian Education* (1996). He has translated works by Italian writers including Alberto Moravia, Italo Calvino, Antonio Tabucchi and Roberto Calasso. His novels include *Tongues of Flame* (1985), *Loving Roger* (1986), *Cara Massimina* (1990), *Europa* (1997), which was shortlisted for the Booker Prize, *Destiny* (1999) and *Rapids: A Novel* (2005). His essays and stories are collected in *Adultery and Other Diversions* (1998), *Hell and Back: Essays* (2001) and *The Fighter* (2007). *A Season with Verona* (2002) is his account of a season spent following the Italian football club Hellas Verona. His most recent novel is *Dreams of Rivers and Seas* (2008).

Jayne Anne Phillips was born in 1952 and raised in West Virginia, USA. She had two story collections, *Sweethearts* and *Counting*, published by small presses before the success of *Black Tickets*, published in 1979 when she was twenty-six. Her first novel, *Machine Dreams* (1984), was followed by another book of stories, *Fast Lanes* (1987), and then three novels: *Shelter* (1994), *MotherKind* (2000) and *Lark and Termite* (2009). She is Professor of English and Director of the Rutgers Newark M.F.A. in Creative Writing at Rutgers Newark, the State University of New Jersey.

Justine Picardie was born in London in 1961. After university she joined the *Sunday Times* as an investigative journalist. Her first book, *If The Spirit Moves You: Life and Love After Death* (2002), was written as a response to her sister's death from breast cancer at thirty-three. Her first novel, *Wish I May* (2004), was followed by *Daphne* (2008). She is a former features editor of British *Vogue* and writes a column for the *Sunday Telegraph* magazine. In 1998 she established the Lavender Trust, which helps raise awareness about younger women with breast cancer.

Anna Pyasetskaya is one of the founders of The Echo of War, an organization that assists the relatives of Russian soldiers who have been reported missing during military operations, particularly in Chechnya. Its members have helped to negotiate the release of Russian mothers taken hostage by Chechen guerrillas, and to identify the bodies of many dead Russian soldiers. In 2000 The Echo of War was officially registered with the Russian authorities. One of its recent achievements has been the establishment of a burial site for soldiers who remain unidentified. Anna Pyasetskaya lives in Moscow. She has one daughter.

Jeremy Seabrook was born in Northampton, England in 1939. Early in his career he was both a teacher and a social worker, and was also a lecturer for the Workers' Educational Association and the Working Men's College. He has written plays for the theatre, television and radio, and has made several documentaries on social, environmental and developmental issues. His many books deal with social and economic justice and international development. Among the most recent are *Love in a Different Climate* (1999), about homosexual relationships in India; *Children of Other Worlds* (2001), about child labour; *Travels in the Skin Trade: Tourism and the Sex Industry* (new edition 2001); *A World Growing Old* (2003) about the problems of an ageing population, and *Consuming Cultures: Globalization and Local Lives* (2006). He is currently preparing a new book, *The End of the Provinces*, on the ways in which global metropolitan culture affects regional identities.

Helen Simpson was born in Bristol, England in 1959 and grew up in London. She read English at Oxford University, then worked for five years as a staff writer at *Vogue* before becoming a freelance writer, contributing to newspapers and magazines and publishing two cookery books. Her first collection of short stories, *Four Bare Legs in a Bed and Other Stories* (1990), won the *Sunday Times* Young Writer of the Year Award. In 1993 she was chosen as one of *Granta*'s twenty 'Best of Young British Novelists'. Her third book of stories, *Hey Yeah Right Get a Life* (2000), won the Hawthornden Prize in 2001, and she was awarded the E. M. Forster Award by the American Academy of Arts and Letters in 2002. Her most recent collection of short stories is *Constitutional* (2005), also published as *In the Driver's Seat* (2007). She wrote the libretto for the jazz opera *Good Friday 1663*, and the lyrics for Kate and Mike Westbrook's jazz suite *Bar Utopia*.

Ali Smith was born in Inverness, Scotland in 1962. Her first book, *Free Love and Other Stories* (1995), won the Saltire Society Scottish First Book of the Year Award and a Scottish Arts Council Award. Her first novel, *Like* (1997), was followed by a second collection of short stories, *Other Stories and Other Stories* (1999). Her second novel, *Hotel World* (2001), won the Encore Award and was shortlisted for the Orange Prize for Fiction and the Booker Prize for Fiction. Her novel *The Accidental* (2004) won the 2005 Whitbread Novel Award. She has also published a play, *The Seer* (2006), and her most recent collection of short stories is *The First Person and Other Stories* (2008). *The Book Lover* (2008) is a personal anthology of pieces by her favourite authors gathered over the course of her life.

Graham Smith was born in 1947 in Middlesbrough, in the North East of England. He studied at Middlesbrough College of Art and the Royal College of Art, London. From the early 1970s he made photographs of his friends and relatives and the pubs they frequented. They were exhibited at the Side Gallery in Newcastle upon Tyne, the Serpentine Gallery, London and the Museum of Modern Art, New York. Though he stopped making photographs in 1990, he continues to investigate his working-class roots through his research and writing. His photographs have appeared in *Granta* 25: *The Murderee* (1988) and *Granta* 95: *Loved Ones* (2006), which also included photographs by his father, Albert Smith, and from which the piece in this anthology is taken. His photographs are held by several major collections including the Victoria & Albert Museum, London and the Museum of Modern Art, New York.

Graham Swift was born in London in 1949. He was educated at Dulwich College, Queens' College, Cambridge and York University. His second novel, *Shuttlecock* (1981), won the Geoffrey Faber Memorial Prize. His third novel, *Waterland* (1983), won the *Guardian* Fiction Prize and the Geoffrey Faber Memorial Prize. In 1983 he was named as one of *Granta*'s 'Best of Young British Novelists'. *Last Orders* (1996), his sixth novel, won the Booker Prize for Fiction and the James Tait Black

Memorial Prize. This was followed by *The Light of Day* (2003) and *Tomorrow* (2007). His first non-fiction book, *Making an Elephant: Writing from Within*, was published in 2009.

Edmund White was born in 1940 in Cincinnati, Ohio and grew up in Chicago. He worked in New York as a journalist then moved to France in 1983. He published two novels before the success of *A Boy's Own Story* (1982), the first in a tetralogy of autobiographical novels, with *The Beautiful Room is Empty* (1988), *The Farewell Symphony* (1997) and *The Married Man* (2000). He has written several collections of essays, and his biography of Jean Genet (1993) won the National Book Critics Circle Award. His most recent books are *Chaos* and *Hotel de Dream* (both 2007), and *Rimbaud: The Double Life of a Rebel* (2008). He teaches writing at Princeton University and lives in New York City.

Acknowledgements

As well as thanking all the writers whose work is reproduced here, a special thanks goes to Ian Jack, editor of *Granta* 1995–2007, under whose editorship most of these pieces were published.

Permissions